Champagne  *Presents*

Siren's Song

By

K. M. Tolan

ALBANY OR
USA

Revision 1

Champagne Book Group
www.champagnebooks.com
Albany OR 97321 USA
Copyright 2016 by K. M. Tolan
ISBN 978-1-947128-50-7
August 2018
Cover Art by Carly Marino
Produced in the USA

Other Books by K.M. Tolan

Dancer Series
Battle Dancer, Book 4
Defiant Dancer, Book 3
Rogue Dancer, Book 2
Blade Dancer, Book 1

Hobohemia Series
Storm Child, Book 2
Tracks, Book 1

Stand-Alone
Siren's Song
Waiting Weapon

Dedication

To my wife and the awesome crew out at wePublish.

Prologue

Harry Rellant pulled off an armored glove to stroke his son's soft cheek one last time. The baby slept in his foam cradle, sedated and blissfully unaware. How many of his men would die for this child without realizing it? *Ought to be me.* Harry dismissed the attempt at self-pity. A little late for that now.

"Get you fixed up soon, Scotty," he promised, his words rasping through his black breathing mask. Bio-weapons from the previous job hadn't just ravaged his respiratory system, they'd poisoned the DNA he'd passed on to his son. Scotty's lungs weren't mature enough to handle the nanobots. Medics said only a miracle would save him. Harry gently closed the ammo case lid. A quick check of the other gear in the assault ship's tiny equipment bay ensured that nothing would rattle itself free during the harsh descent.

One miracle coming up, son.

Turbulence threatened to jerk the deck from beneath his feet. At thirty-five, he was getting too old for this kind of work. Gripping the shelf on which the case rested, he afforded himself a few more precious moments lingering over the disguised life pod. The Valkyrie's pilot was too busy and the strike team too airsick to bother him. What had Boss Mackenzie said about Scotty? Oh, yeah. *Tough luck.* This from the man whose ass he'd saved. Well, what did he expect? Compassion wasn't part of a mercenary's kit. Harry wiped a momentary blur from his gray eyes before affixing his glove. Opening the troop bay's hatch, he turned to give the men a final briefing.

Twenty soldiers greeted him with indifference from benches lining the cramped compartment's green bulkhead. Several of the other "security consultants" had the sense to wear helmets. The rest would learn soon enough to protect their tattooed skulls. Those who still gave a damn. Encased in olive drab combat gear, the troops looked more machine than human. Killing without question did that to a man. Harry didn't linger on the thought too long. He absently rubbed at his own shaven skull. Bad enough his mask made him look like some comic-book villain.

The ship lurched. He seized the overhead weapons rack for support. Engines rumbled in protest, adding to the squeak and clatter of loose strapping. They were deep into atmosphere, trading weightlessness for a rough ride. Time for the speech. Harry prayed this bunch would pay attention for once, considering what he had in store for the poor bastards.

"Listen up!" His boot kicked the car-sized mechanical beetle hogging most of the bay. "We've got one job. Get the drone into the water. Get it back inside. Get paid. Anything moving gets itself shot."

He flashed the fingers on his right hand three times. "Fifteen minutes. Understand? Not a damn minute longer, or I start deducting paychecks. We'll be backing our ass up against an old temple—Plan B if you can't make the ship. That's where the evac bird will pick you up. Questions?"

Of course there were no questions. Just the descending ship's rattle and shake. *Where are we going? What are we picking up? Who's the client?* Like any of them gave a shit. When you worked for Brothers, you didn't waste breath on such trivia. Brothers built its reputation on not asking, and business was good. Most of these guys would figure things out once they saw the sky. Then they damn well better keep their traps shut. He knew who the client was. There would be precious little mercy given for what he was about to do to their benefactor. Harry managed a grim smile behind his breather's grill. Mackenzie said he'd wanted someone he could trust for the job. The man should've seen this coming.

A few more pitch and rolls told Harry they needed him up front. Passing back through the equipment area, he gave the special ammo case a quick pat before returning to the flight deck. The bat-winged Valkyrie was a pain to fly even at the best of times, but the assault ship was reliable and tough. Harry looked through the windscreen at a panorama of boiling cloud tops highlighted by lightning. The weather wasn't the worst of his worries, but you didn't underestimate a dying world, either. Especially this one.

A rail-thin face glanced up at him with wide eyes and a skull's grin. "Lovely weather, mate." The pilot aimed dark spittle at the deck between the chairs, adding to the cockpit's sour tobacco smell.

"Jesus, Mad Jack, get your helmet on." Harry strapped himself into the copilot's seat and grabbed his own protection off a side hook. His helmet fit snugly over what was left of his shaved brown hair. The screens in front of him flashed a collage of warnings. Not just thunderstorms, either. Red triangles pointed out enough tornadoes to make even the most steadfast storm chaser run screaming. He glanced beyond the planet's curve at the bright bar lancing across the cosmos. A plasma jet squeezed from a black hole millions of light years distant, and this system was about to get a close encounter with it. Petal. A disarming name for a doomed world, given for the pattern of circular lakes across the planet's tortured surface. "What's the radiation like?"

"Nominal, but we've super cells above the lakes. Atmosphere's getting baked."

"Believe me, storms aren't our biggest problem."

"Damn straight they aren't, mate. Trust me, you see a siren, don't stop and stare."

He nodded. Mad Jack had been on a previous Petal run. One of the few who made it back after trying to hit the same site again due to a previously aborted raid. There was no fifteen-minute delay before a siren spawn. The same creatures still waited out there for them. This time Brothers was smart enough to find a new target. One far enough north to escape the worst of what pounded the lake clusters below. Harry had seen enough combat footage to take those crystalline bitches seriously. The creatures looked like glass angels when they spread out their dorsal fins. Right up to the point where they screamed and melted you into your armor. Well, Hell had angels, too.

I told them about the temple. I gave them a chance.

Harry tried to feel guilty, but the emotion was hard to come by. Brothers built its reputation on that too, and he was a model employee. He worked the screen between him and the pilot, plotting a descent path to weave around the nastier storms ahead. Most of the cloud piles pierced the stratosphere, a by-product of lakes being heated by the approaching plasma jet. If getting killed by a black hole wasn't enough, Petal was due to be pummeled by ice as well. A mix of oxygen and hydrogen clouds through which the jet passed would hit the planet both coming and going. Fire and water. God was being a real bastard here. Irony barely described this mission.

His client? The Church of Life.

The drop was tantamount to a drunken elevator, the soldiers' comments coming over his headsets with every colorful adjective they could think of. Mad Jack ignored it all, the pilot bucking his way through downdrafts and wind shears with his usual silly grin.

An electronic tone alerted their arrival over Petal's northern hemisphere where the weather thankfully approached some degree of sanity. Harry peered through more interspersed thunderheads and finally spied the landing zone—a series of orange baked-clay towers. Like all Shreen cities, the population center sat on the edge of a lake cluster whose pattern suggested the doomed race had a thing for terrain sculpting. Always four lakes, each body of water forming a near-perfect circle. Their target sat on the western shore of the northernmost lake.

"There." Harry pointed out a long, white cement pier extending from the middle of the city into the lake. "That comes out from the avenue leading to the temple. We'll put down on the street next to those low buildings where we're less likely to be flanked."

"Place should be empty," Mad Jack stated, though it sounded more like wishful thinking.

Harry nodded. "Project Exodus gassed the place almost a year ago. Probably a few didn't get scooped up, so keep your eyes peeled for movement."

The pilot dipped a wing into a gradual turn over the lake. "Think we'll find any beer?"

"Not in fifteen minutes." Harry hit the troop compartment's warning buzzer.

They skimmed crystal-blue waters any resort would be proud of, each ripple diamond-bright beneath the plasma jet's hellish glare. Mad Jack lined them up over the pier. Various sheds along the wharf looked deserted. No signs of life along the cobblestone avenue beyond, either. Harry counted five squat towers surrounded by various low buildings, the structures forming an ideal barrier on either side of the landing zone. He eyed the big domed temple at the end of the street with its iron double doors. The team could hole up there. Keep the sirens at bay.

Just don't stand your ground, Harry prayed in silence.

Mad Jack raised the Valkyrie's nose and brought them to a dust-blasting hover above the avenue just behind the pier. They bounced to a landing, the engines winding down to a fluttering thrum. Harry dropped the rear ramp and locked the engines at idle. He pulled his Hanza-88 from behind the seat. "Let's get this done."

A rush of hot air greeted his arrival in the troop bay as if someone just opened a clothes drier. It smelled about the same, too. He lowered his visor to offset the harsh light flooding the compartment. "Squad out. Mad Jack, give me some anti-personnel. ASAP."

His pilot pulled a launcher from its wall mount and rushed outside behind the hastily formed perimeter. The grenades popped and rolled across the cobblestones.

At least this part of the mission was moving along smoothly. Harry released the drone's clamps and thumbed the console buttons, commanding it to go fetch. Rotors extended and whirred to life. The machine lumbered for the exit, causing a miniature hurricane within the bay. "Heads up everyone. Drone is out and on the way."

The beetle shot over the pier, took a hard left, and disappeared in a splashing dive.

Harry stepped outside, wincing up at the white bar arcing across the sky. He could hardly make out Petal's sun for the invader's brilliance. It was painful looking out over the lake even with the visor. Hell of a way for any civilization to die. The buildings around him were cooked to a crisp—remnants of faded banners clinging to poles around the towers and only suggestions of peeling paint on clay walls. An opaque layer of dust coated glass windows. If anyone recognized either the architecture or the monstrosity overhead, they kept it to themselves. Smart.

"Squad One, extend your perimeter to the pier. Squad Two, give me flanking positions behind the ship and along the boardwalk. Fourteen minutes."

He wasn't sure who bawled out, "Movement, left!"

A shed along the pier puckered with rifle fire. Something hit the water behind it.

"Cease fire!" He ran to where Squad One fanned out along the pier's concrete decking. "Hit my drone, and I'll leave the lot of you here to dry. Get a man up at the pier. Ten minutes, team."

One of the mercs saluted and ran forward. Most likely the nervous trigger finger. The trooper didn't get too far before he reeled back from a single crack of sound. The soldier returned a staccato burst with his rifle. He was still standing. Good.

Harry ran up and inspected the glistening remains of something shattered against the man's breastplate. He remembered this kid. Fresh from Navy Ops, courtesy of one bar fight too many. "Marcus, you good?"

"Sir!" Marcus pointed toward the shed. "Shiny with a shard rifle."

Shiny, eh? Yeah, the kid knew where he was. "Just a hostile," he grated, pushing his helmet against the other's visor. "Got that, professor? You don't get paid to know shit."

"Yes, sir. Make it a dead hostile."

A dead Shreen, Harry corrected inwardly, using the species' actual name. He knelt for a closer inspection. The male sprawled out a hand's breath away from a back ladder inside the shed. The native wore a simple gray loincloth over his glittering brown skin. Near him lay a gas-fed long rifle with a full magazine of crystal needles. Blood ran thin and watery as if from a butchered fish. Hair looking like fiber optic strands ran down the Singer's back. Silicon biology, Harry reminded himself.

He glanced at the Shreen's feet. They were webbed, unlike most of the land dwellers here. Sure enough, those were gills along the neck, too. Great. The kid bagged himself a Quan Singer. The going theory said these amphibious bastards called in the sirens. Well, wasn't this the plan all along?

Harry straightened and turned to Marcus. "Get your ass out to the end of the pier. We're about to have company."

"Yes, sir."

Harry glanced at his wrist display. Shit. He opened the comm channel. "Five minutes."

Mad Jack's voice provided blessed reassurance. "Paycheck's on the way in."

Harry looked north. The drone bobbed to the surface, sending miniature vortexes of water into the air while struggling to get airborne with its load. "Team, collapse your perimeter."

He sucked a shot of hot air through his mask's grill and switched frequencies. Time to see if all the hacking paid off. "Drone. Turn west thirty degrees and proceed sixty yards." His breath became a sigh of relief. The beetle was turning. Heading toward the shore well north of the avenue.

He returned to a squad channel, listening to the kind of curses only the military could engender.

Harry overrode them. "Cut the chatter. Squad One, get after the damn thing. Two minutes."

"I'll shoot the son-of-a-bitch!"

"You do, Mad Jack, and I'll blow that chaw out your goddamned ears. Everyone move your asses and keep sharp. Squad Two, set up a firing line along the boardwalk and pier. Everyone, remember Plan B. Get to the temple if things go to shit." He ran for the Valkyrie, flipping back to the machine's channel. "Drone, ascend fifty feet and hover at Waypoint One."

~ * ~

Ancient memories raced along the Quan, broadcasting themselves into one of the blue-green reception nodules lacing the creature's great ovoid body. So was she conceived. A name occurred to her when she uncurled and split open her humming womb, allowing in a black torrent of cool liquid. *Water.* Something appropriate to couch her dawning self-awareness. She was, after all, only moments old.

She paused above her beloved Quan's rock-like surface, waiting for her memories to settle. She was a Song Guard. Her tribe and lake was Inis Drum. Yes, things were beginning to make sense now. She was here because something was wrong. Why was something wrong?

Water sang a high-pitched questing song through the pressing darkness. Nothing echoed back save for the reflection of her seven sisters emerging around her. Each newborn glowed with life, but the melody Water instinctually searched for was gone. The Song of Inis Drum no longer in the cradle? Her life purpose refined itself. Angry orange ripples shot up her two dorsal fins. She would bring the Song back and kill whoever stole it.

Water straightened her crystalline body, swimming fins spreading from pelvis to ankle. She launched herself toward the surface, arms tight against her side. The questing songs of her sisters painted the depths, finally giving her the distant silhouette of her first potential victim. Water narrowed her own song for a more detailed image. Her racial memories supplied an identity for her. A Quan Singer. One of the other two races her memories told her about.

She chirped.

The return taste told her this one was of Inis Drum. Not killable. Someone she was supposed to trust. Perhaps one who could tell her who her enemies were. She flicked her swimming fins and shot toward him, feeling the water's weight ease as she ascended. The water gleamed a deep azure now, darkness giving way to light.

"Song Guard. Come to me."

She froze, surprised at how the command in his voice gripped her in the penetrating song of Earth, the language one spoke when beneath the waves. Who did he think he was, ordering her like this?

Cutting fins running the length of her forearms vibrated with her irritation. Water swam toward him. Bright beams of light flickered down from the surface above, playing across the Singer's elder face. She searched her Quan's memories for a meaning behind his expression upon catching sight of her. Awe? Fear? Remorse? No matter. The Song needed her.

She sang out in demanding tones. "Release me."

Undaunted, the Singer waited until all of her sisters ringed him as well, their fins glowing in agitated ripples.

"They will kill you if you do not listen to me," he sang. "Your enemy are not Shreen. They wear metal, and have weapons to kill you at a distance. Close upon them silently, Song Guard. Spread yourselves out so as not to be taken at once."

"Not Shreen?" Water asked, her alarm growing. She could feel the Song, but it was moving away.

"Not Shreen?" her sisters echoed, whirling around him in sharp turns, their translucent hair whipping about in exasperation.

The Quan Singer's song was an ode to bitterness. "The Quan should have sent you while we were still a people to save. They have taken all of Inis Drum, and now they steal our future. Go, Song Guard. Save our Song, and give your Drum vengeance."

Water had heard enough, surging past him in a burst of fear.

"Do we believe him?" the nearest sister inquired, keeping pace beside her during the ascent. She hesitated, then added, "I call myself Ping."

"I am Water, and yes, we should. He is older than all of us."

"Everything is older than us," Ping asserted. "Even our memories."

Another Song Guard spoke up, declaring herself in a voice filled with self-discovery. "I am Twitch."

"I am Blue," another sister joined in.

"I...I will call myself Question."

Three more introductions. Memory, Tapping, and Wonder.

Water basked in the music of this newly formed camaraderie, sending green ripples up the crystalline spines of her fins. Moments away from battle, and here was a celebration of sudden life. There was poetry in this. A prayer worthy to be cast in the face of the hated gods. Yes, the waters were warming quickly. She could feel the change, and see the blaze of Kee's Sword flickering through the water above just as legends foretold, all but vanquishing the sun with its brightness. She was legend, too. Of course they would bring the Song back. How could they not?

Water turned westward, following the Song's beckoning toward the shoreline. Along with her sisters, she spread her dorsal fins flat across her back to catch the penetrating shafts from Kee's Sword, letting its cursed light nourish her for the fight to come. Pools of brilliance swept across the rising lake bottom. Her memories supplied her with a name to go along with the cement pilings ahead. Inis Pier. This is where the Song called from, and she and her sisters would answer.

Mindful of the Quan Singer's warning, Water folded her dorsal fins tight against her back and traded the powerful strokes of her swimming fins for a predatory glide among the pillars. Her first sight of enemy came in the moment of Tapping's death. Something, Water couldn't find a memory to place on it, sliced through the water and halved the Song Guard.

"Spread yourselves!" Water sang out. "The Song travels ashore and so must we."

More bubbling trails entered the water. Bullets, she realized. An impossible stream of them clawing up the bottom. Question vaulted upward in a swish of fins next to an algae-stained piling, broaching the surface. When she plunged back in, a bodiless head followed, still encased in a helmet. Thick blood billowed from the severed neck.

The lake reverberated with resonating splashes, announcing the arrival of a new menace. Skimming the sandy bottom, Water spied a cone-shaped metal fish speeding towards her, its tail bright and hissing. She flattened her dorsal fins and chirped. A metallic taste rebounded back, telling her the proper pitch she needed. Shaping her throat and lips accordingly, Water screamed her death song. A narrow cone of vapor replaced the water in front of her, shattering her adversary upon contact.

Gulping water to cool her vocal chords, Water let her spread fins dissipate the remaining heat. Her throat still burned, but it was manageable. And she had other weapons. She looked back and found Blue coming up behind her. And then her sister was gone in a roiling blast of sound, the explosion driving Water into the sand. Gathering her wits, she shot upward to take her chances on the pier.

She landed hard on the pavement, her swimming fins swirling around her like a crystalline dress. Water squinted, the horrid streak of light across the sky all but blinding her. Screeching a curse at the god Kee and his wretched sword, she lunged for the nearest enemy she could find. A metal man, just like the Singer said. He swung on her with a wide-bored rifle. She slashed out with a forearm, her cutting fins sinking into the soft-looking collar beneath her foe's helmet. Thick blood spattered her crystal plates.

Twisting around, Water ran across the pier toward the Song's vibrations, trying to comprehend what she was seeing. A huge machine bird squatted in the middle of Temple Way, its door open wide to admit an equally befuddling insect thing lumbering toward it. She couldn't see her Song, but she knew where it was. The insect had it. She charged forward. These thieves were not going to fly off with her Song!

The armored warriors fought among Temple Way's shops, firing and dying to both death song and fin. Water saw Memory fall beneath a hail of bullets as she and Wonder closed on a beleaguered group of fighters backed up against a tower wall. Wonder screamed her death song. Air wavered between the siren and her victims. Those before her burst and died, the last of their number taking Wonder with them.

The tableau of violence played out on both sides of Water as she ran, giving her an opening among the enemy's ranks. Aiming a chirp at the huge bird, she rushed in, intent on cutting apart the odd insect whose insides sang with the Song's call. The thing was almost inside the bird's waiting maw.

Bright blasts hurled her forward in a tumble, pain shooting through her legs. She slid across the cobblestones, slamming into a storefront. Dazed, Water looked down and found most of her legs gone. Even her own heart's song couldn't stem the life flowing from her.

The machine bird was escaping. Howling like Anasa's wind, the flyer rose, its prize secured in the thing's bowels. Leaving the warriors behind.

Wrenching up on a ruined knee, Water exchanged waves of agony for the dread of seeing her Song taken. The sheer horror inspired her final death song, blistering the air in front of her. The flying machine rocked, a glowing pod flashing into ruin. Bits of metal rebounded across the street, but the flyer rose just the same.

Water tried to scream again, but the heat and weakness overwhelmed her. Her throat cracked, her eyesight leaving her with one last terrible sight of Inis Drum's Song ascending into the harsh glare of Kee's Sword. She collapsed, listening to a dwindling roar mocking her failure. In time, even that faded. Her heart song was stubborn, however. It refused to let her go. Finally, to end the pain and anguish, Water did the task herself. Her ruined throat managed to carry her final keen skyward, broadcasting her toward the Song's dimming presence.

For a brief moment she joined with her people in a dream of welcoming. And then she was…elsewhere.

~ * ~

I'm screwed. Harry's gloved hand hesitated above the red fire handle for the starboard engine. Pull it and this ride was over. He could manage a landing, but not an orbit. No way he'd set down on this dying rock with a bunch of sirens on his tail. Better to let the engine blow its guts out. Alarms bleated like stuck pigs, but the thing still provided thrust. Enough, at least, for a low orbit. The Valkyrie clawed through the deepening blue for the dark sanctuary of space. *Why in hell hadn't they run for the temple? Idiots.* He'd given them their chance. He'd done everything he could.

Harry pulled the encoder from his pocket and jammed it into the comm port. "Maiko, you there?"

The synthesized and heavily encrypted answer didn't hide his wife's anxiety. "Did you get it?"

"Yeah, but won't make it to you. Your orbit's too high. Lost an engine and will be lucky to manage a low pass. I'm exposing Scotty now, and will eject his pod. Head to Petal Gate the moment you've got him aboard."

"They'll see you."

"Yeah, and they'll think I'm sending you the Reliquary. Gonna have to get them to come after me instead." He hung his head, hating himself for the heartbreak in her voice. "Hon, I'm sorry. This was the plan all along. I've got what Boss Mackenzie wants, and he's not above making deals with this big a payday. Not a lot of time so gotta go. Love you…take care of our son. Will join you later."

He pulled out the encoder and crushed it under his heel. Fat chance on that last bit. He'd be lucky if Mackenzie didn't track her down regardless of any agreement they made. Well, the bastard did owe him.

Satisfied the ship wouldn't drop out of the sky, Harry swiveled the seat and headed back to the ammo crate. Perhaps it was better the sedative kept Scott asleep. God only knew what exposure to the Reliquary would feel like. Harry pulled off his helmet. Warm, moist air added to the perspiration along his bare scalp. Taking in a deep breath, he unclipped the releases and removed the black breather as well. He kissed his son's smooth forehead, taking solace in the peace behind those little closed eyes.

"Let's get your miracle." Clipping the mask back on, Harry lifted his son from the pod, pulling away the blue blanket Maiko had wrapped him in. He carried Scott to the rear troop compartment and the empty benches on either side of the drone. "Open."

Still dripping from its immersion in the lake, the beetle obediently unfolded its wings to reveal the wonder inside. The Reliquary looked like… Hell, he couldn't come up with a good description. An opal stuffed with rainbows, maybe. Iridescent nodules lined the large crystal, and damn if he couldn't feel…something. People paid millions for a chance at this. He didn't have millions. Mindful of the short time left, Harry knelt and gently pressed his son against the glowing stone. A halo formed around the baby's forehead where the two touched.

One

Scott sent his oboe's mellow notes floating across the narrow ravine, letting the echoes accompany his afternoon improvisation. He smiled, half closing his eyes in satisfaction. Something worthy of a new opus if he hadn't already started work on his current suite's fourth movement. A crisp March breeze reminded him he'd chosen to wear only a light brown leather jacket and jeans. He didn't have enough meat on his bones for such bravado. But people liked the slender look these days, and he wasn't one to disappoint his fans. Yeah, he should've grabbed the parka.

The sun perched low on the peaks behind him. How long had he been out here? Scott looked over the stretch of pine descending toward Lake Tahoe. Evergreen scents filled the clear air. Easy to forget time up here in the Sierra Nevada. Easy to forget himself, too. That was the whole point to living in the cabin behind him.

He swept back a shock of way too long hair. Better get a stylist up here soon or his manager would have a fit. The Sacramento concert was coming up, and his hermit look wasn't exactly the rogue virtuoso being sold by the media blitz. At least his manager had quit badgering him to switch to black hair. He preferred keeping it brown. One of the few things about himself he did like.

Scott pulled the oboe's electronic reed from his lips. Waning light played across gold keys and a polished veneer of red cocobolo wood. The instrument of his considerable fortune. Fine, so some critics considered the oboe a synthesizer because of what lay beneath the classic exterior, but he wasn't about to explain why he needed ranges well beyond human hearing. He'd spent four years climbing the professional ladder until he could afford having the renowned Wolf company come up with this custom job. All part of a greater plan nearing fruition. He carefully set the oboe within the cushions of its silver carrying case and snapped the biometric locks shut. Grabbing the handle, he headed back up the rutted gravel to his cabin.

His chosen getaway from the human race didn't look like much from the outside where it perched on an overlook. Just another ramshackle afterthought, albeit a rather large one. Nothing to attract attention. Right now he looked forward to what lay under the faux corrugated steel roof. A fat steak, perhaps. Maybe a good movie to—

Scott paused just shy of the front door. Something moved around the old green garbage bin. He let out a slow, frosty breath.

A tawny feline head glared back at him from the shadows between the trash container and the cabin's northeast corner.

Crap. What in hell was that doing here?

The cougar stepped out onto the old road, its belly low to the ground. An adult by the look of it, the cat's gaunt frame telling him the reason for the visit. He gently set down the case so as not to jar its precious contents, and backed away.

The mountain lion snarled, baring yellowed fangs. It should be running for the high country, not swishing its tail at him.

Swallowing back his growing dread, Scott eased two big knives from their holsters on his pant legs. "Get out while you can, kitty. I seriously don't want to do this."

Kitty didn't understand the message. The animal's shoulders bunched.

Fear rose in Scott's throat. He edged closer to a red fir next to the cabin, knowing how nature intended these issues to resolve. Nature, however, didn't figure on his particular madness. The source of his twisting guts had nothing to do with the cougar. It was already dead. He reached into a part of himself a legion of psychologists had failed to lock down. The imaginary fishbowl in his head. Scott shoved the lid back with a shudder. He saw her clearly, coiled up in a crystalline ball. He always saw her, thanks to those damn crystals stuck in his skull.

Water.

His personal demon stirred much like a snake rising from a lethargic torpor. Snakes didn't sing, though. Nor did they look like a murderous sea angel rendered in crystal, fins rippling with bioluminescent menace.

Why do you wake me, thief? Her reply was a melodic vibration through his skull, serrated with venomous undertones.

"Something for you to kill," he sang aloud in her audible language of Air, hoping it might startle the cat into fleeing. No such luck. The animal remained bunched up, as if trying to bolster its own courage. Those bony front legs quivered…then stilled.

A high keen rang in his head like someone running their finger around the lip of a crystal goblet. Water, vibrating her cutting fins right before striking. He braced himself.

Scott jerked forward as if electrocuted. Instead of fighting the involuntary spasm, he threw the fishbowl's lid wide open. He leapt, a throat-burning shriek erupting from his mouth.

To the animal's credit, it tried to scramble out of his way. Maybe it saw the monster behind his eyes, but the revelation came too late. The horror inside him went to work with a vengeance. The first slash opened the cougar's scalp, sending the big animal tumbling against the trash bin. It twisted around and leapt to its hind feet in a vain attempt to claw him. Pivoting in a spray of loose rock, Scott drove the predator's paws against its chest with one arm and cut through its throat with the other. Hot blood splashed across his face. Then Water went for the exposed belly.

Both combatants staggered back. Scott sank against the cabin door, heaving ragged gasps, feeling like his legs and arms had been wrenched from their sockets. His victim's death throes banged against the green container before the cougar dropped into its grisly mess of entrails. Death mercifully stilled the beast.

The pain of strained muscles helped him drive Water back into the fishbowl, but not before she pushed a bloodied blade against his throat. Her crystalline face pressed against the imaginary glass.

Shall we play the cutting game?

"One scratch, bitch, and we don't visit the Tabernacle. No Song for you to climb into."

You are not much fun, today, she trilled back, twisting around to bat at the fishbowl with her swimming fins.

Scott regained control of his arm, wiped both knives against his pants, and holstered them. Her light reply told him Water was in a good mood. And why not? No doubt she'd been thinking of him while eviscerating the hapless feline. Or she was looking forward to their upcoming Visitation at the Tabernacle as much as he was. The goal he'd spent most of his brief professional life preparing for. She would be reunited with her Song, and he would truly be free.

The thought of freedom had him glancing around to make sure the violent encounter hadn't been noticed by a stray hiker. God, if the doctors even suspected he'd been lying to them all this time…

Even Water had pulled off her end of the ruse to perfection. Fourteen years of white walls and humoring smiles. No way was he going back. Just, no way. He was twenty-four, rich as hell, and famous. And technically still crazy, unfortunately.

But this last bit was about to change. Soon.

The ache in his limbs intensified with each step. The human body wasn't supposed to move like that. He inspected the torn lines across his coat and jeans. The cougar had gotten a few licks in after all, but nothing too serious. He healed quickly. Scott winced, feeling the onset of shakes. He glanced at the body, his stomach souring at the sight. He could drag it down to the ravine in the morning and let the turkey vultures have a field day. Right now he needed to go inside.

One day I will have your father lying there. And then you.

She was in a good mood, all right. "I don't have a father. Go back to sleep."

Water floated on her back in her bowl. Her singing turned petulant. *Play me something.*

"Jacuzzi, first." Scott lurched to his feet with a groan, taking a moment to steady himself. The cougar could wait, but not his oboe. Biting his lip, he shuffled across the road for the Wolf's instrument case. It was the last thing he wanted to forget when he arrived for his Visitation.

His cabin basement wasn't big. In fact, it was little more than a rustic hollow hewn out of the granite. Aquamarine lighting rippled across the rocks, extending the submarine grotto effect encouraged by the bubbling marble bowl at the center. He pulled off ruined clothes and eased into the hot massaging waters. The majesty of Holst's *The Planets* rolled out of hidden speakers. Seven movements.

Scott sighed. He'd barely finished *Anasa's Dance*, his third movement in *Song*. He'd reserved tonight for laying the foundation to the fourth movement involving the Shreen sun god Kee, but that was before Miss Mayhem dislocated every bone in his body. The pain would subside, but not the memory of what she had done to the cougar. One last ugly image to throw on the stack before leaving.

Let me swim.

He caught himself moments away from falling asleep. "What? Like at our first and last Caribbean vacation? Nothing like having two guys pushing water out of my lungs."

The ocean reminded me of my Drum, she defended.

"Drum? You talking about your lake back home, or your tribe? Your language doesn't seem to know the difference."

There is no difference, she sniffed. *Both are home.*

He chuckled. "But only one of them can drown me like you damn near did."

Water lifted her chin. *Song Guards do not need air.*

"Cute. And no." Scott wished he could soak in the bubbling comfort all night, but didn't want to encourage Water into any mischief while he slept. Sighing, he pulled himself out of the Jacuzzi and grabbed a white terry-cloth robe from the adjacent hook. He regarded his lanky and uninspiring nakedness in the wall mirror. Gray eyes where they should've been brown, no doubt part of the overall mess in his forehead. A swath of glistening pale blotches marked the start of powdery crystals embedded into his skull. The contact points where he'd been exposed to Water's Song by his father, according to her best guess. The source of his lifelong nightmare about to end.

The cougar's marks were but pink lines across pale skin in need of some tanning. Perhaps some weight training too, so those girls had something worth squealing at. He smiled. Soon he'd be able to take a woman for a drink without worrying about the whole Jekyll and Hyde thing. Oh, yeah. A whole new world of freedom coming up.

He climbed up the basement stairs, his overly stretched muscles complaining. A nod to the automated kitchen, and he was on his way to burying the afternoon's horrid encounter beneath a good steak. He closed his eyes for a moment. This wasn't how the day was supposed to have turned out.

"Sorry, kitty," he whispered.

Once satiated, he lounged in a brown overstuffed chair before the rustic fireplace, and set about playing Water her song. Music was the garden spot in their battlefield where commonality soothed both their troubled spirits. An entire cultural heritage lay behind Water's baleful glare. He'd learned early to tap into those old Shreen memories during her mental and physical tortures, if for no other reason than to maintain his sanity. Much later, well after their desperate truce, he retained a gold mine of ballads and melodies to draw on. Tonight they both needed serenity.

Last Descent told the story of a Shreen merging with their Song. The aliens believed they gained immortality upon returning to their race's collective memories. The Song was essentially a waiting room until it was taken back to some queen-like creature called the Quan. Mythology aside, the journey to the Song's cradle was meant to honor the passing of life, and *Last Descent* did a great job of capturing the grandeur.

Scott pulled his Wolf from its case and put the instrument through a warm-up cycle. He blew softly into the reeds, his fingers plunging the oboe into a sonorous range too deep for anything but a whale to appreciate. Water heard as well, and the vibrations coursed through his mind with equal beauty. Those minute crystals in his head allowed him to enjoy the full range of what his Wolf could do. Doctors dismissed the pale blotch across his forehead as abnormal calcification. He, of course, knew better.

And so he played, giving himself to the music's flow and

forgetting why. *Last Descent* climbed into audible frequencies, then ascended with the grace of a freed soul. Soon, even Water quieted herself to listen, and that was the best part of all.

He woke in the same chair the next morning, still cradling the Wolf. Trading the robe for another pair of jeans and a blue plaid shirt, he dealt first with the mess outside. People were coming over. The grisly task inspired a lackluster breakfast, but his spirits picked up after the arriving stylist brought him back to civilization. Clean-shaven, with a Scott Rellant signature sweep of carefully unruly locks masking a discolored forehead. Black slacks, black shirt, and black sneakers. His wake-up call to a new life without the demon in his head.

His manager's limo appeared in the afternoon sky like a streamlined angel, the pearl-gray flyer settling on the gravel driveway with barely a whisper. Benny stepped out, wearing a lavender satin shirt and the usual red tie stuffed into a pinstripe suit. Benny being Benny, living up to the expectations of being a rock star's handler. Scott didn't even know the squat balding man's real name, not that it mattered. It was all about the performance, and none knew the act better than Benny.

Arms wide, his manager embraced him on the doorstep with an enthusiastic bear hug. Yep. Lavender perfume, too. Fortunately, Water was sleeping.

"Scotty! Sweetheart! Pumped and ready to go." Benny ran an imaginary feather brush over the shoulders of Scott's pressed shirt. "Nice. Gucci makes the man, I say."

Scott went straight to the important question. "You talk with the Church?"

Benny rubbed his hands. "You're in. Baby, the Prophet himself is going to meet you. Jeremiah Jones in the flesh."

Scott let out a caught breath. "When?"

"You said early, so tomorrow. Church limo will pick you up outside the hotel."

Scott savored his long expulsion of breath. How many years had he waited to hear this?

Benny continued to rattle on while trying to keep his custom alligator shoes from being scuffed on the gravel. "You have any idea what kind of publicity we're talking about, here?" he gushed. "Simulcast to all eighteen world temples and audit centers. And then released to the media. You can't buy that kind of exposure, my boy." Benny's delight faded as his words caught up with him. "Okay, so maybe you did."

Clearing his throat, his manager glanced around. His brown

eyes crinkled upon spying the garbage bin.

"Minor accident." Damn, he should've taken a hose to the thing. "Everything's fine. Not my blood."

Benny stepped back, folding his arms. "Then whose?"

"Half-starved cougar. Didn't hurt me. I'm fine."

Benny rolled his eyes. "No, not fine. Mountain lion? You're really okay?"

"I'll go get my oboe," Scott offered to avoid more hand waving on Benny's part.

"Lined up a nice lakeside Tahoe chalet, but no. You get a shack out in the middle of cold-as-hell nowhere where things eat you." Benny followed him in. "One o'clock, and I'm already needing another drink. You're killing me, Scotty."

Scott scooped up his case, relieved the morning's maid service had already been through the place. Otherwise Benny would bitch about that, too. He tacked toward calmer waters. "So, what's Sacramento look like?"

Benny rubbed his hands. "Sold out two weeks ago. Got Angie Carter doing your warm-up with her violin. Quebec Holography brought in the new equipment yesterday. Twice the resolution. How's your fourth movement coming along?"

"Peachy," he lied. Getting started on his newest piece would be a post-Water affair. Getting rid of her was all he could think about. "Let's head out."

Scott pretended to be engrossed in the passing mountain scenery on the flight to Sacramento. He envied Benny's clinking glass of scotch, but knew better than to encourage Water. She remained curled up in the fishbowl, blue-green ripples slowly rising up her twin dorsal fins. No doubt she dreamed of her cherished reunion with her people's memories. Staying away from booze helped keep her that way. People thought him a religious man. No drinking. No parties. Not even a young lady or three to dangle off his arm. If they only knew. He closed his eyes for a moment. If the wrong people knew, he'd be back in a mental hospital. If there were a God, and He wasn't laughing His ass off at Scotty, then this would all end tomorrow. So what if Jeremiah and his "church" were as genuine as a circus sideshow. Maybe it took one big joke to end another.

Scott raised an imaginary glass to Benny, knowing the manager considered him somewhat of a tamed psychotic. Typical for most of his high-end clients, no doubt. The only guy who could repackage fourteen years in a mental institution into an "edgy" persona the people loved. Maybe, with Water finally gone, there would be a chance to actually live the life of a rock star right down to the sex and booze.

Benny raised a manicured eyebrow upon being saluted. "I could still cancel the church visit." His voice had lost its usual Hollywood dressing. "You're not exactly my idea of a religious man, and you're spending a lot of cash. Thirty million just to stare at the thing? What are you looking for, Scott? Redemption, or bankruptcy?"

"A miracle," he returned with a sarcastic laugh. So much truth in Benny's question. He just had to get within range of the Song and let Water do the rest. She claimed to have broadcast herself into him like some glorified radio signal. With the oboe's assistance, she could transmit herself back out.

Redemption, indeed.

"We ain't got the cash for a miracle. This is a Visitation, not a full Intercession. Last guy I know of paid a couple billion to get his miserable life extended, and you're just kissing the Prophet's glass. We're not in that sort of league. It'll take London, Sydney, and probably Frankfurt to cover the rest of your loan." Benny paused for a sip from his glass. "And for what?"

"Publicity, remember? Besides, Beijing sold out, and they want me back. We've got the money."

"You're killing me."

"You said that already."

~ * ~

Backstage green rooms were rarely green, and the Civic Auditorium's waiting area proved no different with bland, tan, panel walls and stuffy smells. He'd already run up and down the Wolf's extensive range of notes twice, ensuring even the low frequencies would catch his every whim. Never mind if the audience heard nothing. They would swear otherwise, however, thanks to both the induced vibrations and what the upgraded holo-sphere displayed.

He set the Wolf aside, its latticework of gold keys and guards glinting in the room's indirect lighting. Scott sank onto a couch, exhaling his tension. The afternoon rehearsals were behind him. The crowd loved *Anasa's Dance* in Beijing. And of course, there was *Prelude*, the first movement catapulting him into fame. Then came *Water*, a flirtation between modern beat and classical divergence. *Water* faced no competition on either side of the fence. He'd be fine. People were starved for something other than computer-composed crap. *Song*'s three movements delivered originality in large doses, the suite giving no excuses in the sophistication department, either. Nobody had heard anything similar. Ever.

And now came his newest movement. *Anasa's Dance* drew

from the Shreen myth of a wind goddess enticing her sun god suitor, the rhythms all about seduction. The tough part was mixing in aspects of the gift she demanded as her bride's price. A crystal necklace made from no less than all of the Shreen Songs. Blending in music containing what Water explained as inexpressible beauty was a challenge and a half. One he'd pulled off, if Beijing were any indication. That was China, though. This was the United States.

Water stirred, lazily circling the fishbowl's confines, her long swimming fins flowing around her. *We will sing well*, Water assured. *Let me begin. Let me curse these thieves one final time.*

He was inclined to be generous since she would be broadcasting herself voluntarily at the Tabernacle tomorrow. It was time to be expansive but not stupid. The Shreen sang in two languages—Air, audible to all and used above water, and Earth, a low frequency reserved for underwater. The latter fell well below human perception. Not a problem for Scott, given his brain's passenger.

"Only if you sing in Earth where they can't hear you," he agreed. "I'll give you the first four lines from *Prelude* to play with."

Done.

"Scott, you singing something?"

He opened his eyes to Benny and his hand wringing. Damn, he'd been talking out loud to Water again. In Air, no less. "Sorry. I do that in my sleep sometimes. Crowd up for it?"

"Angie's got them doing the Texas Two-step out there. It's time to wow 'em, baby."

Scott retrieved the Wolf from its stand. "It's what I do, Benny."

He eyed the burly types waiting at the door, discovering the reason for their presence when they helped him plow through a flurry of journalists crowding the hallway outside. They babbled about tomorrow's meeting with the Prophet. How did he feel about it? Was he begging for an Intercession?

Scott kept walking.

Angie Carter, all flashy in cowgirl sequins and wild brunette hair, raised her electric violin as they passed back stage. "Go get 'em, tiger. All yours."

"Next year I'll probably be your warm-up," he joked, earning a quick smile from the sprite of a girl. Not even seventeen, and Benny had her at near superstar status.

"Damn right," she laughed.

He would've given anything for such confidence a few years back. Everything had been a leap of faith since the hospital. *Prelude* had been written there, and most of *Water,* too. Not out of love for the art as much as a way to escape the hell Water had put him through.

Benny left him at the side curtains. Scott released a quick breath and walked out onto a darkened stage. A dimly lit guideline navigated him safely around the huge holo-globe. His simple stool was a study in contrast to the wizardry around him. He grinned. Benny had left nothing to chance. Behind the props emulating swaying fronds sat a second stool with a fishbowl on top. The man was all about the particulars, even if he didn't understand them.

He took his place on his stool, listening to the restless rumble of an audience just beyond the dark silkscreen. The orchestra pit was already going through the motions, warming themselves to the task at hand. Black-clad technicians flitted about like wraiths. One plugged a broadcaster into his Wolf. Another unrolled his music screen. A row of green dots told him the Quebec Holography bunch were happy with what their displays told them. A single blue mark acknowledged the conductor synching in. The data vanished, swept aside by *Prelude's* sheet music. The conductor glanced back and raised his baton. Scott let Water slide out of the fishbowl, fulfilling his promise.

Her lips closed around the Wolf's reeds.

The silkscreen raised, the floor washing in blue and violet hues. Sea nymphs rose within the holo-globe in dreamy swirls, heralding a sonorous vibration from the oboe only he could feel through the tiny crystals in his head. Water spoke in Earth against the orchestral backdrop of *Prelude's* introduction. His audience quieted. They couldn't hear her, of course, but the infrasound broadcasters throbbed enough to make them think they had.

Surprisingly, Water didn't deliver the scathing tirade he expected. She was almost entreating them. Asking why they stole her people's future. Didn't they understand? Didn't they care? Venom injected itself into her settling on the latter assumption, her appeals darkening into some of the worst death wishes he'd ever heard. This was the Water he knew. Hateful. Desiring to kill everything around her in an impotent fit of rage. All managed in four opening lines. Spent, the Song Guard returned the Wolf to him.

Scott cooled her mood with remembrances of better days plucked from Water's racial memories. Recollections neither of them had experienced. He left the inaudible tones of Earth behind, rising into the salutation of a new sunrise over Inis Drum long before Kee's Sword slashed across the sky. He heard lingering sighs from the audience as they recognized *Prelude's* true opening. The tone, upbeat and full of promise, teetered between classical form and pop in a mad balance he'd perfected and made his own.

The audience clapped their way into *Water*, the second movement.

The orchestra joined in, raising the tempo in a grand salute to the legendary deeds of the Song Guard who defended each Drum when called upon by their Quan. No question as to who this was about. Inside his head, Water sang, lifting her voice in memory of fallen sisters. Wonder. Question. Memory, and others. Not simple words to her, but glittering comrades she'd known only for an instant.

A martial tempo introduced the reason behind the Song Guard's existence.

The stage transformed again, becoming the rainbow cradle to a wondrous orb couched in a bed of jagged crystal. Sure, the people thought he paid homage to both the Church of Life and the Tabernacle's Reliquary. Let them.

He played for Water's Song, and what it would shortly give them both.

Anasa's Song came next. Not only did his latest movement delight, he literally had women out of their seats and improvising the sinuous rhythms for themselves. A thrilled audience refused to let him off stage without an impromptu solo and a few more bows. He felt like a wet rag with all the water twisted out by the time he headed backstage.

Benny met him with a slap on the shoulder. "Did you *see* that? You had them dancing, Scotty. Dancing! I mean, we should think about having a few girls on stage next time. Not just the holograms. Speaking of which, how about ducking into the after-party for once? Just to say hi?"

Scott shook his head. Not with the way Water thrashed about in the fishbowl. The second movement always put her into an agitated state remembering her sisters. The third? Well, she absolutely loathed *Anasa* and every other Shreen god in existence. Scott knew he was better off alone.

"Just get me to the hotel." He waved to the raucous cries of held-back fans down the hallway.

Next time, he'd take Benny up on his offer. He'd be in much better shape after the Visitation. Maybe even human.

Two

Nerves twitching, Scott straightened a contrasting red tie over his expected black-on-black attire. His dark brown hair, just long enough not to be considered conservative, refused to lay down in back. He wasn't sure if the slightly harried look suited him, but it reflected the pensive expression cast over his narrow features.

What to call this momentous occasion? Freedom Day? Rebirth? Or, maybe the day he couldn't get a word out of Water. Not even the usual good morning death threat. She was definitely awake, but the only hatred radiating from the fishbowl felt perfunctory. Her mind, like his, was on the upcoming merge with her Song. Was it anticipation, or resignation? She flat out wanted nothing to do with him. Perhaps this was her way of preparing for the separation. Or, simply finding him not worth the effort to curse anymore.

Usually he wasn't one to prod, but Water's silence shadowed, if not soured, a celebratory breakfast. "If I didn't know any better, I'd say you were sulking."

I would be happier killing you. The retort was listless at best.

He grinned. "Going to miss me, eh?"

Orange ripples of anger shot up her dorsal fins. *I was supposed to save my Song, not return to it a failure. Kee and Anasa laugh at me, along with your thief god.*

"Tough," he spat back, refusing to feel sorry for her even though a part of him did. "You ruined my goddamned life. You, your cutting games, and every other shit torture you could dream up. Wouldn't even let me kill myself those two times in the hospital, remember? Just kept laughing."

He straightened his tie. "Now who's laughing, bitch?"

The fishbowl sang out with the keen of Water's cutting fins, and for a horrid moment he thought she was going to break free of the fishbowl on her own.

Speak to me like that again, and I will refuse to transfer. I will torment you to the end of your days.

"Yes, ma'am," he muttered, her vow's icy sincerity catching him off guard. Bitch till the end. Not that he wasn't being a matching bastard. "Fine. I'm sorry."

Her angry colors dissolved into deep purple waves. *I am sorry, too. Hating you all of the time is hard.*

"So why bother?"

Because I am Song Guard.

He turned from the mirror with a scowl. She was the one who deserved death ten times over. Not him. Today was a mercy she didn't deserve. Damned if she was going to make him feel guilty about it.

Benny met him on the hotel's rooftop landing apron, his manager struggling to hold down a garish yellow golf cap matching an equally obnoxious polo shirt.

Benny pointed toward an approaching white teardrop with wings, the Church of Life's golden hands logo emblazoned on the tail fin. "There's your ride. Just you, I'm afraid. They'll have their own people handling your meeting with the Prophet. Get rid of the sourpuss for Christ's sake. You paid good money for this."

"As if those bandits needed it," Scott grumbled, watching the limousine come to a whispery touchdown. A look through the windshield told him this was one of those expensive pilotless drones, but then money wasn't a problem for Jeremiah and his gang of fraudsters. They were the true thieves, here.

Gift of God, my ass.

The hatch opened. At best, they'd stolen a precious alien relic. At worse, if he believed Water, these bastards were committing genocide. Fortunately for him, he didn't believe in anything. He quickly stepped inside the drone's white leather interior.

He gave Benny a final wave after the man handed him the Wolf's case, then settled in as the hatch clicked shut. The wall in front of him dissolved into a display showing a Latino woman with narrow cheeks framing a receptionist's smile. "Good morning, Mr. Rellant." Her voice carried a rich Castilian lilt.

He did a double take at her half-famished look and slightly sunken eyes. The holier-than-thou smugness. This was no blank-eyed acolyte. Every screen and billboard had this brunette's haunted face plastered on it. Mara Martinez herself. Freshly pulled from death's door via Intercession, this "living miracle" was now Jeremiah's chief huckster.

"Ma'am," he managed, caught without his carefully rehearsed lies. What do you call a bona fide saint these days?

"His Holiness asked me to personally conduct your tour after your news conference. You will meet the Prophet after lunch. Please let me know if there is anything else I can help you with during your short flight."

He mimicked her demure smile. Fine, so she wanted to be God's flight attendant, too. She was reasonably attractive in a down-to-earth sort of way, save for the company she kept. Damn, he hated these people almost as bad as Water did. Best that the Song Guard was sleeping... No, she wasn't. He could feel her pressing against the fishbowl, thrashing those swimming fins of hers.

"Of course," he pushed out.

Saint Mara vanished, replaced with the same introductory bullshit the Church served up to him earlier during his pre-Visitation audit. He had passed the measure of his worthiness with flying colors— or at least his bank account had.

The display yakked on about primitives on a dying planet, and how His Holiness had been gifted with the Reliquary for transplanting these creatures to another world through Operation Exodus. Nothing in the documentary talked about shooting the crap out of the Song Guards rushing to their people's defense. Even less about the Reliquary's true purpose as explained in the Shreen's own religion—a transport meant to carry them to their Quan, a sentient life form humans still knew nothing about. A creature tough enough to protect them as the Shreen slept through the fire of Kee's Sword. According to Shreen mythology, what Jeremiah had done was nothing short of stealing a sinking ship's lifeboat.

Scott ignored the babbling dogma for what he could trust outside the flyer's side windows. Screw all the religions. There was nothing blessed in the hand he'd been dealt. No salvation, save for what he was about to make for himself today. If God meant fairness and mercy, then God didn't exist. This wasn't about miracles. Just about getting his mind back.

The flight to Lake Tahoe was an uneventful glide over the same high country he preferred holing up in. March snows clung to the low areas and shadowed escarpments, although winter was losing its grip along the lake's northwestern shore.

It was hard to miss his destination. Even from this distance, the statue of Gabriel rose above the pines like a marble colossus of old. Seven hundred feet of archangel holding the Reliquary aloft. He smirked. God's magnifying glass. That's what they called the original crystal prism placed in those upraised hands before the thing was hastily replaced. It didn't do for the Lord's Gift to be burning tourists like ants on a hill.

The Tabernacle's golden dome facing Gabriel's statue came into view over the trees during the final minutes of flight. He pressed his nose against the window. Nothing equated to actually seeing this immaculately landscaped cross between the Taj Mahal and Saint Peter's Basilica. The limousine aligned itself over Prophet's Plaza, a mile-long avenue between the statue and the Tabernacle's cascading steps. The vehicle passed between eight sets of columns in the shape of minarets. In front of the Tabernacle, blue-jacketed staff and ropes held back scores of visitors. Apparently, thirty million dollars also bought him some privacy.

The limo settled below the Tabernacle's stairs. Scott peered up at the stained glass windows framed by marble columns, not sure if Jeremiah was going for the look of a mosque or cathedral. A handful of greeters, wearing the Church's pale blue business suits, filed out to meet him. Leading the procession in a white dress with blue trim was Saint Mara herself, right down to the pulled-back brown hair and serene smile.

Stepping forward, she proffered a tentative handshake once he emerged from the vehicle.

Setting aside his Wolf, Scott accepted her hand. Mara's fingers were cool to the touch.

"Welcome to our Tabernacle, Mr. Rellant. Please, allow us to take your instrument for you." She gestured toward a big burly type whose brush cut all but shouted Security. Her greeting sounded perfunctory at best, as if she plodded through protocol reserved for those with more money than sense.

"I'll take good care of it," the fellow assured in a linebacker's gravelly voice.

And have it scanned five ways to one.

Scott slapped a tactful nod over his disapproval and handed over his precious instrument. Well, he was going to meet their Prophet, after all. Thank God they couldn't scan his head. Hopefully, Water would remain on her best behavior. Judging from the steely emotions projecting from his inner fishbowl, Mister Brush Cut was the least of his concerns.

"Problems, Mr. Rellant?" Mara's inquiry cut into his awareness.

Oh, hell. He'd spent too much time staring at the man while worrying about his own inner demon. "Just a bit overwhelmed."

"Tell me about it," she threw back, in her charming Castilian accent. She offered an arm. "Shall we?"

Scott couldn't help a second look at the church's new Saint, not sure he'd heard her correctly. He covered his hesitation with a polite smile, hooking his arm with hers. They headed toward the stairs.

"Relax," she whispered, covering his hand with her free one. "I was an asteroid miner a few months back. Just call me Mara."

And I'm a former lunatic. Probably best not to mention that. He managed a simple response, her abrupt candor catching him off guard. "Scott."

I like lunatic, better, Water interjected, sounding more like her usual biting self. *Or thief. You should feel at home here.*

Hush. We're almost done. Soon you'll be with your people.

But they won't be where they belong, she huffed back.

Ignoring her jibe, he ascended the stairs, feeling like a misplaced schoolboy. Gawking over his shoulder at the huge statue one moment, then up at the marble columns the next. The Church's retinue fell in behind them.

Mara paused at the top of the first tier, holding her side and taking a few breaths. She inclined her head toward Gabriel's statue. "There's an observation room at the top if you're interested."

He studied her staccato breathing and the pinched look around her brown eyes. The Church's first canonized saint drew in slow breaths, her shoulders sagging. Why in hell were they putting her through this if she felt so bad? "You okay?"

She smiled. "I'm good. Still not fully recovered, in case you're wondering. God's miracles can take time."

"Some kind of mining accident, wasn't it?" Scott tried to remember what the talk shows said about her.

She nodded. "Something like that."

Their climb continued, Scott providing a more supportive grip on her arm. Once they'd reached the top, Mara took another brief rest beneath one of the main rotunda's fluted columns.

"The Prophet is pleased to agree to your playing before the Reliquary." Her voice dropped as if finding Church protocol too taxing. "Saw your concert last night. Not bad."

Water kicked at the fishbowl, the tips of her dorsal fins communicating her disgust in orange tones. *You are both thieves, along with this cursed Prophet.*

"*Shut up, Water.*"

"Excuse me?"

Scott's face flushed. Damn, he hated when that happened.

Her fine eyebrows raised. "Some kind of song?"

Luckily, he'd been speaking in Air, the Shreen's above water language. "Sorry. Just a musician thing. You were saying?"

"Your Visitation is scheduled for one o'clock. We'll have your instrument brought to you, Mr. Rellant."

"Scott," he reminded, hearing the fatigue in her voice.

"Scott," she amended with a slight nod. "We've an interview set up in the west wing. If you don't mind, Bob Mackenzie, our head of security, will escort you the rest of the way. I'll meet you again afterwards." She quickly disappeared through a side door.

"Just Mackenzie," the big guy behind him suddenly spoke up, handing Scott's case to an underling. He offered a meaty handshake of his own. "Right this way, Mr. Rellant."

Water stiffened inside the fishbowl, her dorsal fins flattening. *He lies. This is a trap. They found out about me.*

We're not killing anyone today, Miss Paranoia. Got it?

I want this to be over.

"No kidding," he whispered under his breath. One thing the both of them could agree on. It was all he could do to keep the gut-cramping tension focused inward.

Scott followed their Chief of Security into the Tabernacle's right wing. A carpeted hallway or two later, he found himself behind a lily-festooned table. As Benny predicted, most of those asking questions wore Church blue. When did you first feel God's inspiration? What drew you to the Church? How has the Prophet entered your life? All the while, Mackenzie focused on him as if taking mental notes of his own.

Scott was tempted to let Water field the answers. Instead, he disgorged a ready-made pack of lies to keep them off her scent. Audiences he could handle. Especially press conferences. Dropping into a set of canned responses was routine for him, and helped take the edge off his upcoming Visitation. Sure, his music was inspired by the Church's good deeds. Water snorted at that doozy. She was less thrilled by his praising the transplanting of Shreen from their dying world. His complements had her scraping the glass with her claws, sending discordant screeches through his head.

Of course his blotchy forehead attracted their interest, but nothing he couldn't ward off with the usual "abnormal calcification" excuse. He maintained a pleasant temperament despite Water's angry writhing. In a short while he'd be rid of her. It helped keep his nerves from rattling too hard.

Saint Mara rejoined him two floors up in a library atmosphere of oak panels and deep green carpet runners. Instead of books, niches contained both paintings and statues. Antiquities mixed with contemporary works, a few he readily recognized. Especially the face staring out from its timeworn frame.

"Rembrandt's *Self-portrait*," Mara introduced. "The prize of our collection."

"The price of Intercession," Scott guessed.

Thieves, Water added with her usual predictability.

"Along with several minor works," Mara confided, undaunted by his cynicism. She continued with renewed firmness. "God's Gift must be earned. These are tokens, Mr. Rellant. Nothing more. You want to see the worth of a miracle, you can count it in the years our donors gain in life and faith."

"Scott, remember?"

"Well, Scott, we've two floors worth of galleries to view if you wish."

He heard a decided lack of enthusiasm in her offer, but she seemed determined to put on a good show for her Prophet. Fortunately for her, he wasn't interested in the Church of Life's booty. "How about we view the Tabernacle instead?"

She gestured down the hall toward curving brass rails.

They walked out onto a balcony between a set of glass archways. Similar supports ringed the dome, supporting a massive stained-glass mosaic. It was like being inside a lit Tiffany lamp. He stared up at another depiction of Gabriel, wings spread, handing a gleaming Reliquary to a penitent Jeremiah Jones. Incense hazed the air in an almond fragrance.

The glitter of gold plating drew Scott's eyes down to a room-sized miniature castle surrounded by a phalanx of oak pews. The actual Tabernacle, or at least Jeremiah's fanciful notion of what would wow the masses. A tall wrought-iron fence kept the faithful at a distance. He eyed the Tabernacle's single cherub-infested door. Supposedly, the Reliquary sat inside, ensconced behind glass armor.

Water lit up like a green neon sign. *Inis Drum!*

He'd never heard her sound so thrilled.

Scott leaned forward. *You can sense it?*

The Song should be singing louder. Water's observation sounded troubled. Her happy emerald ripples faded. *Can you hear?*

He strained to get past Mara's rambling distractions about the Tabernacle's history and construction. Something tingled in his forehead. Rhythmic, but distant. If Saint Mara would just shut the hell up a moment, he'd probably catch more. Just the same, he was picking up something. Water's Song, not some hoax, waited inside the Tabernacle below. His heart pounded in his chest, and he struggled to keep his breathing nice and even. Finally, the end of his very long nightmare.

Water echoed his thoughts. *Do we really need to have lunch? Can't we just go in?*

He was already fighting the feeling himself. *Just put up with the formalities, would you? Or would you rather I start jumping up and down waving my hands?*

I don't like you.

Lunchtime arrived. Stomach churning for reasons other than food, he followed his hostess to a wood-paneled alcove on the third floor overlooking the dome. The glass Gabriel looked down with beneficence on blue-suited staff serving steamed trout on a bed of rice. Mara seasoned his meal with more awkward conversation. Subjects like his truly believing in the Prophet and his works, or in a loving God.

His appetite dwindled and soured on her probing of the void where his faith should be. Bad enough that she seemed to see right through him without rubbing his face in it.

You only believe in yourself, Water joined in, not exactly taking his side.

You hate your gods, he pointed out.

At least I feel something for them. Tell her the god she worships is a thief. Tell her how empty you will be when I'm gone. Let's see if she keeps smiling.

You've no idea how much I won't be missing our conversations, Song Guard.

He suspected Water would've bared teeth, had she had any.

"Scott?" his host interjected.

Crap. "Sorry, Your Holiness. Just drifted off for a moment."

"Just call me Mara," she reminded him.

"So you were a miner?" he asked, deflecting her from his awkwardness.

"Pilot." She paused between nibbles of trout. "Tugged bits and pieces of asteroid over to an orbiting refinery."

"And then you found God," he speared with just the right amount of manufactured awe. Let's see how she digested a serving of her own baloney.

She forked a mouthful of salad, not batting an eye. "Found a hot rock, actually. Some idiot with bad sensors brought one into the refinery. Radiation would've killed everybody once it got into the grinders. I towed it to a safe distance, and was throwing up blood by dinner." Mara set her fork aside. "How's your fish, Mr. Rellant?"

Her smile reminded him of Water on one of her bad days. "Okay, I deserved that."

She responded with a curt nod, her eyes narrowing. "So let's cut through the hogwash, Scott," Mara continued with a thickening Spanish accent. "What're you really here for?"

Her direct inquiry stopped him cold.

Be careful! Water hissed, fear edging her warning.

"Spending too much money." He could explain all this away as a publicity stunt.

Mara rolled her eyes. "No kidding. I've been trying to get His Holiness to—"

She paused at the sound of approaching footsteps. Four wide-shoulders in blue suits took positions along the balcony rails, their hands clasped in front of them. Each man gave off a "discreetly armed" vibe. Including Chief Security Officer MacKenzie. Did this guy simply not trust him?

Water perched on the edge of her fishbowl in a flash, her screech of alarm bringing Scott to his feet hard enough to topple the chair.

Mackenzie's hand drifted toward the inside of his jacket.

"It's just the Prophet's personal guard," Mara assured him, looking a bit surprised herself. She stood and inclined her head towards Mackenzie, then came around to put a hand on Scott's arm. "You okay?"

"Just fine," he growled, slamming the fishbowl's lid shut before Water launched him across the table.

"His Holiness will see you shortly," she said, her saintly mask firmly back in place. "Nice meeting you, Scott." She beat a hasty exit.

Which left him staring at Bob and his goons.

Mackenzie stepped forward with a reassuring smile and righted the chair. "Have a seat, Mr. Rellant. The Prophet isn't much on formalities." He gestured toward the chair. "Please."

The man's steely tone made Water's cutting fins hum dangerously. *I can kill him where he stands.*

Settle down, Water. Scott eased back into the chair, pulse pounding, fingers curling around the armrests, resisting Water's urge to lash out at the larger man. He forced his shoulder to relax and his jaw to unclench. Must not telegraph his tension.

They suspect.

They don't know a damn thing, Water. We're too close for mistakes, so don't get crazy on me.

Water stomped her foot, jingling her surrounding swimming fins. *They know I am here.*

This isn't the hospital, so stop banging around. We fooled them. We can fool these idiots. God, he hoped so.

His fingers scraped at his seat as Water's claws scratched along the surface of her fishbowl. *Better we kill this Prophet. End the thievery once and for all.*

Had this been her plan all along? He looked away from Mackenzie, his heart pulsating with a rush of blood. Attendants cleared the dishes and set down a fresh maroon tablecloth.

Water, there are four of them. We'd be dead before you got your hands around his neck.

Not if he is close. Her face drew down into the kind of feral grimace he hadn't seen since the bad old days. Dorsal fins flattened as if she intended to scream right through his brain at the Security Chief. *You cannot stop me.*

Scott ground his molars together. *Don't bet on it. I'm not dying this close to being rid of you. Stick to the plan unless you like living in an institution for the criminally insane.*

The threat slid her back into the fishbowl in an angry sulk. Not being re-committed was one of few things they agreed on.

Introductions weren't necessary for the next arrival. Obligatory white suit and pants with baby-blue edging. Perfect blond hair looking as fresh as its spritely one-hundred-and-six year old owner who didn't look a day over thirty.

Mankind's newest Savior flashed a salesman's grin. "Mr. Rellant. What a pleasure to meet such a famous musician." Jeremiah's voice sounded no less well manicured than his hair. The Prophet extended a hand unblemished by the ravages of time.

Scott ignored Bob Mackenzie's watchful glare and rose, albeit slowly, to accept the man's handshake. Damn if he was going to be kissing any of those fancy rings. "Your Holiness."

Muscles twinged along his spine, Water's way of telling him what she would've done just now. Sent them both hurling over the balcony. He sat. Quickly.

The Prophet took Mara's former seat across from him. "I find your second movement, *Water*, to be my favorite piece in *Song*. A brilliant juxtaposition of rapture and remorse. Much like our work here. We share a connection, it seems."

Let me share with this thief.

Inwardly, Scott rolled his eyes. *Jesus, Water, shut up and let me deal with this.* "I've followed your Operation Exodus closely. The Shreen tragedy deserves more than mere words. Hopefully, my music helps advertise their plight as well."

Jeremiah sighed. "You're not a member of our church, yet I

sense more faith in your music than I've seen at Sunday worship. You're a blessed man, Scott. God has watched you for some time. Tell me, what drives you? What brings you to us?"

Singing your death, monster!

Scott froze, hoping he hadn't just blurted out Water's little addition to the conversation. No, Mackenzie and the rest weren't piling on him, so he'd kept her diplomatic jewel in the fishbowl where it belonged. "A search for more inspiration, I guess." Okay, lame answer, but one less likely to get him shot. *Water, shut the hell up!*

"Would inspiration be behind your request to play, today?" Jeremiah breezed on, oblivious to the scintillating violence raging behind Scott's eyes.

"Precisely, Your Holiness." He added some flavoring to the lie. "Perhaps even a new movement."

"Wonderful, Mr. Rellant. You've earned your blessings tenfold, and I'm not one to ignore all that you've already done to put the Church, and Project Exodus, into people's hearts. Please, consider this Visitation as your just reward. The Church asks nothing more from you than your music." Jeremiah rose.

Did he just hand back my thirty million? Scott stood and stammered through the first honest words he'd spoken all day. "I'm...overwhelmed. Thank you."

"Just keep playing, my son." He beckoned toward the Tabernacle below. "It's time."

Scott swore he caught Mackenzie exhaling a sigh of relief.

Three

Scott kept a solemn pace behind the Prophet as they walked among the empty pews, despite his heart hammering to a faster tempo. Water perched upon the edge of her fishbowl, her claws tapping at the lid's rim. Odd that Saint Mara hadn't joined the parade. He had this chill up his back as if Bob Mackenzie's eyes bored into his spine, the Security Chief and his small contingent following at a respectful distance. Maybe Mackenzie did know about him. No matter. In a few minutes there wouldn't be anything left to worry about.

Water started singing. Surprised, Scott paused, narrowly avoiding having Mackenzie bang into him. The thrumming in his head was borderline maddening, yet beautiful despite its intensity. He couldn't even hear whatever the Prophet was babbling on about. Nor did he care, because a counter harmony echoed back from within the golden enclosure. Her Song was singing back to her. He wanted to break into arias himself. Soon this would all be over, and he would have the blessed gift of freedom.

The procession stopped before the fence's iron gate, and his pulse kicked up another notch. So close. Scott's instrument case sat on the purple carpet next to the entrance. He picked up the Wolf with a relieved breath and waited impatiently for Jeremiah to work the elaborate gold lock with a gilded key. And yes, the fellow was doing his best to embellish things with a droning chant. Did this guy believe even half of the mumbo-jumbo he spewed? Again, no matter.

The Prophet finished opening the gate with a final rattle of his "Keys to the Kingdom," as he put it. A narrow walkway led them along the golden castle's jewel-encrusted exterior, an angelic host poking a glittering head out of every available nook.

Jeremiah stepped before the Tabernacle's cherub-emblazoned archway and bowed deeply. The door opened on cue. "Behold, the Gift of God."

If only you could hear the angels I'm listening to, Scott thought. Water sang for her Song, and the chorus of memories inside the Reliquary sang back, beautiful resonances sung in Earth far below human hearing. How strange the singing didn't come from within the opened chamber into which Jeremiah beckoned him. Yes, the Song was here, but it damn sure wasn't in this room. The bastards were serving him up a fake Reliquary.

His expectations of giving a private performance were disappointed when Jeremiah and Mackenzie followed him into a viewing room. Everything was draped in deep red satin, save for a simple stone bench facing thick curtains. The heavy material couldn't hide an iridescence leaking around its edges. Jeremiah and his Security Chief quietly found places in the rear.

Scott swallowed back the premonition that something more than Church protocol was going on here. Time to get to work. Most likely these two wouldn't hear a thing. He unsnapped the instrument case and picked up his Wolf, running the oboe through its warm-up cycle. His mouth ran dry. It was all he could do to keep from gasping from the tension building inside him. At least he wouldn't be the one playing.

The curtains slowly opened on a bright man-sized prism couched in white sand, reminding him of an over decorated fish tank. Scott squinted at the rainbows cascading off the sham Reliquary. How fitting for this bunch of scam artists. He averted his eyes from the distraction, gazing toward the floor on his right from where the Song's music emanated. Some subbasement, no doubt. Well, the joke was on them.

He threw off the fishbowl's lid. *Go, Water.*

Her fingers flew over the Wolf's keys, setting up a deep droning monotone of sound to match the pounding in his brain. She pressed her lips to reeds especially designed for this one purpose. Water claimed she'd originally transmitted herself into his head. Now the Wolf would broadcast her back out again. He didn't understand this odd ability of hers to send her essence through the ether, but he didn't question it, either. Not with having been her unintended recipient. Mentally standing aside, he felt the Wolf literally vibrate in her hands when she aimed a strong carrier signal toward the Song below them.

She *moved.*

Out of her fishbowl. Out through the crystals in his head as if she were some sentient radio signal. Shockwaves rolled through him. This was happening. This was really happening!

But in the next instant she was back inside the fishbowl, thrashing about in a fit of rage.

Knocking aside the oboe, Water lurched to her feet, shrieking.

"It's dying! The Song fades!" She spun on the two humans behind her. "*What have you done?*"

Throat burning, Scott regained control of his body one scream ahead of her lunge. He slammed her back into her fishbowl. Her damage, however, had been done. The muzzle of a wicked-looking pistol pressed against his forehead, with an impassive Mackenzie holding a finger on the trigger.

"I'd say we're through, here," Jeremiah spoke, edging toward the doorway. "Interesting reaction. Guess your hunch was right, Bob."

"I'll take it from here," Mackenzie replied, waiting until the Prophet left before pulling the pistol away from Scott's head. "No sudden moves, Rellant. In fact, how about raising your hands and putting them on your head?"

Scott pointed at the glass, hoping to take some wind out of the Security Chief's sails before things got even worse. "It's a fake! What the hell are you people up to?"

Mackenzie glanced at the Wolf lying on the floor. "That's a damn fine instrument. Really hate to get blood on it. Hands on your head. You won't hear me ask again."

The Song is weak. Water's shaky voice conveyed her shock. *I must touch it.*

Then I've still a chance. Scott grasped at the possibility. He raised his hands in compliance. It wasn't the Church who held all the cards. He just had to get beyond their trigger-happy Security Chief. "I didn't come all this way for a light show, Mackenzie. You take me to the real deal or the whole world's going to find out what you're trying to pull here."

The man's pistol didn't waiver, and the expression on his square-jawed face remained professionally impassive. "Back slowly toward the door or the world's not going to be your concern." Mackenzie's words sounded like the last thing Scott figured he'd hear before being shot. "No, don't look at your instrument. Just keep facing me, and keep moving. That's it. Nice and easy."

Water glowed like a newly forged iron, her eyes staring out at him with a chilling calm. *Release me, Scott.*

You'll get us both killed. He's got his three friends outside, remember?

I don't care. Her voice broke. *The Song is dying.*

We're not. Let me try something else. Scott chanced a slight smile. "Hate to tell you this, but my oboe was set to record to an offsite location. Specifically, my agent's office. I suggest you put the gun down and start thinking…Bob."

Mackenzie smirked as if sharing a good joke. "Nice try, but we block outside transmissions." His tone leveled. "Now I suggest you keep backing up. One move from the siren in your head and I *will* drop you. Understand?"

Scott stared at the man, mentally replaying the words just to be sure he'd heard right. Mackenzie knew? "Who the hell are you?"

"An old friend of your father, which is why I didn't just shoot you now for stopping. Five seconds before I change my mind."

Scott then discovered that not only did the Tabernacle have a basement, it had a special room set aside for anyone whose desperation exceeded their bank account. One with padded beige walls. Hunched down in a corner, he unsuccessfully fought off shuddering waves of despair. How could things have turned around so fast? He cursed the creature inside him. His whole life would be like this room, thanks to her.

The Song is immortal. Water's voice was a mere whisper of its former self. *It shouldn't die. It can't.*

He tried squeezing her from his thoughts. Mackenzie apparently knew a lot about him. Judging from the Prophet's reaction, he'd also been clued in. And Mackenzie a friend of his father? From the look of him, the man couldn't be out of his thirties. Intercession, Scott guessed. Nothing instills employee retention like immortality.

Vague memories of his parents bubbled up from the darkness he'd hid them in. His mother holding him on the stairs while she was crying. Or screaming. He blew out a breath, expelling the unpleasant recollections. Best to worry about the present. Nobody, especially Benny, would be ignoring his sudden disappearance. Scott stood and kicked at the wall. His lawyers would eat these guys for lunch, and he'd live out his days in comfort on the remains.

Water sat slumped into a crystalline heap at the bottom of her bowl. Deep purple rippled along her fins. *They will kill us.*

And explain my absence how, Miss Sunshine? Why the hell didn't you leave? What went wrong?

The Song is weak and fading. Did you not hear me say this? I think it is too long from the Quan. I have no memories to draw on.

"After what you just did back there, I seriously don't care."

How can you not care? My entire Drum dies with the Song. Her voice firmed. *We must return the Song to our Quan.*

"*Your* Quan," he snapped. "The only place we're headed is back to the nut house."

You are heartless. You belong there.

They tensed as the cell door's lock clicked. Mackenzie walked in. Scott kept Water's combative instincts at bay. He wasn't ready to die just yet.

The Security Chief held up a pair of handcuffs. "Turn around, please."

"This isn't going to end well once my lawyers get involved," Scott promised while the man cuffed him.

"Might not come to that." Mackenzie turned Scott to face him. "Jeremiah has a deal for you and your imaginary playmate."

He was sorely tempted to demonstrate just how real Water was, but the Song Guard remained a knot of obstinate silence. "Then why the cuffs?"

"Because the Prophet and I have a little common sense. Come on. We don't keep His Holiness waiting."

Scott walked along the same green cinderblock corridor they'd pushed him down earlier. Desperate to make a deal, were they? Mackenzie led him into a bare-bones interview room. No stained glass here, just overhead light panels and few pretenses. Two guards in military fatigues stood against a back wall holding very big rifles. The reason for the impressive show of force sat across the table with his trademark smile.

"Have a seat, Mr. Rellant." Jeremiah extended a ringed hand to the vacant steel chair across from him. "It appears you have been prepared for God's purpose."

"Let me guess," Scott began, deciding to keep his feet. The need to play ball with this counterfeit preacher had long since passed. "All a big misunderstanding, right?"

"Not at all," Jeremiah countered, sliding a tablet across the table. "Your bibliography is most telling. Committed to New Hope Hospital at age six for self-injury and violent behavior. Diagnosed with severe Dissociative Identity Disorder. Released on your own recognizance after fourteen years of successful treatment. That was four years ago."

Mackenzie bent around Scott and tapped at the display. "This was the day before yesterday."

The video was a bird's eye view of him and the hapless cougar.

Scott stared at the Prophet. "You're having me *watched*?"

Jeremiah spread his arms. "Call upon Me in the day of trouble; I shall rescue you." He folded his hands with another winning smile. "A quote out of Psalms. Appropriate for where you find yourself now, don't you think?"

"Not really."

Jeremiah straightened the gold cufflinks on his ivory sleeves and managed a brief smirk. "Today, God revealed His mighty hand to me. He told me here was a young man who could find a true Reliquary."

"A fading Reliquary," Scott clarified. "Is that what this is about? If you think for a moment I'm going to help you steal another one, guess again."

"What were you seeking, here?" the Prophet inquired, his voice softening with a confessor's empathy. "Bob tells me there was a subsonic carrier wave coming from your instrument."

Scott would've thrown up his hands if they weren't chained behind him. "I was trying to get rid of the siren nobody believes is in my head. Didn't work because I was too far away."

Jeremiah nodded. "Ah yes, the unsanctioned Intercession leaving a siren's memory engrams embedded in your forehead. God's punishment is just, but so is His forgiveness. What would you say if God offered redemption? A second Intercession to relieve you of your burden?"

That caught Scott's attention.

Water uncurled, suddenly taking interest. *No!*

Scott flinched at the intensity of Water's cry. "My other half isn't too thrilled with the idea of stealing more Reliquaries."

Jeremiah shook his head. "We're not heading to Petal. Too dangerous, now. Instead, the Church is seeking to reap the harvest of good will we've been sewing on Sanctuary. We want you to see if the Shreen are creating Reliquaries in the new settlements. If they are, you can help us open trade agreements that will bestow the blessings of God upon both their people and ours."

"You can tell your agent you're giving a concert over there," Mackenzie threw in behind him. "It beats the kind of PR you'll get from having animal lovers come after you."

Animal lovers? Scott glanced at the tablet. The full weight of Mackenzie's statement stepped heavily on his future. Leaked video of the cougar's demise would see him back in a padded cell. Jeremiah had him, pure and simple. He tried not to look as deflated as he felt. "So what next?"

Beaming, Jeremiah rose. "Let us hasten to do the Lord's work, Bob." Nodding to his Security Chief, the Prophet seemed equally hasty in leaving the room.

"Does he ever listen to himself?" Scott remarked after the man left.

"Too much," Mackenzie replied with a snort. "Just hold still a minute, and we'll get you out of these."

The cuffs fell to the floor.

Mackenzie walked around to take the Prophet's chair. He snapped his fingers. "Take a break, guys. Scott, you want a beer? I could damn sure use one."

Scott nodded.

Mackenzie caught one of the departing guard's attention. "Two beers and my suitcase, Marty." He scooped up the tablet. "Cursing out your audiences in a language they can't hear is one thing, but eviscerating mountain lions...not so good."

"Anything you don't know?"

"Sit down, Rellant. We'll start with what *you* don't know. Ever hear of Brothers?"

Scott shrugged. "Can't say I have."

"Good. That's the way we like it. Brothers Security Consulting. A publicly traded subsidiary of Hanza Corporation, much like this Church here. You're looking at the CEO."

"You're mercenaries," Scott guessed, glancing back at the second rough-looking guard loitering near the door.

"Professional soldiers," Mackenzie corrected. "Second oldest profession. Your father worked for me, just as you're about to."

Numbed, Scott sat down. "My father? You blackmailed him into joining, too?"

Mackenzie leaned back with a grin. "You'd be surprised at how many of my recruiting sessions start this way. Now your father, Harry, he was the best commander I've had. Saved me and two squads during a mining colony rebellion. Some kitchen-sink bio-weapons were involved, and your father took the hit while sealing us off. He called in my debt after your first Reliquary incident. Made sure you'd be looked after. So, I've had my eye on you ever since."

"Is he still alive?" Scott asked.

"Retired with your mother."

"Where?"

"We can talk about a reunion later, but first things first."

They were interrupted by the guard's arrival with two frosted beer bottles and a black attaché case.

Scott readily accepted the bottle. Normally, he didn't get near alcohol in public places, but what was left to hide? And now this mention of his father and mother who were apparently still alive? The beer was cold, and a refreshing respite to his confusion.

Mackenzie took a few swigs, not losing a beat in the process. "So here's the deal. A one year, non-combat, analyst contract in trade for thirty shares of Hanza stock. A free Intercession to clinch the deal.

Just as the man promised."

"Seriously? A free Intercession?"

"Figured you'd like it."

Make them take the Song back to my Quan.

A few more pulls from the bottle were needed before he risked spending the rest of his life in an institution. An Intercession. The very thing both he and Water were looking for. Still, the Song Guard had to perform the transfer herself, so he couldn't ignore her. "The Reliquary's dying, right? How about we take it back to Petal where you found it, weather be damned?"

"Let me guess. That's a proposal from your siren."

"More like a demand."

"So, she can negotiate." Mackenzie shrugged. "Not an unreasonable request providing things work out, but we're talking a rough ride. Petal's being pounded by both heat and ice storms from all the water pushed by the plasma jet. I'll see what we can do. Send in a drone if we have to. We'll write the Reliquary's return into the agreement. Even still, your contract's a tourist visa compared to what most folks sign."

I will not join these thieves.

Yes you will, if you want this done. "We're heading to Sanctuary?"

"Nice and quiet like."

Mackenzie downed the last of his beer before continuing. "With all the Hanza stock you're getting, you could play mountain man in the Sierra Nevada for a few years when you get back. All we need is a signature."

I swear, Scott, I will kill you if we steal another Song.

Water's oath sounded half-hearted, her vehemence eroded by a chance to take her own Song home. Scott sighed. "Where do I sign?"

Mackenzie reached for the leather case the soldier had put on the table next to them, then motioned the mercenary over again. "Marty, need a witness. And more beers. We'll be in here awhile."

Four

The limousine glided to a stop on a wet tarmac. "This isn't my hotel," Scott observed.

"I'm getting you out of the public eye," Mackenzie explained, glancing out the window next to him. "We've got a fading Reliquary, so we're all on the clock. Jeremiah's sending you to Norway for operations training."

"Norway?"

"Here's your ride."

A sleek black business flyer taxied into sight around a small hangar and whined to a stop, its tail emblazoned with Hansa Corporation's gold "H" logo. Red-and-green wing lights blinked reflections from scattered puddles. A hatch swung down, transforming into lighted stairs.

"I'll meet you in Oslo after I finish lining up equipment," Mackenzie said as Scott opened the limousine's door.

Scott shivered, his thin shirt offering little protection against a damp Lake Tahoe evening. He'd expected to be shuttled back to his hotel after signing the contract, not spirited out to the airport. "What's in Norway?"

His new boss handed him the Wolf's case. "Training," Mackenzie repeated. He gestured to Scott's blotched forehead. "Keep your private friend to yourself. Double for what you know about Reliquaries. If you need incentive, read Article Thirty-Six of the contract you just signed."

"I take it the incentive isn't a pat on the back."

"Let's just say that we take care of our own. One way or the other." Mackenzie opened the door on his side, stepped out, and regarded him over the vehicle's rain-beaded roof. "I know things are moving fast. They have to, so just get yourself from one day to the next. You'll be done before you know it. Have a good trip."

I do not like to fly.

Go to sleep, Water, Scott advised, having little love for

suborbital flights himself.

Play me a song.

Not tonight. We're both exhausted. No, today hadn't gone well for either of them.

The cabin's indirect lighting welcomed him with a bland corporate atmosphere. There were enough seats in the coffee-colored interior to accommodate a half dozen passengers in comfort. The pilots, if there were any, kept to themselves. He slid the Wolf into an overhead compartment and slumped into the cushioned chair beneath it. Water had fallen silent. He almost imagined himself free of her. That had been the plan, freedom and the rest of his life to enjoy it. Shit.

The cabin's outside hatch remained open. He peered out an oval window as another limo showed up in white Church colors. A young woman in blue jeans and matching denim jacket swung out of the back seat carrying a gray shoulder bag. Slamming the door shut behind her, she waved off two suits attempting to escort her to the steps. Only when the flyer's lights caught her angry Latin eyes did he recognize the Church's vaunted Saint.

Scott stood as she entered, his puzzlement growing.

Mara slung her satchel into the aisle seat across from him before seating herself next to it.

"Saint Mara?"

She raised a hand. "Spare me, okay?"

"I don't understand. This is sort of a private flight."

Her eyes rolled into an expression Scott surmised as being reserved for imbeciles. "You need a pilot to get you into Sanctuary in one piece for your little off-world concert. I...volunteered."

Concert? Is that what Mackenzie told her? "You know who Brothers is, don't you?"

Her manner iced further. "Everybody along the String of Pearls knows them."

Scott recalled Mackenzie mentioning his father had been involved in a miner's rebellion. She used to be a miner. Like hell she volunteered. "Did something happen between you and the Prophet because of me?"

"*Vete,* just leave me alone." She slumped in her seat with half-closed eyes. The cabin door clunked shut behind them, muffling the sound of revving engines.

They were airborne within the hour and climbing high into the California night. He couldn't stop glancing at this possibly defrocked saint. What had he started back in the Tabernacle? Civil war? Okay, she was a pilot. Why would he need his own pilot? Was she doing this as a favor to her church, or to get away from it?

Mara groaned. "What now?"

It was too late to look the other away. He sifted through all the things he couldn't tell her, finally arriving at what he hoped would be a safe question. "So, what did you fly?"

"Energy bars."

"Huh?"

She pulled a thick wrapped wafer from her purse. "Want one? High protein stuff. Helps build up the blood. Got way more than I'm going to need."

He diplomatically accepted the snack and her change of subject. "You do look better." It wasn't a lie. The fine bones along her cheeks seemed less pronounced, and those almond eyes no longer sank into her face.

Mara's shoulders sagged. "I just had a second Intercession."

And this was reason to sound like the world was falling apart? "Wow. Congratulations?"

She gave a tepid laugh. "You know how much my union donated in order to save my life? A quarter billion from the pension fund. People's *retirement money*. Gone. Know how much I paid for this second Intercession? Nothing. Jeremiah thought it would be a good idea to speed things up so the famous Scott Rellant could have a private pilot." She snapped her fingers. "Just like that. Walking down the hall and up comes this idea of his. All so you can sing pretty for his church. See anything wrong with the picture, Mister Superstar?"

So she wasn't so blind to what was going on after all. "Maybe you're looking at the wrong picture," he slowly returned, not wanting to find out what Mackenzie's Article Thirty-Six entailed. One female had already placed him in deep trouble today. He didn't need another adding to it.

"Then finish filling in the picture for me. What are we doing that's worth a quarter-billion?"

He took a breath. "Not singing songs. I'm working for Brothers, now, Saint Mara. Not the most informative bunch."

She scooted to the edge of her seat. "Jeremiah's private little army? Why?" She peered at his discolored forehead with a furrowing brow. "You're buying yourself an Intercession. Is it cancer?"

"Something similar." Not exactly a lie, but one that would hopefully get her off his back.

"And Mackenzie didn't tell you anything about where we're going?"

"Not really," he deflected. Sooner or later someone would have to tell her the truth, but it wouldn't necessarily be him. He had too much on his plate already. "We're heading to Norway for a start," Scott added with a conciliatory smile. Their destination would be obvious soon enough.

"Norway. Lovely," she muttered. "Must be important. Oh, and from now on, it's just Mara, okay? I'm not feeling very saintly right now."

"Not much into the whole saint thing myself," he admitted, hearing the weight of guilt in her words. Her people had been taken to the cleaners in order to save her life. Not something he'd want to carry around, either.

She gave a dry chuckle. "Trust me. Watching people give you Last Rites while floating above them will make you a believer." Mara folded her legs beneath her on the wide seat and bit into one of her energy bars. "Heard the Prophet saying I was in God's hands when I flatlined. Should've seen the look on his face later when I described the Reliquary next to me. They put up a screen so you can't actually see the thing, but they didn't think of someone looking down from the ceiling. The Reliquary wasn't a crystal. More of a glowing stone with bright beads. Jeremiah canonized me on the spot." Her tone soured. "But things are all wrong, now. Miracles shouldn't need to happen twice. God's gifts aren't supposed to be spa treatments."

"Or cost that kind of money," he added, his cynicism wiggling its way from a mouth he should be keeping shut.

"Or cost that kind of money,' she agreed. "Mad Dog Six-Eighty."

"Excuse me?"

She finally smiled back. "MD-Six-Eighty. You asked me what I flew. Asteroid punters. Small three-tonner used by bush pilots and other crazies along the String of Pearls. Probably why Jeremiah had me come along."

"Because you're a pilot and crazy?"

"And sick of hearing me bitch about Intercession costing so much. So this isn't about your giving concerts to the Shreen on Sanctuary, right? Tell me I didn't get a second Intercession for something as petty as you doing a PR stunt?"

"Talk to Mackenzie, he's calling the shots." Scott turned to stare out the window, hating the pleading in her voice.

Damn Jeremiah and his stinking church.

~ * ~

They arrived in Oslo two hours later. The sun cast a pearlescent hue across the early morning, wreaking havoc with his internal clock.

Mara had slept through most of the flight, including the brief weightlessness. He enjoyed no such luck, the Earth's curve a distraction that would've probably bored an asteroid jockey such as herself. Their unseen pilot taxied to a stop upon arrival at Oslo's airport and opened the door onto a deserted parking apron well away from the glitter of commercial terminals. His first impression of Norway came upon a biting cold sweeping the cabin.

Bob Mackenzie poked his head inside after the hatch opened. He'd traded his business attire for a nondescript gray turtleneck beneath a heavy blue jacket and matching pants. He nodded toward Mara. "Welcome to Norway, Your Holiness."

She waved a warding hand. "Knock off with the holiness crap, okay, Bob? I pretty much told Jeremiah where he could stick my halo."

"He'll get over it. Jeremiah didn't start out with a halo, either." Mackenzie entered the cabin and picked up the Wolf's instrument case. "I'll put this in the shuttle for you. We'll be flying up north to a place called Loen. Outstanding hotel there called the Alexandra. If anyone asks, you two are on vacation. Taking in the mountain air for the lady's health and all that."

"And the real reason?" Mara interjected, giving Scott a sidelong look.

Scott shrugged toward Mackenzie. He'd signed a contract, but apparently she hadn't.

"I'll get you briefed in flight," came Mackenzie's curt reply. "Let's go."

They transferred to a small four-passenger green teardrop with yellow stripes along its fuselage. The flyer's cramped interior smelled musty like an overused rental. Mackenzie pointed out landmarks as they whisked over the waking city. Snow dusted the rolling landscape, but not to the depth Scott would've assumed for Norway in March. Their shuttle curved northeast, bumping through rough air over breathtaking snowcapped peaks. He was thankful Water remained asleep. She would've hated the turbulence even worse than he did.

From her vantage point in the front seat next to Mackenzie, Mara pointed down toward plunging cliffs ending in a deep blue strip of water.

"Lustra fjord," Mackenzie provided. "Part of Sognefjord, the largest fjord in the country. We're halfway to Loen. Either of you ever been to Norway?"

Scott shook his head.

Mara's eyes narrowed. "Looks like a lot of Sanctuary's topography. Jeremiah's Canyon, to be exact. I've seen videos of the place. Is this what everything is all about? Mr. Famous blowing his horn for the Shreen? Seriously?"

Mackenzie shook his head. "The whole concert idea is just a cover story for Scott's fans. Yes, we're heading for Sanctuary, but we're doing a direct drop into Jeremiah's Canyon instead of using the access tunnel. You think I'd risk three-hundred-knot crosswinds for a publicity stunt? We've work to do, which I'll cover later."

Mara's eyes widened. "You're going with us?"

"Yeah, and you're doing the driving. Jeremiah and I figured an asteroid dodger like yourself wouldn't have a problem with this kind of run."

She scowled. "Depends on what I'm driving."

Mackenzie's voice took on the same deal-making tone he'd used on Scott. "How about one of the hottest rides this side of anywhere, Miss Martinez? Didn't you wonder how I got to Oslo so fast?"

Mara took the bait. "I did. So, what's the ship?"

"C Class Surveyor. Top of the line. Civie version of the Nightshade. Bet you heard of that, eh?"

Her mute stare said everything her apparently numbed tongue didn't.

Mackenzie laughed. "Thought you'd love it."

"Some sort of military ship?" Scott ventured.

Mackenzie nodded. "Heavy scout. Stealthy. Used for interdiction teams such as you and me once you're trained up."

"Trained to do what?" Mara pounced.

Mackenzie glanced back at Scott before answering. "Spying on our Shreen brothers and sisters to find out why the colony's failing."

So you're not even going to tell the Church's Saint what's really going on? Scott wondered to himself. Just how much of a falling out did Jeremiah have with Mara? Or was it just her getting more airtime than he did?

Mackenzie pointed toward a small city curled around the end of an adjacent fjord. "Right now you both have a few days R&R courtesy of Hansa Corporation. Good food, heated pool, and a damn nice view. Best enjoy it."

Mara's eyes widened. "Project Exodus is failing?"

Mackenzie nodded. "Over half the population's gone. We'll be finding out why." He pointed out the canopy. "Loen coming up to our right."

Scott had to hand it to the man. He was a damn good liar.

The flyer descended along a mountain's rugged shoulder,

aiming for a circular landing apron at a hotel complex upon the north shore. Peaked orange roofs stair-stepped up from the shoreline to end at a multitiered edifice of glass and concrete topped by Norwegian flags. Scott spied a generous swimming pool with a few guests choosing to brave the snow-swept decking. He expected far more of the white stuff this far north, and was surprised at the amount of green spread across the hotel grounds.

Mackenzie escorted Scott and Mara to a luxurious two-bedroom suite on the top floor overlooking Loen's picturesque fjord. After a brief respite, Scott joined Brother's Chief Executive Officer on an attached balcony, both of them taking in the crisp cool breeze drifting across the water.

Mackenzie gestured out over the deep blue fjord. "Do any recreational diving?"

"Not really," Scott admitted. "I have a few problems."

"Siren problems?" Mackenzie frowned.

"Yeah. Water likes to swim but forgets I need to breathe."

Mackenzie wrapped his fingers around the balcony's brass railing. "Then the first thing we work on is your self-control. Underwater training is essential to this mission's success. You and I will head out to the farm tomorrow and get started. Mara will join us once she gets her strength up. I want a lid put on your other personality, understand? We're going to be operating at depths requiring zero mistakes."

As if it were so easy. "No problem."

"Good. I'll pick you up at seven tomorrow morning. And as far as Mara's concerned, this is about the welfare of the Shreen, not about Reliquaries."

"And the bit about shrinking populations?"

Mackenzie took a breath. "Not far from the truth. Forget the rosy pictures Jeremiah painted back at Tahoe. We're dropping into the canyon because the only safe access had to be sealed off. Just do your job when we get there. The less you know, the better off you'll be."

Scott regarded the man, unable to figure him out. "I don't get it, Mackenzie. You know damn well Jeremiah's as fake as his church. Why keep this up? Money still so important to you?"

Mackenzie rubbed his chin. "Fair question. Money, power, life. All the same in my line of work. In the end, the only thing important is a man's honor. When you've got everything, nothing else means as much." He turned to leave. "Get some rest, Rellant. Eat a light breakfast."

Scott spent the remainder of the day fighting jet lag while

purchasing apparel appropriate to the climate from the hotel shops. He emerged wearing a white woolen sweater and heavy gray corduroys to keep the chill away. Several pairs of jeans and various sweaters came along in a shopping bag, including some needed underwear. Brothers hadn't thought of everything in their haste to relocate him.

Mara remained in her bedroom, apparently content to sleep off the trip. To Scott's relief, Water seemed equally content not to bother him.

Mara joined him that evening for a dinner of smoked salmon and other high protein tidbits. She descended the second floor's spiral staircase wearing white pajamas, a quilted brown comforter draped around her diminutive curves.

"Hate this lag," she grumbled, settling at the glass table and helping herself to fish and boiled eggs. She glanced around their lushly appointed living room. "Jeremiah's sparing no expense." Her assessing gaze landed on him. "Nice clothes, by the way."

"They've several shops out front." Scott helped himself to crisp pastry rolls laced in chocolate. Judging from the casual wear, she'd chosen to leave Saint Mara back in Lake Tahoe. "How are you feeling?"

She glanced down at herself and shrugged. "Great, surprisingly. Been thinking about what Bob said about the Shreen colony failing. Maybe God's condemned them, and we're not meant to save them."

He bit his tongue. Okay, so there still was some saint left in her. "Actually, the Shreen have two gods, Kee and Anasa. They can't stand either one of them."

"Then maybe they didn't deserve His gifts from the start."

Scott let out a breath, thankful Water wasn't awake to hear this. "Speaking of which, what exactly happened between you and the Prophet?"

She speared a piece of pink filet off her plate with her fork before speaking. "He thinks I'm getting too much attention. Especially when I talk about giving out Intercessions to those who need them most, rather than those with the biggest wallets. And then there's this whole thing about needing two Intercessions. Miracles are miracles, right? You shouldn't have to ask God twice."

"Assuming you were asking God at all." Scott winced inwardly at the slip. He waited for the blast back, and Mara didn't disappoint.

She set her fork aside. "You're not much of a believer, are you?"

"Just purging my inner demons," he tried to joke, but the truth behind his words wasn't particularly funny. What did he have in his life beyond getting rid of Water? He pushed himself away from the table. "The night's yours. I'm turning in."

~ * ~

Water stretched, eager as never before to watch the fishbowl dissolve under the weight of her jailer's deep slumber. How long had it been since she'd talked to another human? Decades? She breathed as Scott breathed. Paced her own heart's song to his rhythm until she could feel the press of cotton pajamas across his soft, fleshy body. She smiled. Trying to adjust to Norwegian time by staying up all day had come with a cost he hadn't intended.

She pulled the heavy blankets away, relishing the cool temperatures. Water inspected her arms, trying to visualize her cutting fins and glittering skin. Awkward, clumsy, slow, human body. It was hard to imagine herself anymore. Was she even a Song Guard now, or just human?

"Song Guard" she whispered, balling clawless fists.

Her Song was dying. Bad enough she'd failed her Quan once. How many visits from Kee and Anasa had her mighty mother endured, only to come to this? Mackenzie returning the Song to Inis Drum? She snorted. That thief would steal her hopes, too. Nor would Scott help. All he cared about was ridding himself of her. The death of her entire Drum meant nothing to him, and she had no idea how to change his mind. And how much of his indifference was her fault? Had she not given him reason to hate her? More failure to set before her Quan.

She wanted to scream.

Water eased herself from the bed and sought solace in the music she shared with her captor. She pulled the Wolf's case from beneath the side table and unsnapped the clasps. She gently lifted the oboe from its foam cradle and ran the instrument through its warm-up cycle, her thoughts reaching back to the deep azure hues of Inis Drum. She played a long trilling sigh, singing her anxiety away with a faraway dream. Soft blue shafts of sunlight drifting among the Drum's depths. Her sisters swimming beside her, their bodies sparkling and full of life. The warmth of her Quan below. The relaxed roll and ebb of waves above. Tears coursed down her face. Everything was dying.

"Beautiful."

Water pulled the oboe from her lips, her back arching even if there were no dorsal fins to extend themselves in outrage. "Nothing about this is beautiful," she spat toward the unwelcome company.

Mara, wrapped in her blanket, stood in the doorway, still smiling. "What are you singing?"

Of course she wouldn't understand Air. Water switched to human language while gathering her wits. Mara might care about her plight where Scott didn't. "He sleeps. I am Water."

The woman took a step backward. "What?"

Water measured the distance between them, satisfied she could stop Mara if the woman ran for help. "I am Song Guard, Mara Martinez, as you are a saint. Can you tell them to send my Song home before it dies?"

The smile froze on Mara's face, but instead of fleeing, she leaned against the doorjamb. "Okay, this is getting creepy."

"My Song is what you call a Reliquary," Water pressed. "It is fading. Your people stole it from us. You must return it."

"Wow, different voice and everything. Is this some sort of split personality crazy, Scott?" She pulled a small white disk from the breast pocket of her pajamas. "Guess that's why Bob gave me this. You know there are men outside, right? I just press the button."

"Only if I let you," Water hissed. Humans were all alike. "Your church lies to you. Your God is a thief like mine. The Song is *our* gift, not yours, and we must have it back."

Mara took another step back and into the hall. "How about I leave you to your music because you're really freaking me out. Tomorrow, I'll get my own suite and then a ticket out of here."

Scott won't forgive me if you do. I won't forgive me. Water took a controlling breath. "I will not hurt you, Mara Martinez. Mackenzie knows I am here with Scott. I will not give him cause to fear me, so you should not fear me, either. I can find more Reliquaries for him in Sanctuary. I agreed to do this because he says he will return my Song, but I do not believe him. This is why I speak to you now. I need to believe in you, Mara. I need someone to help me bring my people home."

"You're what, a Shreen? Is that it?"

Water nodded. "Song Guard." She brushed a finger across the pale patterns on her forehead. "I was drawn into Scott's mind when his father put him against the Song to heal him. I have been with him ever since. I want to go home as much as he wants me to, but now the Song is dying."

"Dying." Mara repeated the word as a statement, not a question. She slowly walked back into the room and sat at the bed's far corner staring at her. "This explains too much."

"You are a pilot. You could take the Song home."

"So you're not going to hurt me, right?"

Water curled back her lips in frustration. Scott had made one noisome deal and here she was making another. "I will not hurt you."

"Ever."

Clever female. "Unless you help them steal another Song," she spat.

Mara let out a long breath and grimaced. "How about you start explaining to me about all these lies first? Or better yet, about the Reliquary dying."

Five

The smell of cooked eggs wafting up from the hotel suite's living area was a pleasant wake-up call for Scott on his first full day in Norway. Sunshine filtered through the bedroom drapes. He glanced at an ornate clock on the side table, groaned, and rolled out of bed. Pulling on jeans and a brown sweater from yesterday's shopping bag, he headed for the bathroom and a quick shower. He paused at a mirror on the way to the spiral staircase, pushing brown strands of hair over the shiny splotches on his brow.

Mara, wearing her earlier denim outfit, looked up from the remnants of another roll-in banquet. "Still some sausages and scrambled eggs left." She pointed a fork at a covered dish. "They've some awesome crepes." She folded her arms, her voice lowering. "Or would you settle for water?"

"Crepes." He took a plate from the cart and served himself.

"Sleep well?"

"Probably, since I can't remember dreaming. How about you?"

She waved her fork. "Interesting night. Had the strangest dream." Her words trailing off, Mara's expression clouded. "What if I needed two Intercessions because the Reliquary was dying?"

Scott paused between forkfuls of eggs. One instant they were talking about crepes. Now she'd gone deep into forbidden territory, hitting the nail on the head in the process. "Yeah. Crazy dream."

Her brown eyes looked about to spear him. "Yeah, *muy loco.*" She took a breath and smiled. "Bob's out on the balcony waiting for you. He's brought me a flight manual on the Surveyor to study. Said I'll have a simulator by noon to play with."

"Can't wait to get going, eh?"

"You have no idea. Hurry up and finish. Bob's not much for patience."

"You do know he prefers to be called Mackenzie, right?"

Mara returned a knowing grin.

Scott headed out to the balcony, the brief patio affording a chilly but impressive vista of Loen's majestic fjord. The deep green waters were beautiful but also threatening in light of their plans.

Mackenzie, wearing black slacks and a leather jacket, lounged in a deck chair like some stocky movie villain. He raised a cup of what first appeared to be coffee until Scott caught a whiff of chocolate. "Ready for a long day?"

"Are you kidding?" Scott looked across sparkling waters toward white-capped peaks. "Sanctuary going to be this cold?"

"Nah. Generally stays around fifteen to twenty Celsius. Water's warm on the surface, but gets nippy about ten feet or so. "Cold water experience will do ya good." Mackenzie stood, set his cup aside on a small table, and gestured toward the slopes rising behind the hotel. "We're here for the topography. Her Nibs has to drop us down a crack with three-hundred-knot tail winds pushing her ass. Not something you can trust to computers. Takes gut instinct and a touch of insanity. In other words, our saintly asteroid jockey."

Scott glanced back at the patio's sliding glass door and lowered his voice. "She tell you about her crazy dream? The Reliquary dying? Thought the subject was on your list of unmentionables."

Mackenzie's lips thinned. "I didn't tell her anything. What about your other personality?"

"Sleeping. She does that most of the time."

"Like to meet her one of these days."

Yeah, and she'd love to meet you, too. "No, you wouldn't."

Mackenzie gulped the last of his hot chocolate. "Well, keep an eye on your pilot. Last thing we need right now is some crisis of faith splashing us into a cliff."

They hopped into the green shuttle waiting for them on the hotel's pad and headed southeast to a highland lake called Lovatnet.

They skimmed over the startling emerald surface. "The green color's from glaciers and runoff," Mackenzie explained. "Gets a little murky."

Scott could see what drew his boss to the area. Nothing in the Sierra Nevada came close to the granite walls plunging hundreds of feet straight down into narrow waters. Mackenzie aimed for a sloping patch of shoreline barely wide enough to accommodate an old barn and adjacent cottage. The canyon closed in on them like hands clapping together around a gnat.

"Just a little incentive for our pilot," Mackenzie breezed, noticing Scott gawking up at sheer cliffs. "Jeremiah's Canyon is twice this high. Mara's going to give us one hell of a wild ride once she gets up to speed." He set the flyer upon a rutted road leading to a smudged white cinderblock cabin with sloped metal roofing.

Scott puffed out a frosty breath upon exiting and followed Mackenzie up to a door of faded oak planks braced by a rusting iron frame.

"Not much inside," Mackenzie confided, working an antiquated lock. "Fridge, heater, and a couple cots. Bunk the ops teams out here sometimes." He scraped the door open.

Peering inside, Scott glimpsed a single room having more in common with a hunter's shelter than the clandestine mercenary training facility he had pictured.

Mackenzie pulled the door shut again and motioned toward the barn. "Good stuff's out back. Come on, I'll acquaint you with your gear."

The ramshackle building more than met Scott's expectations. A sagging wooden door refused to give way until Mackenzie pressed a hand between two slats. There was nothing rustic about the row of floodlights inside, nor in the arrow-shaped aircraft three times the size of their small rental.

Whistling, Scott walked around the flying machine, trying to discern so much as a hatch on the light-devouring black fuselage. Wings merged into a uniform darkness that swallowed even the glare of overhead lamps. The only feature he could make out was the dull gray recesses from which the landing gear extended. "You park a black hole in here?"

The mercenary chief laughed. "C Class Surveyor. Basically, a Nightshade without the missiles. We replaced the rotary launcher with a diving sled. Gets us in fast and silent. Mara's going to wet herself seeing this thing. Here, duck your head and take a look at the bay." Mackenzie ran his hand along the undercarriage. Scott half expected the man's fingers to disappear into the featureless skin.

Shadows moved and shifted, revealing a gray square in the Surveyor's belly. Mindful of the low clearance, Scott crouched and made his way along the aluminum decking. He looked up at a cross between a navy blue toboggan and sporty wave rider. The thing hung from an overhead cradle by four cables.

"Two-man sled," Mackenzie said as if reading from a manifest. "Self-contained eight-hour air supply. Rated to a depth of three hundred feet, though we won't go much beyond a hundred. Can reach a top speed of twenty-six knots and outrun anything. Even sirens if we're really unlucky."

"You expecting to be really unlucky?"

The other man shrugged. "We've not been in direct contact

with the Shreen in Jeremiah's Canyon since they started killing each other. Figured those left aren't going to be too hospitable."

"*Killing* each other? It's that bad?"

"Yeah, that bad. You think those idiots would've worked together, or at least teamed up on us, but no. Goddamn tribal wars. Only one bunch left now, and barely enough to remain a viable colony." He motioned Scott toward a row of tables to the Surveyor's left. "Your embedded memories have anything able to explain what went wrong?"

Scott searched through his conversations with Water. A wealth of information about Inis Drum, but precious little about the other lakes. Anything outside the periphery of her Quan was apparently not worth remembering. "Absolutely nothing."

"Says something in itself," Mackenzie commented.

Scott nodded, not looking forward to their upcoming dive. Water slept now, but naptime would end the moment they hit the water. He walked up to one of the stainless steel tables and picked up a helmet consisting of black fabric fused to a clear facemask.

"Not much different than a vacuum suit," Mackenzie said. He indicated one of the backpacks on the table. "That gives you twelve hours of recycled air without bubbles. Plug into the sled and you've an extra eight." He tossed a suit lined with thin black cords. "This responds to both pressure and temperature, so don't worry about freezing your ass off in the lake. Shuck down to your skivvies and put it on."

The suit slid easily over his narrow frame like loose fitting coveralls, at least until Mackenzie strapped on the backpack. Only then did those thin cords constrict to mold themselves into a second skin. The helmet barely cleared his nose, leaving few gaps between itself and his face as the mask mated to the suit's collar. A fresh circulation of tinny-tasting air quieted the sensation of having a plastic bag stretched over his head.

Mackenzie's voice, calm and assuring, came over tiny speakers. "How you doing?"

"A little claustrophobic," Scott admitted, his heart rate not encouraged by a new stirring inside his head.

"Just focus through the mask. You're doing great. Hop on the table, and I'll slide on your flippers. We'll put the ballast belt on last."

Water stirred in her fishbowl. She leaned over the lip, looking at him. *What is this?*

Scott slid up on the table, the suit proving only a mild restriction. He sucked in a helping of air, relieved the effort didn't fog up his mask. *We're going for a swim. Go back to sleep.* Fat chance.

A swim?

The eagerness in Water's voice wasn't encouraging. *Look, I can't deal with you and this at the same time.*

She cupped her chin in her hands. *I remember swimming.*

Mackenzie hesitated halfway into his own suit. "Scott? You alright?"

"Getting used to it," he replied, standing up on the awkward shoes. Walking was a chore. More so when his instructor finished helping him affix gloves and a thick belt. Scott concentrated on just breathing normally.

Stop being afraid, Scott.

Have you forgotten almost drowning me in the Caribbean?

Water's grin looked too eager. *Then give me control. I know how to swim.*

Scott winced at the idea. *Oh, hell no.*

He practiced breathing and trying to walk. No doubt he looked like a goose with a pole stuck up its butt.

Mackenzie was into his own suit in a quarter of the time, complete with a broad grin. "Let's head to the dock. I'll be right behind you. This is gonna be fun, Scott."

"I'll keep telling myself that."

Calling the meager planks arranged at the water's edge a dock was charitable at best. Water sloshed over the lichen-spattered wood the moment he stepped on them. As promised, he felt a slight coolness through his ankles, the fabric guarding him against both the freezing waters and the Norwegian morning.

Mackenzie joined him on the narrow perch, instructing him on the use of a wrist display—air flow, lights, and even the equivalent of a panic button to inflate the belt and send him popping to the surface like a fishing bobber.

"Can't drown in these things unless you want to," the mercenary assured him. "And then you'll have to work on it." He nodded toward the darker waters a few yards out. "There's a little bit of shallow, but it drops off quick. I'll start you on the edge until you get used to it. Then we'll swim out a bit. Nothing deep. At least not for today. I just want you getting a handle on the suit."

Water slapped at the fishbowl with her hands. *Let me go.*

No. He focused on Mackenzie. "What about currents?"

"None up here. For starters, just sit and slip off."

Grimacing, Scott obeyed, coolness closing around his thighs. Of greater concern was Water pressing against her fishbowl's glass, her long glittering swimming fins swishing back and forth. Begging for trouble. He sucked in some courage and slid off the wooden planks. The lake rose midway up his chest, giving him a dry-yet-wet chill. He swallowed back an urge to jerk his helmet off and call it a day. Water wasn't helping. He sensed her leaning half out of the fishbowl as if wanting to tip him forward into a dive.

Mackenzie joined him, startling Scott with a slap on his shoulder. "Doing fine. Now crouch and get your head under. Nothing's going to change but the view."

Scott obeyed, trading a blue sky for a slightly greenish landscape of round pebbles. Being in the frigid water felt similar to sticking his head in a freezer, but again the temperature seemed manageable. No hint of leaks, thank God. Water continued being a good little nightmare and kept her mouth shut.

"Let's go down slope a little," Mackenzie suggested.

"Let's," Scott muttered, turning toward a great aquamarine abyss. He straightened and took a few hesitant steps, the lake's weight pressing on his chest. Looking up made things worse. The guy wasn't kidding about a drop off. The rippling surface looked to be a good couple feet above him.

Mackenzie kept to a casually professional demeanor. "The suit changes the air mix and pressure the deeper we go. You might feel stiffer, but everything's being handled for you. You're doing just fine, Scott."

He wished Mackenzie would stop saying that.

"A couple more steps. Your belt's set for neutral buoyancy. You can't sink."

Gritting his teeth, Scott moved carefully across the gravelly bottom, staring at the yawning gulf ahead. A ragged edge of bare rock brought him to the edge of the precipice. He saw no sign of bottom. Just a flawless emerald nothingness.

"Stay put. Slow your breathing. No rush. You're fine."

Scott fought the urge to tear everything off. "Just…give me a moment."

"Got all day. Work on your breathing. Slow, deep, and even."

Hell with this. He clawed at his helmet, only to roll on his back in a desperate fit of thrashing.

"Hold on, Scott. I got you."

Water was half out of the fishbowl before he knew it. *I have you. Give me control, Scott.*

It was the cougar all over again. He gave her the reins. She slipped from Mackenzie's grasp with a leisurely sweep of fins, rolling into a vertical dive.

"Scott!" Mackenzie's shout made the comm crackle.

"He is fine," Water threw back. "I am teaching him."

Mackenzie's voice in his helmet was all command. "Stay with me."

"Come catch me," she retorted, the beckoning depths a welcome homecoming. Sliding through the darkening water in Scott's body was almost like being herself again.

Scott's thoughts intruded on her bliss. *Damn it, Water. Listen to him.*

"I will teach you far better," she shushed him, skimming along the granite cliffs. The suit began to harden around her. Annoying.

You won't teach me anything if you don't let me do the swimming, idiot Song Guard.

Then stop being a child, Water dismissed. *Feel the smoothness of your passage. The rhythm of your fins. Curl gracefully...like this. Move back up toward Mackenzie. See? Simple? You even breathe this time. You cannot drown.*

Water relinquished her control of his body, settling back into her fishbowl with a satisfied smirk.

"Coming back," Scott said, seeing Mackenzie diving toward him with helmet lights flashing. Water's joyous familiarity with the elements bolstered his self-confidence, his heart settling back into a steady beat.

"You have your head on straight again?"

"Yeah." He glided to a stop before the grimmest expression he'd ever seen from the man, save for when Mackenzie held a gun on him. "You said you wanted to meet the siren in my skull. You just did. She's helping me swim."

"I'll help her into a frontal lobotomy if she pulls her shit again, Rellant. There's no room for mistakes down here."

Not if you die, thief.

His hand drifted of its own accord to a previously unnoticed knife sheath on his belt. *Don't you dare, Water. Just swim and be nice. He's trying to help.*

I would have been nicer all along if you let me swim. I am so tired of hating you.

Just play along, and we'll both be free of each other soon enough.

She remained perched on the edge of her fishbowl, instructing him to use his flippers more like her powerful swimming fins. Scott swore he felt fins along his back and arms as well, as if someone had glued crystal plates to him. He swept aside a curtain of anxiety to appreciate the green waters. Silver flecks darted around the rock face, seeking the darker clefts as he glided by. Water was beside herself with glee, encouraging him into deeper investigations along the submerged cliff.

Mackenzie kept checking to ensure he was okay, but otherwise shadowed his explorations. "Seems you've a good teacher."

"Mostly solo, now," he replied, angling up through a shaft of light. If only he'd gotten his hands on one of these suits back in the Caribbean, things might've turned out better between him and Water. Still, his arms seemed like sponges and he was dog-tired. Time to head back to the cabin.

Water folded her arms upon the fishbowl's rim and rested her chin on her hands. *You did reasonably well for an addle-headed fish.*

Because you didn't drown me for once. And thanks, he threw in, not used to sending gratitude her way. The swim had put her into an uncharacteristically good mood. Only one death threat today, and it hadn't even been directed at him.

~ * ~

Water plucked at the flimsy pajama sleeve covering Scott's aching muscles. "I do not look like this, Mara Martinez. My true skin is hard and strong. It shines like rainbows."

She let out an exasperated sigh. Her last talk with Mara hadn't ended well. Too many truths for this saint to digest. Had Mara believed even half of what she'd been told before running out? Was there even a chance left of enlisting her help?

Mara sat on the edge of the bed wrapped in a white hotel robe, her expression no less pessimistic than Water's hopes. "Scott said you hate your gods."

Water frowned. The last thing she wanted to do was darken Mara's doubts. "Not at first. Kee brought us light and warmth. Anasa gave us cool breezes. We loved and trusted them."

"And then what?"

Water drew in a long breath. "Betrayal. Anasa asked Kee to fashion her the most beautiful of necklaces, and he demanded our Songs for the jewels. The Quans refused, so Kee drew his sword from the sun and Anasa summoned her winds. The Quans shouted, using the water to make their voices loud. It is why we call our lakes drums. The sound drove the gods off, but Anasa and Kee keep returning. She will not marry him without her necklace, and he is as stubborn as she is selfish. How could we not hate them?"

"And then we came." Mara stood, shaking her head. "Another

thieving god. Is that what you think, Water?"

"Is this not what you think?" Water countered. "Is this why you come to talk to me again?"

Mara fidgeted with the hem of her robe. "I wasn't always a saint. In fact, until I was reborn, I didn't believe much of anything beyond the next paycheck. I don't want to go back to such meaninglessness. Or...emptiness." She pressed a hand to her chest. "I saw God in what those miners did for me. They gave everything. Our God's not a thief, Water."

Water saw a chance to finally get Mara on her side. "Yet your Prophet steals our Songs in your god's name. Prove to me that the one you worship is not a thief. Help save my Song, Mara Martinez. Help save my people."

Six

Scott could barely swivel his head, his suit reacting to the foreboding depth by stiffening to the point where the suit had the flexibility of medieval armor. He blinked at his wrist display. "Says one hundred and six meters." He panned his helmet lights across a field of grayish pebbles. Beyond the narrow beams of his lights he could see nothing but blackness.

"Welcome to the bottom of Lovatnet," Mackenzie quipped, waving a gloved hand beside him. "I'd say we met our goal. Not bad for your second day."

"If freezing is your goal, yes," Scott retorted. This was the final of eight dives, and by far the deepest. "Begin ascent?"

"Roger that. Use your voice mode."

"Suit command," Scott began, no longer needing to fumble for his belt's control pad. "Initiate slow ascent."

His belt hissed in acknowledgement, lifting him slowly off the fjord's rocky bottom. Scott spent the next twenty minutes thinking of how comfortable his warm hotel bed would be by the time he crawled through the door.

Mackenzie had other plans in mind after they'd surfaced. Instead of hopping into the flyer after changing in the barn, the man took him inside the cottage. "Had your stuff brought out. Fresh beer and sandwiches inside the fridge. I'll get you a decent oven tomorrow."

Scott stared at an overworked space heater trying to keep the Norwegian night at bay. The Wolf's instrument case sat next to a stack of blankets adjacent to one of three cots. His extra clothes were laid out on the other beds. "What's all this about?"

Mackenzie folded his arms. "Mara doesn't want you back at the hotel. Seems your other half has been blabbing away at night and upsetting the shit out of her. It was either bring you out here or watch our pilot take the next flight to Oslo. I told you to keep a lid on it."

Scott kicked at the floorboards, his stomach sinking. "Mind telling me how? Because until now I thought I had."

"I don't do miracles, aside from holding this team together. Suggest you have a long talk with your siren." Mackenzie turned for the door. "Tell it to shut its trap or forget sending the Reliquary home."

"She doesn't believe you, anyway."

"Not my problem. Fix this."

"Fix this," Scott repeated through gritted teeth after Mackenzie's abrupt departure. "Water, wake your ass up. What in the hell you were thinking, talking to Mara?"

I wanted her to be a friend and help save the Song. Nobody else will.

The hopelessness in her voice told him how far her little ploy had gotten her. "We just have to stick to the plan. Mackenzie promised to send your Song back."

He is one of the thieves who stole it. My people are fading inside the Song, and I am the only one who cares.

Scott huddled against the space heater's meager comfort. The whole idea of the imaginary fishbowl was to stop her nighttime sojourns from happening. "How long have you been popping out while I slept?"

Shall I cut you again so you can keep track? She sank to the fishbowl's bottom, curling into a glistening ball, purple waves traveling up her flattened dorsal fins. *You do not care about anything but yourself. My people die, and this means nothing to you. I have failed at the one purpose I had, and this, too, means nothing to you.*

"Maybe it's because of all the cutting you've already done," he spat. "Your sick idea of revenge is what got us thrown into the nut house in the first place, remember? Mom holding me while Dad bandaged my arms. You do remember, right?"

I want to die.

Scott cut his tirade short at her dark statement. She'd never said that before. Ever. Water was always the one keeping him from ending it, sometimes forcefully.

He softened his voice. "No, you don't, Water. Mackenzie gave us a chance we'd never have gotten on our own."

He lies. You never cared. Mara refuses the truth. My people will never see their Quan because of me. Inis Drum dies, and I will, too. Her cutting fins abruptly sang out in a high-pitched burr.

Water surged through the fishbowl. Her desperate ferocity, fueled by bleak despair, rushed through him. He turned for the door, but not by his own volition. "Let go, damn it!" His demand had no effect on arms opening the door, the night's biting cold unable to dislodge her grip on his body. He reeled outside in a drunken stagger toward the lake. "Water, no. Don't do this."

Do you feel hopeless? Scared? This is me. This is what you do not care about.

"I'm not like that," he gasped, trying to drag his feet or trip himself up during her headlong rush down the darkened road. Except... *I am like that.*

An awful realization to die with. "Stop," he yelled, hoping someone would hear him. Mackenzie's flyer was gone. "Somebody help me!"

Water screamed, sending a flood of hurt through his head as if her soul were tearing itself apart. Alone. Terribly alone.

"I didn't know!" he pleaded.

They hit the shore. His feet slipped on a bordering crust of ice, tumbling him forward. An icy shock tore the breath from his lungs. The water burned, engulfing him in total blackness, sapping strength from his limbs.

Water tried plunging them deeper. Shit. He didn't want to die. Heart pounding, muscles pumped, he seized control and pulled them toward land. His shoes found purchase in the gravel. Thank God, some leverage. He dug in and pushed up. His face broke the fjord's surface, and he sucked in a needed breath.

"Not...letting you die!" Scott plowed forward on numbed legs, dragging himself back to the embankment. Head spinning, he collapsed on the half-frozen ground.

Let me go, Scott.

"Never," he gasped. "You're stronger than this."

You do not care about my people.

"No," he admitted, trying to stand. Stay here long enough in the cold and Mackenzie would find his dead body the next morning on this very spot. But Water's hopeless screams chilled him far worse than the paralyzing cold killing him now. "I don't want you dying too, Water."

Because you do not want to die, yourself.

"Because you're...better than...me," he forced through teeth-chattering spasms.

Scott struggled to sit up, his dripping hair stiffening into icy layers. An unforgiving wind threatened to claw him back into oblivion. He lurched to his feet, barely feeling them at all. Focusing on the cottage's beckoning lights, he counted victory in each step taken.

No Reliquary felt as good as the space heater welcoming him back inside. Scott fell back against the door, slamming it shut behind him. He tried working the lock, but his numbed fingers couldn't manage the keypad. Groaning, he crumpled in a sodden heap. Water was the strong one. The third leg of an unstable stool he laughably called his life. A source of vehemence he relied on. Tonight, that support had finally broken under the strain of his not giving a damn.

"Sorry," he whispered, having no idea what else to say. A great weariness overwhelmed him. Maybe she'd try again if he dared sleep. Maybe he deserved it.

He woke sometime in the early morning, feeling like an undecided rag with one side hot and the other sopping cold. His muscles were beyond weak, every movement requiring a moment's thought before expending effort. Not a word from Water, who lay curled up and staring blankly through the glass, as if she too were at a loss for what came next. Puddles dotted the wooden floorboards around him. God, if Mackenzie walked in on this, the man wouldn't let him remain unsupervised for the remainder of the mission.

His timepiece told him he had roughly three hours before dawn. A sandwich from the fridge helped restore strength to his limbs. He shed his dripping clothes for a black zippered flight suit on the cot next to his other clothes. He hung out his pants and shirt to dry as best they could on the cottage's third cot, and curled up on a dry spot with some of the blankets Mackenzie sent.

Play for me.

"Too tired," he whispered. "How in the hell am I supposed to get that Song for you, Water? All I have is what Mackenzie gives me. Best I can do is make him deliver on his promise, even if I have to put a gun to his head."

Water lifted her head, clear hair fibers falling across her face like a veil. *Play for us, then.*

She sounded no less wrung out than he felt. Scott dragged over the Wolf's case, not wanting her to slip back into the yawning desolation he'd just extricated her from. They both needed a fresh start, one served with a brimming ladle of hope. He reached back into their shared mind for visions of a new dawn rising over Inis Drum's sparkling waters. *Child's Morning* was a lighthearted song from Water's racial memories, one he hoped would carry both himself and his Song Guard far from these troubling waters. He pulled the oboe from its cushion and sent it through a quick warming cycle.

Scott began to play the melody, but didn't remember finishing it. He opened his eyes to find Mackenzie and Mara staring at him, both wearing leather coats atop dark flight suits similar to the one he'd found last night. He followed their gaze to the clothes he'd draped over the cot near the space heater.

"Rough night," he explained, sitting up amidst the blankets. "Slipped on some ice down by the lake."

Mackenzie shook his head, but Mara's lips formed a silent, "Bullshit," behind the mercenary's back.

"You're looking well rested this morning," Scott shot back at her. "Good sleep for once?"

"For once," she returned, surveying the cabin's Spartan interior. "Mackenzie, can Scott and I have a moment?"

Their boss shrugged. "Thought you didn't want to be in the same room with him."

"Just go, please." She blew out a long breath after the man disappeared out the door. "I figured he'd give you another place at the hotel. Not this."

Scott stood, stretching aching muscles. "He knows better, unlike you, apparently. Water's not some figment of my imagination, Mara. She's real, and she's deadly when she wants to be."

Mara glanced at his wet clothes. "Such as last night?"

"I slipped."

"Yeah, I bet you did." Her lips thinned. "Let's bring this all out in the open, okay? Mackenzie told me everything. Even showed me your commitment papers. Look, I'm sorry. I can't imagine what a split personality must feel like, but that's all your Water is to me. She might seem real to you, Scott, but to us she's just your messed up head trying to compensate for those crystals stuck in your skull."

"So I'm just crazy," he surmised with a scowl.

Mara returned a relenting grin. "Hey, I can work with crazy. Just don't ask me to join in. I've issues enough without your imaginary friend cooking up stories of dying Reliquaries and genocide." Her voice hardened. "So here's the deal. The only bitch aboard my ship is going to be me, got it? Your little friend stays put without me hearing her crap. You just do your job, and I'll do mine."

"Fine." Maybe it was better for her to swallow Mackenzie's lies whole. "You're the insane asteroid pilot, and I'm just plain ol' insane. Works for me."

Her response was delivered with a relieved breath. "Good, and don't worry. Half the pilots I've flown with back home are certifiable. Comes with the career choice."

Water glared out of her glass enclosure with obvious disgust. *She will not help us. She believes nothing of what I told her.*

Then we'll just have to make her a true believer.

Accepting Mara's response as the closest he'd get to a buried hatchet, Scott switched to safer venues. "I take it you saw your ship?"

She nodded. "Took a few hours saying hi to her." She extended a hand. "Come on. Let me show you what I'm good for."

Grabbing his jacket, Scott followed her across the frosted grass to the barn, not wanting to dwell too long on last night's outing. Hard to blame Water. He'd pushed the Song Guard to her limits just as surely as she'd driven him into the lake. Water managed to put him inside *her* head for once, and he hadn't liked what he'd seen of himself from that perspective. Is it any wonder she'd reached out to Mara?

Mackenzie waved at them from beneath the Surveyor's opened rear bay. "Are we a team?"

"I'll do the driving," Mara chirped. "You two do the diving." She put an arm around Scott's shoulder as if to indicate they'd come to an accord and patted the ship's prow with her free hand. "So how about I take her out?"

Mackenzie shook his head. "Not yet. I've set up the flight controls for some hands-on simulations. This isn't one of your rock hoppers."

Mara released Scott and stalked up to the mercenary, her lips pulled back in a smile that was all teeth. "Why don't you let me worry about that?"

"Because I'm not letting you." The man stepped back, clearing the way for the underwater sled as it lowered in a soft whine of unspooling cables. He grinned at her growing frown. "I've locked the computer on my bio, Sweets. This bird sits in the hangar until I say differently. You work on your simulations. Scott and I are going to suit up and take the sled out for a spin."

Mara offered a suspiciously cheery, "Okay," gripped the edge of the opened bay, and disappeared inside.

Scott exchanged a look with Mackenzie before helping him detach the sled and move it out from under the Surveyor. The machine's blue composite frame wasn't heavy as much as awkward due to its size. He changed into his suit with some misgivings about reentering the lake, taking what reassurance he could from the sober feelings radiating from the fishbowl. It appeared Water didn't want to talk about last night, either.

Geared up and masked, they carried the sled sideways through the front door rather than use the disguised hangar door, Mackenzie obviously not eager to expose the barn's true nature to prying eyes. They set the sled down along the embankment where Scott had fallen in.

Mackenzie glanced at ice-laced footprints embedded in the dirt. "Slipped, eh?"

Scott detected a hint of exasperation in the man's voice through his helmet's speakers. He tried imagining himself in the other's boots for a moment. "Hell of a babysitting job you have here, Mackenzie."

The mercenary's face mask momentarily fogged with the first genuine guffaw Scott had heard from him. "We'll do alright, Scotty my boy. Let's get this rig into the water and have fun for once. Clear sky, so visibility should be as good as it gets."

The sled's neutral buoyancy made getting aboard a lot easier than Scott expected. At Mackenzie's instruction, he straddled the left saddle designed for both sitting and supine positions. Lying down, he grabbed the handlebars behind the narrow windshield, watching displays wink to life across the glass.

Mackenzie took position beside him, the sled sinking just beneath the surface. "Left handle is the throttle. Right handle is up and down. Turning left on the yoke is left, and right is right. Simple. Take us out, Mr. Rellant."

This is not swimming, Water observed, her tone glum.

But it's faster," Scott encouraged, twisting the left handle.

Scott angled them along the brief shelf comprising Lovatnet's banks. The soft whir of recessed propellers replaced the sound of slopping waves against his mask. The swift passage of rock and gravel beneath them encouraged Scott to push the throttle more, jetting them into an exhilarating flight over the submarine terrain. Water rushed over his body like a hard wind, the sensation nudging Water from her sullen mood as well. He sensed her brightening.

I remember swimming like this.

"Quit petting and show her what you have," Mackenzie encouraged beside him.

He's talking about the sled, Scott realized after an initial start. He turned the handlebars right and sent them plunging over the drop-off, the emerald expanse giving him the assurance he needed to open the throttle. He braced his heels in a set of stirrups as acceleration drove them downwards into twilight. His suit stiffened, the sled's windshield flickering once before displaying a clear view of the craggy topography below. The propellers pitched into a high drone.

Their dive exacted a cry of delight from his unseen passenger. *This is almost as fast as I remember swimming.*

"So, Mackenzie, is this our top speed?"

"Yep. Nothing's going to catch us."

Scott grinned. "Don't bet on it."

He actually enjoyed himself. The sled proved a perfect toy for darting around Lovatnet's secret recesses. Did the cold bother him?

Yes, but he didn't mind trading discomfort for discovering a sudden patch of freshwater plants in the shallows, or a mysterious cave mouth gaping from within a recessed cleft. Thanks to the clever electronics, he discerned the ancient grooves left by glaciers forming the narrow lake, rather than having his vision clouded by murky runoff.

His sled mate took it all in stride, offering various facts about the sled's performance and handling as they zoomed along. Mackenzie showed him how to connect up to the craft's reserve oxygen, and familiarized him with displays meant to help them rendezvous with their mother ship.

They drifted over a silt-choked ravine near the bottom. "Rather odd," Mackenzie commented. "Getting an active beacon."

Scott looked at the bright red dot moving through a series of concentric rings. "That supposed to be a simulation of Mara's ship?"

"Simulation hell, that *is* the Surveyor," came the mercenary's testy answer. "Take us up."

At this depth of over a hundred meters, Scott's gloves had stiffened into useless clamshells. "Sled command," he ordered. "Begin a slow ascent."

The machine obeyed, rising slowly to allow their suits to compensate. The water around them brightened, the fabric covering Scott's body slowly softening from its steely consistency. Scott glanced at the battery readout. Four hours and cold as hell, but the sled hadn't lost more than a quarter charge. Just how long a search was Mackenzie planning on Sanctuary? The only feature not aboard their clever little toy was the hot lunch he craved.

The mystery of the rendezvous beacon solved itself when something tore across the lake to their left, near the surface, sending a V-shaped wake nearly flipping them off their saddles. Swearing, Scott leveled the sled and broached. He and Mackenzie sat up in their seats atop the bobbing waves and looked around for the cause.

Mackenzie pointed above them. "There. Just finishing her loop."

Scott watched a black dot drop from the sky. The Surveyor expanded into a black arrow against blue skies, the ship rearing to a hover a few feet over the waves with engines keening. The flyer slowly eased its way toward them, the flutter of maneuvering thrusters swirling the aquamarine waters beneath.

Mara's voice boomed at them. "Afternoon, boys."

"Definitely Brothers material," Mackenzie muttered, pulling off his mask. "Out for a morning spin and a kiss-my-ass, are we?"

A chuckle embroidered her amplified rejoinder. "Hey, next

time lock out the fire suppression subsystems, *cariño*. Emergency protocols override everything, or didn't they teach that in mercenary school? I don't have the cradle deployment figured out yet, so I guess you'll have to head to shore on your own. I'll put this back in the barn, then you can bitch at me over something better than those sandwiches you left in Scott's fridge." The Surveyor turned on its tail and jetted off.

"You hired her," Scott reminded the man.

"She volunteered," Mackenzie corrected, shaking his head. He slapped the sled's side. "Flank speed, Rellant, before she decides on a high-priced restaurant in Oslo."

Seven

"Okay, yell at me for taking your pretty toy out for a spin." Mara perched herself upon the equipment table next to the Surveyor and propped her chin in her hand.

Mackenzie set his diving helmet beside her then walked over to an adjacent locker. He slapped at the palm reader. The door swung open to reveal a rack of wicked-looking pistols. The mercenary pulled one out and tossed it on her lap.

Mara looked down with distaste. "What's this for?"

Mackenzie grabbed her hand and curled her fingers around the grip. "Your predecessors, Sweep Team Alpha, got themselves caught. The Shreen took their time with them. This, Your Holiness, is so you can put a bullet in your head before they get to you."

Color drained from her face. "Don't call me that." She pushed the gun back into his hands and hopped down. "Spare me. The Church has missionaries going to Sanctuary all the time with food and supplies."

"Sound about right to you?" Mackenzie asked Scott with a sardonic grin. "Nothing but happy Shinys out there?"

Scott studied the pistol. "We probably could use some training."

Mara raised a forefinger. "Excuse me? Thought you told me he was full of crap?"

Mackenzie leaned against the Surveyor's hull. "His embedded memories aren't."

"The Shreen hate us about as much as they do their gods," Scott explained.

She shook her head. "Yeah, I already heard that from your make-believe monster. And now I'm supposed to *believe* it?"

Mackenzie handed her a pistol holster. "Chocolates and roses are over, sweetheart. You're bunking out in the Surveyor tonight and hereafter. You will be armed at all times in order to impress yourself with the seriousness of what we're doing out here. Tomorrow, we see if you're the shit-hot pilot we hope you are."

She glanced at Scott. "He getting one?"

The mercenary chief narrowed his eyes in Scott's direction. "No. And since I can't seem to trust either of you, we'll all be staying out here for the duration of the training."

Scott ended up back in the cottage eating sandwiches for a solitary dinner, the other two having elected to remain in the barn.

She begins to believe, again, Water observed with approval after he wound himself in a few blankets near the heater.

He pulled over the Wolf's case. "It's a start. I still haven't figured out how we'll end up with the Song without Mackenzie's help. Any suggestions?"

Let me kill him, and we will have Mara help us.

"Don't be so naïve. There's still Jeremiah between us and your Song. Any *useful* suggestions?"

I will kill this false prophet, too.

"Along with the army of mercenaries guarding him. Got it."

She rolled on her back. *Play for me.*

He sighed, having few ideas himself beyond sticking with the plan. "Don't fret, Water. I'll get you back to your Quan with your head held high. Either with Mackenzie or in spite of him."

Why? Because you do not want me to kill us both? I should have. Just to teach you a lesson.

"Love you, too, Water."

Scott played *Anasa's Dance* for her, letting the seductive rhythms pull them a world away from dying Songs and devious mercenaries. Wind was the goddess Anasa's providence, woven into the blue folds of her long dress. His oboe mimicked the soft rush of an evening breeze, keeping each lingering note in tempo with Anasa's swaying hips. Water sang in a trilling accompaniment, embellishing their performance with a duet worthy of any Shreen mythology.

A cold rush of air interrupted their reverie. Mara peeked her head inside. Like Scott, she was still attired in a black flight suit. She also wore one of Mackenzie's pistols. "Nice music. So whom am I talking to, tonight?"

Water shot Scott a warning look. *Be nice to our pilot. Do not tell her the truth.*

"Just me. Sorry to disappoint. Come on in before we both freeze."

She shut the door and rubbed her shoulders. "Was listening to you outside. Didn't want to interrupt. That something new you're working on?"

"Something I recently finished, actually. *Song's* third movement. I call it *Anasa's Dance*." He gestured to a cot. "Have a seat. There's sandwiches in the fridge if you haven't eaten."

"I came over to invite you for pork chops. Boss man flew back dinner from Loen." She slumped down on the proffered cot. "Your other half told me about Anasa and her *imbécile* lover. A religion where they hate their gods. So what about you? Hate your god, too?"

The question, delivered without a hint of sarcasm, caught him off guard. Scott set the Wolf in its case. "Can't say He's done me any favors. How's yours doing?" The last part slipped out before he could stop himself.

Mara's expression softened from her usual self-confidence, her eyes losing their determined stare. "Mackenzie keeps changing the story about what we're doing. Why we're doing it. How long before Water's version is closer to the truth than what my own Church tells me?"

Scott frowned. Mackenzie would have his ass if Mara quit now. "Look, Mara, just because I'm a faithless pig doesn't mean you should jump into the sty with me. I'm a nutcase, remember? You're the saint, here."

"Then why don't I feel like one, lately?" She stood. "You really don't believe in God?"

"He doesn't visit insane asylums, apparently. Just makes the arrangements and walks away." Scott took in a long breath, not meaning to sound so bitter. "You find a loving God, Mara, you let me know, okay?"

"I thought I had. Doesn't believing in nothing make you feel hollow, inside?"

"I'm never alone. Trying to change the situation."

One miracle at a time.

He laughed. "Yeah, Water. That's exactly what it would be." Scott caught his tongue too late to keep the conversation from passing his lips.

"Tell her I said hi," Mara threw back while heading for the door. "She's probably the sanest one here. Just the same, I'll be locking the hatch doors tonight. Goodnight, Scott."

"Night, Mara. Tell Mackenzie he can have my dinner."

Scott didn't eat much better the following morning, either. Mackenzie pounded on the door just after daybreak and handed him a protein bar with the consistency of wet cement. "Let's go, hot shot. Drop practice. Mara's already running through her pre-flights."

Scott didn't need to throw on a flight suit, having slept in it. He followed the man outside, letting the chill finish waking him. The barn's southern wall facing the lake had been rolled aside, exposing the Surveyor's dark prow. The ship's engine's purring throb rebounded across the narrow valley.

Suiting up next to a running spacecraft was all the impetus Scott required to be dive-ready in record time. Scooping up fins and helmet, he crouched and followed Mackenzie along the ship's belly. He swallowed the remainder of his joyless breakfast to free up a hand for the forward hatch's brief ladder.

The Surveyor's interior was a cramped mix of equipment racks and conduit with four gray cushioned seats crammed into the fore section. Everything hummed, clicked, or whined against a droning backdrop. The cockpit held the acrid tinge of warm electronics. Mara, looking at home in her flight suit, gave a quick wave from the pilot's position. "Grab a seat."

Mackenzie was already in the copilot's position to her right, pointing out readouts and graphs crawling across the dashboard display. "Middle display's our audible signature. We can't be heard. Not a whisper. That's what the flutter baffles on each of your thrusters are for."

"Wouldn't want the Shreen knowing we're about to screw them over again," Mara remarked with an acidic smile while patting her side holster.

Mackenzie frowned at her. "How about we get to work?"

She turned. "Buckle up, back there."

Scott dropped into the seat behind her and strapped in. The sled swayed slightly in the rear bay, the submersible tucked up tight in its overhead cradle. The Surveyor's sweeping forward display made for a broad windshield, allowing him to watch Mara ease them from the barn.

"Hangar clear," Mackenzie reported.

"Hangar clear," Mara crisply parroted, sending them into a left turn low over Lovenet's banks. They sped over the water, giving Scott a view normally reserved for speedboats. An early sun reflected orange ripples across waves rushing beneath them.

"Ten meters," she said, skimming the surface as if trolling for fish.

Mackenzie shook his head. "Fifty-eight decibels. Too damn loud. Descend to six meters and slow down."

"Six meters," she acknowledged. "Slowing to eight kilometers per hour. Fore and aft thrusters at twenty percent. Fluttering fifty percent."

Scott wasn't too happy with how the Surveyor quivered, as if it were about to drop from what little sky they had.

Mackenzie frowned. "Six meters altitude and thirty-eight decibels. Give me four and thirty. Come on, woman. Teach this damn boat."

She scowled. "I've crap for flaps, you know. Five KPH and bringing thrusters to thirty percent. Baffles extended one hundred percent."

Cold water rose to claim them. Scott braced for the expected impact.

Mara grinned. "You've got your four meters. I own this dance, *perra.*"

Makenzie tapped at the dashboard display. "Twenty eight decibels. Nailed it. Lock into the flight computer."

"Locked." She lifted the Surveyor. "Breaking off."

The lake dropped away. She pointed them skyward, the engines rumbling with an eagerness for altitude. Mara executed a right bank that glued Scott's stomach against his ribs.

She let out a breath. "Now we'll see how this goes. Engaging program and rolling in from three hundred meters." She leaned back, removing her hands from a pair of joysticks.

The ship banked sharply and dove for the lake, its engines cutting back to a whisper. Hull quivering, the Surveyor drifted across the surface in a faithful mimicry of Mara's earlier efforts.

"Four meters at twenty-eight decibels," Mara said with satisfaction. "What now, boss man?"

"Bring us to a hover."

Show time. Scott unbuckled his straps and pulled on his fins and helmet.

Mackenzie had already lowered the sled to the deck by the time Scott joined him. "Got to be quicker than that, Rellant."

Ignoring the jibe, Scott straddled the sled's left saddle. Mackenzie joined him on the right.

"Drop us when ready, pilot," Mackenzie ordered.

The deck below them slid back to reveal green water. The cradle's cables spooled out, lowering them into the lake with little more than a few added ripples to mark their passage. The wires detached.

Scott pushed the yoke forward, the surface closing over their heads. Above them, the Surveyor's shadow slid away.

"Come back around for pickup," Mackenzie said, motioning to stop their descent. "We'll take another look at the acoustics once we're aboard."

Scott used the beacon display on the dashboard to guide them beneath the Surveyor. Magnetic grapples clicked into recesses and drew them back aboard, rivulets sliding off their sled and spattering the deck.

Mackenzie dismounted and peered over the copilot's seat at the display. "Terrible, but not bad, guys. Other than waking the entire village with our drop and retrieval, we did okay. That just gets us shot on the way out instead of captured."

Mara sighed. "Everyone back in your seats for another go-round."

Mackenzie snickered through his face mask. "Wait until we start doing this at night." The humor faded from his face. The man's brush-cut grimace was all military. "We must drop inside of two minutes. Retrieval will take one. Twelve minutes for the entire op, then fly as if hell's coming after you, because most likely it will be."

"Sirens?" Scott guessed.

The man nodded. "A safe bet if we find what we're looking for. We'll be out here all day, and all night if need be. Once we hit the mark, I'm upping the ante. We'll come in from near orbit, hot as hell in order to simulate what we'll be faced with on Sanctuary. Do good tonight and it's steak and lobster. Otherwise, we're talking sandwiches and ration bars."

The pre-dawn sandwiches that night weren't too bad.

~ * ~

I miss our songs, Scott.

Scott couldn't agree more, not having touched the Wolf in three days. *I miss them, too, Water. Just been too tired. Hang tight, this is the last exercise if we do okay. Graduation day.*

He checked the buckles crisscrossing his black diving suit, not wanting to be caught floating above his seat once Mara kicked in the Surveyor's engines.

"Oslo reports clear traffic," Mackenzie said from the copilot's chair. "Mission clock started. Make me proud, Mara."

Mara busied herself with dashboard checklists, ignoring both Mackenzie and Earth's majestic azure arc in front of them. She started humming *Arrorro Mi Niño*, a lullaby she claimed her mother sang to her during storms.

Scott grabbed his armrests, having picked up her odd habit early into this high-speed insanity. Eighteen rollercoaster rides down, and he had yet to get used to this.

I do not like this, either. Too fast.

Close your eyes, Song Guard. We'll be swimming soon

He hung on to his stomach as Mara somersaulted the Surveyor one-hundred-and-eighty degrees and lit the engines, the sudden deceleration pushing him against the harness. Another flip to orient the nose and they dove hard, the ship's windshield obscured by bright pink plumes of heated plasma. The buffeting seemed worse this time, but he always thought that during reentry.

They tore through the atmosphere like a hell-bent meteor, mimicking the three-hundred-knot winds they would face on Sanctuary. It wasn't the best part. Oh, no. They would approach Lovanet from the northeast, a full ninety degrees off the narrow canyon they had to drop into. "Drop" was too kind a word, but Mara already had come up with a more appropriate term.

She interrupted her lullaby. "Slam in ten minutes." Her laconic statement rose over the rattling cabin.

Scott tensed. Damn if she wasn't smiling. He slid on his flippers despite the ship's rock-and-roll, intent on shaving a few more seconds off the clock while ignoring the swirl in his guts. If Mara screwed up, nobody would have the chance to realize it.

Mackenzie's voice echoed Mara's apparent confidence. "Three hundred knots on the money. Target coming up."

Mara started her lullaby again.

Scott sucked in a breath and pushed his head back into the cushion. Damn, he hated this part.

She stopped humming.

The ship pitched upward at a horrific angle, the cabin ringing with the sound of multiple shock waves. Scott's straps dug into pre-existing bruises. Gritting his teeth, he endured the pain, half expecting to see his stomach come flying out his mouth.

With a sickening jolt, the wrenching forces ceased. The ship dropped, guided by Mara's adroit corrections on the thrusters. Since it was nighttime, he couldn't see the sheer cliffs rising on either side of them, but he knew from several daytime practice sessions they'd arrived. His practiced fingers quickly released the buckles restraining him. He swung from his seat, one step ahead of Mackenzie. They were both fully suited up and lying prone in the sled's saddles by the time Mara brought the ship to a hover.

The hatch slid open on darkness. The lake had hardly closed over Scott's head when he felt the distant singing vibration along his brow.

Water surged to the edge of the fishbowl with wide eyes. *The Song!*

Scott raised in his seat, trying to keep his breath steady. *Sure does feel like it, Water.*

Quickly!

Mackenzie started to say something, but Scott cut him off. "Turning left, angling eight degrees at full throttle. What the hell have you got down here, Mackenzie?"

The man said nothing beyond acknowledging their sudden course correction.

Scott pushed the throttle, hardly believing what his inner senses told him. The Reliquary, here? They closed on a rock shelf. He could feel Water already half out of the fishbowl in anticipation. The heat signature of six divers were silhouetted in the sled's visor. Damn if there wasn't a big crate with them. "The Reliquary. You brought it here?"

Mackenzie tapped on his shoulder. "Full dress rehearsal. Had to be sure you could sniff this thing out."

Inis Drum calls, and I must answer.

Scott was right there with her. Whether or not Mackenzie was toying with him didn't matter right now. Nothing did. *Damn right we will, Water. Hang on. Going to push us right through those bastards.*

Scott jerked the throttle forward, barely holding on as the sled darted for a gap between the waiting divers. He wasn't sure if they were holding weapons, and right now he didn't care. Maybe, just maybe, all he needed to do was touch the box. This close and Water might not need the Wolf's assistance to broadcast herself back into the Song.

"Sorry about this, Scott," Mackenzie said.

Scott shot toward the surface like a bubbling comet as if the sled had ejection seats. Water shrieked with rage and frustration. By the time he realized Mackenzie had pulled the cord on the suit's inflation collar, he was already bobbing helplessly amid Lovanet's shallow waves.

"Mara, this is Mackenzie. We have a swimmer in the water. Prep for retrieval."

She acknowledged with the curt confidence of someone who had repeated this emergency exercise several times over the last few days. "Swimmer in the water. Lowering the hook."

The sled surfaced beside him as Scott struggled to deflate his ballooned collar.

"Figured you would make a go for it," Mackenzie said from the sled's saddle.

"Damn you," Scott swore. Sudden inspiration hit him. If the Song was already here, it should stay here. "The Reliquary goes with us, or I don't go. Understand?"

"Not in the contract," Mackenzie answered.

"*Understand?*" Scott grated. "It's insurance for Water's people. A guarantee they'll be returned home. She didn't sign your damn contract, Mackenzie. Might want to consider that."

"The plan all along was to take it to Sanctuary, so tell your siren to relax. It's just not coming with this ship. That's *our* insurance your other personality will behave. Head's up."

The Surveyor blotted out the evening stars with its whispering descent. Mackenzie grabbed the descending clasp and clipped it to the ring on Scott's back. "Hook secured. Bring him aboard."

Mara was waiting to retrieve him in the open bay. She swung Scott to the side and lowered the cradle's cables.

We could jump, Water suggested.

Scott regarded the open hatch. *Not with all those divers waiting. He's bringing the Song. We'll hold him to his promise.*

She swept aside a lock of crystalline hair, a predatory grin stretched across her sparkling face. *Kill him, and then jump.*

Would you please just shut up?

The sled arrived. Mara jumped back in her seat and was underway by the time Mackenzie had secured the vehicle in its cradle.

"They have the Reliquary down there," Scott told her with a glare toward Mackenzie.

Mara turned, her eyes wide. "Seriously?"

"Dangling like a piece of cheese," Scott added, wondering if he could get away with hitting the bastard. Probably not, though Water would be delighted if he tried.

Mackenzie pulled off his helmet. "Just making sure we got what we contracted for. Scott's job is to sniff out a Reliquary, and he passed with flying colors. You both did. Got out of there within twelve minutes. Steak tonight, boys and girls, but not here. Mara, punch your Bravo Four button on the navigator."

She looked at her display. "That's orbital coordinates. We doing this again?"

Their boss shook his head. "We're done playing around. Those coordinates are as close as I can get to the ship taking us to Sanctuary. She's called the *Deep Explorer*. Has a great bar aboard. First round's on me."

Eight

Twelve hundred and twenty-three kilometers above the Indian Ocean, Scott watched Mara engage the Surveyor in a slow motion ballet with a stadium-sized sphere whose bulk shielded them from the sun's harsh glare. The *Deep Explorer's* strobing lights beckoned them toward a central hangar.

"She's about the size of a mining hotel back home," Mara observed while matching rotation. Her voice turned professionally brisk. "*Deep Explorer*, this is *Alicia* riding in on Beacon Six."

"Copy, *Alicia*. Assume station keeping. Handover on nine-zero-eight."

"Copy. On station keeping and channel nine-zero-eight for handover."

Mackenzie, sitting in the copilot position, regarded her with a raised eyebrow. "*Alicia?*"

"*Alicia* was my mother's tug," Mara replied with an imperious tilt of her chin. "I traded up to *Alicia* number two. She was the ship I was in when I pushed that radioactive rock out of the refinery at the mining station. She was too hot, so they scuttled her." Mara's eyes narrowed. "So this Surveyor is officially named *Alicia* until you take her back."

The mercenary chief returned a lazy salute. "*Alicia*, she is. Heads up. They're rolling open the doors for you."

"*Alicia*, this is *Deep Explorer*. Handshake confirmed on nine-zero-eight. We're bringing you in."

"Copy that, *Deep Explorer*, I'm hands off." Mara leaned back in her seat and folded her arms behind her head. The Surveyor closed in on the hangar of its own volition.

"Fresh clothes are waiting on our bunks," Mackenzie informed as the rectangular maw drew them in.

"And gravity, I hope," Scott complained, his stomach not appreciating the feeling of constant falling.

"Decent enough," the man replied. "Matter compression is

about three-point-five Earth." He laughed. "Enough to put the color back in your face, Rellant. I've another ship bringing in your effects, including your instrument. Figured you might want it."

"Much appreciated."

"You ever do a jump?" Mackenzie asked.

Scott shook his head. He'd never taken a liking to cruises, extraterrestrial or otherwise. Too many people. The Surveyor glided to a stop inside the *Explorer's* cavernous hangar, the craft's wheels unfolding to settle on a yellow striped platform.

Mara gave a low whistle. "You've never been flushed?"

"Slang for being shot out of a gate," Mackenzie explained. "It's like being spat across hell. Get to wave at ol'Hobb on the way through."

"Don't worry," Mara assured. "They give you sedatives. You'll sleep."

Mackenzie unbuckled his restraints and cycled open the flight deck's hatch. "Low gravity in the bay, so step lightly unless you want to smack the ceiling. Aim directly for the elevator across from us. On the off chance you see someone, don't talk to them."

Scott followed his boss down the ladder and toward an elevator's double doors. The man was right about the gravity here. Moving across the deck was similar to walking underwater at neutral buoyancy. He saw no sign of any crew beneath the overhead lights, though loudspeakers were echoing "Code Black" across the bay. Behind them, the hangar door finished its rumbling traverse with a deep-seated thud. An intervening magnetic barrier crackled into silence.

"Where's everyone?" Mara asked.

Mackenzie placed his hand against the elevator's palm reader. "Locked down. We are to be neither seen nor heard. We're headed for the *Explorer's* black deck. We're ghosts, people. Keep it that way. Green arrows on the floor will direct each of you to your cabin. Change clothes and meet me in Conference One. It's time for a larger slice of the big picture."

"Thought we were going drinking," Mara reminded with a cross look.

"Afterwards. You'll probably need it."

Scott's cabin was an olive-drab shoebox where everything capable of being built into a wall, had been. The gravity was at least strong enough to keep his stomach happy. The place smelled used and reused, with a helping of bleach in between. He struggled out of his diving gear and into a green felt jumpsuit with Velcro strips. He looked like a long-haired string bean. He tried to comb a semblance of order into his brown tangles.

Putting on a pair of matching slippers, he was back in the hallway following another green line with his name on it. The ship's padded walls, done up in a sandy brown, were uneasy reminders of the darker days when he was institutionalized.

He saw no one until his arrival at the conference room. Mackenzie wore similar attire to his own, though the mercenary's big frame easily filled out any loose folds. Mackenzie motioned him to a seat at a faux-maple table.

Mara poked her head in, the woman's aristocratic features offset by unruly black hair and the same unflattering apparel. She stepped inside, plucking at the material. "Military pajamas?"

Mackenzie gestured to the chair next to Scott. "Have a seat."

The table's circular design showed its practical side after the lights dimmed. A hologram plunged down an impossibly deep chasm, following sheer cliffs into a long jagged lake. A web of yellow lights spanned the valley floor.

"Jeremiah's Canyon in Sanctuary," Mackenzie introduced, "at the height of its population. Three transplanted tribes. Over three hundred thousand souls plucked from their home planet of Petal and deposited together in what was widely proclaimed to be a safe place to prosper. You probably recognize some of these shots...they were broadcasted all over the world at the beginning. The Church got great PR from these views."

The hologram flickered. One yellow dot.

"This was last month," Mackenzie continued. "Sixty-eight survivors."

"That's a lot less than you told me," Scott pointed out.

Mara's dark eyes widened. "Survivors of what? What in the hell happened?"

Mackenzie let out a breath before speaking. "Tribal warfare, apparently, as I explained to Scott earlier. To say Project Exodus failed is an understatement at best. We screwed up. Badly."

Water's grief surged up to blur Scott's vision. *My Drum.*

Mara banged her hand on the table. "How come Jeremiah never said anything about this? According to him, everything's fine. Exodus is the church's crowning achievement. It's not..." She sank back in her seat. "It's not like that."

Mackenzie pursed his lips. "How to say this? Jeremiah's too busy talking to God to see the big picture. Dealing with reality is left to grunts like us."

She buried her head in her arms. "We might as well have left them to burn on Petal."

"They wouldn't have burned on Petal," Scott blurted in disgust, having had enough of this con job. "The Shreen have been through these firestorms before. Water told you about her Quan, didn't she? That's how her people survive. This creature is essentially a big lifeboat. There's a Quan in every Drum…every lake."

"Except this one," she spat, jabbing a finger at the hologram. "What was Jeremiah thinking? Where's God's plan for them?"

Water's rejoinder was as livid as her bright orange fins. *Your God's a thief like mine. I have no people because of Him.*

You've some people left, Scott reminded. *We can get your Song home.*

The Song is not aboard. Can't you feel its absence? Mackenzie lies. I will kill both him and his false prophet for what they've done!

Mackenzie's fingers snapped in front of his face. "You with us, Scott?"

Scott blinked, swallowing back Water's outrage. The chair next to him was empty, Mara apparently having bolted from the room. He groaned. "Why did you have to tell her about the mess on Sanctuary? She was fine until now."

Mackenzie dropped into the seat next to him. "Better now than later. Think we'll be fine when she starts doing a head count after we're in the water? Mara's not stupid, and I don't need her freaking out while we're up to our ass in sirens." His big jaw tightened. "That didn't give you license to blab out the rest."

Scott got up and put some distance between himself and the mercenary. "Didn't the Church know about these Quan before coming up with Project Exodus? Wasn't there even a little speculation over what those things were for?"

Mackenzie shook his head. "We got nothing on these Quan. Sure, we detected anomalies in the lakes, but dismissed them as geology. Lifeboats, eh?"

"According to Water, yes. Didn't you guys do *any* science out there?"

His boss shrugged. "Jeremiah did some field work on Petal when he was just Frank Hanza. He was an anthropologist back then. Dove down to discover the first Reliquary, and got opened up like a pillowcase for his troubles. The Shreen line these things with sharp crystals to keep the uninvited out. Frank lands on the Reliquary and gets healed. The rest you can figure out for yourself."

"Science took a sudden back seat," Scott guessed.

Mackenzie rubbed his chin. "Hey, I'm not Jeremiah, so I can't speak for him. Miracles aside, he saw an opportunity and grabbed it. I'm not going to blame him for that. Besides, he pays well. Look, I've some leeway, so tell you what. I'll order the *Explorer* to Petal right after we leave. Have them take a closer look at these lifeboats of yours. If these Quan are the real deal, and assuming we can even get close to the planet at this late stage, then maybe we can send what's left of these villagers back home."

Scott wanted to believe the man. Mackenzie sounded sincere enough, but the rumbling from the fishbowl suggested Water didn't buy his story for a moment. "You said we'd be bringing the Reliquary aboard."

"It's on its way." Mackenzie rose. "I keep my word, Rellant. I suggest you keep yours, and tape your mouth shut when you're around our pilot."

"While you and Jeremiah wash out what little faith she's still got? Mara's better than either of us." He cringed at the ugly truth behind his admission.

The mercenary nodded. "Yeah, she is. Since we've shit on her halo, I'll have to offer something else she can hang her hat on." He pointed to the door. "Bar's out to your left. Make sure your first drink's a stiff one. I'll collect our fallen angel."

Turned out the *Deep Explorer's* bar wasn't the graffiti-smeared dispenser he'd expected for a mercenary ship. There were potted plants for one thing, and a ceiling fashioned to look like the ship's hull was made of clear panels. The galactic arm spread in glowing blue-and-violet depths above an aquamarine Earth.

Scott eyed the stainless steel auto-vendor waiting behind a genuine oak bar. "I'm just one of the boys, now" he muttered, raising his voice. "Rum on the rocks, four ounces."

Water waited until he was halfway through his second drink before commenting. *You risk dissolving the fishbowl separating us. Why?*

"Why the hell not?" he retorted, feeling the alcohol's effects. "You're part of the crew, right? Probably the better part. Besides, Mackenzie keeps saying he wants to meet you. Ought to give him the pleasure. Get you and I thrown into the brig for murder." He moved to a nearby table to take in the view outside, since the view inside his head was getting uglier by the moment.

Scott sipped from his glass. "Mackenzie's right. I should've just kept my mouth shut."

Mara has been lied to. You tell her the truth.

He nearly choked. "Truth? What, that there's nothing worth believing in? I'm an asshole, Water."

"I'll second the last part," Mara's voice broke in.

Cursing to himself, Scott turned in the chair to see Mara entering the room. The once confident look he expected on her face wasn't there, replaced instead by drying streaks. She went straight to the bar and ordered a watered down whiskey. She slumped into a chair across from him and followed a long gulp with a grimace.

Scott frowned. "What'd Mackenzie say to you?"

She gave a serrated grin. "What does *diablo* always say? Sign here, *amiga*." Mara took another swig, slammed down the glass, and pushed herself from the table. "Just traded my sainthood for a ship. I guess faith and miracles aren't enough for me, these days. What about you, Scott? What did you sign your soul away for?"

"You contracted with Brothers?"

"Aye. One year. Then I hop aboard *Alicia* with her papers in hand, and fly off into the sunset." She returned to the table. "Let me guess. You want an Intercession in order to rid yourself of Water. How's she feeling about that?"

I cannot leave now. You know this. I am Song Guard, and I must see my Song home to my Quan.

Like hell you're staying. Scott swept aside a lengthy argument Mara didn't need to hear. "We're still negotiating. You shouldn't have signed. You're still Saint Mara to everyone. You have leverage."

"Leverage with a church that's only in it for the money? We're both assholes, Scott. You're just admitting it. I'm still coming to grips with being no better than when I was back home towing rocks." She took another drink. "I was conned into this. Came walking out of this big ol' white light into a new life, and for what? To watch my family and friends give their future savings to a son-of-a-bitch masquerading as a savior. Your crazy half's been right all along, hasn't she? Our God's no better than hers."

"Then maybe you're not looking at the right God."

"Says the man who doesn't believe in one." She stood. "Come on. Mackenzie wants to see us in the infirmary."

Scott welcomed a distraction in the overhead view as an excuse not to fumble for a retort. Red-and-green wing lights blinked in the darkness, heralding the approach of something three times the Surveyor's size. The ship on approach had the guise of a scaled raptor with dull gray plating running down its spine.

Mara turned. "That would be a Valkyrie from the looks of it. Big, badass assault transport."

Scott rubbed his forehead, feeling a slight rhythmic itch. So Mackenzie did keep his word.

Water's fins brightened in emerald waves. *My Song.*

"Reliquary's coming aboard. Surprised they were willing to let go of it."

"Why not?" Mara turned for the hatchway. "It's dying, isn't it? I'm sure Jeremiah will steal another after we find one for him."

Water lost her cheerful bioluminescence. *Another reason for me to stay. So I can kill him.*

We're just full of purpose, aren't we? Glowering, Scott followed Mara out the door, albeit on unsteady legs.

The infirmary was a no-nonsense trauma facility watched over by a row of medical bots resembling white lozenges with appendages. Everything was either blue or white, with red crosses and various warning labels providing contrast.

Mackenzie stood across from a medical cabinet with a clutch of medical cuffs in one hand. "Roll up your sleeves. Make sure you're already lying down when we reach Heron Gate, because you damn sure will be when these babies go off. Alcohol makes the effects hit faster. Trust me, you want that. You'll be monitored from here. Something goes wrong, one of these bots will come get you."

Scott watched with misgivings as Mara slid on her cuff. "May have to pass on this. Sedation's not a good thing for me."

Mackenzie pushed one of the devices up his arm just the same. "See the little yellow button? Don't want to go under, don't press it." He locked eyes with Scott. "Your Reliquary just arrived."

"I felt it."

"Good, because that's all you're going to do. The Reliquary is being locked up in Bay One until we're through on Sanctuary. It'll be guarded, so no shenanigans from your other half, got it? Now get yourselves to your bunks."

Scott waited until Mara left before confronting the man. "You actually signed her up? This is your idea of handling the situation?"

Mackenzie nodded. "Everybody's got their price, Rellant."

"What was yours?"

Surprisingly, the mercenary grinned instead of decking him. "Hell, gobs of money and a long life."

"Should be the Church motto," Scott snarled.

Mackenzie just slapped him on the shoulder before heading out. "Something worth believing in, eh?"

The mercenary's words chased Scott back to his cabin. He lay down and watched Heron's Gate come up on a screen at the end of his bed, and tried not to think beyond the moment. The jump gate reminded him of an ore refinery with a barrel at one end. Rings of bright lights illuminated a broad bore fashioned from huge girders, giving the station an appearance of still being under construction. The *Deep Explorer* drifted into the framework like a chambered bullet.

Scott fingered the cuff on his right wrist. A choice of hells. The institute doctors learned early on that sedating him only made matters worse. Remembering Water's delightful little swim in the lake, he decided to see just how bad being shot through a wormhole was.

The only thing exciting about their jump was the sound of klaxons before everything outside disappeared. No big flash. No flickering lights. Just the kind of unsettling feeling one got from peering over the edge of a high tower.

It was easy to shrug off the entire event, except after a while the tower he looked over decided not to have railings between him and the chasm below. The platform narrowed, and the sensation of losing his footing kept getting worse. He tried to fixate on the cabin's blank screen and shake off the feeling of being one breath away from falling forever. Minutes took hours. Then years. All contained in the moment of a convulsing throat wanting to scream. Maybe hell was better. His muscles froze. Fearing any movement at all would send him tumbling, Scott pressed the cuff's button.

Counting each second became a surreal race between nightmares. Behind him yawned a reasonless gulf of oblivion making vertigo a welcome friend. Ahead lay the fishbowl, and the lithe sparkling entity swirling inside with predatory anticipation.

His world collapsed and reformed.

"And here you are, monster," Water slid effortlessly around him in a leisurely ripple of her thigh-to-ankle swimming fins. Fine translucent filaments streamed from a vaguely female head, a snub nose and large gem-like eyes rendering a false image of youth and innocence.

"Keep your distance," he warned. "You need my help, remember?"

Tiny motes of green bioluminescence traveled up the crystal spines of her twin dorsal fins. Yeah, she was enjoying this. Water rested her arms on his shoulders, letting him feel the retracted threat of more specialized fins along her glistening forearms. "What game shall we play?"

"Spare me your bullshit, Water. We're not kids, anymore. Let's talk about you getting out of my head as we agreed."

"I was not supposed to, as you term it, grow up," she returned, her emerald colors fading. Water folded her legs beneath her, her swimming fins pooling around her. Her finely articulated lips pulled down. "You made me live too long, so now I also fear. I should never have learned to fear. You might not help my people unless I am here. I thought Mara stronger, but she is too much like you."

"You're not going to leave," he surmised.

"I have to stay with you, or you will not be me. Only inside you can I save my Song. We will return the Song together. I will return to my Quan, and you will be alone." Her abrupt smile seemed forced. "You can drink, have females, and play music."

He fended off the foreboding crawling up his spine due to her disingenuous grin. "Sex, drugs, and rock and roll. Not exactly your idea of a future, eh?"

"I hear your thoughts. Better if you and Mara were me. We would return the Song, kill Mackenzie and his prophet, and make sure nobody steals our Song again."

Scott almost preferred the cutting game to a reasoning Song Guard. Things seemed so simple and clear when put that way. "Murdering the Church of Life's head man isn't much of a future."

Her dorsal fins took on a dangerous orange hue. "Something worth believing in," she hissed, parroting Mackenzie.

"We're not going to find squat on Sanctuary, are we?"

"Without a Quan?" She shook her head. "You already know this. What will happen when everyone knows? You must be me when this happens. Mara must be like me, too. Without her we cannot go home."

"Good luck with that," he sighed, sweeping a hand through the fishbowl's fine white sand upon which they sat. "She's got little more to believe in than I do. Jeremiah really did a job on her, but now she's seeing the light, and it's not pretty."

"She needs a god," Water stated with an air of decision. "I will find her one between our gods and yours."

"Sorry, fresh out of gods," he reminded her.

"You lie." She unfolded her legs and performed an effortless loop in the water. "Your god is the cruel one who let me punish you for your father's sins. So, you need a new god, too. One to take away the fear."

Water floated back and softly butted her forehead against his. "The god who helped Mara save her people would help us save mine. We will call this new one our God Between. Better than Kee and Anasa. Better than yours. You will believe in this god instead of sex with females and drinking."

Scott laughed. "It will take a miracle."

Water drifted into a growing darkness as something pulled him from the fishbowl. "That is what gods do, Scott."

Scott woke to bright lights, blue walls, and the wet sensation of a moist towel on his forehead. His heart tried to hammer its way out of his chest.

"Adrenil Six effective," a monotone voice reported. "Heart rate one hundred sixty eight and dropping."

Mackenzie's voice intruded into his awareness. "You're going to feel like shit for a while. Had to coax you back out with some adrenalin. Happens, sometimes." The man scraped over a stool and crossed his arms over an olive drab T-shirt. "You were giving quite a performance when the bot brought you in. I've never heard Shreen spoken so fluently by a human. Might come in handy."

Wincing, Scott accepted Mackenzie's help to sit up on the gurney. He endured the robot's prod and poke while it continued to babble out statistics. His boss finally waved a hand, sending the machine back to its spot on the wall.

The infirmary's hatch opened to a bleary-eyed Mara wearing her rumpled, green, ship's outfit. "He okay?"

"If you don't count the pounding headache," Scott grumbled. Everything about him ached, but without the soul-sucking disorientation. "We there?"

Mara tapped at a wall screen. An ochre crescent spread itself across the panel. Cloud tendrils raced across the terminator, blue flashes highlighting deeper formations streaming as if from a fire hose. "Welcome to Sanctuary, *hombre*."

Nine

"Good luck, *Alicia.*"

"Rodger that, *Deep Explorer,*" Mackenzie replied. "Good hunting on Petal, Captain. Bring us back some news on those Quan."

"Fast as we can, Boss," the Captain replied. "*Deep Explorer* breaking orbit."

Mara aimed the Surveyor toward the roiling world beneath them. Scott drew the seat harness tight across his black diving suit.

"Roll and pitch completed," Mara intoned, her voice devoid of its usual cockiness. "Flight path set. Two minutes."

"Your track is good," Mackenzie acknowledged in the same unemotional tone.

Scott didn't know if the humorless interchange provided a professional façade over sheer terror, or a reflection of the sour mood Mara displayed earlier during breakfast. He could tell she preferred to get the mission over with and leave everyone behind while she sailed off in her new ship. Not a happy crew, this.

This wasn't Norway, either. One glance out the windshield at the storm-wracked planet made that fact abundantly clear. Sanctuary consisted primarily of water. Tidal-locked to its sun, the stationary world remained hot on one side and freezing on the other, with three hundred knot winds making up the difference along the terminator. Somewhere amid the maelstrom, Jeremiah Canyon waited eagerly for their first and probably last misstep. Grimacing, Scott slipped on his diving flippers.

Mara began humming *Arrorro Mi Niño*.

She pitched them one hundred and eighty degrees. Sanctuary dropped from sight. The engines kicked in with a vengeance, throwing him forward in his restraints. She flipped the nose forward again, the planet swooping back into view. Bright plasma streamers ran across the windshield, marking their entry into the atmosphere.

"Braking maneuver on the money," Mackenzie approved.

"Picking up a little turbulence," Scott added just to hear

himself pretending to be calm. The cabin shivered and groaned during their plunge into Sanctuary's eternal night.

"*Alicia's* built for worse," Mara assured over the vibrations. "*Esta bien.* We'll catch the winds on the dark side and ride them all the way over to the canyon."

He tried to imagine the Surveyor as a bright pink fireball streaking above ice fields that never saw the light of day. A brief flash of rose sweeping across frosted grays. The serene image helped take his mind off the cement mixer ride. Water was no help. She remained silent and brooding within her fishbowl, having spent the morning giving bleak predictions of how this mission would end. Would Mackenzie honor his promise to return the Song, or was the *Deep Explorer*'s departure just a ruse to encourage cooperation?

"Thirty kilometers and dropping," Mara spoke up. "Five minutes to dayside. About to enter the jet stream. It's going to get really bumpy back there, Scott."

He realized Mara deliberately directed her conversation away from Mackenzie. "We should've used a few hurricanes for practice," he joked, hoping to offset her ill humor. She'd signed the contract of her own free will, after all, just as he had.

Any retort was lost when Sanctuary's high winds kicked the Surveyor across the sky.

"Little early, but okay," Mara assured them with an annoyed frown, leaning into her control sticks. She sent the ship into a dive with a suicidal exuberance, aiming between two lightning-laced storm walls. The Surveyor rolled and slewed its way east toward the planet's sun-facing side. Daylight came in a rage of boiling yellow-and-orange streamers, clouds tearing themselves apart in the slipstream alongside the bucking craft.

A brief hole in the turbulence revealed monstrous whitecaps below, the frothing waves easily topping eight hundred meters. Moments later, thunderheads closed over the chilling view. He let the deceleration push him back into his seat, enduring what amounted to a controlled crash. Even Mackenzie remained tight-lipped during their descent.

"Ten kilometers," Mara said in a clipped voice over the rattling cabin. "On track and approaching terminator." She released an exasperated growl. "Screw this, I'm taking us lower. Need to scrape those peaks coming up, or we'll be blown into the cliffs. Going fifty percent manual."

"You're the boss," Mackenzie acknowledged with a nod.

Scott peered across her shoulder at a display showing an

onrushing land mass. Suddenly, the clouds in front of them parted, giving him an unbroken look at Sanctuary's ocean in all its violent glory. Heaving gray giants rolled across the twilight surface, their crests torn away by insane winds. The behemoths surged up against jumbled cliffs, megatons of water exploding in geysers of raw fury.

The craft shot into a low-lying cloud bank, the windshield brightening from surrounding lightning as they reentered Sanctuary's night side.

"Full manual and here we go," Mara warned. "Hang on!"

The Surveyor shuddered as if running across washboards, sending Scott's stomach into a prolonged plunge. Mara resumed her lullaby, her crooning voice punctuated by quick jerks on the joysticks. Engines howling, the ship pitched up, heated vapor momentarily graying the windshield. He gritted his teeth. Every buckle on his seat straps dug in hard through his diving suit. The Surveyor flattened out once more. Shadowed granite peaks whisked by on either side of them.

Mara stopped humming. The ship's nose rose even higher, engines screaming in a vicious breaking maneuver worse than any of her Norwegian drops. Forward thrusters roaring, the Surveyor fell tail first down a sheer cliff wall.

The buffeting ceased.

"Welcome…to Jeremiah Canyon," Mara brought them to a level hover. "Piece of cake."

"Slow descent," Mackenzie advised. "We've an eight hundred meter drop. It's pretty dark. We've sunlamps down there, but they'll be off at this hour."

"This how we brought the Shreen in?" Scott asked.

Mackenzie shook his head. "No. Part of this place's selection criteria was that it would be hard to reach. Didn't want anyone coming in to bother them. There's an old research site to the northeast. They used a tunnel to get here. Access was sealed off once things started going to hell."

"Sounds perfectly irresponsible." Mara sneered. "Approaching valley floor. Extending baffles and engaging flight program. Get ready, guys."

My people will kill us, Water warned while Scott headed for the sled.

Like they killed each other? Sure they're still people you understand, Water?

She shook her head, her voice lowering. *No. I am too much like you.*

"Mission clock starts when we hit the water," Mackenzie

reminded them, unbuckling his harness.

Scott scooped up his helmet from a bulkhead hook next to the cradle controls. He lowered the sled and mounted the left saddle.

Mackenzie swung on beside him. "Just like we practiced. You see something, we'll head in and take some recordings. That's it. No funny stuff with your other half. You feel about to lose it, you tell me."

Scott eyed the man's holstered pistol. "And get myself shot?"

"The gun's for worst case scenarios." Mackenzie patted the leather case on his belt.

"Ten meters," Mara reported, glancing back at Scott.

"Keep your nose pointed at the village on the western side, Mara," Mackenzie directed. "Let us know if you see even so much as a splash."

"Got it. Eight meters."

Scott pulled on his helmet. The bay hatch slid aside to reveal rippling black waters.

Mara's voice lowered. "Four meters and at hover. Good luck, guys."

The cradle dropped. He had a few moments to see distant lights on the far shore before tepid liquid closed over their heads. The cables released. The sled's narrow windshield displayed a V-shaped topography below the surface, the lake essentially a water-filled crack. A deep one from the looks of it. He pointed the sled's prow into a shallow dive and advanced the throttle.

Mackenzie's voice came over his helmet's headset. "Getting anything?"

"Nothing," Scott admitted, studying the sled's visor. There was an odd aquamarine blob of brightness across the submarine canyon. "You seeing a light over there?"

His boss nodded. "Yeah, let's check it out. Mara, you copy?"

"Affirmative," she replied. "Seeing nothing around the village. I think they're all still asleep."

"That was the plan," Mackenzie said. "Steady as we go, Rellant."

The sled glided over the chasm. Scott wondered if the water grew colder further down. It felt like bathwater up here, a pleasant departure from Lovenet's chill.

His brow furrowed as if someone were strumming their fingers across his forehead. There it was again—an ultralow frequency humming in the Shreen's Earth language.

Something I remember from my beginning, but this is impossible. I was in my Quan's birthing receptor.

"We...I got something," Scott warned. "Not the same as Norway, but it's coming from the same spot of light ahead of us.

"That's what I want to hear," Mackenzie said. "Close on target for a good visual, then we run like hell."

Water sounded both annoyed and perplexed. *This is not a Song. Then what is it?*

Something I remember, she repeated. *Take me there.*

The clump, he didn't know what else to call the crystalline lump perched on an outcrop, was about the size of a small room. Only when they closed to within five meters did he put a name to the vaguely glowing thing. *Charnel house.* Fused bodies merged into an irregular egg-shaped form, a horror of arms and legs sticking out at angles.

"Not what we're after," he said with a shudder.

Water strained at the fishbowl's glass confines. *Yes, it is. You do not have your instrument to play, so we must touch it.*

He frowned, not understanding her excitement. *Why?*

Her lips fluttered between a smile and a desperate grimace. *Because it will free me. I will take Inis Drum's Song home myself.*

He stared at the grisly formation. *In that?*

It will do. I just need to broadcast myself inside. She whipped her hair in obvious frustration. *We must touch the crystal before Mackenzie kills you.*

What?

He is pointing his gun at you.

MacKenzie's razor-edged voice boomed in his comm. "I said hold up. Now. Don't make me do this, son."

Water reared back, her entire crystalline body glowing as if dipped in fire. She flattened her dorsal fins. *Time to see if there is a God Between.* She screamed, shattering the fishbowl they'd built between them.

Water lashed out with Scott's right arm, knocking aside Mackenzie's extended wrist and sending the mercenary's pistol tumbling into the depths. She followed with a spin and vicious kick to the man's helmet. The blow sheered off Mackenzie's mask, leaving a trail of bubbles erupting from his suit.

Scott regained enough control to stop Water's next fatal kick. He pulled the stunned man's emergency release cord. Their team leader inflated like a puffer fish and shot to the surface.

"Mara, we have a man in the water," Scott blurted before lunging from the sled. Water started a high keening vibration, sending throbbing waves of fire through the tiny crystals in his skull. He didn't know if it was Water or himself who pulled off his mask, ending the sound of Mara's shouts. Holding his breath, he banged his head against the glowing crystal lump. Eyes squeezed shut against the increasing waves of agony, Scott felt his brain explode.

~ * ~

The first thing Scott noticed while coughing up metallic-tasting water was the gravel beach upon which he lay on his stomach. The second was the webbed hand holding a crude dagger against his convulsing throat.

"Whall youll dooll?" a voice croaked, the broken and heavily accented English difficult to discern. Obviously the fellow didn't realize he spoke their language, a hopeful plus that might keep his gullet from being slit.

An awful emptiness in his mind told him what he, or Water, had done. He answered in fluent Air. "I released a Song Guard into your...she called it a reception node."

The knife pulled away at his fluent response in Air. He dared raise his eyes to see a crowd of Shreen forming upon the beach. Most wore shreds of brown or green fabric, reminding him of coarse canvas bags. Their pale skin glistened, much like the crystals embedded in his forehead. Most of those scowling at him were male. However, a few females stood among them, their black hair knotted into multiple ponytails. Several rifles pointed at him, a few more skyward. The air seemed thick with a nonchalant hatred. From their expressions, Scott figured they already saw him dead. They just hadn't decided on how.

His captor rolled him over on his back none too gently. A wrinkled face glared at him with large, malevolent black eyes. Scott noted the silver main flowing down the Shreen's otherwise bald scalp, along with the gills running along the sparkling neck. It was hard to collect thoughts through the throbbing in his brow, but he recognized this elder as a Quan Singer. Possibly their leader.

"Song Guard?" the Shreen sang in contempt, crouching to push the point of his blade against Scott's chest. "Song Guard live only as legends, thief. What did you do to our Quan? What sings there? Tell me, and I will end you quickly."

Scott coughed up more lake water, took a few wheezing breaths, and vocalized his own surprise. "Quan? That obscenity down there is no Quan."

The Quan Singer straightened and regarded the ring of villagers. "See? Even the thieves know better. Those who stole our lives now laugh along with Kee and Anasa. My brothers sacrificed themselves to create nothing. Three Drums killed each other to possess this...nothing. Even the thieves do not want it."

Mara's booming voice interrupted the Quan Singer's apparent I-told-you-so lecture. "Kill him, and we open fire on the village."

The Quan Singer's brow furrowed for a moment before he nodded. "They say they will kill us if we kill him. Hold him so they can see us kill him. We have nothing left but our meaningless lives. Let these thieves take them, too."

A pair of Shreen rushed forward and hauled Scott to his feet, nearly wrenching his arms from their sockets. The *Alicia's* dark shadow hovered overhead with the unmuted growl of her twin engines.

The Quan Singer brandished his dagger at the Surveyor before advancing on his prisoner.

"She lies," Scott rushed out, to halt the sweeping blow aimed at disemboweling him. "They have no weapons. They won't be what kills you. Anasa and Kee will laugh even harder when the one created to save Inis Drum's Song avenges me, instead. Her name is Water, and she has lived her life inside me. Now she is in your crystal, and she will neither forgive nor show mercy."

Eyes blinking, the Shreen elder sheathed his weapon. Scott's respite was brief. The Quan Singer's stinging backhand rocked his head.

"How, thief?" Another blow. "How?"

Spitting blood, Scott swayed on his feet. "See the crystals in my forehead? That is what happened when I was pressed against your Song. One of your Song Guard was inside. She transferred to me."

The Quan Singer stepped forward and struck him again. "I am Kohl, Quan Singer of Inis Drum. Song Guard are the statues we raise, the songs we sing. They are stories."

Scott's legs crumpled, earning him painful jerks on his arms until he stood again. "They are real. Beautiful. All crystal with dorsal fins like wings, and legs wrapped in flowing glass. Water fought hard against my people to save your Song. She made me pay for my father's sins. She will make you pay for yours." It was a good threat, even if he doubted Water would ever emerge from that ghastly artifice she'd rushed into. Too bad. He'd love to see the look on these bastards' faces.

A different vibration joined the constant throb behind his eyes. "Does she speak to you like this, thief?" It was Kohl singing, but not with his lips.

"Sometimes she speaks in Earth," he acknowledged in Air, unable to vocalize the low frequencies without his oboe. "It is the language of her Quan."

Grimacing, Kohl ran a finger along Scott's forehead, tracing out the glimmering discolorations. Shrugging, he slammed a fist into

Scott's stomach.

"We deserve death," Kohl hissed. He raised his voice, glaring at the crowd. "I told you we insulted our Quan by making that thing out there. You would not listen. There is a new song being sung in the crystal. If a Song Guard comes, let us face our Quan's judgement with honor."

Kohl kicked his ribs. Hard. He cried out and fell back upon the gravel, curling into a defensive ball.

"Let this thief face our Quan's judgement, too. Tie rocks on him and throw him back in the water. Let his Song Guard save him if she will."

They bound his hands behind him with coarse fibers, then knotted a chunk of granite to his legs. Too weak to struggle, Scott could do nothing but brace himself. The time for reasoning with these people had passed, if ever it existed at all. Water tried to drown him once before. At least this time the lake would be a lot warmer.

His tormentors tossed him from the end of a brief wooden pier. The Surveyor's engines shifted and rumbled above him, Mara helpless to do anything but watch. There was time for a long final breath before the lake claimed him.

A gloved hand grabbed his arm, pulling him down even faster. It was Mackenzie, wearing a new mask. The mercenary pulled an air hose from the sled he rode and shoved it into Scott's mouth before helping him onto the saddle. Lake water flowed swiftly around Scott's aching skull as the sled sought distance from the village. Finally, they surfaced.

"You'll live," Mackenzie growled, offering a steadying hand. "You can thank Mara for that, because I'd damn sure have left you here."

Scott just looked at the man, in too much pain to offer any clever riposte.

The Surveyor descended like a fish hawk and pulled them up into the bay. Scott lay on the sled unable to move, and not really caring about the pistol Mackenzie now aimed at him.

"Relax," Scott slurred through swollen lips. "She's gone." His head sagged, as much from the heavy void in his psyche as the fire raging behind his eyes.

"Put the gun away," Mara scolded. "He's beat to shit. Come on, Scott, stay awake."

"Damn miracle they didn't kill him," Mackenzie muttered, easing Scott into a rear seat. "Damn miracle I didn't, either," he added with a growl. "Take us up, Mara. Let the winds carry us eastward once we're topside, then go north over the ice fields. I'll punch in coordinates for the research facility."

"Thought you said it was abandoned," Mara replied while inspecting Scott's battered face.

"Just said it was old," Mackenzie replied, buckling Scott into the chair restraints. "Start your ascent, pilot. We're through here."

Ten

"Come out, Song Guard. If you are in there, obey my voice as the legends say you must."

Water's eyes sprang open at the summons. Barely able to move, she glared through the blurred crystal shell at this Quan Singer who swam around the nodule in indecisive circles. Her muscles twitched at every command. Where was Scott?

"Song Guard!"

Her birthing chamber was crude and thick. The voice irritating. Her temper short. Even Scott wouldn't dare talk to her like this. Being curled up tighter than a knot was not bringing her closer to freeing the Song, and time was short. *Enough of this.*

Water screamed, shattering her prison.

The tepid lake embraced her in an exhilarating rush. Water cried out in the sheer exuberance of feeling her dorsal fins expand as she arched her back. This wasn't her imagination. This was real. This was her. She inspected her gleaming arms, shivering her cutting fins with delight. Glancing down at her legs, Water tested her broad swimming fins, sending an undulating ripple from mid-thigh to ankle.

The movement propelled her from the nodule's broken remnants. Bright green ripples raced up her wing-like dorsal fins.

I am myself! Water spun around, delighting in the swirl of translucent hair across her crystalline cheeks. *Whole!*

And alone.

Not quite alone, she corrected, spying the annoying Quan Singer floating at a distance. Had he been the one to wake her? She reared up before the Shreen, observing his rapidly fluttering gills. No commands now. She emitted a brief chirp, tasting his rebounding echo. Yes, he was of Inis Drum, so killing him was out of the question. "Where is Scott?" she sang in Earth. "Where is my thief?"

His lips quivered but said nothing.

Water swished her swimming fins, pushing past him for the last place she remembered the Surveyor. Breaking the surface, she looked up at a bright orb. *Sunlamp*, she remembered. The artificial sun the humans had provided for this failed colony.

Scott's expected rejoinder didn't come. She pushed aside her unease. Water surveyed the valley floor, metallic-tasting water cascading down her hair. Odd stunted trees with huge leathery leaves crowded the shoreline save for a cluster of huts spiraling around a half-finished tower. In the distance to her right, a low wall loomed, fashioned from roughly hewn granite. She didn't see Mara's ship. Heart sinking, she swam toward a tongue of rock jutting out from the brief embankment across from the village. She was hungry, and right now even the sunlamp's weak radiance became a banquet.

Water climbed up on the granite ledge and spread her dorsal fins flat against her back, soaking in the light. She rested her head on her arms, taking a moment's delight in wiggling her very real claws. This was no fishbowl. But how long had she been caught up in that lump of malformed crystal? Her colors drifted into deep purple.

"You weren't supposed to leave me behind," she whispered to the emptiness inside her.

Approaching ripples interrupted her darkening mood. What if they'd killed Scott? She pulled herself to the slab's lip and looked down at the Quan Singer bobbing there, his silver mane pooling around him. She sang in Air, slowly and deliberately so he wouldn't miss one note of her concern. "Where, Quan Singer, is my Scott? What have you done with him?"

"I allowed his people to take him, Song Guard. He said you would be displeased if we took our justice before yours." He pointed a glistening webbed finger northward down the narrow lake. "The thieves have an underwater passage. We believe they originally brought us through it. They will take Scott where the tunnel leads."

She nodded. "Then I will go there, too."

"Not alone," he replied. "You will come with me. Carry my people to a new home."

Water shook her head. "The humans aboard that ship have our Song. I must return it."

"And we are what remains of Inis Drum," he countered. "I am Kohl. I am the last Quan Singer. You must take us back to our Quan as well."

"Impossible. Your people are not like us. They will drown in this tunnel."

Kohl pressed a hand against his chest. "Not if you migrate them. Become a Song Mother instead of just a Guard. This is whom we sought to create here, and now you have come."

She had no reply. No memories from her Quan to give meaning to this idea of a Song Mother.

Kohl apparently caught her blank look and took on a teaching tone. "Song Guard, you were meant for a brief life. You may not have been given the same memories from our Quan as I. How do you think our Quan came to be in the lake that we call our Drum? It has no legs to walk with. It is far too great in size."

It was a good question, but all Water saw were hours slipping by. She couldn't save her Song if there wasn't any ship to take her off this planet. Satiated by the sunlamp, she folded her dorsal fins and stood. "I have no time for this."

Kohl kept talking, obviously undeterred. "A Song Mother appears when a Drum's population becomes too large. She is like the Song Guard escorting her, but she is also a Song." Again, he put a hand to his chest. "She carries us as the Song does. She finds a new lake to call her Drum."

"And then what?" Water finished, giving Kohl a hard look. "Becomes a Quan? Are you listening to what you are saying?"

He pulled himself out of the water and stood on the ledge behind her. "I can make you a Song Mother. You will carry my people inside you."

"No." The mere idea was ridiculous.

"Do you have time to find this tunnel by yourself, Song Guard?"

She advanced on the Quan Singer with her cutting fins humming. She was easily a head taller than this male. To his credit, Kohl didn't even flinch when she poised a clawed finger inches from his forehead. Water paused, her intended threat dwindling in her throat. How could she convince him to help when death was already in his eyes? She withdrew her hand. He was right. It could take days trying to find this submarine passage of his. "I am Water."

He nodded. "Follow me."

She slid back into the lake, though not without a tinge of orange lacing the tips of her fins. Scott never liked taking orders. Neither did she. Hopefully it wouldn't take too long for this Quan Singer's madness to run its course.

A number of Shreen already gathered on the gravel beach bordering the village. The dwellings were far removed from the towers of Inis Drum she remembered from her brief battle. The villagers pulled back into a semi-circle upon seeing her and Kohl emerge from the waters.

Shaking her dripping hair, she regarded the clay brick homes and thatched roofs, some of the ceilings sagging or collapsed altogether. The huts circled a central courtyard featuring the tower of what she guessed would've been their community temple, except that her first assessment of its present state had been in error. Not half finished—half destroyed, with blackened and pockmarked walls attesting to recent calamity.

The people didn't look much better. They stood on the cobblestone street in clothes harvested from scraps. Most of them barely looked alive, many with eyes no less vacant than the emptiness inside her. A few of them had the impudence to hold shard rifles at the ready. How dare they? She expressed her indignation with a sharp chirp that shot through them to rebound off the surrounding cliffs.

The Shreen dropped their weapons and fell to the cobblestones, heads lowered in submission.

"You fought too much," she accused.

"We did," Kohl admitted, shoulders slumped. "But not over nothing as I had feared. We sacrificed, and you came."

"Scott sent me," she corrected. Or had it been this God Between she hunted for? Water frowned at what was left of a once mighty Drum. This new god needed to be smarter. She folded her arms as Scott often did when confronted by idiocy. "So now what? I guard Songs, not pretend I'm one of them."

Khol stiffened, but his rebuttal was interrupted by a little girl, perhaps in her first ten years of life. The child rose from her knees and walked around the prostrate Shreen to stare up at Water and tugged at her clawed hand. "Take us home."

"Her name is Yeaka of the family Tene-Inis," Kohl quickly explained in entreating tones, trying to push the girl back.

Water smiled down at this slip of a female who defiantly stood her ground, wearing little more than a homespun adult shirt as a dress. She brushed her hand across Yeaka's forehead, smoothing the little one's fine black hair. "How can I take you home?" she asked. "You are not Song Guard, nor are you Quan Singer. You cannot breathe beneath the water."

Yeaka pressed her hand against Water's crystal chest plates. "You will take us here."

Water sighed inwardly.

"Please take us home." The little one's song trembled, carrying all the tears her listless eyes could not. "Take my sister Teny first. She is ill."

Water's heart sank, sending purple waves rippling through her fins. Without a word, she followed the girl, ignoring the other Shreen scrambling to their feet to make passage. She didn't ignore Kohl, though. Glaring, she motioned with a claw. She wanted him next to her when these delusions he wove crashed around them.

The child led them to one of the huts having little more than a few bent rafters to serve as a roof. An effort had been made to sort out and organize the debris of what once had been someone's home. Broken cupboards propped up by brick. A makeshift table and stitched up, blue room divider.

Ducking, Water pushed aside the divider's drapes and entered a bedroom softly lit in yellow hues by a corner lamp. The teenaged female on the broadleaf mat barely moved to acknowledge their presence. Glassy eyes on a sunken face cracked opened to regard her. She remained otherwise still beneath a thin green blanket.

Kohl positioned a stained pillow beneath the female's bandaged head. "This is Teny, Yeaka's older sister." He inclined his head toward the long rifle laid out beside her, its barrel twined with red honor threads. "She took up her brother's weapon in the final battle against Osaga Drum."

"You should have joined with Osaga," Water fumed. "This is how the humans defeated us. One by one. And what did you do when you got here but make things worse? This was a good valley."

"We follow only one Quan," Khol grated. "You know this."

"I knew too little. So what now, Quan Singer? Did you bring me here to kill everyone, because that is all I do." She looked down at the stricken sister, her anger subsiding. "I can at least do that," she continued in softer tones.

Fear finally entered the child's eyes, and she recoiled into Kohl's arms. "No! You're supposed to take us home."

"She will," Kohl assured the girl. "She simply doesn't know, so watch and I will teach her." He stroked the child's head. "You'll see Teny soon, and she will be all better." He sat the girl down on the mat across from her sister.

Water's eyes narrowed. This sounded exactly like he was asking her to kill them. Starting with this young warrior right in front of her little sister?

The Quan Singer bent down and cradled Teny's injured head, eliciting a moan from the woman. Khol crooned in the low tones of Earth, his voice sharpening. Narrowing. Became more intense.

Déjà vu struck Water. This was the same transference song she sang through Scott's oboe at the Tabernacle. And in the aftermath of her very first battle when she was dying. Her realization came with Teny's long exhale, and the brightening of a new light deep beneath her crystal chest plate. Her heart's song now had an accompaniment.

Kohl rose, and clasped his hand toward her. "Song Mother."

Yeaka once more grasped Water's hand. "Her tiny voice wobbled. "I don't like it here. Can I be next?"

Water looked over at Kohl, then down at this beautiful new radiance inside her. She felt warmer. More complete. "I can take you to my Quan."

"Please?"

And so Kohl sang again, this time for the little girl. When he'd finished, a second rainbow shone next to Teny's spark.

Kohl gently laid the tiny body aside next to her older sister's still form.

Water stared in wonder at her chest. "You are changing me."

He inclined his head. "And I will escort you safely through the tunnels. Are you ready to take the rest of us, Song Mother?"

She found it difficult to look at the two corpses. They looked asleep. Peaceful. Water closed her eyes, listening to the faint reverberations of two new songs inside her. Yes, they were asleep, and alive. Finally sharing a peace they probably never knew here. "I am ready."

And so the migration began. Not with banners or a hurried gathering of supplies, but with her quiet entrance into one hut after another until only silence saturated the cobblestone street. Her body sang of its own accord, a galaxy of scintillating hues swirling inside her. Water slipped beneath the lake's surface with Kohl, not knowing who or what she was now. No longer empty, yet very much alone.

The human tunnel wasn't hard to find. It lay below a cul-de-sac of swirling currents where the lake sought out deeper avenues. A simple concrete tube jutted out from the rocks, one large enough to accommodate a human bus. There was even a rail leading out from the closed metal doors.

Kohl looked at her expectantly. Water motioned him to remain well behind her. She undulated the flowing fins around her legs enough to maintain her position in the current. She chirped, tasting both the door and its surrounding material. The cement promised the easier task.

Water emitted a long droning cry. Pebbles danced in response along the tunnel's base. Vibrations built, one upon the other, until a latticework of cracks shot across the concrete. One tight focused shriek vaporized the liquid before her. Boiling water gurgled in her throat, the heat drawn off by her flattened dorsal fins. *Almost there…*

Kohl advanced with a disheartened expression at her apparent lack of progress. Not wanting him hurt by the heated metal, she held him back. Water gripped the crumbling gap between the metal and concrete and jerked half of the door free.

Her guide grinned and swam into the tunnel. She followed, her body's glow sending iridescent hues across the inner surface. She became their lantern as the pipe stretched out before them. Swimming toward a constant black circle eventually became boring, then tedious, and finally worrisome.

"This will lead to a better lake," Kohl assured in Earth, the low frequency song laced with uncertainty. "We could resettle there. Catch them as they caught us. Unaware and in their sleep. Our Quan will see justice."

Pacing his slower progress with leisurely strokes of her swimming fins, Water found his conversation no less weary than her effort to keep moving forward. Was he thinking of migrating to another lake? "Would you prefer slit throats, or should I simply take their heads off?"

"Either would do."

She shook her head. "I will take everyone back to our Quan. Now be silent."

Her command wasn't lost on Kohl, buying her a few more hours of blessed quiet from his ranting. When he finally sang, he did so with an unexpected fragility. "I didn't want this hate, Water. It hurts...always hurts. Presses against my skull and makes me forget who I once was."

"A teacher," she reminded, her response softening.

"I didn't ask for this. None of us did. Living apart from our Quan. Just dying forever." His eyes darkened enough to lose the beauty of her reflected lights. "They must pay."

"I'm sorry," she murmured, having felt similar vengeful emotions from Scott in those first years when she tormented him.

"The thief claimed to have kept you inside him. I find that difficult to believe."

"He was embedded with crystals from our Song," she explained.

"Surely you must hate him and his kind as much as I do?"

"Of course I hate him." She sighed. The problem was not having Scott around to hear it. Water found a much better subject expanding ahead of them. "The tunnel ends."

"Finally. This was a much harder swim than I anticipated."

She gave a weak nod. "I am so very hungry. We must find light. Another sun."

There was no light. No habitation. They traversed what her

sounding chirps outlined as a narrow cavern reminding her of cracks in a shattered rock. They kept swimming and hoping. Her fatigue caught up with her when she became conscious of Kohl's hands supporting her beside the rail.

"Hungry," she explained, wanting to curl up and sleep.

How long had he waited before shaking her? She blinked, finding herself lying next to one of the rail's support pillars.

"There is heat flowing from the left," he said, shaking her again. "I think we are close to the sun side. You will find your strength there."

"I am tired."

His voice hardened like a vise around her will. "Follow me."

Disobedience required more strength than she had, so Water obeyed, trailing behind his approach to a side fissure. He kept ordering her. Swim this way. Go up. Go down. Squeeze through here. She really wanted to kill him, but that too required more impetus than she could scrape up from her dwindling reserves.

His pleading and prodding drove her to a steaming pool. He dragged her from it. A distant wall radiated heat, the small chamber a natural sauna that would've scalded Scott's skin had he been here. Unfortunately, it wasn't Scott who pointed toward the rocks and ordered her to break them.

She tried refusing, sinking down on her knees for a much-needed nap.

Kohl would have none of it, his voice lashing her mind. "I said sing, Song Mother!"

His command was all but lost in a rhythmic pounding as if the ground were being struck by huge mallets. Was this the God Between calling her, or laughing? It didn't matter. He told her to sing. She flattened her dorsal fins and chirped, tasting battered rocks that would soon give way on their own. Water hung her head. So tired.

"Sing!"

She shrieked out the last of her body's reserves.

The granite exploded. Its violent blast threw her back into the pool, shards bouncing off her plates. Water sank and wanted to keep on sinking, but a tantalizing orange glow beckoned her failing eyesight. She shoved off in a final push of her swimming fins.

The chamber was a thundering howl of wind, the pool's lip sheltering her from the worst of the maelstrom. What mattered was the renewing strength emanating from a low hanging sun. Crouching, she spread her dorsal fins, chancing having them ripped off by an errant gust. New life flowed. Focus returned to her gaze. She looked around for Kohl, seeing only the whipping vapors scouring the small room. Alarmed, she dove, and found him.

He lay half buried by a pile of rubble. Enough blood oozed from the creases between the rocks to tell her that the Quan Singer was beyond the healing abilities of her heart's song. His head moved, Kohl's gills working in a belabored rhythm.

"You saved us," she sang in Earth, touching his cheek with the back of her hand.

He shuddered, blood diffusing into the water from between his lips. "Raise our people to be strong. The thieves must not take them from you."

"They won't," she promised, pressing her forehead against his. "No more hate, Kohl. No more fear." She pulled back and chirped.

"I was a teacher, Song Mother."

"I know." Water wished she could transfer Kohl inside her, but putting another's life into herself was beyond her abilities. She sang her death song for him instead then rose to finish feeding with renewed purpose. Mara's false prophet should have died like this, his soul twisted and shorn of compassion. Maybe the one between her gods and the human deity was a vengeful being. Right now she felt it easy to worship such a thing.

Kohl's silence joined with Scott's, chasing her back down the dark galleries and through broken halls until she returned to the cavern. No need to swim slowly now so Kohl could keep up with her. She shot down the railing with meteoric ferocity, pitting speed against the sucking darkness around her. Another tunnel, a smaller cavern, and finally nothing more than a simple shut gate whose bars she quickly melted.

Water rose to the surface of a lake that would have pleased Kohl greatly. To the west, mountains silhouetted orange skies. Ahead of her, two bright sunlamps hung over a shoreline of office buildings and neighborhoods.

She wasn't going to be alone for long, either. Not judging by the blinking red-and-green lights skimming toward her across the surface. Drones of some sort. Her arrival hadn't gone unnoticed. Water glanced right toward darkened skies. No, she'd had enough of being famished. The mountains, then. Barely enough light to sustain her, but far more than what she'd had in those caves.

There was one vital task to perform before fleeing westward toward some submarine cleft. She chirped hard enough to see her broadcast sweep across the lake in waves. Eyeing the approaching machines, she waited, and was rewarded. The rebounding echoes had

Scott's taste all over them. Faint, but discernible. Most likely from inside one of those buildings whose windows she nearly shattered.

Hissing at her onrushing assailants, Water bet on Scott's embedded crystals being able to still hear Earth. "I am here," she sang. "I am whole. Sing to me with the Wolf, and I will come."

Eleven

He still hurt. Why did he still hurt? The cabin jostled, Scott's seat straps eliciting another cry from his lips. A ball of pain pounded his chest where the Quan Singer had kicked it. Even the cougar's injuries back in California hadn't stayed with him this long.

"Hold on," Mara called out from the front. "We're almost out of the jet stream."

"Two minutes to waypoint," Mackenzie directed. "Head north once you hit it. We'll be on the cold side where there's not so much turbulence." He looked back at Scott. "We'll have you in an infirmary within fifteen minutes."

The Surveyor turned. Scott glimpsed ice fields and frosted ridgelines beneath dark gray skies. He gingerly reached up and felt his puffy cheeks. Yeah, he'd been beat to crap. Water should be laughing her ass off at him, but silence greeted him instead. He groaned. Not silence. *Absence.* Not as easy to get used to as he'd thought.

A new no-nonsense voice filled the cabin. "Aircraft, you are entering the Sanctuary ADZ. Identify."

"I'll get this," Mackenzie said in a hurried voice. "Sanctuary, this is *Alicia*. Squawking particulars on Channel Six. Encode is Nancy Sierra. Repeat, Nancy Sierra. Be advised, we've an injured crewmember aboard."

"Copy, *Alicia*. Reduce your speed to one hundred sixty knots. Approach vector five degrees. Do not deviate."

The ship slowed. "Turning five degrees," Mara acknowledged, staring at Mackenzie. "I've a tight signal beaming me. Please tell me that's not what I think it is."

"Just don't deviate," Mackenzie advised.

"Where you taking us, again?" Scott pushed through throbbing lips, matching Mara's concern.

"A research facility," Mackenzie returned.

Mara stared at him. "Research facilities that put missile locks on you?"

"A *Brothers* research facility," Mackenzie dryly embellished. "The one tracking you would be Site A. Everyone lives at Site B."

Mara pointed to craggy silhouettes back-dropped against a perpetual sunrise. "Mountains coming up on our left."

A yellow grid pattern appeared across the windshield.

"Sending me a road." She banked toward the peaks. "Looks like sunlamps to our left down a canyon. Is this where we're heading?"

"Negative," Mackenzie said. "That's Site B. Just follow the road. Site A's a little north. Keep low, and you'll stay beneath the winds. Mountains are shielding us only up to a hundred meters."

Their electronic guide brought them west over a shallow basin, icy slabs giving way to equally uninviting vistas of arid gravel pans. Mara slowed the Surveyor upon approaching a concrete pad near the foothills. Spotlights tracked them from the roof of a single story office building.

Mara hovered above the landing apron, gesturing to a much larger military flyer. "That the Valkyrie from *Deep Explorer*?"

"Bringing in supplies," Mackenzie said. "Set down next to it." He nodded back to Scott. "Med team's coming out."

"Not much of a research center," Mara observed with a scowl, settling their ship.

Getting out of his seat proved even more painful than being strapped in. Both Mara and Mackenzie did their best getting him on the gurney, but every twist and jostle pounded his chest like blows from a hammer.

Two soldier types strapped him down to the gurney and rolled him across the tarmac. Mara held his hand. Double doors banged open, the dark sky replaced by white roof tiles. Two more olive drab uniforms arrived, complete with side arms.

"Take Miss Martinez to Briefing," Mackenzie ordered after exchanging casual salutes with the men. "Get her a coffee...steak, whatever the lady wants. She's earned it."

Mara crossed her arms. "I'd rather stay with Scott."

"He'll be fine, Mara," Mackenzie replied. "I'll join you once they check him over."

"It's okay," Scott muttered between gritted teeth, noticing the indignation in her eyes when one of the men put a guiding hand on her shoulder.

Glowering, she pulled away from the guard. Scott lost sight of her.

The first white suit he saw belonged to a disgruntled black woman with a pocked face and graying hair. She swept a tablet across

Scott's chest with indifference and spoke to Mackenzie with a casual drawl. "Two cracked ribs, multiple contusions, and so on. Couple jabs of cement and some happy pills."

"Full prep, Doc," Mackenzie replied.

"Haven?" she inquired with a raised eyebrow.

"After you patch him up." Mackenzie put his hands on the gurney's railing. He looked down at Scott with a grimace. "The Prophet considers you a liability. He wants you gone, and that's one place you don't want to be. I swore to your father I'd keep you safe. This is how I'm doing it." He took a breath. "I'm sorry. "

Scott frowned at the uncharacteristic apology. "Where are you sending me?"

"Back home, Rellant."

~ * ~

Scott woke up. What the hell? He'd been sleeping? He looked down the fresh-smelling blue blanket covering him. What was that last thing Mackenzie said about being home? Okay, this had the look of a small hospital room with a screen replacing his bed's headboard. No place he recognized. He tried peering beneath his green paper pajama top at what he suspected was a series of bandages where his ribs used to hurt. No such luck, his movements limited by heavy leather cuffs binding his wrists to the bed rails. Not good. He licked dry lips, intending to coax an equally parched throat into getting some attention from a nurse.

He didn't have to. The door across from him opened to admit a middle-aged woman with short black hair wearing a flowery, pink, medical smock.

She smiled at him. "Going to stay with us this time, Scott?" Her voice sounded British.

"Where am I?" he croaked. Scott raised his hands as much as the straps would allow. "And why this?"

She clasped her hands in front of her. "You are in Haven. Otherwise known as Site B." The woman inclined her head to his straps, her words softening. "Otherwise known as Brother's answer for those who know too much. Those restraints are for our protection, Mr. Rellant. Some of our new villagers get violent when they realize they've been retired."

"I've been sent to a prison?" His heart plunged into an abyss of disbelief.

"Haven," she quickly corrected. "And we're villagers, not inmates. You were brought over by water-bus while under sedation. Standard protocol. Again, for our safety. Many of our citizens are ex-military, you understand." She grasped his right hand. "I'm Dr. Paris, chief psychologist. You can call me Abby. Nobody's much on formalities, here."

"My pilot? Mara Martinez?" Mackenzie wouldn't dare imprison her too, would he?

"Next door. We've given her a mild sedative. She's a bit upset as you can imagine. Nothing my staff and I can't handle. How about I remove those cuffs? You don't impress me as a violent man."

I used to be. He missed Water's death threats. Now she was trapped forever inside a ghastly attempt at a Quan. His freedom from her came at too high a price, thanks to Water's reckless impulsivity. He couldn't leave her like that. "People know me. *Lots* of people. I won't be staying here long."

Surprisingly, the psychologist grinned while releasing his bonds. "Good. A healthy reaction. I felt the same way when I retired." Her laugh sounded edged with cynicism. "I was originally part of the staff at Site A. One debriefing too many, I guess. Karma can be a bitch."

"How long?" he couldn't help but ask.

"Eight years, four months, and three days. Care for some water, Mr. Rellant?"

"Scott." He sighed. "Just Scott."

She retrieved a pitcher and glass from a side table. "Well, you've got a leg up on everyone else. Your parents are anxious to see you."

"My parents? Here?"

"You were raised in Haven, Scott."

Back home, Mr. Rellant. He washed down Mackenzie's last statement with the doctor's offered drink, though it did little to cool his rising anger.

Abby's eyes narrowed. "Starting to sink in, eh? I can get you a sedative if you want. Helps dull that sharp pain you're feeling from a good Company backstabbing."

"My parents...outside?"

She shook her head. "Not until tomorrow. Your mother's not the Mayor on this floor, I am. I get my twenty-four hours observation before cutting you loose." Abby folded her arms. "Assuming you behave."

"Mayor?"

Abby walked over to a window to his right and made a sweeping motion to dismiss the opaque tint.

Scott winced while pulling himself out of bed. Damn, he

should've fully recovered by now. He never had to put up with this much healing time when Water was inside him. He stared out at a wide lake glimmering beneath a bright sunlamp. White painted piers hosted everything from kayaks to sailboats. And did he see an actually a golf course curving around to the left? Beyond a broad beach he glimpsed rows of Mediterranean style houses beneath a second artificial sun. The only thing missing was a margarita stand.

The psychologist drew up beside him with a smile. "As I said. Mayor." Her expression sobered. "I'm not going to kid you, Scott. First few months are rough. Denial, anger, and all that good depression stuff. You won't be facing it alone. We're family, here. We'll carry you through."

He tried not to ball his fists, having no desire to join Mara and end up sedated to the gills. "I won't be staying here, Abby."

Her hand on his shoulder suggested otherwise. "That's the spirit. Get dressed. I'll bring you back some morning coffee if you'd like."

He nodded, not too surprised at the double click of a lock when Abby shut the door behind her. Scott shuddered. No, this wasn't another mental institution. He had to get such feelings out of his mind. Swearing, he turned to a closet door, expecting some quip from Water and being met with only his own fears. Nobody to even argue with. The absolute quiet was worse than any ache, allowing his anxiety to run wild. Freedom never tasted so alone.

"Get used to it," he muttered, inspecting the stack of jeans and flowery polo shirts waiting on a shelf. Sneakers, too. One big tropical paradise, this.

His gaze settled on a familiar silver box. His Wolf? All nicely prearranged by Mackenzie. He gave the case a cursory inspection. Yes, the oboe was still inside. How were they going to cover up his absence back home? Benny would give them hell. One didn't go from worldwide concerts to sudden obscurity. Unless you died, his cynical side reminded him. Of course. Big crash that claimed both the famous musician and the Church of Life's celebrated Saint Mara. Something conveniently tragic to help Jeremiah squeeze a few more donations out of his flock.

He dressed, taking a moment to inspect a series of small round bandages peppered across his ribs on the right side where the Quan Singer had kicked him. He carefully prodded the area, eliciting some soreness. A far improvement over the stubborn lingering pain he'd endured. He couldn't bring himself to match the anger the Shreen elder must have felt. Those people around him might as well have been dead, for all the hopelessness he'd seen in their eyes. Had he been their Singer, he'd have kicked himself, too. Was Mackenzie really intent on taking those survivors back to Petal? He laughed. Yeah. Sure. Of course the bastard was. Man of his word.

The doctor wasn't kidding about his being under observation, nor that it would last a full twenty-four hours. He spent much of his time either staring out the window or fiddling with his Wolf, not having enough focus to do anything more than meander through a few loose tunes. A few curious staff members had peeked in, a few even wanting autographs. Scott finally put the oboe aside. He had enough on his mind already, such as seeing his parents, for one thing. People he hadn't talked to since they'd had him committed. It was easy thinking they'd died. He hadn't anticipated facing a day like this. What did you say to parents you didn't remember?

Scott bumped his head against the windowpane, once again pulling himself away from one anxiety in order to concentrate on another. Like getting out of here. He could see he was on the third floor of a horseshoe-shaped building. The hospital straddled a narrow river leading toward the modest lake. Almond-colored brick and orange tile roofing continued the Mediterranean theme carried by the small neighborhood beyond the golf course.

No watchtowers. No fences. Brothers obviously meant Site B to be a long-term facility where the inmates would grow content with their incarceration. Their *retirement*.

Damn you, Mackenzie.

He glanced through a thick brochure of "Haven" sitting on a side table, touting the place more as a resort than the high security rug he and Mara had been swept under. No mention of Site A where Mara's Surveyor waited. And how long before the *Deep Explorer* came back? Scott figured any chance at escape would end when they returned to scoop up both Mara's craft and the larger Valkrie. Assuming the whole show of the *Explorer's* leaving hadn't been little more than a ruse. If such were true, he was already marooned.

Abby made several visits throughout the morning, sitting patiently while he vented his frustrations or made inquiries about Mara or Haven. He told her about the Shreen and Jeremiah's dashed plans for farming Reliquaries. Why not? He had the feeling she'd listened to worse. Scott had no intention of telling her too much about himself, but apparently Mackenzie had been busy covering all the bases.

"I'm surprised you haven't said anything about Water," Abby commented, while he ate a reasonably good chicken stew late in the afternoon.

Scott's guard went up. He set the lunch tray aside on the small table where they sat near the window. "That's because she's gone."

"Well, that's good news, isn't it?" Abby replied with an unconvincing smile, folding her arms on the table. "You were treated at New Hope Psychiatric in upstate New York, yes? Dissociative Identity Disorder?"

"Fourteen years," he grated. "As I said, she's gone."

"Well, I haven't seen any symptoms," she agreed. "Usually there's some externalized dialogue or behavior changes while under stress. Your medical records advise no medication, and suggest that sedatives are counterproductive." Abby grinned. "Judging from your concerts, you certainly seem without issues. Yes, Mr. Rellant, we get regular updates to our library here, including your performances. Your parents haven't missed one show. I suspect you're going to be quite the celebrity once word gets out. Speaking of which, you'll be released after—"

The broad window beside the table rattled sharply, making them both jump. Outside, people on the bridge in front of the building stared and pointed across the lake.

"Some kind of explosion?" Abby wondered aloud. "I don't see anything."

Scott's forehead burned, each minute crystal vibrating. Wincing, he turned away from the psychologist, not wanting his clean bill of health to become soiled again. Water? Could it be?

I am here. I am whole. Sing to me with the Wolf, and I will come.

Shit.

"Scott? You okay?"

He nodded. "The noise...it set off the crystals in my head. It's okay, just startled me." Scott faced her, pasting a snarky retort over his shock. "Let me guess. Your records just happen to mention these crystals, too."

"Yes. Something about a bad Intercession. You sure you're okay?"

"Peachy," he assured. Water was alive, and out there. He let out a deep breath, feeling better than he had all morning. Did she look anything like the crystal nightmare coiled up in the fishbowl? Should he warn everyone they had a real live siren swimming in their lake? Sure, if he wanted to be locked in here for the rest of his life. As it was, he couldn't broadcast back to Water. Not without the Wolf. Nor was he sure he should dare.

Scott rubbed at his forehead, flashing a good-boy grin back at

Abby. Assuming Water didn't kill him on sight, he might have a way out of here after all. "You were saying something about being released? It's been twenty-four hours."

Abby glanced back out the window. "Yes, after breakfast. Your parents will be by to pick you up."

"Can't wait," he lied. "When can I see Mara?"

"How about now? She's awake, but still under a mild sedative." The psychologist led Scott down a typical hospital hall and paused before one of the ubiquitous faux-wood doors. "Scott, she's gone from being literally a saint, to being given a life sentence no more deserved than yours."

"In other words, she's as pissed as I am."

"Yes, so try and avoid arguments." She opened the door.

Mara's voice made Abby's cautions quite clear. "Get the hell out!"

"It's me," Scott said, easing in.

The door locked behind him, leaving Scott alone to face a pajama-clad Mara with an orange food tray raised in her grasp and ready to hurl. Her eyes widened. She tossed the tray on the bed's tangled sheets and rushed over. "Scott!"

He winced when she hugged him. "Easy. Ribs are still on the mend."

"Sorry," she said, stepping back.

Scott eyed her disheveled brown hair and streaked cheeks the soft blue flowers on her pajamas couldn't offset. "You look a mess."

Mara wiped at her eyes. "They've had me on meds since I got here. Damn, Mackenzie. Damn that *bastardo* to hell! This is a maximum security prison, Scott. They tell you that?"

"Yeah, they told me. Same place where Brothers have my parents, apparently."

She stepped back. "Your *parents* are here?"

"Yeah, long story. My father apparently worked for Brothers, too."

Scott looked around. No doubt there were cameras. How to tell her about Water? He motioned around him to indicate they were probably being monitored. He began by choosing words Abby would expect. "I'm going to get us out of here, Mara. Trust me."

"How?" she sneered. "Sick Water on them?"

"Something like that."

She shook her head. "Scott, all you're going to do is get yourself thrown into a padded cell if you give in to your other side."

"Remember the crystal we found in the lake?" He tried to put a meaningful tone in his voice. "Did Water ever tell you how she was born?" Scott walked over and rapped his knuckles against the window hard enough to replicate the earlier noise.

Mara paled.

Twelve

Scott faced off with the bathroom's steam-fogged mirror. "You up for this?"

He wiped his hand across the surface to reveal the stranger he had turned into. A hospital barbershop managed to chop the ragged mess above his eyes into something resembling business casual. Not that it helped soften the hunted look. Despite a garish Hawaiian shirt, he looked older in all the wrong ways. Slipping on jeans and tennis shoes, he considered his upcoming reunion with his parents. No, he wasn't ready for this.

"Ready?" Abby had to ask when he emerged from the room.

"They realize I could walk right past them and not have a clue who they are, right?" He cringed inwardly at one hell of a damning admission.

"I told them what I tell you. Patience. None of this is going to be easy."

Scott glanced out the window. If the sunlamp's orange hue was any indication, it was late afternoon. He retrieved the Wolf's case, about the only artifact he had left of agents, stages, and unfinished symphonies. Music wasn't on his mind right now. Mara and Water were. "My pilot getting released anytime soon?"

Abby shook her head. "No, not yet. Partially because we're still arranging for Mara's apartment. Also, I would like some more time with her. Speaking of which, I'll be seeing you tomorrow after you get settled."

Her narrowed eyes suggested she preferred he stay under lock and key as well, but had been overruled. "My parents are here in the hospital?"

"In the lobby." She put a reassuring hand on his shoulder. "Just take things one small step at a time."

"Haven't been particularly great at that," he muttered, following her into the corridor.

The hallway led into a small circular triage center where a

handful of staff carried out their business much like any city hospital. Abby exchanged chatter with a few of whom he guessed were inmates. He stumbled through a few perfunctory greetings. A couple of the nurses referred to his performances, much to his surprise.

His apparent notoriety extended into a reception area where he collected waves from more tropically attired denizens. He waved back, preoccupied with growing knots in his stomach while Abby guided him to a side room.

The psychologist left him at the door to the kind of place where doctors told families the bad news. Inside were a few green chairs and a box of tissues on the windowsill.

A couple rose from their seats. He didn't recognize them. The older looking of the two, a graying Asian woman slightly smaller than himself, wore dark business pants and a white shirt as if defying Haven's vacation-standard style. She reminded him of a strict math teacher you didn't dare cross. Her husband dwarfed both her and Scott, a thinning brown brush cut hinting at a skull festooned with tattoos. His gray eyes sunk deep in his head, stern, and yet haunted. The man's jungle-patterned shirt and shorts seemed only a step away from regulation camouflage.

The woman walked up and placed soft fingers on Scott's cheek. Her words clung to a faint Japanese accent. "Do you remember me? I am Maiko, your mother."

The sound of her voice penetrated the darker folds of Scott's mind. He briefly closed his eyes, remembering encircling arms and sobs, but little more. Sensations he could've gotten from anybody. "I'm sorry," he finally spoke through the bitter recollections.

She stepped back, giving the kind of hesitant smile one gives after an aborted hug.

"Harry," the man said with a nod. "I'm your father."

"Sir," Scott responded, exchanging a firm handshake. God, this was awkward. He didn't know either of these people.

"We followed your concerts," his mother intervened, gesturing to the Wolf's case in his other hand. "Is this your famous oboe?"

Scott nodded. "This is the one. Hadn't planned on a concert here, though."

"Article Thirty-Six got you sent here," Maiko said in disgust. "Same old prejudicial disposition excuse bringing most of us here."

"Any way out of this?" Scott asked. "There a good lawyer around here?"

Harry shook his head and rumbled out a cynical laugh. "Not the point of this place. Whatever you know, Son, it was decided that you knew too much of it. Did you actually contract with Brothers?"

"Needed an Intercession," Scott supplied, tapping at the discolorations across his brow. "The name Mackenzie mean anything to you?"

His father swore softly. "That son of a bitch? Is he still around?"

"Said he owed you, which is why I'm supposedly here and not buried in some hole."

"Why another Intercession?" Maiko demanded with a stung look. "You were cured."

It took Scott a moment to realize she was talking about him and Water. "Oh yeah," he replied, unnerved by her even bringing up the subject. Should he even breathe a word about Water to these two?

"You're cured," his mother repeated, touching his arm. "I mean, they wouldn't have…"

"Released me?" he finished, assuming she meant the mental institution these two consigned him to. Not that they had a choice with Water and her cutting games. Still, this conversation had him glancing toward the door. He'd already be walking if he didn't need allies here.

Harry placed a diplomatic hand on Scott's shoulder. "We can talk back at the house. Let's get you home."

"I'm not staying long," Scott warned.

"None of us ever are," his father replied with a dry smile while opening the door.

"Anything we can do for my pilot? Your doctor won't let her go just yet."

"Abby didn't want to let you go, either," his mother added. "Don't worry about Miss Martinez. Abby's good at what she does. She'll have Miss Martinez integrated into our society in no time."

"So you're the Mayor?" Scott asked, trying to establish a rapport during their walk to the reception area's elevator.

"Three years running," his father answered with obvious pride. "Haven's run like any other community. We are self-governing for the most part. Those in Site A stay put there, and we do the same here."

"Save for the fact that you can't leave," Scott remarked. Did either of these two even want to be free?

"Haven started out as a research center," Maiko stated with determination. They walked out on a ground floor lobby. "It can be one again."

"I'd rather see Jeremiah stopped," Scott countered. "There aren't enough Shreen left to bother researching, thanks to him."

"We've people here who tried that, too," his mother added with a resigned breath.

The first real jog on Scott's memory was a familiar brimstone and ozone tang to the air upon leaving the building. And the sound. Especially the sound. He looked up, unable to see anything beyond the sunlamp's glare. But he could hear the constant rushing, as if from a distant flooding stream.

Once outside, he took a good look at the hospital itself, the facility occupying the office complex's top third floor. Across from him and his parents, a few people fished off the wide concrete walkway in front of the glass-paneled façade. Several folks exchanged waves with his mother.

Scott leaned over the stainless steel railing and took in the lake, golf course, and a wide swath of imported white sand. A warm breeze from the west kept things at a pleasant temperature, reminding him of his Hawaiian concerts.

Harry gripped the bar beside him. "Brothers wants it known that they take care of their own. Helps with recruitment."

"Unless you're retired early," his mother added, voicing Scott's own thoughts.

"You actually have retirees out here?" Scott asked.

She nodded. "Believe it or not."

Scott gave a start, his forehead burning.

I see you. Wave your hand.

Water? Of course there was no answer. He held up a hand and waved, his eyes scouring the lake surface in vain. "Another fan, apparently," he hurriedly explained to the couple's puzzled looks.

"People out here would love a concert," his father suggested.

I see you. Come play me a song when it is safe. They hunt me.

He tried to keep the alarm out of his voice at Water's last statement. He needed to get Water out of there. "How about we discuss things when there are fewer ears around…Dad."

Maiko quirked an eyebrow. "Something you're not telling us?"

"A lot I'm not telling you." Nor did he know how much he should tell them. It was a hell of a concern to have about one's parents. Did he have much choice? If Water were discovered, those staffers in Site A would blow her—and his chance of freedom—into pieces.

"Save it for the house, then," his father replied, motioning him left toward a line of parked golf carts.

A narrow asphalt road took them past the golf course and into the neighborhood he'd glimpsed from the hospital. Either the perfectly manicured lawns and bushes were artificial, or soil had been brought in. Either way, he could imagine himself entering a plush community straight off the Monaco coast. Another sense of deep familiarity struck him when his father rolled the cart into a driveway. The two-story home prodded frozen memories with its stone archway and bay windows. Especially the surrounding hedges. Places to hide where people couldn't see the monster inside him. No, this wasn't going to be a great homecoming. Not by a long shot.

"Your old room has a regular bed, now," Maiko said when they entered the house. "You can stay here until you're assigned an apartment."

Scott braced himself as best he could, but couldn't suppress what welled up inside him once he saw the oak stairwell with its twisting balustrade and speckled brown carpet. This was one nightmare he remembered clearly. How many times had he and his mother ended up here? One or both screaming. He finally placed the woman beside him in his memories, or at least her voice on these stairs.

"Think I need a drink," he muttered.

Maiko stared up the stairs, seemingly no less transfixed than he was. "Make that two, Harry."

"Coming up." His father led Scott to a corner leather sofa adjacent to a maple dining table.

Setting the Wolf down, Scott accepted the glass his father handed him from a cabinet. A bottle of light-colored brandy followed.

"The Company doesn't hesitate providing the good alcohol," Harry said, retrieving two more glasses. He poured out a swirl of brandy and took a seat next to his wife in lounge chairs opposite Scott.

Scott sipped at his drink, letting the liquor pour its calming blush over his nerves. He dismissed the automatic concern of Water taking advantage of his dropping guard and adding to the conversation in disastrous ways. He wanted to feel a bit happier over the new freedom, but he couldn't. Not hearing her snide voice was going to take some getting used to.

"They don't monitor the houses," his father mentioned. "They wouldn't dare. No way we wouldn't catch them. Besides, staff really don't want to hear anything. Keeps them from ending up here too."

"So I heard from Abby," Scott agreed. Well, his father gave him his lead-in. He sucked in a breath. "Mara and I didn't come here alone. We brought another, or more to the point, she found her own way in." He took another long pull from his glass. Might as well get it over with. "Either of you remember Water?"

His mother's face turned ashen. "Of course we do. Your other personality made the name hard to forget."

Other personality? Oh man, this was going to be a lot harder than he figured. Scott downed the rest of his glass in a gulp and charged in. "Well, guess who's in your lake right now? She's being hunted, so I need to pull her out. Tonight."

His news was received as he expected—with silence and stunned expressions.

"She's real," he pressed. "I'm guessing you guys thought she was all in my head, but that's never been the case. Water transmitted herself into me when I touched the Reliquary. She broadcast herself out again using a crystal we found in Jeremiah's Canyon. Apparently she's reconstituted herself, if that's the word for what she did. She called to me outside the hospital."

Maiko swallowed, then glanced at her husband before speaking. "That's who...you were waving to?"

Scott touched his discolored forehead. "I picked up her voice. Look, I'm not expecting either of you to understand this. Just accept that I can't just sit here and let her be hunted down. Water could be my ticket out of here."

Maiko set her glass aside, her voice trembling with horror. "So the doctors did...nothing? Just let you out of the hospital like this?"

The weight of two terrible days threatened to buckle what little patience Scott had left. He shook his head. "Mother, just...stop. Forget the doctors. Listen to *me*. Water is real, alive, and in the lake. Tonight I need your help getting her out."

"Here?" his father asked, his voice strained in obvious disbelief. "You actually think your siren's in the lake, now?"

Maiko put a hand on Harry's shoulder, her tone collapsing into an abrupt reasoning purr. "It's alright. I'll take him." Wincing, she looked away.

Taking me back to Abby and her sedatives. Scott's chest squeezed at the crumbled expectations visible in Maiko's expression. He fought the urge to hurl himself off the sofa and leave. These two were little more than strangers, yet they weren't. It hurt seeing his mother treat him no different than she probably had when he was little. So little had changed here. Trouble was, where would he go? Who else in this cozy little prison could he turn to?

Damn, but he needed these two. He hated playing the part of a humored nutcase, but so be it. After all, he'd had years of practice. "Any chance you have a tarp? Something that will hide her?"

His father finished off his drink and stood. "Sure. In the garage." He let out a breath soaked in disappointment. "You really want to do this, son?"

"I have to."

Harry sighed. "Then let's get it done." The only thing missing in his father's tone was a pat on the head. "You'd best stay here," Scott suggested. "According to Water, you two have a history."

"Sure, son. Whatever you say."

Just going to have me committed all over again, aren't you? Scott dismissed emotions that rushed blood to his cheeks. He couldn't gloat at what was coming. You had to know a person in order to invest a modicum of spite in them. Besides, there was a good chance his reunion with Water could go very wrong once she laid eyes on his father upon her return from the lake. "Dad, any chance you've a gun?"

The man shook his head. "You've got to be kidding."

"Well, just take it easy and don't do anything rash when you see her, okay?"

His father said nothing and headed for the garage.

Scott picked up his instrument case. "I'll need this to call her."

"You do that," Maiko replied with a broken voice. "I'll be outside waiting."

She rushed off, leaving him feeling like crap. These were his parents, after all. He owed them something. Especially if they'd ended up here for saving his life. But he had neither the time nor opportunity to stop the onrushing train wreck when he returned home with a real live siren. He had to get Mara and Water off this planet. He owed them, too.

The yard was lit in soft blue hues, the sunlamp having transformed itself into a reasonable facsimile of a crescent moon. Excellent. Darkness he and Water could use. His father wordlessly dumped a canvas tarp into the cart's rear cargo area, a few bits of rock and soil bouncing across the floorboard.

Maiko sat in the driver's seat, her face a frozen mask hiding thoughts Scott didn't want to hear. "So where are we meeting her?" she asked, her tone deadpan.

"Someplace secluded and dark," Scott said, hopping in beside her. He set the Wolf between the seats and turned to his father, but the man had already gone back into the house.

His mother looked away from him as she spoke. "And when she doesn't come out? What then?"

"Then I settle in and start giving music lessons," he lied. "Let's go."

Instead of heading back toward the hospital, his mother took him alongside the golf course. With the sunlamp dimmed, the mountains reminded him of a great wall holding back the fire, which wasn't too far from the truth. He couldn't see much sky overhead other than an occasional sweep of lightning, but each flash allowed him a glimpse of impossibly swift clouds. Scott decided to keep his eyes focused on the job ahead.

They crossed over one of the fairways. "Might kill the lights," he suggested.

She tapped at the dashboard controls. "Anything else?"

Asphalt gave way to gravel. Scott sorted out the gray shadows ahead. There was the lake, a black swath reflecting the western glow. He pointed toward a layer of rock stair-stepping down the embankment like a stack of pancakes. "Yeah, go there."

Maiko pulled up next to the granite shelf and slumped back in her seat. "The only thing coming from that lake exists in your mind. You know this, don't you?"

Scott released the locks on the Wolf's case. "I promised to teach music, remember? How about you promise not to run screaming?"

"I'm a bit past screaming."

Doubtful.

He lifted the Wolf from its foam and ran it through its warm-up sequence. This could go so wrong. Would he encounter the same Water? Now she could kill as idly as she had threatened. Scott shook his head. His parents weren't the only ones he had to trust.

Keeping the oboe tight against his chest, he searched along the granite slab until he found the least treacherous way to the water's edge. The lake's slight waves made lapping sounds against the rock. He regarded the lights along the shore to his right. Far enough away as not to attract curious eyes or drones. He crouched on the ledge and blew into the oboe, seeking the ultra-low frequencies of Earth to call Water's name.

His mother peered over the upper ledge's lip, still trying to sound reasonable. "So what song are you going to play?"

"I've already called her," Scott said, peering out over the surface. "You couldn't hear it."

Maiko sank to her knees with a moan. "Is your monster taking you away from me again?"

Scott swore softly, imagining what the woman must be going through. She'd thought him cured. The house of cards she'd built around their future was collapsing about her. He handed her the Wolf. "It's not like that, Mother. You'll understand in a moment."

She carefully set the instrument on the rocks beside her. "I don't want her coming back, Scott."

"A little late for that," he muttered, spying a series of V-shaped ripples heading toward them. Twin dorsal fins broke the water, rippling in violet luminescence. He swallowed. She was big. Almost a head taller than him.

"Oh God," Maiko gasped, scrambling to her feet. "That...that's her?"

"Yeah," he said, hoping like hell Water hadn't reverted to her old, more vicious self.

Water heaved her glistening body halfway onto the granite beside him. The Song Guard's dripping crystal plates scraped against rock, a multitude of swirling colors dimming beneath sagging fins. She slipped, nearly tumbling back into the lake. "Tired."

Alarmed, Scott grabbed her around the waist before she fell. "Water!"

"So hungry," Water replied with a listless trill.

"She's starving," Scott translated from Air, throwing introductions aside. Water's body felt cold, glassy, and surprisingly heavy. For everything he knew about her, what she fed on was something he hadn't bothered to ask. He did remember her cutting fins, and was careful to maintain a firm grip beneath her arms.

Water's opalescent eyes whirled slowly beneath dangling strands of crystalline hair. "Tired."

"Yeah, I got that. Going to take you home." He looked up at his mother, who seemed ready to collapse. "Help me get her into the cart. She's weak."

"This is...Water?"

"She won't hurt you. Just keep away from the fins along her arms. They'll slice through anything like butter."

Maiko slid down the staggered granite layers, her eyes wide. "She looks like she's made out of crystal." She helped support Water's left side. "Are those lights inside her?"

"Bio-luminescence," Scott explained between grunts while they hauled the Song Guard up to the cart. Indeed, Water had far more rainbow colors emanating from inside her than he remembered from the fishbowl. Damn, he was actually *holding* her.

Water lifted her head to regard Maiko. "I know you." She spoke in English, sounding like a chorus of violins.

Maiko wasn't gentle about dumping the Song Guard into the back of the cart. Much of the initial awe had left her voice. "And I know you," she said in a shudder of shock and disbelief.

"Easy," Scott warned, catching his mother's scowl.

Maiko stepped back, holding one arm. "I can't believe it's real."

That makes two of us. He went to toss the tarp over Water, only to find her lying on it. "She'll be real enough to Dad. Any ideas on how to break this to him?"

Maiko gaped at the torpid figure. "This is really her? The thing that tortured you?"

Scott found his oboe lying where his mother had set it, and returned the instrument to its case. "She's less of a bitch these days." He hopped in the front seat and looked at his mother expectantly.

Maiko slid beside him and glanced at their passenger. "I don't understand. All this time? In your mind?"

"In the crystals, actually." He glanced in the back. Water barely moved. Hardly the kind of meeting he'd anticipated. "Let's go."

She backed the cart around. "God, what am I going to tell your father?"

Scott had no answer.

His mother slowed upon returning to the neighborhood, then brought the cart to a stop a block from their house. She tapped her fingers on the wheel and looked over her shoulder. "Okay, think. She's one of your father's sirens, right?"

"Pretty much," Scott affirmed. "They call themselves Song Guards, not that Dad's going to care when he sees her."

"Is there somewhere else we can take her?"

"You're asking me? Water's my ace in the hole for getting out of here. At least she will be once I figure out how to use her. For now, we take her home."

Maiko shook her head. "You don't understand. Your father still has nightmares about these things."

"She's practically been raised as one of us," Scott stressed, stretching the truth as far as he dared.

Maiko's words iced. "What she did to you, to us, wasn't human."

"Neither is what we've done to her kind. Would you start driving before I lose her?"

"Better if you did," his mother hissed, continuing toward the house.

They pulled into the driveway. His father waited just inside the door.

Maiko was out of the cart the instant it stopped. "Stay put. I'll talk to him."

Scott leaned back, singing in Air. "Try and look harmless. You're about to meet my father."

Water propped her head over the edge of the cart's rear bed.

"He will kill me."

"I think he's done with killing, Water. You'd better be, too. We've your people to think about."

"I am Song Mother."

He raised an eyebrow. "Song *Mother*?"

"I am more than Water," she asserted. "I must defend them."

"You must behave," Scott sang back softly, trying to hide his rising anxiety. By now Water had to realize she wasn't in a fishbowl he could slam the lid down on. He'd gone from having very little control over her to having none at all.

Both he and Water watched the hurried words exchanged between his parents, Maiko gesturing more excitedly up to the point where her husband abruptly pushed her aside.

"Behave or we're both finished," Scott warned before intercepting his father halfway up the driveway. "Easy, Dad. She thinks you're going to kill her."

His father blocked Scott's attempt to stop him with a sweep of his arm, Harry's eyes set on the cart as if not seeing anything else. Two steps later he recoiled like being struck by a viper. His hardened expression froze into sheer horror. "Jesus, Scott! What the hell have you done? That thing will kill us all!"

"It's Water," Scott said, pulling his father back after spotting an orange glint in the Song Guard's dorsal spines. "She's not harming anyone."

"I am not harmless," Water stated listlessly in English, raising herself up on an elbow.

Harry's jaw sagged. "It can speak?"

"*She* can, and right now she's half-starved." Hoping to dispel his father's fear, Scott walked up to the cart and eased Water into a sitting position. "Come on, harmless," he coaxed in English. "Let's get you inside."

His father shook his head. "Scott, no. You don't know what that thing is."

"The hell I don't," he retorted. "I've lived with her all my life. She's how Mara and I are leaving this place. We're the only chance those Shreen back in Jeremiah's Canyon have left. Don't repeat the same mistake you made stealing the Reliquary."

His father just stood there, as if Scott's remark had hit him with a mallet.

"It's alright," Maiko cooed, touching Harry's shoulder. "Harry, you're just—"

"Scott's right," Harry stated with a deathly grim expression.

"Maybe this is how I fix things."

"She *is* beautiful," Maiko reasoned.

His father's laugh made Scott cringe. "Yeah…beautiful."

Scott wasn't sure what they were talking about, but recalled Water telling him how her sisters managed to kill most of his father's raiding party. So what was this? Guilt over lost comrades? Post-traumatic stress?

"She's not hurting anyone," he pleaded. "Just get her inside so I can see what's wrong with her."

"Wrong with her?" his father repeated, walking up to the cart. For a moment, the two combat veterans just stared at each other, as if trying to pick the other out among the chaotic memories of battle. Finally, Harry spoke. "You can understand me?"

Water nodded. "I remember you, thief."

"How can I get you to swear you'll not harm anyone?"

She pointed a claw-tipped finger at Scott. "I will swear on him. I will not kill, even if you deserve nothing less. Now *you* swear. We will both be like your son."

Harry's brow wrinkled. "Alright, siren. I swear on my son that I won't call staff to blast you to hell, provided you keep your word."

"Song Mother," she corrected in a distant voice, her head sinking to her chest.

"Get her in," Scott said. "Watch the arms, Dad."

"Yeah, believe me, I know," he grated, helping to lift Water to her feet.

"And careful not to step on those lower fins around her legs," Maiko added while half dragging Water toward the door. "Sounds like we're moving a chandelier."

"Carbon crystals," Harry explained. "Basically, diamond body armor. Sirens weren't made to look pretty."

"You don't have to tell me what this thing's like," Maiko rebutted, holding the door open while peering both ways down the street.

Water jerked away from their grasp once they entered the living room, her eyes fixed on the cluster of lights hanging over the table.

"Watch it," his father barked, barely getting clear of Water's swishing leg fins.

She clambered up on the table. Claws scraping across the veneer, she knelt on her hands and knees. Her dorsal fins flattened out to their full length.

Harry pushed Maiko back toward the door, his face paling.

Yellow ripples flowed *down* from the tips of Water's dorsal spines, instead of in the opposite direction. Interesting. Surprising. He looked up at the lights. "She's feeding."

His father sagged against the wall, his forehead beaded with sweat. "Not what I thought she was doing. This is God damn insane." His voice went up a notch. "Honey, your arm."

Maiko glanced at her left arm's drying rivulets. She traced a long thin mark near her shirtsleeve. "I thought I'd gotten cut while loading her," she spoke with a wondering voice. "But it's already healed."

"Looks about right for me," Scott remarked with confusion, wondering why his ribs hadn't been so merciful.

"The hell it is." His father pointed at stains spattering his wife's left pant leg. "She must've gotten you good." Eyes narrowing, he eased up to Water and gingerly touched the glittering plates along her ribcage.

Water regarded him, a slight orange hue lacing the tips of her fins.

The two once more exchanged less than endearing expressions. "May, bring me a kitchen knife."

"I wouldn't do that," Scott advised, watching Water's combative colors heighten.

"Not for her," his father said. "For me."

Water's articulated lips pulled back into a venomous grin. "Allow me." She offered an arm, its cutting fins unfolding like crystal fans.

"Take it easy," Harry growled.

He ran his right palm over her fins, grimacing at the resulting bloody gash. Ignoring Maiko's cry, he placed his injured, hand against Water's glowing side. He waited a moment then walked into the kitchen.

Scott listened to a faucet's splash in the kitchen sink. He exchanged looks with his mother. What was the point, here?

His father reappeared, his fingers spread wide over little more than a crimson line. "I always wondered why you healed so fast when you were young, son. Now I know why. Your siren's just like a Reliquary."

Thirteen

"Can you tell it to get off my table?" Maiko fumed, glaring at the furrows gouged into the polished maple surface.

Water folded her dorsal fins and eased herself back onto the carpet in a crystalline swish. "*It* can hear." She pointed a claw at Harry. "I am not the monster, here. He stole my Song. No one will rise from my Quan when Kee and Anasa have left."

"Mythology is how the Shreen interpret the plasma jet," Scott interjected, getting between Water and his father. How to explain all this? "Imagine you want to survive the winter, so you ride a bear into its cave for protection. You can't get into the cave any other way. Water's Song is what we call the Reliquary. It's the bear. The cave is a creature we've not encountered before called a Quan. That's how the Shreen get through the firestorms. It's just like hibernation."

"Church is committing genocide," his father surmised, rubbing his forehead.

"You have killed us, thief," Water hissed.

"Easy," Scott snapped at her. "Without their help neither of us is going anywhere, got it?"

"Tell him what he has done," Water demanded, her dorsal spines glowing orange with her anger.

Scott took a breath. "The Shreen can't be stored inside their Song, what we call a Reliquary, forever. They have to be reabsorbed into this Quan of theirs or the lives inside will fade. That's what's going to happen if we don't get her Song back to Petal. Her entire tribe gets erased. Therefore, we have to get off this planet and find a way to force the Church to return the stone."

"Also the people inside me," Water added, tapping at her chest plate.

"You could've told us, siren, instead of melting people," his father growled.

"My sisters and I were too young," Water said, her orange hues diminishing. "You would not have listened anyway. You do not listen, now." Disgust peppered her melodic vocalization. The siren brushed by Scott and tromped her way up the stairs, jingling with each irate footfall.

His mother stared up the stairwell. "Scott, I want that creature out of here."

"She thinks this is her home, too," Scott answered bitterly. Yeah, he remembered those steps. Trouble was, so did his mother.

"The hell it is," Harry interjected.

Scott faced them. "She can't go back to the lake. You saw what a mess she was in without enough light to feed on."

Maiko folded her arms. "I'm not letting that beast stay in this house."

"Is that what you said about me?" Scott accused, feeling the flush of resentment he'd thought long since buried. "Just toss it in a goddamn cell and walk away?"

Maiko's eyes brimmed. "To keep you from hurting yourself, yes!" She gestured upstairs with a trembling arm. "That...that *thing* up there tortured you."

"I didn't exactly make living easy for her, either," Scott said, reigning in his temper. "Neither of us meant to be crammed into each other's heads."

"Nobody meant it to happen," his father agreed. "Can you control her?"

"As long as she knows I'm trying to help her," Scott guessed. "We know each other. She's not the same siren you fought, Dad. You heard her. Water's articulate, smart, and can be reasoned with. Where do you think I got most of my music from?"

His last statement seemed to have an impact on his mother, judging by the way she glanced back up the steps again.

Harry encircled Maiko in his arms. "Here's the deal. I'll help you get out of here with your siren. Just keep a leash on her. She threatens or harms *anyone* in this house, and I call in the troops."

"I'll keep her in check," Scott promised, doubting that task would be any easier to fulfill than his father's assistance. "Aren't you worried about repercussions if you're caught?"

"Isn't your concern," came his father's curt answer. "Just one thing, Son. Nobody here owes you an apology. Not me, and especially not your mother. We clear?"

Scott's cheeks flushed. "Not even for throwing me in a nut house?"

"Better than watching you butcher yourself on the steps," Maiko threw back. Her voice trembled. "Did you think we wanted to do that? Think we had a choice?"

"No," he admitted. "But it still hurts."

Part of him wanted her to reach out and hug him. Say she was sorry. Say anything other than just look away.

Harry released his wife and stepped back, his tone hardening. "We've three days tops before the *Explorer* returns. You've got a siren, and your pilot claims her ship was a converted Nightshade. I'd say you've a shot. We'll probably have to grab Mackenzie and use him as leverage."

Scott smiled. "I don't have a problem with that."

"Neither do I," his father replied grimly.

They sat around the table that night eating fried rice balls and celery sticks, the latter smeared with peanut butter. Conversation was stilted. Scott struggled to even force small talk through his lips, having written off his parents long ago. "Thanks, by the way," he finally pushed out.

"I'm not saying I wanted your monster in here," his mother asserted.

Scott shook his head. "I meant for saving me in the first place." He gestured around him. "And ending up here because of it."

"Nothing you're not risking yourself," his father pointed out. "You're welcome in any case. We'd do it again. From what I've seen, you'd probably do the same."

His mother ran her fingers over the table's deep scratches. "I'll have another maple top printed at the shop," Maiko said in a relenting tone. "So, Water actually helps you with your music?"

Scott nodded. "All three movements of *Song*, the symphony I'm working on." He brightened. "How about I play something?"

Maiko smiled. "I'd like that."

Scott liked the idea, too. He picked up the Wolf's case from next to the doorway. Music was a bridge he knew how to build. He glanced up the stairs, suspecting Water was still in a foul mood. He knew how to cure that, too.

He returned to the sofa and pulled the Wolf from its silver case. He inspected the instrument's red cocobolo veneer for any sign of scuffing, relieved to find the oboe unmarred by its earlier adventure on the rocks.

"I promise you'll hear this one." He tapped keys to start the warm-up sequence. "This is a song called *Last Descent*. It's about a Quan Singer, a Shreen priest of sorts. It's one of the songs I got from Water's memories. He's returning to his Quan for the last time. I play it when she gets moody."

"What exactly is a Quan?" Harry asked.

Scott raised his brows. "Some big life form out in the middle of a lake. Used to think it was just a Shreen god like the others, but lately I'm not so sure. That's why the *Explorer* took off, by the way. To figure out what the things really are."

"How much does that instrument of yours cost?" Maiko's question was more to the subject at hand.

He grinned. "A little north of seventy thousand. The oboe is custom made by Wolf to hit both ultra-low and high frequencies per my specifications. The idea was to get close enough to the Tabernacle's Reliquary for me to broadcast Water into it. Looking back, I could've saved myself some money."

The oboe's tiny jewel-like lights were green, telling Scott he could start at whatever frequency he chose. He chose to remain in the audible range of Air, feeling more nervous around his parents than any stadium performance. Straightening his back, he brought the Wolf to life, flirting on the edge of the low frequencies to please his listener upstairs.

His mother's furtive nod from her chair made him look at the top of the stairs. Water sat on her haunches, quietly listening. Her swimming fins spilled down the steps in a glittering cascade.

Tucking his lower lip tightly beneath the reeds, Scott plunged into *Final Descent's* opening refrain, a long sonorous halleluiah played against a backdrop of gratitude and humility. He thought of the Quan Singer sinking into the lake's deepening blues, enraptured by the Quan's return song. Scott realized he wasn't playing alone when a serene chorus cascaded and wound its way around his central theme.

He raised his gaze to Water at the top of the stairs, singing in accompaniment, her dorsal fins expanded to either side like angel's wings. The rainbow colors reflected along the stairwell's walls were nearly indescribable in their beauty as the siren joined in with a voice equal to an entire string section. Each note laced his music with a crystalline hum, elongating *Final Descent's* lingering tranquility. She performed on behalf of the Quan, he realized. Water was welcoming the song's old Singer home.

His parents were transfixed by the spectacle, encouraging Scott to coax Water's accompaniment along subtle improvisations as they often did together in the fishbowl.

Water didn't disappoint. She followed his altered melodies, even using the subtle vibration of her dorsal fins to add a background harmony. The room filled with a performance like none other.

"Not the Water I knew," his mother breathed, staring up the

stairs.

Water ceased singing, the bioluminescent lightshow fading. "But you are still the thieves I know." Folding her fins, she stood and disappeared back into Scott's room.

"Same old drama queen," Scott sighed, putting the Wolf down.

"You two sounded beautiful just the same," his mother replied.

"She's not all pretty lights," Harry cautioned from his seat beside Maiko. "I doubt you've seen the side of her kind I have."

Scott bit back a reply. That cougar hadn't been a pleasant sight by the time Water finished with it. Then again, the cat hadn't been human, either.

"Might want to sign her up for one of your concerts," his mother suggested with an offsetting smile.

"One thing's for sure," Harry continued. "When word gets out that she can heal like a Reliquary, things will get complicated."

"Very complicated," Scott agreed. He eyed the ceiling, hearing Water pacing around. "Think I'll use the sofa tonight."

~ * ~

Scott woke the next morning with far fewer sheets covering him than he remembered pulling from a hall closet the night before. His disorientation wasn't helped by the crystalline light show on the carpet between him and the table. He looked down at Water's supine form. He'd always imagined her smaller for some reason. She lay there with most of his blankets wrapped around her, though he suspected it was more out of habit than necessity. Her covering did little to hide the rainbows glittering inside her.

Water twisted around to regard him. She brushed aside long silicon filaments, her face's crystal facets crinkling around an annoyed frown.

"Too many bad memories upstairs?" he guessed.

"Your bad memories belong here with you," she sang softly in Air.

Apparently he wasn't the only one needing to fill the silence in his head. "Feeling's mutual. Move a fin, would you?" He sat up, straightening his flowery shirt.

Water rose and sat beside him in a tinkling cascade. She looked him up and down. "You are smaller."

He snorted at her observation, feeling only a little put off by her close quarters. Not much different than the fishbowl, and her proximity made him feel whole. Scott flicked a finger at one of the iridescent motes behind her armored chest plates. "You're glowing a bit more than usual."

"I am Song Mother."

"Which means what?"

She pointed to the miniature galaxies inside her. "I am migrating what remains of Inis Drum, save for the Quan Singer."

"The Quan Singer that kicked the crap out of me?"

Water nodded. "Kohl said he let you go. They would have killed you."

Scott stared at the lights, their significance dawning on him. "Those…they're all the villagers?" He didn't like the darkness where his conjecture took him. "How will you get them back to the Quan?"

"I will merge," came her simple explanation.

"Die?"

"Merge," she repeated. "Become one of my Quan's memories. Be reborn when it is time to be Song Guard again. I will not die like Kohl. He died during the swim here." Her statement sang with loss. "I was hungry, so he took me to the dayside. The winds were too great."

"He saved us both," Scott realized. Kohl had to know Mackenzie was in the water waiting for him. The ass-kicking had been a show for the others' benefit. "What's left in the village?"

Her opalescent eyes swirled slowly. "Bodies." Water bumped her warm forehead against his. "I do not know what I am now. Maybe I will become Quan. I am not sure I like this God Between I found."

He could sense her fear. "You said you were being hunted."

"Machines came. I had to hide in dark places."

"We'll get you home," he promised.

"Jesus." They both looked to where his father stood in the living room hall wearing a brown robe. Muttering, the man walked back into his bedroom.

Water straightened. "I will not kill him, today."

Scott shot her a wry grin. "How charitable of you. Try and be a bit more polite, okay?"

"No."

"Try, damn it. He's putting his neck on the line to help us."

She smiled. "No."

Throwing his hands up, Scott headed for the kitchen. He'd better warn his parents about what had happened in Jeremiah's Canyon before they jumped to awful conclusions. "I'll fix up some breakfast with a side order of bright lights for you."

Odd how his selective memory worked. The fridge and oven didn't jog any recollections, but he vaguely recalled the copper skillets hanging neatly over the island. He picked a pan, watching with amusement as Water pulled open the fridge door. "Easy with the claws, okay? She's already pissed about the table."

"Four eggs," Water hummed, deftly using two talons to scoop up the shells from their cups along the door.

He slid the pan toward her. "Triple it. Got two extra to feed. No, idiot, don't try and cut the damn things…"

"They cut," she announced, dropping the contents of a neatly halved egg in the pan. She fixed him with an accusatory expression. "You did not grease the pan, first."

"You want to cook?"

"Yes. I will make everyone too afraid to eat anything."

The smirk on her lips told him the Rellant family siren was working herself into a good mood. He allowed Water to finish with the eggs. At least until his mother walked in.

Maiko tightened the cloth belt around a brown robe similar to her husband's and eased the pan out from beneath the siren's hands. "We do not stir with our claws."

"I no longer have his fingers," Water pointed out, inclining her head toward Scott.

His mother set the pan on the stove. "And thank God for that. Sink's behind you. Clean up and go back into the living room before you scratch something else. Scott, there's fresh clothes in the bathroom for you."

"I do not obey thieves," Water crisply sang back in Air.

"She says good morning," Scott hurriedly interpreted, grateful Water had the sense to be snarky in a language his mother wouldn't understand. He shepherded his siren back into the living room.

"She was not polite," Water huffed.

"Just have patience," he sang in turn. "All she remembers is holding me on those steps until I stopped bleeding from your cutting games."

Water's fin tips tinged orange. "I could do worse, now. You know this, so stop reminding me of why I am hated here."

"Point made, and sorry," he apologized, sensing the thin ice he'd stepped on. There wasn't much preventing her from turning threats into reality at this point.

She faced him, her luminescence descending into deep purple. "Please do not fear me. I am already afraid."

He bumped his forehead against hers once more, relieved to hear her admission. "Then lighten up, Song Mother."

She issued an exasperated trill. "It is not easy being outside of you. You do not stop me from speaking."

Nodding, Scott headed for the bathroom to change into another

Hawaiian holiday ensemble. "Practice."

"Would you please turn the lights on?" Water's request in English, couched in an effort at politeness, wasn't aimed at him.

His father, now dressed in jeans and an olive print shirt, flicked on the dining room lights.

She responded with a slight bow. "I will not get on the table this time."

"Appreciate that," Harry managed, watching her soak in the illumination. "Maybe you should stay upstairs. People will be coming over, and I don't want them upset."

"What people?" Scott asked.

"Software infiltration tech who got sent here after his job caught up with his nerves," his father explained. "We call him Crazy Eddy. He'll be joined by a gentleman specializing in underwater ops. Guy made his own re-breather suit."

They were interrupted by Maiko, dressed in another of her business suits and looking every bit the part of Haven's mayor. She aimed a frown toward Water, then motioned Scott and Harry into the master bedroom behind them.

"I just got a call from Staff," she whispered, glancing out toward the dining room. "They want everyone to stay in their homes." Maiko took a breath. "They lost two drones last night while inspecting what's left of the old tunnel gate into Jeremiah's Canyon. Some kind of sonic disruption."

"They figured there's a siren in the lake," Harry surmised. "Not too surprising."

"Not the half of it," Maiko continued, chancing a second look out the door. Her voice lowered even further. "Staff sent a drone down to the canyon. Nobody's left. They were all found dead in their homes."

"That's because they've been migrated into Water," Scott supplied, kicking himself for not bringing up the fact earlier. "Remember my talking about life boats? She's being used as one right now. Those lights inside her are collected lives."

"You've got to be kidding me," his mother answered.

"We're not the only ones with escape plans, Mother," Scott reminded. "You said she destroyed drones?"

"Two of them," Maiko answered.

He shook his head. Great, just what they didn't need. *Thanks a lot, siren.* "Hey, Water!"

The siren poked her face around the corner. "Why are you all in here?"

"You didn't say anything about destroying drones," Scott

accused. "How many?"

Water held up four claws. "I do not like those machines."

"*Four?*" Maiko asked with a groan.

"Tell them about saving the village," Scott added, wanting to fully dispel his mother's notion that she had a mass murderer on her hands.

Water stepped inside the room and pointed to the sparkles inside her. "My people are here. I will take them to my Quan."

"They're still alive?" Harry asked.

"They are as alive as I was with Scott," Water asserted, pointing a claw at the pale discolorations across Scott's forehead. "I am Song Mother. My people will live again."

Maiko attention switched from Water to Harry. "Didn't Brothers think to study these creatures before shooting them full of holes?"

"Just the slice and dice parts," Harry defended. "You flew for the Company, May. You know how military intel works."

"So we end up killing the very life giving artifacts Jeremiah was after," she groused. "It would be hilarious if it wasn't so tragic. You know Mackenzie's going to send teams into that lake. I'd better get the lockdown started before he puts two-and-two together and sends them here, too. I'll use the excuse of an emergency meeting here to cover our guests' arrival."

"And get my pilot," Scott reminded. "Mara Martinez. Make sure she's not sedated to the gills this time. How many of us are breaking out?"

"Too many," his mother spat, brushing past him.

"I'm going with you," Harry clarified. "You're mother doesn't like it, but there's not a lot of choice." He jabbed a finger at Water. "You and I are going to get Mackenzie. We'll force him to take you to Petal, and Scott and I back to Earth. The only way we'll save ourselves is by threatening to blow this whole Reliquary business wide open. We'll have to make a deal, otherwise Jeremiah will bury us for good."

"A deal to do what?" Scott asked. "Return here?"

His father gave him a long look. "What? You thought everyone would just walk away? Your good intentions carry a steep price, Son."

"Not enough of a price," Water chimed in coolly.

Harry's face reddened. "Maybe you'd prefer Mackenzie hanging you from the ceiling with a pole jammed up your ass. I'm not doing this if I have to watch my back, so make up your damn mind."

"I'd better go with her, instead," Scott offered.

"Not your skill set," his father brushed off, still staring Water down. "You're not the only one with payback coming, siren, or did you forget what your bunch did to my squad?"

"They deserved to die!" Water shrilled.

"We all do," Harry threw back in a disgusted voice.

"We all do," she repeated after a pause, her colors deepening. "I already promised Scott I would not kill you. You must promise to die for my Song if need be. Not steal it again."

"If that's what it takes," Harry agreed. "We on the same page now?"

Water folded her dorsal fins and hunched down. "We do not have to like each other?"

"Hell, no."

Water nodded. "Good. Scott and I will wait in our room until you bring the other thieves."

Scott held a hand up to keep his father in the room after Water left. "Got a question."

Harry folded his arms. "Shoot away."

"Why are you doing this? You know I barely remember you, if at all. I've given you no reason to risk your neck. It's enough you saved my life and were tossed in this prison for your reward."

"Guilt's a hard thing to ignore, isn't it?" his father returned with a dry laugh. "If it makes you feel any better, I'm not doing this for you or that bitch you finally got out of your skull." Levity fled his voice, and with it any remnants of compassion. The man facing Scott now conveyed the demeanor of a drawn blade. "I killed my squad to save you, boy. Used the sirens to distract them while I stole the Reliquary. My decision. My responsibility. A man pays his debts, and this is how I'll be paying mine. I suggest you don't get in the way."

Having no words to answer with, Scott headed for the door.

"And one more thing," his father added. "I don't give a damn whether you remember us or not. You're family."

"Thanks, Dad," Scott replied heavily.

Glowering, Scott headed for the stairs, bracing himself to face a snake's pit worth of bad memories upon entering what used to be the center of his childhood hell. He vaguely remembered the low-gabled ceiling, but nothing else. He stared at the quilted guest bed and neatly arranged white shelving. Lace curtains and eggshell blue paint? No, this wasn't where a younger and savagely angry siren waited to pounce in his sleep. Still, the irony of sitting in a rocking chair across from where she now perched on the bed wasn't lost on him.

"Is there any word in your vocabulary for diplomacy?" Scott sang in Air, wishing she would realize what her ex-adversary was sacrificing for her.

"Two words," Water replied with a melodic snort. "*No*, and *thief*."

"A husband and wife are about to risk being broken apart in order to save your people, and this is all you can say?"

"They remember more of me than I do of them," Water admitted, fidgeting with her leg fins. She looked around. "I am too much changed, like this room. I made you swim in a shallow Drum."

"Huh?"

"I have caused you not to love your parents as I do my Quan," she clarified. "You only believe in yourself."

He chuckled through the discomfort of Water's accuracy. She still knew him inside and out. "Fine. Show me something deeper."

"I will find a good Drum for you, and Mara, too."

"You like her, eh?"

Water nodded, and pointed a crystalline claw at him. "She is better than you. She wants to believe in more than herself. I will give her my God Between."

Scott was tempted to ask how her new god was working out for her lately. He bit his tongue. There wasn't any fishbowl separating them this time.

A flurry of discussion and opening doors announced the arrival of his father's guests. One voice stood out from the rest. It was Mara.

Footfalls raced up the stairs. "Just take it easy with her," Scott cautioned.

Mara stopped at the doorway like hitting an invisible brick wall. Her almond brown eyes widened. "Wow. Water, is it really you?"

"I take it you were briefed," Scott observed.

Mara nodded, smoothing the same tropical shirt and jeans as he was issued. "By your mother. Does she speak?"

"Does she speak?" Water repeated, injecting enough sarcasm into her musical mimicry of English to elicit a laugh from their pilot. "We have already met, Mara Martinez." She slowly eased herself from the bed, allowing Mara a full view of her glittering form.

Mara let out a low whistle. "You look like a Reliquary."

Water swept a hand over her chest. "I carry what remains of Inis Drum. You must help me take them home."

"And you're playing nice?" Mara asked, glancing at Scott as she stepped inside.

"I promised not to kill," Water assured.

Mara boldly reached out to touch Water's left shoulder plate. "Might want to stay away from those fins on her arms," Scott cautioned.

"You're warm!" Mara exclaimed with a half-laugh. She carefully lifted a few translucent strands draping Water's face. "You have hair."

"I will not hurt you, Mara Martinez," Water said, bumping Mara's forehead with hers. "I am finding the God Between for us. See what She has done so far?"

Mara gasped as Water extended her dorsal fins. Green ripples danced up crystal spines. The rainbow motes inside the siren's body shown bright. "Water, you're beautiful!"

"She's also healing like a Reliquary," Scott added. Your Jeremiah's been barking up the wrong tree. Instead of grabbing Songs, he should have been cutting deals with the Song Guard who came up to defend them."

Mara's jaw sagged. "You're kidding me. Water, is this true?"

Water's claw poked Mara in the arm, drawing a bead of blood before the woman had a chance to wince.

"I had to ask," Mara ruefully said, putting a distancing step between herself and Water. She wiped away the red smear on her forearm. "Hey…not even a scratch?"

"I am Song Mother," Water stated.

"Dad had a little more dramatic demonstration," Scott said, offering Mara his chair while delivering a sideways look at Water. "Opened up his hand. I didn't even see a mark this morning. I think he's lost a little gray in his hair, too."

Mara finally gave him her full attention. "Tell me we're getting out of here, Scott."

"My father's planning it as we speak," Scott replied. He regarded Water. "No impromptu displays, okay? We're supposed to work with those guys downstairs, not scare the hell out of them."

"Thieves," Water ground out.

Mara folded her arms. "Oh yeah. That's Water."

Water inclined her head. "I must be Song Guard again, Mara. You must be Song Guard, too."

"My father's enlisted her to grab Mackenzie at Site A," Scott clarified. "Basically, we're going to use the bastard as a hostage to get a trip to Petal, and then to Earth."

"Love to," Mara hissed.

"Water won't be singing songs, Mara."

Mara's eyes narrowed. "Neither will I. Maybe we can bag Jeremiah while we're at it."

Water placed an approving arm around Mara, the siren's

cutting fins carefully out of the way. "This is why I like Mara Martinez."

"Just Mara, to you," Mara replied with a grin. "Let's go downstairs and get introductions out of the way." She looked at Water. "Hey, you. Enough with the thieves bullshit. Be nice."

"I will be nice," Water agreed.

They headed downstairs. "Better than what I got out of her," Scott grumbled.

His mother met them at the bottom of the stairs, her attention switching from Scott to Water. "We all in control, here?"

Water nodded. "I will not kill them."

"That's so reassuring," Maiko muttered, ushering them into the living room. She raised her voice. "No sudden moves, guys."

His father's guests rose from their chairs, mouths agape. One reminded Scott of a gray-haired social dropout on holiday. "A real siren, eh?" he remarked with a scratchy voice. "Looks more like a glass doll."

"Real enough," the other new arrival said, his dark eyes fixed on Water.

The island clothes did little to hide a muscular frame dedicated to Brothers' core purpose. He looked a bit younger than Scott's father, his shaven skull showing off a stylized anchor tattoo.

The man swallowed. "Saw her kind take on the east bank team as we bugged out. None of the squad made it back. So why aren't we fricasseed?"

"Because she's sentient, Doug," his father spoke up. "Like it or not, and she doesn't, we're all on the same team. Boys, meet Water."

"A little less orange in your fins, please," Scott whispered to her.

The gray-haired fellow promptly extended a hand "Well how do you do, little lady."

"Easy, Crazy," Harry warned. "Trying to get your hand chopped off?"

"I said I will not kill," Water reminded, staring at the man's outstretched arm as if it were a sacrificial offering.

"It can speak," Doug gulped, having not moved a muscle.

"Sounds like a drunken string section," Crazy embellished, dropping back into his seat.

Water surprised Scott by sitting down on the steps, rendering herself a bit less intimidating.

"Can she burn through armolite bars?" Doug asked, slowly edging his chair around to face her. He took his seat, but kept his gaze on the siren.

"Already did," Scott's mother informed. Maiko took a seat next to her husband. "That's why we've at least two swim teams in the lake right now, and three squads patrolling the shore with drones and heavy rifles."

"Which means they're not watching home turf," Harry interjected. "We'll use it to our advantage. Water and I will hit Site A and take Mackenzie. My son and Miss Martinez here will follow in a water-bus once we secure the access station."

Doug nodded. "I have a suit in the back of the cart you can use, Colonel. You know this'll be all or nothing. People start dying and Mackenzie won't be…" He trailed off at Maiko's glare. "Sorry, Mayor, but you know the score just as I do."

"And it's why I'm not asking for volunteers," Harry rumbled, cutting off his wife's reply. "Crazy, tell us about the stick you're holding."

"Universal key," the man proudly announced, twirling the thumb-sized gray rectangle. "Missy Martinez said her ship's skin was hard to see. That tells me they never tore out the passive suite, so the active jammers are part of the package. Means we're just looking at your run-of-the-mill spec lockout. Usual quantum encryption." He twirled the device on the table. "This eats such shit for breakfast. Plug it in, wait a few, and she'll be up on the *Explorer* like two turtles humping." The tech eyed Water. "So does she roll over? Play fetch?"

Doug slapped the man's shoulder. "Ease off, dammit. You have *zero* idea what she can do."

"I am not a doll," Water interjected, irritation grating across her violin voice.

"One of those sirens cut through my starboard engine like it was butter," Scott's father pointed out. "You might want to think about it before getting too cute, Crazy."

Water looked at Harry for a moment before giving a smile that would've exposed teeth, had she possessed them. "I brought down your ship, thief."

The two ex-combatants stared at each other through the ensuing silence.

Scott fought the urge to give her a hard kick. "Thanks for sharing."

"I do not *play*, either," Water seethed, rising. She chirped out a window-rattling note, bringing everyone else to their feet. "I am Song Mother!"

"I think social hour is over," Scott said, guiding the irate siren

150

back up the stairs.

"What the hell was that?" Mara demanded once they returned to Scott's old room.

"I should be killing them," Water fumed, passing through a confusion of colors. "I am not some pet!" She flopped down on the bed. "I am Song Mother. I must be feared."

"To protect them?" Mara guessed, bending to inspect the swirls. "Are they aware in there?"

"They sleep, and yes. I must protect them."

Heavy footfalls came up the steps. Scott pressed a cautioning hand against Water's shoulder.

His father slowed upon entering the bedroom. He leaned against the doorjamb next to Mara and folded his arms. "You know, I'm about ready to call this off after the shit you pulled downstairs."

Scott stepped aside, realizing his father was speaking directly to Water.

"You are thieves," came the predictable answer.

"And you're why I never made orbit and ended up here," he shot back. "Reason enough to call those teams over and blow you straight to hell. Might ask yourself why I'm not. It's time to be soldiers, again. You ready to start acting like one?"

Water rolled to her feet in one smooth motion. "I am Song Guard, now."

Harry's brow furrowed. "That a yes?"

"That is a yes," Water affirmed, her eyes glowing orange. "They will not call me a doll, or they will be *dead* soldiers."

Scott's father scowled. "Believe me, they've got the message and left." He glanced at Scott and Mara. "We're about to leave, too. *Explorer* just popped through the gate and is hauling ass here as fast as it can. Apparently Mackenzie pulled them back early to find Miss Congeniality here. We head out now, or we don't bother trying."

Fourteen

Should I kill him? Water wrestled with the question during the bumpy journey in the back of the electric cart.

Lying beneath the dirt-stained tarp, she weighed her responsibilities to her Quan and vanquished sisters against her one constraint—Scott. Not only did Harry Rellant deserve his fate, he might even agree with it. Scott's father had said as much in the hushed late night arguments with his wife, thinking they couldn't be heard. Scott, however, would never forgive such justice.

Water cursed her humanness.

The cart jerked to a stop. The gentle lapping of water against rock and the subtle echoes told her they were in some kind of grotto.

"It's clear," Harry said. "Come out."

She threw off the tarp, glancing around the dimness of a bowl-shaped cleft in the rocks beneath red granite cliffs. The river pooled in aimless swirls, as if stymied.

"We're just behind the reception center," Harry informed her, hurriedly pulling a cumbersome-looking backpack over his black suit. "Get in the water before a patrol sees you."

"You are not Scott," she hissed back in Air, sliding out of the cart. One sweep of her arm would end his audacity.

"Easy, siren," he grated, as if guessing the intent behind her words and accompanying expression. Her foe pointed toward the pool. "Blow the gate and swim like hell, because they'll know we're coming. Anything, and I mean *anything* shows up, you take it out. Understand?"

She hated receiving orders from this creature. "Yes."

"Good. Get going."

Just one slash. Fighting instinct, Water slid into the water, distracting herself with the sheer joy of being back in her natural environment.

A guide rail led to a lifting platform on the right side. To the left, a massive sliding door guarded the entrance into a concrete tube extending out from the rock face.

A burst of bubbles announced the clumsy entrance of her irksome counterpart. She flicked the tips of her swimming fins, gliding in a tight spiral around this human in his ridiculous outfit. Fake fins, and weights to keep him from bobbing back to the surface. She rocked him with a contemptuous swish of her fins, propelling herself to the bottom and back up again before he finished cursing.

"I can hear you," she warned, narrowing her voice to vibrate that stupid mask he had to wear.

"Yeah, and I can hear you, too," Harry replied in a mixture of surprise and annoyance. "Stop showing off and get to work on the gate. It needs to be off its hinges so we can send the water-bus through."

She arrived at the barrier in a single stroke, tasting the unforgiving metal with a quick chirp. Water frowned. This was far more protection than the bars she had encountered before. Shattering these thick plates would suck every bit of strength from her body. She shook her head at Harry when he joined her. "It is too strong. I would have to rest too long afterwards."

"So you do have limitations. What about the tunnel?"

The reinforced concrete tube jutting out from the rock behind the gates tasted far more brittle. "Easier."

"Good. Knock a hole far enough back as to not damage the gate. Nothing too big. Remember, we've got Scott and Mara to move through it once we secure Site A."

Water motioned the human back and spread her dorsal fins. Her lips and throat shaped a suitable song to create a precise puncture. Poised above the large tube, she screamed, the water blurring in concussive waves. A section of gray concrete shattered, revealing its metal bones. Water chirped again, narrowing her focus to the exposed rods. Her next scream brightened and sagged the obstructions enough for a following kick to clear a path.

She pivoted to Harry, her dorsal fins shimmering with heat. He floated listlessly above her. "Thief?"

No response.

Alarmed, Water swam up and peered through the mask at his unresponsive eyes. Gripping him, she pushed herself to the surface and had him halfway onto a ledge before he started moving again. She pulled off the mask. "You were too close."

His eyes focused on her. "Yeah…" Harry shook his head. "You do it?"

"Yes, and the gates are undamaged. It is a nice hole."

"And nice alarms are now going off," he finished with a grimace. "Come on. We're on the clock." Sliding on his mask, he lowered himself back into the river.

Water stared after him, reluctantly impressed at his determination. "Thief," she reminded, propelling herself after him.

Satisfied the resultant rubble wouldn't impede the bus, they started toward Site A. The tunnel was just that, the same black nothing ahead and behind much like the tubes she'd traversed earlier. The only difference was the metal rail leading them on. She sent a sharp chirp down the pipe, earning a cross look from Harry whose mask now glowed with some internal wizardry of its own.

"Very long," she reported. "And you are too slow."

She whipped around him in emphasis, jetting ahead and flipping over to pass him again in a rainbow blur. Water flashed back in front of him, pulling at her hair in hopes of his understanding her frustration. At this pace, she'd be starving by the time he got to the other end. Exasperated, she finally rolled on top of him, grabbed his harness, and surged ahead as hard as her swimming fins could push her.

"What the—?" His voice cut off in apparent realization. Scott's father pressed his arms against his sides, offering the least resistance.

"Stupid thief," she replied with a scowl, hating having to do anything for this human that didn't involve separating his head.

Fine, so he was being brave. And yes, he was helping her escape to save her Song. Water sneered at the other part of herself that allowed a modicum of admiration to infiltrate a Song Guard's proper sentiments. Her sense of gratitude sneered back. Water's fin tips rippled with orange irritation. *Too human*, she snarled to herself, letting her temper help fuel their travel. She could do this without him. Mostly. Some of it. She emitted another harsh chirp. The passage ended just ahead.

They broke out into an oval-shaped underground cavern large enough to contain at least three houses like the one she'd spent last night in.

A buzzing fish shot out from another tunnel at the far end.

"Stay back," Water warned, happy to have something to tear apart. She shot forward, her quick chirp identifying her quarry's torpedo-shaped skin. Plastic? Not bothering to flatten her fins, she sang out in a turbulent voice, each successive wave building on the other. The machine hurled itself into satisfying pieces against the cavern wall. "It was a drone."

"Next ones won't be," Harry warned.

"You stayed back this time," she added with begrudging approval. Smart thief. Water twisted around, found him again, and wrapped her claws around his harness. They jetted forward into the second tube, though not without her noticing a tug on her endurance. "I will be hungry, soon. We must hurry."

"Relax. I brought a flashlight."

Very smart thief.

They entered the far pipe, which proved to be a short one. She sent out another questing chirp. A second room-sized opening revealed itself, and beyond, another tunnel. The upcoming passage, however, hinted at something else. The taste of metal and churning water. Her sensitive ears picked up a high-pitched whine that stirred up memories of her first battle. "Missiles! Two of them."

"Don't let them catch us in here!"

She drove forward. "They won't."

Water pushed him away from her the moment they cleared the pipe. The missiles' keen shrieked throughout the room, the sound amplified by the passage through which the weapons traveled. Water eyed the pipe in front of her. If being caught inside was bad for her, it would be worse for those incoming projectiles. She aligned herself with the other tunnel, sending out a series of chirps to track the missiles as they closed on her position. Wait too long, and her prey would clear the opening. Too soon and her song might not claim them both.

Water glanced back to ensure her companion kept to a prudent distance then spread her dorsal fins. The missiles reached the entrance. She sang her death song, frothing water into a compressed vapor trail no thicker than her arm. Her throat boiled, waves of heat dissipating through her fins before real damage could be done to her.

Two bright flashes heaved and buckled the concrete, sending out a concussive wave to knock her back into the previous tunnel. Recovering, she swam to where Harry gestured next to the guide rail. "You are not hurt?"

"Rattled," came the man's response. "You damn near brought down the ceiling."

"Next time *you* sing," she retorted. Water inspected the sagging concrete ceiling across from them. "Can your bus get through?"

"I can get it out, but probably not back in again," came the brief appraisal. "Let's move before they send a second volley."

Strength ebbing, she hauled him through the final pipe, a section hanging loosely along the structure's upper lip. They emerged in a subterranean room where floodlights shone through a mirrored surface several meters above them.

Several egg-sized objects plopped in the water as she rose with her charge in tow.

"Grenades," Harry shouted.

She whirled him away from harm and dashed for the tunnel. The water erupted in bright, concussive spheres. Metal shards bounced off her plates.

More plops.

Water lashed her hair in a building frenzy, every inch of her crystal fins brightening like an open forge. These weapons vanquished her before. Not again. *Not again!* She shot up, broaching the surface as geysers erupted harmlessly around her. Her momentum sent her up and clear of the water. She banged her head against the bottom of a large lifting platform. Startled, she fell back with a splash, managing to catch sight of an adjacent gantry lined with soldiers.

Collecting her senses, she shot through the water.

Thieves shouted in triumph, "We got her!"

Stupid thieves. *You have nothing.* She vaulted to the metal deck and slashed her way through screaming soldiers. Limbs and heads splashed into the water below. The cries stopped.

Water stared across a tumble of uniformed bodies, save for two whose white shirts and ties she had shredded to crimson rags. A clang turned her attention to a heavy steel door, closing a gap between the platform and a concrete wall. Wide-eyed thieves stared out at her from a window adjacent to the door. She snarled at the face with its familiar square jaw and close-cropped hair. *Mackenzie.*

Movement behind her turned her toward the corpses. Harry climbed up a ladder, his face unmasked and strained.

He slipped off, falling back into the water.

Water dove in and grabbed his limp body by the harness. Red trails oozed from his suit. Her thief must have been hit by shrapnel intended for her. She supported his hips while he struggled once more onto the gantry before collapsing to his knees. Wincing, he clamped a hand over a profusely bleeding wound in his belly.

Keeping an eye on the door, Water cradled Scott's father, spreading her dorsal fins to bring in the welcome nourishment provided by the overhead lights. "My heart's song will heal you," she assured him.

"Get...Mackenzie." He looked up at her, his words spoken with effort.

She inspected his riddled suit. "You will die."

"No shit. Go."

And what would Scott think if she abandoned his father? She held him closer. "No, thief, I will not." She looked toward the window. "They are already gone."

"Help me up. We've got to send the bus." He indicated the

yellow lozenge-shaped vehicle resting upon the platform next to them.

Reluctant to stop the energizing warmth flowing down her fins, Water heeded his request. She helped Harry struggle to his feet, the man in obvious pain. She supported him while he staggered to the doorway.

"I'm tired," she warned, eyeing the heavy barrier.

"Just get inside the bus. One end of it is locked into a boarding hatch you can use."

Water eased Harry to the gantry's deck, grabbed one of the lift's dangling chains, and leapt atop the vehicle. A quick inspection revealed the bus had doors at both ends. She hung over the roof's edge at the vehicle's exposed door, fumbling with the access lever until the hatch cycled open. She swung inside and ran past bench seats to the second door. It opened without resistance, allowing her into a small room where spilled drinks and tumbled console chairs attested to a hurried retreat.

Shouts and running footsteps sounded. Water poked her head into the hallway. Tempted to give chase, she forced herself to open the armored hatch instead.

Harry stumbled in, headed to the other room and sank into a seat to work on a console. Water stayed close, letting her heart's song staunch the man's bleeding. The bus closed both its doors and descended into the water on rattling chains.

"Go after Mackenzie, damn it," Harry yelled.

"You sound stronger," she observed with a rueful frown. "I will get him."

"Alive," he ordered.

She sped down the corridor, following thrown-open doors to an empty intersection. She skidded to the left, colliding with flower vases bordering a small cafeteria. The tables inside were empty. Where were those humans and Mackenzie?

A door opened behind her.

There was a sharp crack, followed by a stunning impact in the back of her head. Water fell. Screeching, she leapt back to her feet, fins blazing bright orange at the human standing there with a raised pistol.

A rifle barrel appeared beside the man's head, followed by Harry. "Wouldn't do that, Commandant. You're just pissing her off. Drop it."

The pistol clattered to the floor.

Harry looked ready to collapse, but at least he wasn't soaking the floor in blood. "You okay, Water?"

She pulled aside hair tendrils and ran fingers along the scored plate on the back of her aching head. Kicking at the spent bullet, she advanced on the shooter, her cutting fins vibrating in earnest.

Harry raised a hand. "Don't. This is Commandant..." He peered at the name sewn into the man's blue shirt. "Grissom. He's going to help us get into the Security Center."

"Not on my watch," the man ground out.

Water raised her right forearm to remove his head, her limb's ridged fin quivering like an eager sword blade.

"Easy, siren," Harry cautioned, shaking his head. "Trust me. The Commandant's going to help or see his men melted into puddles." He prodded his prisoner into the right hallway. Harry looked over his shoulder at Water. "You okay?"

Stomping a foot, Water lowered her arm. Better to see her enemy's head bouncing down the hallway. "Head hurts," she growled back. "You?"

"I've felt better," he admitted.

"We've a fully equipped infirmary," Grissom offered. "You don't have to do this, Colonel."

They stopped at a plain gray hatch flanked by two thick windows. She eyed the armored plating with a disheartened trill. Surely he wasn't expecting her to sing through that?

Sagging against the wall, Harry glanced at her behind the Commandant's back and shook his head, as if guessing her dilemma. He addressed the grim-faced officer. "Colonel, I'd like to formally introduce you to Water. Maybe you've seen combat footage of what these sirens can do. Maybe not. What's important is she'll be singing a song able to melt hearts on the other side of that wall, and I'm not talking figuratively. You saw what she did with those missiles. Tell your boys to open the door."

"Not happening, Colonel," Grissom returned stiffly.

Water played along with Harry's bluff, knowing she hadn't enough in her to even shatter those windows. She managed a sharp chirp, watching the officer flinch as the sound wave rebounded off the door.

"We figure that's how they get the right frequency," Harry added. "What comes next isn't pretty. Like being boiled from the inside out. We just want Mackenzie. The rest of your staff can go free. Their lives aren't worth a paycheck, Grissom."

"You're looking mighty pale, Colonel Rellant," the man returned. "Give it up, and I'll get you on the medi-bed."

"I *will* kill everyone inside," Water pressed, rattling her cutting fins with all the ebbing strength she could muster.

"Go to hell, bitch."

Harry glanced around then swung his rifle's butt against the man's head, dropping the Commandant to the floor.

"Can I hit him, too?" Water asked, happy to see her headache would be shared.

Harry swore. "He's evacuated everyone aboard the Valkyrie outside and is stalling us. Right hallway behind you goes outside. Move your shiny ass!"

Using the last of her reserves, she bolted down the hall and hurled herself out a set of double doors onto a wide swath of concrete. The howl of engines made her look up. A great bat shape silhouetted against the sunlamp's brightness. An attack ship like the one she'd damaged in her first battle, but this time she hadn't enough energy to produce a proper death song.

Bright flashes erupted around her, glancing blows all but knocking her to the ground. Her enemy had its own death song. Screeching, she scrambled back inside the building, followed by gouts of pulverized cement. More holes tore through the ceiling until she found the safety of the inner hallway. The firing stopped, allowing her to inspect cracked and scored plates along her shoulders and chest. Nothing that wouldn't heal. The enemy's engines pitched into a stronger thrum. Then the sound receded. She staggered back outside, hoping this wasn't just another ruse to lure her into the open.

No ship. Only Mara's smaller Surveyor remained on the ramp. She hurried to rejoin Harry, each step bringing with it a deep-seated ache.

But Harry wasn't at the Security Center's door, and neither was the other man. Water stared at the only thing remaining—Harry's rifle. Emitting a saw-edged cry, she followed the faint sound of breathing and found both of them in a white room. Harry lay unconscious on a blue table with a mask over his face and small devices crawling over him. Slicing into his chest and belly.

She regarded the officer working intently at a wide screen, her cutting fins humming.

"I'm saving his life," Grissom explained, glancing up at her. "Stop me, and he'll be dead. You understand what I'm saying?"

"If he stops then you will be dead," she spat, noting the retrieved pistol stuck in the man's holster. Water kept an eye on him as she hovered over Harry. Machines extricated bloody bits of metal from his skin. She unfolded her dorsal fins, soaking in the bright lights so that both of them would benefit from her heart's song.

The officer regarded her for a moment then studied his screens with widening eyes. "Don't know what you're doing, but keep it up."

She studied this Commandant with growing perplexity. "Why are you helping?"

"Because Colonel Rellant and I are both soldiers," the man replied.

She inclined her head toward Harry beside her. "No. He is Song Guard."

Fifteen

Standing on the dock, Scott watched the arriving water-bus rise on the lift, water streaming down the yellow hull's sides in tiny waterfalls.

"Your father made it," Maiko said, placing a hand to her chest.

Scott eyed the fresh-looking gouge along the yellow hull's roof, but kept his worries to himself.

His mother lifted the Wolf's case. "You'll need this."

"I'll carry it," Mara volunteered, taking the instrument. Of the three of them, she was the only one dressed for the occasion in her black flight suit.

Scott and his mother kept to Haven's required holiday fashion, though what ran through his mind wasn't particularly festive. Would he even see her again, let alone have the chance to treat her as someone other than a stranger? He walked next to her, but at an arm's length, having no idea how to say a meaningful goodbye.

His mother acknowledged Scott's sudden awkwardness with her own nervous smile. She actually retreated a few steps. Her smile faded into a stoic expression. "Stay safe."

"I'll do my best, Mother." He opened the bus's hatch, not knowing what else to say.

Maiko shut the hatch behind them. Without saying a word.

Mara laid the Wolf on a bench seat and gave him a long look. "You could've at least hugged her."

He watched his mother work the docking console outside the water-bus. She didn't even wave when the river closed over the hatch's window. "We hardly know each other," he lamented. "Too much of Water under our bridge. Yeah, this whole thing sucks. She's probably blaming me for risking Dad, not to mention dragging Water back into her life." He kicked at a bench seat, wishing he could feel more than guilt.

"She still bore you," Mara pointed out. She looked at the empty seats. "At least Makio knows your father's okay, otherwise he wouldn't have sent this thing." She picked up the handle of a phone hooked into the wall midway down the bus. "Anybody there?"

Silence.

The bus bumped and rocked for a moment before beginning a smooth traverse down the tunnel toward Site A. Small external motors purred along the cabin walls. Scott could see nothing outside due to the lack of lighting. He found a dial to lower the inside lights, but it didn't help.

Mara peered out one of the windows next to the seats. "Pitch black out there."

Scott found a console along with an adjacent joystick on the bulkhead next to the other hatch. Pressing the control's top button produced a wide swath of illumination from a floodlight atop the vehicle's outer hatch. "Looks like we're on a rail along the river bottom."

"And what's waiting at the far end?" Mara voiced his own worries. "Nobody's answering the phone."

"I'd say they're a bit busy grabbing Mackenzie," Scott guessed. "They made it into the building far enough to send the bus back."

"Assuming they're the ones who sent it," Mara replied, dropping into a seat.

"We'll stick to the plan, okay?" Scott sat next to her, wishing she'd quit second-guessing what awaited them ahead. He had no answers, and the lack of communication with Site A didn't help. "Know how to use that dongle Dad's friend gave you?"

"Beyond plugging it into the access panel?" She shook her head. "Even if it helps us get to the *Explorer*, there's no guarantee we'll be let in even if we have Mackenzie as a hostage. Especially if they see Water. These are mercs we're talking about. Hardly the epitome of compassion."

"A little late to worry about that," Scott remarked.

"Not to mention holding off a boatload of trained soldiers until we get to Petal? You'd better hope they're loyal to Mackenzie. Not sure we'd end up back in Haven again if things go wrong."

He glared at her. "I'm waiting for a better idea. Got one?"

Mara sighed. "We're just playing it by ear, aren't we?"

Scott rested his head back against the seat's cushion, not daring to think beyond the next hour. So much could go so wrong. "I'm a musician, remember? Playing by ear's what I do, and so far we're doing alright."

"Miracle of miracles," she added with a frown.

The ride was maddeningly uneventful, right up to the moment

the bus jerked to a stop to the accompaniment of a warning chime.

"Now what?" Scott walked up to the front console and gripped the searchlight's joystick. He played the light across a tunnel entrance ahead. "Think I found out why we stopped."

Mara pressed her nose against the thick glass window. "Whole front end of the tunnel's sagging down. What'd Water do to this place? She walked back to the phone and spoke into the receiver. "Is *anyone* listening?"

"Easy," he cautioned, studying the on-screen map. "We're just on the other side of the dock." Scott looked around, spying a yellow case bolted beside the first row of seats. He broke the plastic seals and flipped open the lid. "Breathing masks here."

"Just lovely." She shook her head, glancing around as if seeking any alternative. "I drive around in space. I live on a moon. Scott, I don't know how to swim."

"It's like floating, but thicker than air," he lied, tossing her a clear mask. "You want to wait out here and see which side picks us up? Straps go behind your ears."

She inspected the cartridges on either side of the faceplate. "Says three hours of air." Frowning, she slipped the safety gear over her head and pressed the side button. A gasket popped, sealing the mask to her face. A string of lights winked on along the cartridges.

Scott followed suit, wishing he wore something better than a flowery shirt and shorts that begged to get caught on obstructions. Air hissed across his face. "Can you hear me?"

"Yes," her tinny voice quavered across the speakers. She gripped an adjacent seat with whitened knuckles.

"This is nothing compared to your dropping us into Jeremiah's Canyon." He pulled a couple flashlights out of the case. Luckily, these masks didn't include a heart monitor or she'd see just how calm he really wasn't. *Just like diving in a suit*, he reminded himself. *Yeah. Sure.* He read the emergency instructions next to the hatch screen. "We have to flood the compartment first. Ready?"

"I can't see crap out there."

He handed her one of the lights. "Grab on to a seat."

He unclipped a small red hammer next to the hatch. A warbling alarm and flashing yellow lights announced his breaking a plastic cover over an adjacent red handgrip.

"Here we go." He pulled the lever down.

The hatch's thick black seals bulged and popped. A spray of water forced them back to the middle of the bus. The floor flooded quickly, warm water rising to their chests before the hatch abruptly swung inward. A green wall of liquid followed.

Water rose over his face. "Stay with me, Mara," he encouraged. The mask's seals held, much to his relief. Mara stared at him with wide eyes through her mask. Heart pounding, he gave her a thumbs up and moved toward the open hatch. He paused. *Oops, almost forgot. Idiot.* Scott grabbed the Wolf's case. The thing was supposed to be waterproof, but until now he hadn't put it to the test.

As much as the unexpected swim unnerved him, what lay beyond that tunnel worried him far more. Not only was there no word from his father over the bus's phone, but Water hadn't bothered with even one broadcast. Neither boded well for the kind of reception awaiting them.

"Least the water's not freezing," Mara commented, following him outside.

Judging from the weight on his chest, Scott guessed they weren't too deep, which helped when he kicked away from the tram and swam for the tunnel's cement lip. He looked back. Mara thrashed more than swam. Her eyes bulged behind the mask. Remembering his first panicked reaction to diving, Scott waved his flashlight around, looking for anything resembling an air chamber above them.

He was pushed aside by a rainbow streak. Water. Fins rippling, the siren curled around Mara, bumping her forehead against the woman's mask before taking her hand. Water extended her other hand toward Scott.

He released his flashlight and gripped it, mindful of her claws. Scott's other hand closed tightly around the Wolf's case.

They sped through the blackened tunnel, Scott noting bits of shrapnel embedded in the damaged concrete. Emerging below the dock, they shot toward the surface. Scott's stomach cramped at what floated above him, backlit by overhead floodlights.

"*Madre de Dios!* Are those…arms?" Mara choked out through her mask's speakers.

"Mara, it's going to be bad up there," Scott warned, his worst fears realized. His father and Water hadn't walked in without a fight.

Water released them just below the surface, her voice pitching low to vibrate through his mask. "I am Song Guard now."

Scott caught the irregular glint of star-shaped cracks in her plates, including a mark above her luminous eyes. "Water. You've been shot."

"My heart's song is strong," she assured. "I am mostly healed." Water rolled around and touched Mara's chest over her heart. "You must be Song Guard, too." The siren tapped Scott's shoulder and gestured to his case. Nodding, he handed it to her.

"I'll go first," Scott offered, swimming up to grasp a ladder protruding into the water. He lifted himself out on a side platform next to the bus's lift and paused at what he saw. So much worse than the cougar remains back at his cabin. "Mara...I want you to close your eyes when you come up. Just...don't look." He pulled off his mask. The metallic scent of blood mixed with the cavern's mineral smells.

Mara popped up below him, her hands reaching for the rungs. When she climbed up, there wasn't much he could do but watch the grisly sight take hold in her horrified eyes. Mara ripped off her mask with a small cry then clasped her hands over her face.

Gripping her shoulders, Scott helped Mara pick her way through the bodies, keeping her aimed toward the open hatch.

The gantry vibrated with Water's leaping onto the deck, exacting a yelp from Mara as the siren advanced through the carnage with indifference.

"Just get away from me," Mara exclaimed, edging past Scott into the main building.

Scott exchanged glances with Water before launching down the hallway after Mara. "Where's my father?"

"In the infirmary with the only remaining human," Water replied. "He is injured but heals. The rest fled aboard a ship. Not Mara's ship. A bigger one."

"Shit," he swore, catching up with Mara. "Mackenzie got away. Harry...Dad's hurt." He grabbed her shoulder. "Hold up. Let Water make sure it's safe ahead of us in case there are others."

"Safe?" Mara replied with a hysterical laugh, squeezing herself against the wall as Water brushed past them. "After what I just saw?"

Water paused long enough to point a claw at her. "I am no glass doll, Mara Martinez. I am Song Guard. You must be Song Guard, too."

"Did you have to *butcher* them?" Mara shrieked after Water ran ahead.

"Are bullets any better?" Scott growled, heading after the siren. He followed Water into a small hospital room where another man, an officer by the look of him, backed away from a blue operating bed. His patient lay there, pointing a pistol at his apparent doctor.

"Dad!" Scott exclaimed, running up. He inspected his father's torn diving suit. The man was a patchwork of bandages.

"Move your ass," his father ordered in a groggy voice. "Mackenzie's high-tailing it to the *Explorer* aboard a Valkyrie." Harry nodded to Mara upon her entrance. "Your Surveyor's still on the ramp.

165

I'll keep the Commandant Grissom here company until you're out of range."

Scott grimaced at the bloodied shards lying in a glass dish on a side table.

"He'll live," Grissom stated, edging away from Water who moved to Harry's side.

"Go," Harry repeated.

Scott squeezed his father's free hand, not knowing what to say. "Thanks doesn't really cover it."

A smile managed to spread across Harry's strained face. "Try and remember us this time."

"We've got to move," Mara joined in, touching Scott's arm. She favored the officer with a steely expression. "You going to take care of him?"

The man nodded with a grimace. "Just the same, he'll have to answer for this. All of you will."

Harry raised the pistol. "We'll settle up after they're in the clear, Commandant."

"Settle now," Water seethed, raising an arm.

Scott held up a hand and shook his head. Mara didn't need to see further examples of how vicious Water could be. He looked down, wishing he knew his father better. One debt settled. Another begun. "I'll come back when this is over, Dad."

Mara pulled Scott away. "We've *got* to leave." She rummaged through a drug cabinet behind the table and rattled an amber bottle of pills at Scott. "Now."

Sucking in a breath, Scott nodded at his father. "Whatever you think you owed your men, you've paid it."

"Down payment," Harry grunted. "Good luck, son."

"Same to you, Dad," Scott replied.

He joined Mara and Water in the hall. They broke into a run.

"I will keep us safe," Water said, taking the lead.

They charged through a bullet-riddled foyer for a set of shattered double doors.

'You just like killing people," Mara accused.

Water jingled to a stop, her dorsal fins rippling orange. "I am Song Guard!"

"How long are you going to keep repeating that?" Mara threw back, coming to a halt with her fists clenched.

"Until I am not your pretty glass angel!"

"No time for this," Scott reminded, dashing outside. He spied the *Alicia* sitting by itself across a pockmarked apron. Overhead hovered a solitary sunlamp. He stopped and spun around, his voice rising over the distant howl of insane winds. "Ladies, stop the drama and get the hell out here!"

Water charged out in a ruddy glow, swimming fins whipping around her legs. "I will not be her monster," she sang in Air.

"Then don't let her become yours," Scott returned, greatly relieved to see Mara coming behind Water in one piece.

They ran underneath the Surveyor's fuselage where the forward hatch lay open. Mara was first up the short ladder, followed by Scott and then Water with his instrument case. He dropped into the copilot's seat, watching anxiously while Mara flipped overhead switches and tapped at screens. To his relief, the cabin quivered with the thrum of wakening engines.

"Didn't break my lockouts," she said with satisfaction. "Hatch closing." She pulled a dongle from her pocket. "No idea what this is going to do." Mara plugged the device into a console's receptacle. Every display darkened, along with the cockpit lights. Even the engines quit.

"Damn hacker crap!" She slapped at her armrest.

Scott reached over to pull the dongle out, only to be blocked by her hand.

"Just…wait."

"My seat is not comfortable," Water complained behind them.

"Wasn't made for dorsal fins," he sympathized. "Try flattening them out."

"The harness does not fit, them," the siren stated, flicking her fins in emphasis.

Mara slapped at a control stick. "And we're stuck…" Her anger was cut off by reappearing cabin lights. Screens blinked back to life.

The display in front of Scott came on. "Uh, got something new here. Letters spell out PSAP, whatever that means."

"No idea," Mara snapped, once again flipping switches. "Engines spooling up."

The cabin quivered with the return of the Surveyor's propulsion plant. The floor hatch thumped shut.

"Grab onto something back there," Scott warned, hearing Mara start humming one of her lullabies. He fixed his harness. "Remember, we've got winds up there."

The *Alicia* jerked forward then rose a few feet over the tarmac. More clunking noises announced the gear tucking in.

"Pitching ninety and max," Mara announced.

The next moment saw everyone on their back and pressed into

their seats, Mara's vault skyward underscored by Water's annoyed screech.

They rushed toward a stream of torn orange clouds. "Crosswinds," Scott warned.

"Oh, really?" Mara derided between hums.

The Surveyor flipped on its belly and merged with the jet stream in a shudder of acceleration.

"I do not like this!" Water shrilled. "You do this to me!"

"I don't like what you do, either," Mara threw back amid the buffeting. "Suck it up, Song Guard."

"Not now, ladies," Scott broke in, catching the anger in Mara's voice. "Mind leveling us out?"

He received only a scowl in response, but the Surveyor rolled over and continued its climb. *Great. Both females are pissed now.*

Space was a stomach-twisting pain in the ass, but he gladly traded shaking around in a can for simply floating in one.

Hair suspended about her, Mara bent toward him, her gaze on his screen. "I think the bracketed blip's the *Explorer*. Press on it. Good, it's selected. Okay, see the button saying *engage*? Press that."

He obeyed. The Surveyor abruptly rolled to one side, corrected, then eased up on the engines. Scott saw a new display on Mara's screen, looking similar to the same electronic road guiding her earlier to Site A.

"Even a Song Guard could do this," Mara remarked, easing a representation of her ship toward the middle of the displayed corridor.

"Song Guard could take your head off right now," came the caustic response behind them.

Mara flipped a right hand over her shoulder.

Scott reached over and pulled down Mara's extended middle finger. "I wouldn't if you plan on keeping it."

She twisted around to see Water waving an extended set of cutting fins along her forearm.

"That's not exactly helping, either," Scott added, scowling at Water. "Remember who we're doing this for." He turned back to Mara. "By the way, how are we going to do this? We haven't got Mackenzie, and I don't have any idea how to sneak about that ship."

"They're going to Earth, right?" Mara asked. "Well, we will go with them. I think I can get us close enough to make the jump when they do."

He swallowed back doubts. "Without being spotted?"

She shrugged. "It's all up to what we uploaded into the computers. If we're really configured like a Nightshade, we can nudge right up alongside them and they'll never know it. Have a little faith, huh? Contact in one hour, seventeen minutes just shy of Sanctuary Gate. I'll have to program *Alicia* to stay up against the Explorer during the jump, because we'll be sedated with those pills I grabbed for the occasion. We're already crazy enough without ending up even worse on the other side."

Scott glanced at Water, who sat hunched forward in her seat to accommodate her dorsal fins. The siren's claws were firmly embedded in the side rests of her seat. "What about Water?"

"I am already insane." Water reached up to an overhead conduit and used it to slide forward until she suspended herself upside down between them, her silicon hair waving like tiny serpents in the weightlessness. Her claw gently tapped Scott's discolored forehead. "I have been in there too long."

"Great, so we all wake up in pieces when Miss Slice-And-Dice loses it," Mara grumbled.

Water's fin tips glowed a slight orange. "How would you have me kill them back at the dock?"

"By hacking them to death?" Mara hissed. "Damn it, couldn't you have negotiated first?"

"They were dropping grenades. Those are what hurt Scott's father." Water pressed her face close to Mara's. "So I ask again. How would you have me kill them?"

Mara's voice lowered. "I get it. Welcome to the war. Now, how about you get your sparkly mug out of my face?"

Water withdrew to the rear seat. "I have found a new God Between for you, Mara, but I do not think you deserve Her yet. This god saves my people, and will not let me harm you when we reach Earth."

Mara's lips turned down into a near snarl. "Sorry, not in the sainthood business anymore."

"As I said. You do not deserve Her…yet."

Mara rolled her eyes. "Fine. Anybody here have a plan for when we get to Earth? Someplace we can hole up while every merc in the world searches for us?"

"I've a place in mind," Scott thought aloud, his mind automatically supplying a well-worn answer to escaping the unwanted public eye. "It's in the Sierra Nevada west of Lake Tahoe. Assuming Mackenzie doesn't detect us hitching a ride, we'll hunker down at my cabin there."

Mara folded her arms. "And then?"

What always comes next after the cabin. He smiled, an idea far better than a blindfolded Mackenzie forming in his head. Something Jeremiah and his fake money-sucking church would do anything to avoid. Including helping them get to Petal.

"We're going to give a concert." Scott decided. The look on Benny's face was going to be worth the trouble.

Their rendezvous with *Deep Explorer* was just as anti-climactic as the chase. Save for blinking navigation lights, the huge orb was simply another blotch of darkness set over more darkness. No alarms, and no evasive maneuvers.

"And we're not being blasted into space or even hailed," Mara said, her voice dropping to a whisper. "I guess *Alicia's* a Nightshade, now." She adjusted her screen to a second cluster of lights among the stars. "And there's the gate. I'll ease us into that shadow beneath the *Explorer's* hangar door, engage the autopilot, and hope for the best."

The Surveyor glided beside the larger ship's hull, Mara using a combination of maneuvering thrusters and the *Explorer's* own microgravity to keep them all but touching. The approach to Sanctuary Gate proved a nail-biting wait to see if either Mackenzie's crew or the automated station detected their presence. When they finally glided into the skeletal bore of the gate, bright floodlights along the barrel's superstructure made a mockery of their hiding place.

"Somebody just has to look out a window," Mara said with a hopeless laugh, peering anxiously at the hangar door next to them.

"We will test our God Between," Water spoke up. "See if She is better than the thieving gods."

"She, eh?" Scott replied, looking for any excuse to lighten the mood.

"The God Between gave me my body. Of course a She."

"Makes perfect sense," Mara added smugly. "Ought to make Water the Prophet."

"Or you," Scott threw in, thinking of the concert to come. The Saint and the Angel. Neither Jeremiah nor his lapdog Mackenzie would see this coming. "Make sure we're as unnoticed on the other end when we reach Earth," he added to deflect Mara's scowl at his comment.

The universe abruptly lost its footing and fell into an abyss. Scott bit his lip, trying not to show his building panic.

"We jumped." Mara pulled the pill bottle from her pocket. "Water, are you sure you can't take one of these?"

"I will be safe," the siren promised.

Scott's world plunged in on itself. He swallowed the sedative. Water's answer became clearer when he found his face enwrapped in her translucent hair, her forehead pressing hard against his. She dug her claws into his chair's armrests to anchor herself.

He let himself swirl down the medicinal drainpipe, the sedative depositing him in a familiar place. The fishbowl. Water was there waiting for him. They floated above powdery white sands, the siren curling herself protectively around him.

"You left your body?" he asked.

"Not all of me," she sang. "You still have the Song's crystals in your head. Much like a Quan Singer. Maybe, when we return home, I will see if my Quan will take you, too." She smiled. "I do not want the emptiness in my thoughts. This is better."

"Yeah, you left a hole, too," he admitted, surprised to actually be relaxing in her company. So eager to get rid of her without thinking through the consequences.

She nodded. "Your emptiness needs my fulfillment, Scott Rellant. I have such purpose inside me now. Do you not hear the voices singing? This is the song of our God Between."

Water had a knack for odd conversations, even if he suspected she was just being overly dramatic to suit her mood. How much of the sedative flowing through him contributed to it? "Isn't the Quan actually your god?"

"Better," she replied with a snort. Water raised three glittering fingers and, one by one, pulled them down. "Kee's Sword burns us. Anasa's wind tears apart everything we build. Mara's god sends thieves to murder our future. My Quan does none of these things."

He propped his head up on an elbow. "You know, you're going to depress the hell out of Mara with such talk. She was really wanting to find something to believe in."

"So we give her a new god. One closer to our Quan. We will be her miracle, and she will be a saint again."

Scott tapped at one of her crystal plates, tracing out the swirling rainbow galaxy beneath. It sounded like a tiny choir. "What about them?"

Water's voice dropped an octave. "I do not know. I bring them back to my Quan who suffers under Kee and Anasa's wrath. Is that wrong? Should I have stayed in the lake and given them a new home?"

Scott digested her statement for a moment. "You mean...become a Quan yourself? Is that possible?"

"I am Song Mother. It is possible, but then I would have to leave you. Maybe it is I who does not deserve a God Between. I am too much like you. Only think of myself."

He stroked her crystal cheek, not sure how to respond to her admission. "Then we need a miracle."

Sixteen

A constant tinkling sound. Claws clicking on the glass of a mental fishbowl Scott thought vanished for good. Water's voice interrupted his disorientation. "Wake up."

He blinked away the fog, catching a glimpse of Water gliding behind him. His ears picked up the whirr and beep of cabin electronics, reminding him of his location. He twisted in his chair, feeling each crease in the cushions. Amber light shone through the Surveyor's cabin, casting golden sparkles off Water's body.

The siren reached out and tapped Mara's sagging head in the pilot's position next to them.

Mara's hand batted listlessly about, then with more purpose. "You mind?"

"That Jupiter?" Scott leaned forward to peer out at ochre swirls filling the windshield screen.

"As programmed into the flight director," Mara confirmed, rubbing her eyes. "Old smuggler's trick. Find a big gasbag and let its background radiation do the rest. If *Deep Explorer's* looking for us, they'll have to look harder."

"Thought you were tugging asteroids back home," Scott ventured, stretching an aching back.

She looked over at him. "Thought you were tooting horns."

"An oboe."

Mara tapped at the dashboard in front of her. "Okay, guys, I've been thinking. You needed me to get back to Earth. I got you here. This concert you talked about...I'm guessing it's to force the church to get you to Petal."

"Close enough guess," Scott agreed with a frown, seeing where this conversation was heading. "I need you as part of the show, Mara. Someone people can believe in."

"That Saint Mara crap was *Jeremiah's* idea," she replied with a scowl. "I'm done. I'll take you home and sneak a jump back to the String of Pearls."

Water poked her head between the two of them. "Mara knows I am not her angel."

"And Mara doesn't need your shit, either," Mara retorted. "You're no better than the mercs that'll be hunting me if I stay here." Her words tumbled into an awkward quiet. Mara sent more instructions to her console. "Next stop, Sierra Nevada. ETA roughly two hours."

It took them five, with Mara working in close concert with the Nightshade software to slip undetected into Earth's busy traffic patterns. Scott used the time figuring out how he could talk Mara out of leaving. He came up empty. Any sympathy she had for the Shreen ended upon seeing the results of Water's darker side. Mara also possessed the ship of her dreams—fast and undetectable. Hell, if it weren't for Water's plight, he'd be sorely tempted to join her.

Scott tried to make sense out of Mara's displays, but finally gave up. Scott observed the Surveyor finally biting into atmosphere a carefully executed quarter mile behind a freighter's glowing wake. The cabin quivered, bright pink plumes wrapping around the windscreen. "How we doing?"

Hands locked on her joysticks, Mara scowled at the green corridor on her screen. "Damn plasma stream's trying to knock me out of the safe zone. My fingers aren't the only things cramping."

"Just be damn glad this Nightshade software is working." Scott wanted to give the dongle stuck into her console an appreciative flick of his finger, but decided otherwise.

Mara nodded. "We'll follow that tub another five thousand kilometers, and then we'll have your departure angle for Sierra Nevada."

Back where I started, with everything I wanted except peace of mind. He shook his head. "Never thought I'd come crawling back like some miserable thief. And Water, not a word out of you."

"You are no thief," Water asserted. "I will find something to hang on to. Mara does not like me."

"I'm too tired to be bitchy," their pilot answered. "Hang on just the same. I'll have to turn a few lazy-eights to burn off energy when we're close to landing."

They angled away from their unsuspecting host over eastern California. The *Alicia* descended in broad turns, vapor trails curling off black wingtips refusing to reflect the afternoon sun. Scott studied the upcoming terrain on his screens, trying to discern a familiar line of wooded slopes while the cabin quivered from Mara's braking.

Water leaned over his shoulder. "There," she spoke up.

"I don't see it." He tried to follow her pointing claw.

"I remember the color of rocks," Water explained. "Mara, go right."

"Going right," Mara repeated, skimming along escarpments. "Sure these are the right coordinates, Scott?"

"More or less." *Let me be right...* He grinned. Success. "That brown tile roof perched on a lower hill, see it?"

She scrunched her nose. "Weren't you supposed to be rich?" She slowed the Surveyor to a hover over the sparse clearing offered behind the small building. "No porch. Fake log siding. Ever heard of paint?"

"Didn't build it to impress visitors," Scott muttered, stung by her comments. Who cared what she thought? He liked it as is.

The Surveyor landed in a flurry of dust and loose pebbles. He waited for the cloud to settle before opening the cabin's floor hatch to almost forgotten evergreen smells.

"I can hunt mountain lions," Water quipped, green ripples racing up her fins. She slipped past Scott in a crystalline rustle.

"Not now," he yelled after her, not needing to attract the attention of another Brothers satellite. Great, just what he needed right now. Water annihilating the local fauna for sport. Couldn't she wait until *after* they saved the day?

Mara unsnapped her harness. "Lions?"

"Rarely," Scott assured her, dropping down from the hatch. God help any cougar unlucky enough to encounter his siren.

Mara slid down the ladder next, the Wolf's case in her hand. "Might want this."

Scott grinned. "Weren't you just dropping us off?"

Mara ignored the jibe and rapped on the cabin's door while casting a meaningful look his way. "I *seriously* need a bathroom."

Water walked up to the entrance, reached around her, and tapped the access pad to no avail.

"Need fingerprints for that to work," Scott said with a grin, entering the combination.

"Not if I use my cutting fins," came Water's saucy reply in a tone suggestive of a stuck out tongue, had she possessed one.

"Would one of you just get me inside?" Mara snapped, bouncing from one foot to another.

The inside of the cabin extracted an appreciative whistle from her once the lights flickered on. She favored the comfortable interior with a wide-eyed glance before spying the bathroom door.

Water disappeared down the narrow basement stairs in a jingle of fins, no doubt heading for his Jacuzzi.

Scott inspected the auto-kitchen in the corner, satisfied the management company had yet to stop their upkeep. "Anyone for steak?"

Mara returned from the bathroom and ran a hand across the couch's curved leather back while admiring the wall screen occupying the opposing corner. "Sounds good. Any beer?"

He peered in the fridge. "Ale, lager, or malt?"

Mara laughed. "Malt. So, this is where you spend your days?"

"Just when I need to get away. Have a studio on Maui where I do most of my composing. People might notice a Surveyor parked outside over there, though."

A bright light shone up the stairs. Water had found the tanning lamps. Apparently, everyone was hungry.

"She loves the bubbles," he explained to Mara's raised eyebrow. "Water would keep me down there until my skin wrinkled. Now she's got it all to herself."

Mara eyed the open bathroom door. "Saw your granite walk-in shower. Nice. You mind if I take advantage of it?"

"Robes are in the right closet. I take it you're hanging around a bit longer?"

She rolled her eyes. "Look, I'm dog tired, no? I'll be out of your hair in the morning."

Mara headed for the bathroom.

"We'd all be better if you'd stay," he threw after her.

Scott sank into one of the ultra-soft couch cushions. He couldn't do this concert by himself, not if the theme was all about faith as he intended it to be. Godless bastards such as himself didn't hijack a religion. That was a job for bonafide saints. Somehow he had to corral a disillusioned pilot and a crystalline nightmare into becoming something Jeremiah couldn't afford to ignore. Or crush. Scott smiled. Water had her God Between. He, on the other hand, had Benny.

Shortly after the auto-kitchen presented dinner, Mara reappeared in a robe with a towel wrapped around her hair. Two steaks and accompanying twice-baked potatoes filled the room with mouthwatering smells. He grabbed more beers to hand out, and soon they both had their feet propped up on the coffee table beside the couch. The mutual blur of weary contentment was apparently contagious. A soft vibrating hum drifted up from the basement, accompanied by a gurgling Jacuzzi.

Mara half-raised her head. "That Water?"

Scott listened to the soft sonorous melody coming up the steps as if from some mystic temple. He grinned.

Water was singing the first movement of *Song*, the introduction of his newest, unfinished symphony. Doing a fine job of it, too. Raising a finger, Scott pulled himself off the sofa and grabbed the Wolf's case. He warmed up the oboe and joined Water halfway through the second movement's epic rise. Water followed, her voice matching the Wolf in offsetting tones to both compliment and lift the music even higher.

The siren emerged from the basement in a rainbow of colors, each iridescent hue splashing itself off the walls. Water stood at the top of the stairs, her mouth open in song, her dorsal fins spread wide in a glitter of frozen fireworks. Mara's angel reborn.

Mara seemed to think so, too, judging by the rapture in her eyes. At least until her eyelids fluttered, as if memories of the carnage back at Site A fought against the beauty of the moment. Her soft smile crumbled.

Almost brought you back to us. For a second he'd glimpsed Water's God Between touching Mara's soul.

Water must have seen it, too. She stepped forward in the same manner, reminding him of a cat testing uncertain ground. Her song ended on an entreating note.

Slowly, carefully, the siren reached out and lifted Mara's hand, placing it against the miniature galaxies swirling in her chest. "Please take them home."

Mara drew back. "Damn it, Water, I wish you'd make up your mind about what you are. You can't be both monster and...and *this*." She pushed herself off the couch onto unsteady legs, sending several bottles tumbling across the coffee table.

Scott raised a hand to ease Water's disappointed expression. He nodded approvingly while steering Mara toward the upstairs loft. "Let me get you up the steps. Bed up there is yours. We'll figure out what's what in the morning."

Mara sagged against the paneled wall next to the stairs. "How in the hell are we supposed to get her home? I mean, this is the plan, right? It's only a matter of time before Brothers comes looking, and this'll be one of their first stops. You know that, don't you?"

"When they find us, they'll have to squeeze their way through several thousand others." Scott pointed to Water, who watched intently from the edge of the couch. "You're Saint Mara, remember? Guess what miracle you just discovered. A walking, talking Reliquary."

"So your father told me." Mara closed her eyes for a second. "Jeremiah's going to shit bricks when he finds out. He'll try and take her from us."

"And that, my dear, is exactly what I'm hoping for."

~ * ~

The following morning, after pepper-jack cheese and sausage omelets, he and Mara stood outside to watch a small dot descending from scattered clouds.

"Nice to see you're still with us," Scott observed, keeping his tone carefully neutral. Didn't want to spook her. He needed her to stay.

"About the only miracle you'll get out of me, *hombre*. Hear the news, this morning?"

"Hadn't bothered," he admitted with a frown. "Why?"

"Because there's no mention of us or Mackenzie coming back. Don't know if it's bad or good." Mara shielded her eyes from the sun. "Think your guy told anyone where we are?"

"Not after I explained to him how much money he'd make." Scott brushed remnants of breakfast biscuits off his jeans. He'd assumed his lumberjack look, though the unruly sweep of his brown hair had more of that mountain-man wildness than he preferred.

Mara, on the other hand, looked fresh and professional, having cleaned and worn her black flight suit, as if reminding him her tenure here was iffy at best.

"And your agent's name is Benny." She crossed her arms. "Seriously? I mean...*Benny*?"

Scott shrugged. "Welcome to show business. His real name is probably George or something. Never bothered to ask. Thanks, by the way."

Mara's expression went south of skeptical. "For what? Helping the Church with their bullshit? People deserve better than the crap we're about to serve up." Mara kicked at the granite lip, watching pebbles bounce down the slope. "You're doing this to get Water home. I'm doing this just to get myself home. Some Saint, eh?"

"Water thinks so. Even came up with a God Between for you."

"Funny how an alien has more faith than we do."

He shrugged again. "Something miraculous is at work here. Consider how things are falling into place to get Water home. Hard to keep calling this pure luck."

Mara lost her snide expression. "I just wanted to believe we weren't alone in this universe. I like the idea of something out there taking care of us. Not too much to ask, is it?"

Scott watched the black limo angle for a landing up the road from the Surveyor. "Not really."

The two of them walked down the gravel ruts to greet the short man in a canary-yellow suit and red tie as he stepped from the flyer. For a moment, the balding man just stared at them, his bushy eyebrows raised in genuine surprise.

"Holy...crap!" Benny stretched his arms out. "You *are* back from the dead!"

The agent's exuberant hug seemed genuine, as well as the hearty pats on Scott's back. Benny stood back and jabbed a thumb toward Mara, who stood back from them. "And...that's Saint Mara? How'd you two do this? I mean, Church said you'd crashed into a cliff on Sanctuary. Had themselves a big ol' memorial for you two. The video was seen by millions across the planet."

"God gave us another miracle," Mara smoothly broke in, taking up the story she and Scott concocted over breakfast.

Benny's narrowed eyes switched between them. "This on the level, right? Not Church PR?"

Mara's smile was a celestial masterpiece. "Would you like to meet the angel who blessed us with life?"

Skepticism crept into the man's tone. "Yeah, sure. Let's see this *angel*, Your Holiness."

They took him inside the cabin. Scott held his breath. Water ascended the basement steps with a queen's majesty, her chin high and swimming fins flowing like the hem of a bridal dress. The siren spread her dorsal fins, their spines bright with iridescent ripples.

Benny swallowed, his Adam's apple working overtime. "Sweet Jesus." His voice lost his usual harried Hollywood agent accent.

Now for the hard part. Scott stepped forward. He sang in Air just to keep things a bit more mysterious. "Show him what your heart's song can do, Water."

She stepped forward. "Cutting game?"

Scott nodded. He hardly felt the sweep of her forearm's fins across his left cheek. The result even widened Mara's eyes.

Water held his face against her in an embrace, her warmth dampening the electric pain even as it registered itself. Her violin voice emitted a genuinely apologetic croon.

"I'll get a towel," Mara hurried into the bathroom and returned with a wet washcloth. She dabbed at his face, then wiped crimson rivulets from Water's chest plates for good measure.

Scott ran a finger along his smooth cheek, suppressing a satisfied smirk at Benny's stunned expression.

"Behold God's new gift," Mara intoned, precisely on cue.

Scott could imagine her biting her tongue. "And we want you to present us to the world," Scott finished. "A concert. As many people as you can get in the shortest amount of time."

Benny shook his head. "Guys...this is big. This isn't a show, this is Church stuff. Hand of God and all that. You don't want me."

Scott clamped a hand on the man's shoulder. "Nobody can get the word out like you, Benny. It's why Water chose you. You're the best."

The manager licked his lips and looked at the siren. "Water...your name's Water? You chose me?"

Scott's breath caught in his throat. Water wasn't the best at improvisations unless there were a dire threat attached to them.

Water bowed her head. "You must be Song Guard."

"Song...Guard, yeah." Benny produced a garish purple handkerchief from his shirt pocket and dabbed at his beaded scalp. He straightened his spine, chest puffing out. "I can do this. How long do I have?" His voice had regained its snap.

"Days," Scott cautioned the man. "And no forward publicity. Not everyone in the Church will welcome a living, sentient Reliquary. We have to hammer the point home, Benny. Water can sing as well as I can play, so we'll do *Song* just like at Sacramento."

"Hammer, yeah." He dropped into the sofa beside the door. "You're killing me, Scott."

Scott raised a silencing hand to Water before she said something they'd all regret. "Nobody but you can pull this off."

"It's still fifteen percent?" Benny swallowed and glanced around, as if expecting a bolt from the blue or from the Almighty, or worse.

"And nobody the wiser, Benny. You've no idea how much is at stake, here."

"And she...your angel's okay with this?"

Water folded her dorsal fins. "We fight thieves."

Mara looked away and mouthed a curse behind Benny's back. Scott settled for glaring at Water and her loose mouth.

Benny gave Mara a long look then regarded Scott as if catching his hand in the till. "Wait. You guys aren't with the Church. You're going against it, aren't you?"

"Let's just say we're dragging it along," Scott revised. "Maybe start with a branch of our own. A little more affordable Intercession, perhaps." He tried on Mara's earlier smile. "Think what fifteen percent of that would look like."

Benny finally tore his gaze off Water and regarded Scott with a bit more clarity. "Get me a screen."

Rolling her eyes, Mara headed for the door. "I can't keep this up. Just...can't."

Scott ran after her, with Water close on his heels. He'd be

dragging the Church nowhere without Mara's help. He found her leaning against the cabin's weathered exterior rather than hightailing it for her ship.

"Fifteen percent," she spat. "So this is what faith goes for these days. Should start calling myself Saint Mara of Perpetual Whoredom."

Scott found a small pine across from her to lean on, its roots stubbornly clinging to the granite ground. "A few months ago, I wouldn't have given a damn either way. A few months ago, you would've killed me for even suggesting this. I never said this idea of mine wouldn't suck."

Water finished nosing around where she'd eviscerated the cougar some months back and walked over. "Maybe you are ready for my God Between."

Mara sneered. "The one that chops up people alive?"

Water looked up at the sun, its light sparkling off the tiny plates along her cheeks. "Our god burns us. Yours steals from us." She walked over and bumped foreheads with the pilot. "You should like me, Mara Martinez. I defend those I love. Is this not better?"

"I tried liking you," she replied, pushing Water's arms away. *Mierda*! Mara drew back a bloodied palm.

Water folded her hands around the injury. "Do not choose your god. Do not choose mine. Find the one living between the other two. The one who will save us now." She released her grip, revealing Mara's mended hand. "Maybe you will like me then."

Scott flicked a finger at Water's left dorsal. "You could apologize while you're at it."

Mara studied her stained but now unblemished hand. "Why? She heals about as fast as she cuts. Maybe being between gods isn't so bad a place."

"I am Song Mother again," Water added. "I could be the miracle you look for. The real one."

"Better than no miracle at all," Scott agreed, wanting to put his own emptiness behind him. Getting Water home with her precious cargo was all he had left, but it was better than nothing. Maybe he'd find something along the way to inspire his own lack of faith other than Jeremiah's sideshow religion. "I know you're fed up with the whole Saint thing, Mara, but we need you to tolerate the bullshit a little longer. Make it harder for the Church not to play ball."

"Saint Thief," Water offered, drawing long looks from them both.

The cabin door creaked open, Benny's face aglow as he grinned at them. "London. Eight days. Royal Albert and over five thousand tickets already sold."

Scott's eyes widened. "Eight...days? It took us almost two years to get a gig scheduled there."

"Yeah, and thank you so very much for getting yourself killed. Gave your tour to Angie Carter. Remember her? The one you pointed out to me? Kid's a natural. Topping the international charts with *The Crying Hand*. That's a eulogy to you, by the way. Real tear jerker. Song's all over the Net. Speaking of dying, she's dying to meet you."

Scott frowned. "We're supposed to keep this to ourselves, Benny."

"She's *giving* you her concert. Says she owes ya. What was I supposed to say? No?"

Mara shook her head and walked up to him. "Benny, whatever your name is, you need to understand something. There's more to this than Scott's telling you. People might not appreciate our message. Some are out to kill us. Literally. You might want to think twice before getting involved."

The small man raised his eyes skyward for a moment before giving her a moronic look. "I wasn't born yesterday, Missy. I met those goons who grabbed Scott after Sacramento. Security outfit my ass. They're Brothers, a bunch of mercenaries on the Church's payroll. You kids are supposed to be dead, and those guys probably got cash on the table to keep it that way."

Mara folded her arms. "So why are you helping us?"

Benny looked at Scott and jerked a thumb toward her. "She's kidding, right?" He put his hands on his hips and all but stuck his pudgy face into Mara's. "*Fifteen* percent, lady," he drawled out. "Don't worry, Your Holiness, I told Angie the score. She'll keep her mouth shut, too. So now we'll figure out what your story is. The bull you fed me earlier sounds like a good start."

Scott raised an eyebrow. "What bull?"

"I've been in this business too long to believe in miracles." He jabbed a finger at Water. "Or angels. You kids be straight with me, and I'll make sure the audience buys into whatever you're selling."

"Over lunch?" Scott offered.

"Got booze?"

"Plenty."

It took most of the afternoon, along with more beer and a stack of hamburgers, to explain the true nature of Water's Song, but Benny took the story in stride with a healthy chaser of cynicism.

"So you exposed the Church's little racket of passing off this alien Song thing as a holy relic," Benny summarized between chews at the table. "Now you're gonna make 'em an offer they can't refuse in order to get the crystal queen here home with her babies. Kinda like blackmail. You'd make a good agent, Scotty my boy."

"Not babies," Water objected, the edges of her dorsal spines glowing orange.

"Plays better that way," Benny corrected. "So what's in it for Jeremiah, honey?"

Water stared at him for a moment as if not realizing he was addressing her. "They will not be thieves."

Benny let out a long breath and glanced at Scott. "And she's been living inside you *how* long?" He leaned forward. "Sweetheart, that's not how it works. Church is in it for the money. They don't do charity work unless there's an angle, so we give 'em an angle."

Scott regarded Water, seeing what Benny was getting at but not sure as to her reaction. "Are there any Song Guards left in your Quan?"

The siren nodded. "In a way, yes. My Quan remembers, and they are created. But by now my Quan has little strength. This should be a time of sleeping."

Scott licked his lips. Now for the hard part. "Could you convince other Song Guards to come here?"

Mara snorted. "Wouldn't take much to find them. Just hang around Water's lake for fifteen minutes. That'll be the easy part."

Water straightened from her resting place against the wall next to the basement steps. She hesitated then spoke. "My Quan must decide after I return."

Benny threw up his hands. "Please, guys, you're killing me."

"No I am not," Water countered.

The agent waved a dismissing hand. "Yeah, she learned a lot from you, Scott. Look, I don't care about the how, okay? It's the offer that counts. You tell the Church they can have all the living Reliquaries they want, and they'll kiss your ass all the way to Petal."

"Or more to the point," Scott clarified, "they won't kill us and go after my parents for good measure. Then we come back, and you start collecting your percentage with each Intercession."

Benny rubbed his hands. "Now we're talking. So, about this concert, Scott. What do you have in mind?"

Scott leaned back into the couch. Albert Hall. The place was huge. "What've I got to work with?"

"Same crew you had here in Sacramento, including those Canadians doing your special effects. Usual worldwide media stuff. The works. Audience might be a little more Country Western than you're used to, but we can work with that."

"And one Saint," Scott added with a wink toward Mara. "Along with one angelic ambassador."

Mara waved her recently injured and healed palm. "And one miracle. You got to have a miracle, Scott. Remember who we're really selling ourselves to."

Scott groaned, but saw her point. "Okay, we'll need a knife. Water should just heal. But it's going to be me, not you, Mara. You're already the miracle lady here."

Water's colors rippled with green delight. "The cutting game?"

Scott glanced over at her. Oh yeah. Nothing but fun.

Benny whooshed out a breath. "We've eight days. We'll need Angie for our opening act. She'll front us for the equipment and props. I'll arrange some rooms in London. We'll head out in the morning." He aimed a finger toward a briefcase. "One last thing before we get started, kiddies."

"Not again," Scott muttered, staring at the stack of unsigned papers the man produced. Benny never failed to get things in writing. It was his hallmark.

The agent gestured toward Water. "You too, bright eyes."

Seventeen

London was London, a confusion of modern and archaic merged together in a strangely compatible whole. Scott had visited the city several times, but not by being secreted from a hangar in the back of a lorry along with a defrocked saint and an alien. The horizon was a sweep of pearl gray in search of dawn by the time they arrived at Albert Hall. The Victorian-era concert dome probably looked magnificent, but there was only so much Scott could see from beneath the blankets Benny's handlers tossed over him and the others when they were secreted inside.

Benny waited for them in the hall's green room, a stately affair of off-white panels, paintings, and red carpeting. For once, the small man almost looked respectable in a gray suit in contrast to the outdoor clothes Scott and Mara wore.

"Brought you in some breakfast," he offered, gesturing to a teak, serving table. The manager eyed Water. "She eat sausages and mashed potatoes?"

Scott watched the siren spread her dorsal fins below a bowl-shaped chandelier. "Our Shreen ambassador prefers a light breakfast."

"Cute," Mara tossed in. "I suppose you found a robe for me?"

"Same as in the church posters," Benny assured. "Why the face? You are still Saint Mara," he reminded her. "Folks are going to love you."

"Not exactly loving myself at the moment," she muttered sourly, crossing the carpet to help herself to the meal.

Scott caught her wrist. "Mara, in a few hours we'll be meeting with Angie and the crew. You'll need your game face from that point forward. Just like when we first met."

"The difference now is I know it's a lie," she snapped, pulling her arm away.

"Not a lie," Water spoke up in her melodic voice. She folded her fins and approached Mara, bumping the woman's forehead with hers. "You are a Saint of the God Between now. You only have to believe."

Mara shook her head. "You've more faith in your new god than I do, Water."

"Then test Her like I did." Water tapped at one of the rainbow swirls beneath her plates. "She gave me this miracle. Make Her give you one, too."

Scott didn't know what to make of Mara's utterly stoic expression.

Angie Carter arrived a few hours later in everyday jeans and a blue pullover. The country singer and violinist got as far as the green room's hall entrance before stumbling to a halt. Her hands flew over her mouth. "I just don't believe it! You're really alive, Scott."

"All true, honey," Benny assured. He put an arm around the singer's shoulder and coaxed Angie to where Scott sat with Mara at a side table.

Rising with Mara, Scott motioned to the third member of their trio who stood warily to the side. "Angie, I'd like you to meet Ambassador Water. She represents the Shreen people. Water found us after the crash and saved our lives."

"You're…beautiful," Angie gushed.

Water took her place beside Scott in a tinkle of fins. "I am Song Mother."

"She is also a living Reliquary," Mara added. "See all those lights inside her? You're essentially getting an Intercession just by being around her. This is the miracle we're announcing tonight."

Benny motioned members of Angie's retinue into the room and handled the introductions. Scott stayed close to Water, making sure she dealt with all the new adoring faces without lapsing back into her old self. It took a while, but conversation turned from the miraculous to more down-to-earth subjects like wardrobes and choreography.

The real work began with the arrival of Quebec Holography and the Royal Philharmonic, whose initial displeasure at having to change programs vanished upon meeting with the concert's honored guests. New stage marks were set, and compositions altered for the transition from Angie's country pop to Scott's symphony. They practiced one rehearsal after another before tiers of empty seats, the hall's famous pipe organ serving as a grandiose backdrop. Lunch came and went. What emerged toward the evening was a performance unlike anything Scott had ever imagined.

Everyone entered wardrobe as the final hours ticked down.

Mara was the first to be transformed, trading loose-fitting hiking apparel from the cabin for a pale blue dress and flowing white robes. Hairdressers pulled her hair back, Mara's uncertain smiles making it clear she was anything but comfortable reassuming her previous role as Church saint.

Scott found familiar black pants and slacks waiting for him as well, along with a barber who wrangled dark twists of hair into a style more conservative than edgy.

And then there was Water. Costumers wanted to clothe her, but the siren wasn't having any of it. Being au naturel had its advantages when one sparkled like lead crystal. Angie's handlers settled for sponging the siren down with scented window cleaner before wiping each armored plate with microfiber cloths. Water soon outshone the chandeliers.

The evening saw most everyone ready for their unsuspecting audience. Scott took the swelling numbers in stride. Water, on the other hand, paced back and forth behind the stage, her fins rippling between violet and a color Scott rarely saw. Blue. A rare display of trepidation.

"So many," the siren said, eyeing the ramp leading up to the main stage.

"Just think of them as a den of thieves," Scott reassured her. "You'll do great."

"I will stand on the tape marked with a W," she stated with a nod.

"And you need to slow down," Benny reminded Scott. "Give Henri time to synch the hologram with you."

"We nailed it last time," Scott replied. "We're good, Benny. Just smile and make money."

"Scott, I can't protect you afterward." His manager's voice quavered, and for a moment Hollywood was gone. "Not against those boys you signed with."

Scott smiled, knowing he couldn't thank his agent enough, even with the royalties. "Not every day we save an entire race, Benny."

"That what we're doing?"

He put a hand on Benny's shoulder. "That's what we're doing. Don't worry, we'll be fine."

Angie began her show as she always did, with a mournful violin solo of *The Crying Hand*, her signature song and ode to Scott's reported passing. He never realized she'd considered him a mentor, but the theme of his ghostly hands guiding her over the strings would hit home even harder tonight. Angie had foregone sequins for a plain pair of jeans and matching jacket, her hair loosened to a more natural look. She almost made him feel guilty for being alive.

Now it was his turn. Technicians affixed a microphone to his neck and led him to the darkened alcove behind Angie. Directly ahead of him stood his chair, and a cleverly wrought image of himself playing on a dais. His hologram provided a ghostly accompaniment to Angie's mourning violin. Scott slowly moved toward the chair, his eyes on an overhead series of tiny lights he had to keep green or face a lot of angry French words from Henri afterward.

He reached the chair at the same moment Angie hit her final bridge in an uplifting salutation to a departed teacher. All eyes focused on her. He merged with the hologram, the crisscross of photon emitters fading on cue.

Angie's hands fell to her sides, her instrument and bow brushing against her jeans.

Scott looked across a huge rotunda of burnished woods, plush reds, and shining brass. All topped by arches and a domed ceiling covered by acoustic spheres. Below the Victorian splendor, a sea of faces looked back from three tiers and a packed floor. Perfect.

He picked up his Wolf.

Angie bowed her head. At this point, the hologram behind her was supposed to vanish. She waited until her silence instilled a wave of murmurs across her audience. Then she spoke. "Miracles." And stepped aside.

Scott waited for the aquamarine glow as the marine backdrop enveloped him in all its three-dimensional splendor. Sea fronds waved and fish darted, but this time no nymphs swirled and spun.

Please, Water, find your mark this time.

He opened with the rising glory of *Prelude*, the First Movement of *Song* responsible for catapulting him to fame. The Royal Symphony rose in accompaniment, but they couldn't compete with the nearly indescribable voice coming from behind him when Water made her entrance.

He couldn't see her from his stool, but knew she sauntered out from between two crystalline outcrops, her dorsal fins spread wide in angelic glory. Her earlier performances had rendered even the musicians speechless. Now she stunned her audience, her voice matching his oboe measure for measure.

Scott couldn't see much beyond the stage lights, but he could hear the gasps as it sunk in that this wasn't a hologram. Reflections across the stage floor told him Water pressed the point home by stepping up her own bioluminescent light show.

He dove into his masterpiece with vigor, wanting to project all the beauty and tragedy he'd endured over the past month into his composition. His Wolf was up to the task, issuing tones in the mellow richness only oboes could deliver. The orchestra kept up the pace. So did Water, right through the thunderous concussions and final notes she capped with an echoing aria as if from Heaven itself.

If anyone still thought he might be a product of Quebec Holographic, Scott ended the notion when he stood and joined Angie at the front of the stage to exchange hugs. Water came forward, too. The result was near bedlam from the audience.

"Ladies and gentlemen," Angie repeated over her microphone, her pleas all but lost in the uproar. A line of security hurriedly formed before the stage.

Water didn't bother with the mike. For a harrowing moment Scott thought she would vaporize the first row.

The siren's violin voice pierced through the clamor with an almost painful clarity. "Be silent."

Scott had never seen five thousand people quiet down so fast.

Taking a breath, Angie tried again. "Ladies and Gentlemen, Saint Mara of the Church of Life."

Mara walked on from the side stage wearing her poster smile, eliciting additional gasps from an already reeling crowd. She exchanged embraces with both Scott, Angie, and carefully, with Water, before turning to the hall.

"Ladies and Gentlemen," she began, pausing until utter silence fell over the seats. "As you no doubt have seen on the news, five weeks ago, Scott and I were involved in what should have been a fatal crash on Sanctuary. We were given up for dead, but once more our God saved us. This time, He sent us His messenger to heal us."

Hearing her cue, Water sent green ripples through her fins and bowed.

The audience appeared transfixed. Good. Scott put his hand into his pocket, fingers closing around the small folding knife that would provide the next moment's drama.

But Mara chose to go off script, and take Water with her. "Behold God's justice!" she cried, pulling back her right sleeve. "And His mercy."

Water struck like a serpent, laying open Mara's forearm in a horrific slash. Brightening with an intensity he'd never seen before, the siren pressed the bloody limb to her chest. The bleeding stopping immediately.

Scott rushed to Mara's side, fearing she'd collapse from the shock, but she shook her head. Her breath rushing out in spurts while she watched the wound close.

The crowd's screams vanished when Mara, her face pallid but

firm, raised her arm for all to see. "Behold the miracle of Intercession!"

"Behold our God Between," Water sang out.

~ * ~

Scott turned from the prim little reception area's wall screen at their hotel across from Albert Hall. The Net was flooded with commentary, and media coverage extended well beyond anything he could have hoped for. He didn't need to see more videos of police barricades and crazy-eyed people, however. Sirens blared through the hotel's third floor windows. "Okay, so we started a riot."

"Stop looking at us like that," Mara grumbled standing next to Water by the room's red brick fireplace. "It worked, didn't it?"

"Mara has her God Between, now," Water joined in. "The miracle she wished for."

"By laying her open to the bone?" Scott peeked out the maroon drapes covering the windows. "Cops have the whole street blocked off. Surprised Mackenzie's not already here with an assault force. Assuming he could make it through the mess outside."

Mara, having changed back from her spattered robes into the hiking apparel Scott found for her, left the glowing comfort of the fireplace and joined him. "Relax. It's only been a couple of hours. You wanted Jeremiah's attention, I'd bet you got it. At least your manager's gotten Angie and himself safely out of town."

He glanced uneasily at her arm with an inward shudder. "Mara, did you really need her to cut you like that?"

She took his hands in hers. "Call it an act of faith. Something real to believe in for both me and all those people Jeremiah's fleecing. Seriously, Scott, you don't see the hand of God in this? The real God, whatever He or She is?"

"I saw Water beating all previous records healing you," he returned. And thank whatever God for everything working the way you hoped. If it hadn't …

"And maybe Water *is* a messenger for something closer to God than Jeremiah ever hopes to see." She released her grip on him. "Trouble with you, Scott, is being too close to the answer to see it. Everything happening up to this point. All the things not going wrong when they easily could've. You've said the same yourself, but you still don't get it, do you? We're going to save her tribe, if not her race. You can't get away with doing these things without some kind of divine guidance or inspiration."

"All the help I see is in this room or back on Sanctuary," he pointed out, suspecting she wasn't kidding by the earnestness in her face. Saint Mara was apparently back again.

She snorted with a shake of her head. "And what were you expecting? Angels from on high? God Himself on stage?" Her expression darkened. "This is how people like Jeremiah exist. They show God as a candy machine or genie dispensing wishes…for a price. You don't have to believe, you just have to put your money in. Well, I'm going to change that."

Scott's eyebrows raised. "You're going to try and take over the Church?"

"Damn right I am. Half the reason Jeremiah ditched me was because I was getting more press than he was. Well, this time I've got a real message. Her."

Water nodded with a smug look. "Mara has found the God Between."

A chill of distrust pooled in Scott's guts. "You can't keep her, Mara. She's got to go home." Water wasn't some doll to be taken out of a closet and shown around when it suited Mara. No way in hell would he allow such a thing. New religion be damned.

Mara glared at him. "That's not what I meant. Did you ever think beyond getting Water home? What if we could convince the Shreen to come back with us?"

"We tried." Scott spoke softly, not sure what was going on in her mind. "We didn't bring back the most important member of their society, the creature at the bottom of the lake they worship. Their Quan. That's why Operation Exodus failed."

"I am Song Mother," Water interrupted, tapping at the lights inside her. "Song Mothers migrate to a new lake and become Quan themselves."

"Her own Quan might reject her," Mara added.

"I take it you two have been talking," he realized, surprised Water would keep him out of the conversation.

Water walked over to stand beside Mara. "She is not a thief. We did not know if you would understand."

Scott eyed the siren, wondering how long they had been hatching this idea. He dove to the core of what he suspected drove Water's involvement. "Why would your Quan reject you?"

"Because I am too human."

Scott groaned. "So you're telling me what? You don't want to go home? You want to go *back* to Sanctuary and prison? I'm sure the boys at Site A would love to see us again."

"No," came the firm answer. "You must take me home to Inis Drum. Our God Between must speak with my Quan. Together they will decide."

His own fears surfaced. "Is there a chance other sirens would kill you?"

Water nodded. "It is why I must bring our Song home, too. So the Quan will see I am not a thief."

"You'll disappear inside that creature of yours," Scott said, remembering their earlier conversation. "How is this not like dying?"

She gestured to the lights inside her. "Because I will live as they do."

And is that much different? Fine, she was alien. This was a good thing, at least from her perspective. Not so much from his, though. Either way, the plan hadn't changed. Just the admission that it might not end well for any of them. Mara had a revitalized Church to hope for, and Water a new future. Which left him with what? Sure, he could keep on playing music, but every note would have him thinking of the silence in his head where Water used to be. Maybe he'd find their God Between, too. The prospect was better than staring into an empty fishbowl for the rest of his life.

One thing not showing up tonight ended up being Brothers. Everyone eventually tired of waiting for the doors to be kicked in. Maybe the Prophet didn't care much for concerts after all.

Scott went to bed in a room straight out of a Victorian novel, right down to red brocade bed drapes and cherry paneling. Benny spared no expense. Unless all of this fit into his agent's idea of a last meal. He slept fitfully, caught between his own doubts and expectations of masked men in combat armor swooping through the window. Water insisted on remaining on guard in the hallway, just in case.

The following morning began with nothing eventful other than their trio making the front page of most London papers. He waved at Water who paced the hallway in a listless manner suggesting she'd been doing it all night. "Nobody showed up, I take it."

"Nobody to kill," she sulked, slumping against a paneled wall. "Mara is in the reception room ordering breakfast."

He decided to bump her head with his for once. "You really that blood thirsty?"

She sang back in Air. "I am bored."

"So where's the army?" Mara asked when he and Water joined her. She plucked at her borrowed clothes. "I'm about to say the hell with it and go shopping. Find something I can run fast in."

Scott glanced out the window and groaned. "Half of London's still out there. Police still have the entire block cordoned off." He frowned. "We can't just sit in here. People are going to want to hear something. Oddly enough, I was hoping the Church of Life's glorious

Prophet would have stepped in by now."

Water perked up at a discreet rap on the reception room's door.

"Easy," Scott cautioned her, seeing the wrong kind of a smile on the siren's face. "Mercs rarely knock."

"They do now," Mara observed.

Well...damn. Smartly dressed waiters with rolling trays entered the room, accompanied by large men in ubiquitous brown suits sporting an embroidered russet "B" above breast pockets. The Brothers security detail said nothing, and more importantly did nothing. They simply stood off to the side while the waiters set out tea and scones. The men eyed Water, and she eyed them in turn. The rising tension dissipated when both groups left in a wordless rush.

Mara sampled a scone and chuckled. "Wonder if we should've tipped them?"

Scott hazarded a second look outside. "There are four brown vans parked in front. My guess is they've cleared the entire floor up here."

Water poked her head through the curtains.

He wagged a finger at her. "Easy. You're an ambassador now, not a siren."

"All they know are sirens." Water gestured toward the door. "Footsteps. One person."

Scott raised a cautioning hand. "I can guess." Taking a calming breath, Scott opened the door.

Mackenzie stared down at him then across at Water. "Good morning," he rumbled with a dry smile, straightening his brown suit. "I believe you're expecting me?"

"Come on in, Bob." Scott fought an urge to wipe the smirk off the man's smug face. "Like the show last night?"

Mackenzie walked in, nodding toward a sneering Mara before helping himself to a buttered biscuit. "Didn't know it could sing."

Water's sharp chirp knocked the man back, and rattled windows. "*She* can sing, thief."

"We're good," the man blurted. "Stand down."

"Others outside," Water reported, leaving the window. She stalked up to Mackenzie with a predator's grace. "I did not come here to kill."

He stiffened. "Tell it to those men back at Site A."

Mara slid between them and pushed Water back. "How many of her kind did your goons shoot up?" she countered. "Oh, by the way..." Her slap held more meaning than real force. "That's for leaving us to rot, you backstabbing son of a bitch."

"That was for your own good," Mackenzie grated. "Both of you. How long did you think you'd last back here with what you knew?"

"This long," Scott replied with a slow smile. "Tell Jeremiah today's his lucky day. We're going to make a deal."

Mackenzie eased himself into a chair at the table, his eyes traveling from Water's orange colors to Mara's wolfish grin. "Somehow I doubt it." He folded his hands on the table. "Look, guys, getting Article Thirty-Six'd on Sanctuary was business. The men your pet siren killed? They remain unfinished business. Spare me the ambassador crap. I know damn well what she is."

"After last night's coverage, there's a few million who think otherwise," Scott retorted. "You here to pout or negotiate?"

Mackenzie folded his arms. "Sounding more like your father with every moment. So, is it true? Sirens have the same ability as a Reliquary? Or was last night a parlor trick?"

"Have Water cut his leg off so he can find out," Mara brightly offered.

Scott waved Water away and sat down across from the man. Maybe leaving them on Haven had been a mercy in Mackenzie's eyes. None of that mattered now. "The Reliquary is fading and Jeremiah's about to lose his cash cow. Petal's becoming unapproachable. He needs sirens, and I've got the only one who might not kill him on sight. So how about we do what we should've done from the start with the Shreen? Negotiate."

"We could've done things better," Mackenzie admitted with a grimace. "So what's the deal?"

Scott swallowed his surprise at what sounded like genuine regret from the man. "Jeremiah puts the Reliquary back where he found it, and there's no reprisals against my parents. In exchange, Water recruits her friends to come back and take the Reliquary's place."

Mackenzie tossed Water a measured look. "You'd do this?"

"If my Quan decides," Water replied, her tone as sharp as her cutting fins. "You will return Inis Drum's Song, thief."

"So there's our deal," Scott finished and stood. "I suggest you head back to your boss, Mackenzie, before the Ambassador forgets herself."

"I wouldn't leave this hotel," Mackenzie replied, rising. "I pull my boys, and the mob will be up here after your siren's miracles." He paused before letting himself out. "Wouldn't want her showing them that Hell has angels too, right?"

Scott glanced out the window after the man left. "Police have all gone. Just a lot of Brothers men out there. I would've thought the British government might have stepped in by now. Was counting on it, actually."

Mara frowned. "Half of their Parliament's up for Intercession. They're being told to back off."

His suspicions, as well as Mara's, seemed to bear out over the following hours when the only news reports gaining traction on the Net made brief mention in the entertainment segments. Private forums were another matter altogether. He and Water sat at the top of all social media discussions, complete with videos. Especially the images where Mara volunteered to have her arm laid open. The various talk show hosts and televangelists had a field day. Everything from declarations of the Second Coming to scathing conspiracies and counter accusations. Some of them chillingly close to the mark.

Mara tapped at the wall screen. "Look at the Foundation forum. That's the Church of Life's unofficial outlet. They're welcoming us back. Comparing Water to Gabriel? A bit of a stretch. Looks like you're a Saint, too, Scott."

"Saint Scott," he said with a laugh. Nice ring to it."

"Here we go." Mara's voice roughened. "They're announcing a press conference tonight at the London Temple. With us." She looked at him. "The Prophet just left Tahoe."

Eighteen

The white limousine settled on the hotel roof's landing pad, sending ripples along puddles left by afternoon rain. The Church's golden hands emblazoned the flyer's hull.

Scott studied the wet splotches in the concrete at his feet, having the same doubts as when he initially signed Mackenzie's contract. Talk about dealing with the devil. Actually, he'd prefer having the devil across the table rather than Jeremiah. The devil didn't take himself so seriously.

Mara folded her white robes around her and glowered toward the emerging passenger in his brown suit. She looked at Scott, her voice dropping. "Are you really going to recruit sirens for those bastards?"

"No," both he and Water chorused in hushed tones as Mackenzie approached them. Scott took comfort in having Water on the same page with him.

"Then I guess I'll have to put up with this," Mara muttered.

"See you had your robe cleaned, Your Holiness," Mackenzie wryly observed.

Mara pulled back from his outstretched hand. "I hope you prepped Jeremiah on my not being his *puta* anymore."

The large man's face sobered. "Now, now, little Miss Sainthood. None of that. Better look like you'd kiss his ass when you're seen in public."

Scott felt his face redden along with Mara's at the man's impertinence. "I'm beginning to like the idea of Water kicking yours, actually."

Mackenzie just grinned before turning his attention to Water. "Speaking of protocols, your siren keeps six paces away from the Prophet at all times."

Water's contempt rippled up her fins in orange bursts. "He sees himself dead from my claws. So should you, thief."

Mackenzie's demeanor darkened further. "An armed team will

be shadowing your every move. One twitch. One sound I don't like, and nobody goes home. Got that?"

"Are we through with the pleasantries?" Scott coolly interjected, putting a warning hand on Water's shoulder. "I'd like to get going before somebody gets himself killed."

It took some creative fin-folding for Water to nestle into a leather upholstered corner, but soon they flew along the Thames for a landing at what Mara told him was once the site of a Catholic college.

Mara smirked during their descent. "The Brits forced Jeremiah to make Gabriel's statue atop the Temple a foot shorter than Saint Paul's dome. Temple Square used to be part of a tennis court."

"Big crowd," Scott observed with satisfaction, seeing a city block's worth of people pressing against security lines beneath the basilica's floodlights.

The flyer settled along maroon ropes next to the Temple's marbled steps. And there, at the top of the stairs, stood Jeremiah Jones with his coiffed blond hair and white wool sweater. All eyes, however, focused on the limousine.

"Look pretty," Scott encouraged, gesturing Water out first.

"I will be Mara, not Song Guard," Water vowed.

Water emerged into the moist night air, her dorsal fins stretching out in prismatic ribbons of light. Cheers erupted across the plaza. Blue-suits strained to keep the faithful at bay, falling brass stanchions clanging like bells.

"Might want to keep this brief," Scott suggested, taking Mara's hand. They paused beside their newly minted Shreen Ambassador to endure a barrage of camera shots then ascended the stairs.

"Watch your distance…Ambassador," Mackenzie warned, coming up behind them.

"Like to see you try and shoot her now," Mara snapped back in a low voice.

Scott was relieved just the same to see Water prudently stop a few steps from where Jeremiah stood. No threats of evisceration. She certainly was trying to behave herself.

Mara's words were picked up and amplified as she presented herself with the smoothness of a career politician. "Your Holiness, I present Ambassador Water of Inis Drum."

The Prophet was the epitome of beneficence, right down to his outstretched arms. "Ambassador, holder of God's true Gift, I welcome you to His temple. May this be the beginning of a blessed new relationship between our races."

"My Song is here," Water blurted, looking past their host.

Scott could feel it, too, the odd thrumming picked up by the tiny crystals embedded in his skull. "They've brought the Reliquary from Tahoe," he whispered to Mara in a voice too low for the microphones to pick up.

Mara maintained her saintly smile and whispered back, "Watch her."

"Your Song's presence has graced us all with its radiance and will return home as our heavenly Father has ordained," Jeremiah rushed out, as if fearing she might charge right past him. He swept an inviting arm inside.

"*Do not run to your possible death,*" Scott sang out in Air, touching Water's arm. There were human shadows beyond those ivory columns ahead, and they didn't appear to be well-wishers.

The Church of Life's leader led them through an entrance rivaling any Venice-inspired portal. The heavy brass doors boomed closed behind them, making Scott want to crawl out of his skin.

Water took one look at what lay on a gold altar at the end of the blue marble colonnades and broke into a run, dashing past the startled Jeremiah. Armored soldiers emerged from either side of the dais, weapons raised. She skidded to a halt on the granite floor halfway down the Nave. Water's dorsal fins flattened. Her sharp chirp shook the overhead chandeliers. The guards raised their rifles in a rattle of released safeties.

"Hold on!" Scott dashed in front of her. He spread his arms in a gesture far different from Jeremiah's welcoming embrace. Chest heaving, he stood between unattractive deaths, his eyes locked on the siren's baleful eyes. "Jeremiah, order your people to stand down. *Now!* That Reliquary isn't yours, anymore. Water, get a grip on yourself!"

"I am Song Guard!" she screeched.

"Song *Mother*," Scott corrected. "You've a responsibility, remember? Now fold those fins of yours."

Jeremiah took a composing breath. "Gentlemen, let her go to the Reliquary."

"Slowly, siren," Mackenzie added, lowering his own weapon.

Water straightened, her eyes focused upon the large oblong crystal resting on the altar's purple cushion. Fists clenched, she folded her twin back fins.

Scott released a long exhale. Thank God Water still listened to him. He took another long breath while watching the squad melt back into the dark places behind the columns.

"Thieves!" Water spat.

She vaulted over the intervening oak railing to land astride the altar. She crouched, unfolding her fins around the crystal like a mother hen protecting an egg almost as large as herself.

Scott approached the railing, not daring a closer inspection of the Reliquary due to the bright orange outlines along the siren's fins, a clear sign she was one move away from annihilating them all.

"You have a hold of yourself?" he asked, locking his eyes on hers. "You remember what we're here to do?"

Her angry ripples faded. "I know I will not leave my Song again...but yes. I will be Ambassador."

The Song hummed in his head, its mottled translucence matching the iridescent glow inside Water's body. Instead of the magical prism presented in Church literature, the object resembled an opaque chunk of football-shaped quartz with beaded seams running along its sides.

"God's Gift was much brighter in its day," Jeremiah observed, coming up beside him.

"Careful," Scott said, catching the return of orange hues in Water's agitated fins. "As I said, it's not yours anymore. She's running on instincts at this point, and they're not particularly healthy for us."

"Just keep her under control," Mackenzie advised, his voice heavy with threat.

"Then get your goons out of this room," Mara suggested, brushing past him. "She's just trying to protect the Reliquary. That's her job, after all."

"Practical advice since you're close enough to be cut up," Scott reminded her. He smiled up at the irritated siren. "You alright up there?"

"Trying to be like Mara," Water quavered. "It is hard not to be Song Guard."

"Squad stand down," Mackenzie ordered after Jeremiah's nod. Tucking his pistol back into its concealed harness, he kept his eyes on the crouching siren.

Water's colors cooled to blue-green, but she remained in place, like a glass gargoyle frozen over her prize.

Mara leaned forward to pat Water's leg. "You going to stay up there all night, honey?"

"I am both Mara and Song Guard." Water brushed a clawed hand across the brightness in her chest. "I am Song Mother, too."

"Think that's a yes," Scott surmised.

She pointed a claw at Jeremiah. "Get him out, too."

Jeremiah raised an eyebrow, his expression rich with disdain. "This is the one who's going to help me recruit more of her kind?" He aimed a finger back at her. "This is a temple of God, creature, and I am always welcome in His house."

"Your God is a thief like you." Water replied, her voice dripping venom. "We are with the God Between. This is now Her house."

Mara clutched Jeremiah's arm. "Let's uh, not debate theology with the siren, shall we? Come on, we've a press conference to practice our lies on."

Jeremiah regarded his Saint with disgust. "You've fallen, Miss Martinez. You are no longer in His grace."

She shot him a saccharine smile. "Speak for yourself, *pendejo.* There's a special place in hell for people who whore out God for profit."

"Blasphemer, too?" Jeremiah accused with an unruffled air, pulling away from her.

"Let's cut the holier-than-thou shit, *Frank*," Scott interjected, having had enough of this huckster. "Whether you knew it or not, or just didn't give a damn, you've committed genocide with every Reliquary you stole. It's why you and your hired man here put Mara and I out to dry. Your cover-up ends the moment you stop cooperating with us. If you're lucky, Water will convince some of her kind to forgive and forget, but don't count on it."

Jeremiah took a long breath and shook his head, an expression of saddened patience on his face. "My poor child. It will be due to God's mercy that we even reach Petal at this stage in its destruction. Yes, I was a scientist named Frank Hanza before being called by God. I can tell you about the oxygen clouds being pulled into Petal's system by the plasma jet. How those gases will mix with an abundance of hydrogen. The planet will be struck by fire and ice in truly Biblical fashion, Mr. Rellant." He glanced up at the siren glowering from her perch. *"Anasa's wind has come,"* he spoke in crude Air.

Water straightened, her fins shining as if drawn from a furnace. "You knew. You knew what you were taking from us!"

"I knew fables when I was just Frank Hanza. Myths and legends handed down by the Shreen, including tales of Song Guards like you. It must've shocked those Shreen land dwellers to no end seeing your kind rise from the lakes much like our dragons of old. The End of Times proclaimed for all to see. I but carried out God's will on an undeserving race."

Water leaned over her Song, her eyes on Jeremiah. "You must die."

"Careful," Mackenzie cautioned, grabbing his boss by the

shoulder to pull him back.

Jeremiah shrugged off the mercenary chief. "She won't touch me. She can't, because she will suffer through anything to get home. I'm guessing those lights inside her are what's left of the Sanctuary colony. According to legend, her kind aren't just defenders. Comes the need to migrate to a new lake, they're conquerors. The last thing we want here on Earth is another Inis Drum full of vengeful Shreen."

Mackenzie's voice drew down to a dangerous deadpan. "So, no deal?"

"Not at all, Bob. It is God's will that she return home and fulfill her part of the bargain." His voice drifted to a silky purr. "Otherwise, Song Guard, I will bring God's justice upon your lake and boil away what's left. *Anasa will have another Song for her necklace if you fail me,*" he sang.

"Our God Between will destroy you," Water promised, her violin-voice modulating into a withering tone.

Jeremiah grinned. "There is only one God, and I am His mighty Right Hand."

"You know where you can shove that hand, too," Mara growled.

Her vehemence bounced off of Jeremiah's icy expression. "Tell me, Miss Martinez. Would you call your recovery from radiation any less miraculous now?"

"That wasn't *your* miracle."

The Prophet inclined his head toward the Reliquary. "But it still was a miracle."

"You really believe your own bullshit, don't you?" Scott added, shaking his head in disbelief. "You wrap religion around a money-making scheme robbing whole Shreen tribes of their future and you still want to play holy man behind closed doors?"

Jeremiah laughed. "I'd call such a thing a miracle all in itself. Everything you're doing is actually His work."

"Everything *we're* doing, yes," Mara retorted. "We're not playing along for the money, you sick bastard."

"But you *are* going to play along," Mackenzie growled from next to the Prophet. "And show respect while you're at it. So, I suggest you fetch your halo, and get it nice and shiny for the upcoming press conference. Same goes for your pet siren, too. Otherwise, the next miracle will be the Ambassador staying in one piece."

"Close off the Temple," Jeremiah instructed with a dismissive briskness. "Since our Ambassador chooses to remain here, we will position cameras around her and make them high enough not to show the Reliquary. I don't want anyone realizing how faded it is. The rest of us will have our meeting in the reception area." He nodded toward Scott and Mara. "Take these two sinners to the chapel. Let them seek forgiveness in private."

The two of them were hustled off to a small room with stucco white walls and low rafters. Soft light reflected off the glinting statue of Gabriel holding out the Reliquary as if in offering.

Mara slumped into one of the pews. "How in hell can you look yourself in the mirror, Bob?"

"How in the hell can either of you be so damn stupid!" Mackenzie shot back, slamming the chapel door shut on accompanying guards. His voice lowered. "You have no idea what you've stepped into. I stuck you in Haven for a reason, damn it. That wasn't Jeremiah's plan for either of you, trust me on that."

Scott gaped at him. "Jeremiah was going to do what? Kill us?"

"You are absolutely out of your league, sonny. You should've stayed put, but no. Had to be heroes. Well listen up, heroes. First chance you get when we reach Petal, grab your siren and head out in the *Alicia*. Dump her in the lake and run for the gate. Doubt you'll make it, but if you do, I've programmed in access codes for a jump to the String of Pearls. Mara, you make damn sure you two disappear when Jeremiah sends me after you, understand?"

"So Jeremiah's going to finish the job and murder us on Petal," Scott guessed. No doubt there were countless ways to have an "accident" there. "Why are you telling us this?"

Mackenzie backed him up against the wall. "Look, hotshot, I don't give a damn about you, understand? You're just lucky your father and I made a deal long before you became such a pain in my ass. This is the *last* time I stick out my neck for you. Got it? I filled my part of the bargain getting you to Haven, and you screwed it up. Now you're on your own."

"Wow," Mara remarked after the man left. "What did your father do? Give that son-of-a-bitch a heart?"

"Saved his life." Scott sank on the pew beside her. "Know any places to hide out where you live?"

"You like rocks?" she replied with a lackluster grin.

The press conference was an extravaganza of yellow carnations, white satin banners, and even a full choir in the reception room's upper balcony. Heavenly arias and contrasting red rose petals heralded their grand entrance. Scott tried to avoid tripping over the white and blue robes an acolyte hurriedly threw over his shoulders to hide his black attire.

Jeremiah led them to a linen-covered table choked with even more flowers. Scott wrinkled his nose. The room smelled like a florist's shop. Behind them, a large screen displayed Water watching the proceedings via cameras like some crystalline queen, though care was taken to only show her upper torso. Judging from a meager three rows of reporters lined up before an intervening wall of lilies, Scott suspected the public relations was less about candor and more about propaganda spewed for the benefit of a select audience.

Jeremiah played the Prophet with his usual flair, leading everyone through prayers and introductions after the choir died down. Scott endured the hypocrisy, and even received confirmation from the journalists' Church-prepared questions that Jeremiah was indeed taking them back to Petal as promised.

"What will happen to the Reliquary?" Jeremiah repeated a journalist's question as if authorizing the subject for discussion. He took a drink from the glass in front of him. "In seven days, I will be leading an expedition to return God's holy gift back to those who gave it to us. I will be joined both by Her Holiness, Saint Mara, and her Steward Mr. Rellant, to oversee this unprecedented exchange."

And now he was Mara's Steward? Scott waited for more divine revelations. If he already didn't hate Jeremiah's pompous piety, now he had more reason to. And then there was whatever catastrophe might be waiting when Water started answering questions.

"Once we have proven our faith through the return of the gifts lent us," Jeremiah continued with practiced assurance, "we will receive the greater blessing of more emissaries such as Ambassador Water. Through their acts and miracles we will continue to open the path to renewed life for those in our church who've earned their place in God's house."

"Emissaries, Your Grace, or invaders?"

The direct question from the press woke Scott from his attempts at ignoring Jeremiah's entire agonizing march of lies. Some woman in a maroon dress had spoken out of turn. He could tell from Jeremiah's frozen smile that this was most certainly not part of the program. The Prophet glanced to the side. Yep, there was Mackenzie and a couple of his boys lurking in the back. Two brown suits began moving forward discreetly.

The woman beamed a smile along with her clarification. "I mean, their planet is dying, isn't it? Are you sure these are emissaries we're bringing back? Are you familiar with the term *siren*, Your Grace? A formidably hostile life form rumored to inhabit Petal." She looked up at the projection screen. "Perhaps the Ambassador might

202

elaborate?"

"I am Song Guard," Water smoothly countered over the speakers.

The security men edged beside the outspoken journalist.

Undaunted, the woman hammered home her point with another polite observation. "Song Guard. Is that a military designation, Your Holiness?"

"What was your organization, again?" Jeremiah took another sip of water.

At least Scott assumed it was water. Beside him, Mara's smile looked more genuine than it had all night. Scott smirked inwardly. Seeing Jeremiah squirm was the highpoint of the night.

"Home Office," the visitor answered with a prim nod. "Perhaps you misplaced our invite?"

The Brothers' suits slunk back into the shadows.

"Perhaps we did," the Prophet answered with a disarming chuckle. "The Church is always honored to have governments give witness to our Lord's work. To answer your question, you needn't worry. I doubt a dozen or so emissaries can make much of an invading force."

"Perhaps your Ambassador could field the question herself?" The woman's smile shot past him to the large screen. "Madam, is your kind also referred to as sirens? Have you yourself killed humans, Ambassador?"

Scott's chest tightened. *You already know that answer, don't you, lady?* Surely Water would see the trap being prepared for her.

The siren stood, slowly spreading her dorsal fins in an angelic poise. "Yes."

~ * ~

"Her name's Georgia Kohen," Mackenzie explained, hustling Scott and Mara out through a garage exit. "My sources put her with British Intelligence. MI6." He thrust a phone into Scott's hand. "Calm her down. She's got a phone on speaker beside her."

Scott put the phone to his ear. "Water, it's okay. We need to move both you and the Song. Looks like the government's getting involved."

"Where are we going?" Water's voice held little compromise.

"Home," Mackenzie replied. A phalanx of brown suits opened another set of doors leading outside and the group raced through. "You have an idiot for a siren, Rellant."

"Thought you had the government handled?" Mara shot back as they rushed through a darkened courtyard.

"Apparently not," Mackenzie rumbled. "Maybe Jeremiah should've lined up King George for an Intercession. Doesn't matter, now. We've some surprises up our sleeves, too." He gestured to a familiar bat-winged shadow sitting next to a pool. "I had your *Alicia* brought from the airport in case this sort of shit happened."

"Wow...thanks." Mara gave him a look of profound surprise and gratitude before disappearing up the forward hatch.

"Open the back," Scott called up, guessing who would arrive next.

Pounding feet and shouts sounded behind them. Both he and Mackenzie looked back toward the Temple. Water staggered down the pebble-lined path they'd just traversed, an oblong crystal in her arms.

Mackenzie gaped. "She's *carrying* it?"

Water stumbled up, barely able to hold her weighty cargo.

"No touch!" Water shrilled at the man, her fins giving bright orange warning. She inclined her head toward Scott. "You touch."

Nodding, he grabbed one end of the glowing oval. Its vibrations coursed through his embedded crystals. The damn thing was heavier than it looked. With extreme effort and an aching spine, he helped her heft the Reliquary up into the Surveyor and place it below the ship's hanging sled.

"Tired," Water complained, scrabbling up after her Song.

Scott hauled himself over the back hatch's lip after her. "Might not want cabin lights just yet," he cautioned her. "The less people see us leave, the better." He tried to keep the panic he felt out of his voice.

Mackenzie was already in the copilot's seat and busy at the screens.

Water clung to her Song. "Be very careful flying, Mara. You like me now, yes?"

Mara gave a curt laugh and closed the rear hatch. "We're good. Hang on just the same. Company coming."

Scott buckled himself in. "What company?"

"Three British troop transports and escorting gunships," Mackenzie spat, staring at his screen. "Nightshade software's engaged. Get your ass out of here, pilot."

"And the team's back together, again," The acidic edge in Mara's voice could've melted the hull. She brought up the engines. "Next stop, *Deep Explorer*."

"Not this time." Mackenzie rose from his seat. He opened the forward hatch and swung onto the short ladder. "Plan's changed. I've just given you three pirates your clearance to Petal through Heron's Gate." He paused then glowered in Water's direction. "I'm going to need a good reason why I let you escape. Take your best shot, bitch."

Scott thought he'd have to explain what Mackenzie meant, but she moved so fast he didn't have time to do more than yell, "Don't kill him!" when she struck.

Mackenzie fell back down the ladder, his scalp laid open.

"He does not act like a thief," Water said with an air of puzzlement, peering down the ladder. "So he lives."

Scott brought the ladder up and sealed the hatch after watching the mercenary stumble clear of the Surveyor. Mackenzie definitely had a code of honor all his own. "Mara, go!"

Nineteen

The Surveyor streaked skyward, pressing Scott into his seat. He took his last look at London. Not exactly how he planned on leaving. He twisted his head around with effort to see Water bracing her Song against the back seats.

"Mara, be careful," the siren complained, her voice strained.

"We'll be better once we've cleared atmosphere," she declared.

"*Alicia*, this is *Deep Explorer…*"

"Kiss my ass," Mara spat, slapping at her console to end the transmission.

The acceleration eased when the Earth was but an azure curve, weightlessness taking over.

Scott's screen woke with an irritated bleep, showing converging lines and signal patterns fanning out in their direction. Not good. "Um, Mara?"

She glanced at the display and sneered. "That's the *Deep Explorer*. Don't worry, we can easily outrun that glorified beach ball."

The display, which Scott assumed was part of the recently acquired Nightshade upgrade, quieted down.

Mara fished a familiar bottle of pills from a seat pocket. "Same tranquilizers we picked up in Sanctuary. You know the drill. Pop one before we jump. I'll program *Alicia* to head like a bat out of hell for Petal once we hit the other side."

Water surprised Scott by releasing her charge and floating up beside him. She bumped foreheads with him. "The Song is safe now. I will go with you to our fishbowl like last time."

The blinking lights of Heron's Gate grew closer. Mara lined them up on the barrel-like superstructure.

Scott's screen came to life once more with yellow colors. The narrow-beamed signal originated from behind, and with it an ominous warning. Shit. He didn't have to be an expert in stealth technology to understand the words sweeping across the bottom of the display. "My screen says we've a fire control system sweeping for us," he warned.

"Eight thousand kilometers and closing fast."

"Sweeping and not locked?"

He nodded. "Think *Alicia's* giving them the slip."

Mara swept a lock of her floating hair out of the way. "Heron's Gate just cleared us. Hang on back there, Water."

"Range seven thousand," he managed, the Surveyor's engines kicking him deep into his seat. "That's no beach ball coming after us. Damn, that thing's accelerating fast. Six thousand."

"Bet it's a Valkyrie," Mara replied. "Too little and too late. Here we go!"

The Surveyor plunged into the swirling vortex ahead of them.

The universe fell away. "Pop your pills," Mara commanded.

Scott already had. Grimacing, he tried to pretend he wasn't falling headlong into an abyss.

Water gently gripped Scott's head and leaned her forehead against his.

He managed a quick smile. It was too late to ask her if she really wanted to do this. They were on the way to her home, and he would never see her again once they got there. She would return to her Quan, and merging with this mysterious creature of hers would be a one-way trip.

~ * ~

Scott roused to the sound of something banging. Wasn't he in space? On the Surveyor running for his life, his thawing awareness reminded him.

Another thud shook the cabin. Okay, this wasn't a good thing to be hearing.

"Wake up!" Scott shook Mara as *Alicia's* hull reverberated from another impact. Barely able to focus due to the damn sedative's lingering effects, he stared at a thick fog strewn across the planetary system. Except it wasn't fog.

A fist-sized chunk of ice careened off the windshield, helping Scott to draw her from her stupor. "Wha...? They firing at us?" Mara jolted upright with a wince.

"They haven't come out the gate, yet. What you're hearing is ice. It's everywhere."

"We are home?" Water questioned from behind them. The siren pointed out the windshield at a small gray disk. The orb she indicated looked like a spotlight shining amidst heavy mist.

"That look familiar, too, Water?" Scott asked her. He indicated a painfully bright bar sweeping over the solar system's planetary plane.

"Kee's Sword." Water's voice quavered with anger, orange

ripples lighting her fins. "Kee and Anasa have come to steal from us again."

Another impact rattled the cabin, eliciting a screech of defiance from the siren.

"Easy back there," Mara growled, running her fingers through floating dark curls. "Jeremiah mentioned the black hole's plasma flare tossing oxygen and hydrogen clouds into each other. Basically, we're going to fly into a fire hose."

Well, that sucked. Was there a choice? They'd made it this far, and no way in hell would he let down Water now. Even if it meant losing her in the process. Scott nodded. "You're right, there's no getting clear of this stuff. Any sign of whoever was chasing us to the gate?"

She frowned. "Couldn't have been Mackenzie. Water certainly made his injuries convincing. The only place he was heading was a hospital."

"I just played the cutting game," Water objected. "Remember, he told me to hurt him."

Scott shook his head, still amazed at the last person he ever expected to help him. "Mackenzie knows how to look after himself."

Mara tapped her screen. "Our former employer sent us navigation waypoints all the way to the planet's northern hemisphere. He's pretty good for a bad guy."

The Surveyor accelerated toward the planet. The ice caused a constant clatter against the hull. Scott tried in vain not to tense for a big explosion that never came.

Scott's screen bleeped, streaming symbols along with crimson lines extending from Petal Gate's exit to a second vessel's entrance into the system. A ship's graphic rotated in the lower right corner.

He read the screen to Mara, his heart notching up a beat. "Assault ship. Valkyrie class. Four thousand kilometers distant. Damn."

Mara leaned toward him, her lips curled back. "Now we know who jumped us. We'll head to Petal's dark side and see if we can't blend into the shadows." She released a long breath. "Hopefully, we'll reach it before that crew wakes up."

Scott gut clenched. He did not like the *hopefully* in her statement. This had to work. "This is bad. Looks like Jeremiah didn't wait to send the *Deep Explorer*."

"It's probably next out the gate." She slapped at the pursuing ship's image. "This jerk here is meant to catch us for them. Buckle in and hope they want us alive."

Water poked her crystalline head between them. "Will we get home? Inis Drum is north where the sun stays low."

Scott tore his eyes from his screen's foreboding display. "Water, it'll be alright. We're going to drop you off with the Song just as soon as we reach your lake. Make sure you tell your Song Guards not to come up to the surface. Ever. If you can, warn the other Drums to do the same." He pushed aside the thought of having made things worse for the Shreen. Why hadn't he come up with a better plan than just getting Water home? "Jeremiah's after sirens now."

"I'm all for hearing ideas on getting back home, too," Mara added, her gaze on Petal's lightning-laced night side expanding in the windshield. "That Valkyrie coming up our ass knows exactly where we'll head. Once they realize Water's gone, we're target practice."

"Not if we lose him in those things," Scott said, pointing out whirling clouds visible along Petal's terminator.

"Those are mezzo-alpha cyclones, bright boy. You don't lose people in those things, you die in them." She tapped a side screen and whistled. "Atmosphere's scalding—showing fifty-five Celsius. Water, can you handle that sort of thing?"

Water stood in her seat, her silicon hair waving like serpents in the weightless cabin. She spread her twin dorsal fins and flicked the blades along her forearms. "I am Song Mother."

"Well we're not," Mara shot back. "Jump just as soon as the hatch opens. Better yet, grab your Reliquary and just stand over the doors. I'll drop you in."

"Song," Water corrected. "Not Reliquary. You must fly careful, Mara Martinez, pilot."

"Fat chance that, hon. Just hold on tight to your Song and pray to our God Between. We make it out of this in one piece, and I'll personally convert everyone in the Church."

Water tapped her shoulder with a claw. "This is why you are Her saint now."

Mara laughed. "*Her*. Yeah, I like that. The guys haven't done such a hot job if you ask me."

"A god who helps our Quan instead of trying to steal Songs. A better one for us both to believe in."

"And one you don't have to pay a fortune to," Scott agreed, happy to be part of something halfway decent for once. Who knew? If they got out of this mess, Mara might well start Jeremiah's Church down the right road. Preferably without its Prophet.

Petal drew closer. Mara's brief smile faded, the clatter of ice now sounding as if they flew through gravel.

"We are being hurt?" Water's musical tone tittered with anxiety.

"*Alicia's* military grade," Mara assured her. "She should be able to handle worse." Grimacing, she patted the dashboard. "Won't you, baby?"

Scott didn't like what his screen was trying to tell him. "Our friend's course just changed...toward us. Crew must've woken up." He tapped a blip on his screen. "Shit, the Valkyrie's accelerating." I thought you said they couldn't see us?"

Mara switched the view on her screens. A contrail of pulverized ice reflected the plasma jet in a sparkling trail behind them. "It sees this."

"That ship's moving fast. Closing to under three thousand kilometers. Now what?"

"Now we try your plan."

He looked at her. "You mean the one you said would get us killed?"

"Unless you've a better one. We'll be harder to catch in the mess down there."

He grimaced and tried to keep his eyes on the screen in front of him. It was too easy seeing bits of burning Surveyor and body parts raining down over Water's lake.

They plunged toward Petal. Nature's pyrotechnics crackled and branched across hundreds of kilometers of shrouded surface. Fiery bright streaks arced across the stratosphere. Several exploded with enough force to light an entire hemisphere. The most beautiful and terrifying thing Scott had ever seen. And they were streaking into the middle of it.

"Meteors?" Scott asked.

"Very big ice cubes," Mara clarified. "About the only thing we're missing for a wonderful trip is Sanctuary's winds. Brothers knows how to plan its vacation spots."

Scott looked back at Water, who held tight to her Song beneath the suspended sled. "We need to get you tied down." He released his restraints and flipped up the rear seat armrests to form more of a bench. The siren didn't protest when he lifted the weightless Song and secured it across the chairs with the harness straps. He directed the siren to wedge herself into the middle aisle. "Slide your legs underneath the Song and grab each seat. Hold on for all you're worth."

Water slid into the narrow space. She tucked her swimming fins around her legs. "The Song is safe?"

Mara cut off his reply. "Scott, get buckled in. Atmosphere in ten seconds. I'm going in hot."

He dropped in his seat and fastened the harness. "Readout shows the Valkyrie fifteen hundred kilometers away and still closing."

The cabin lurched. Pink ion trails twisted into glowing vortexes across the front windshield. The hot plasma spread into a solid rose-colored incandescence. A constant rumbling replaced the pounding ice.

"Find us now, *pendejo*." Mara smirked, pushing the Surveyor's nose down further.

They descended into a soupy twilight broken by lightning-laced thunderheads. Gravity returned with a vengeance. The fires of reentry diminished. Mara slammed the ship through braking maneuvers in the thicker air, the *Alicia* swaying and bucking like a drunken bull.

Once she seemed satisfied with their speed, Mara plunged the ship into a lower cloud deck.

Outside, the grayness flashed yellow-green. The ship rocked, a hollow boom following.

"They shoot us!" Water cried.

Mara shook her head. "Meteor exploding. Not even close." Her fingers whitened around the control sticks. "Approaching day side. Seventy thousand meters and dropping. Pulling left so we don't fall into that crap ahead of us."

Scott focused his eyes on the jiggling screen in front of him. He discerned outlines belonging to one of the more horrendous storm cells whipping around the planet. He gaped at boiling towers silhouetted against a brightening horizon. The Surveyor sank into a huge rift between green piles. Shards of ice clattered along their hull, interspersed by heart-jarring bangs.

"We must not die!" Water sang over the bedlam.

"You must shut the hell up!" Mara shouted back, fighting her way through the turbulence. "We'll make it."

Scott scrutinized the huge anvil heads looming ahead. "We're running out of room."

"No kidding," she grated, raising her voice over the rattling cabin. "Rough sledding here on in, folks. We're still following Mackenzie's nav beacons…more or less."

"Nightshade system's gone," Scott reported, studying his darkened screen.

"So's our friends," Mara added with a grin. "Couldn't take the heat down here." She started humming one of her lullabies.

The Surveyor leapt clear of the hail long enough for him to glimpse a black-green wall cloud before they hit it. The deck flipped sideways, nearly wrenching him from his seat. The image of flaming debris over Water's lake became too vivid in his mind to dismiss. "Easy, damn it!"

"Easy, my ass." Mara jammed the throttles open and shot into the darkest skies he'd ever seen. The engines sent thrumming vibrations through the cabin. One of her lower screens showed them streaking over a cluster of four lakes.

"Altitude fifty thousand," she called out through the buffeting. "Four hundred kilometers from target. How you doing back there, Water?"

"I do not like flying!"

After this hell ride, neither did he. "We're coming out the other end," Scott said, spying daylight ahead.

The Surveyor slewed sideways again, this time in the opposite direction. Mara straightened the craft over a steamy canyon between storms. The battering ice let up, offering a moment's breather.

Scott stared up at thunderheads rising like giant roiling pillars. The Surveyor dove into the left wall cloud. A giant's hand slammed them into their seats.

"Downdraft!" Mara shouted over warbling alarms. She pitched the Surveyor's nose up and put renewed thrust into the engines. "And I thought running Angel's Rim was fun."

"Asteroid belt?" Scott guessed while trying to keep his stomach in one place.

"And much prettier than this mess." She whooshed out a breath. "Okay, heavy rain ahead. Water, your home world *sucks*."

"It is Anasa's fault!"

They plunged into a deluge that slung the ship around as if on high seas.

"Two thousand kilometers to target," Mara tersely reported. "More storms ahead. Starting my deceleration program. Dodging what I can."

Scott's harness dug into his shoulders. Mara kept her eyes glued to her screens, ignoring the outside maelstrom altogether. Water clung to the seats behind them, her claws digging in deep.

"Next set of lakes should be ours," Mara said. "Five thousand meters. Looks a lot clearer ahead than I...*shit!*"

They banked hard toward a ridgeline to avoid a three-kilometer-wide tornado plowing across a shallow valley. Mara hopped their ship over a rock-strewn crest, swinging in behind the huge storm. They aimed for a wind-whipped lake visible through the thick haze.

"That your city, Water?" Scott asked.

The siren scrambled to her feet, half-falling between them

before steadying herself. She pointed to a jumble of flat buildings stacked along the shore. "Enna Drum," she said. "Inis is to the north."

"Enna's the tribe and city name," Scott explained. "Drum...well, she tends to mix up the meaning between tribe and lake."

"As long as we end up where we're supposed to be," Mara dismissed with a grimace.

The Shreen city swept beneath them. Several terraces sagged or lay collapsed upon rubble-filled streets.

"Less turbulence near the surface," Mara said, bringing them low over stunted trees. "Guys, it's sixty Celsius out there. That's one hundred and forty degrees Fahrenheit, Scott."

He twisted around to face Water. "Are you sure you can withstand such heat?"

Water tapped on one of her armored plates with the equivalent of a musical snort. "I will ready the Song." She straightened then lashed an arm across the harnesses, cutting the oblong crystal free.

The clouds outside the cabin brightened. The deck shuddered from the resounding blast.

"Okay, that one was close," Mara squeaked, pointing at a huge plume of water erupting from the lake.

Scott glared at her. "Less turbulence, eh?"

"I didn't include meteors," she growled. "Water, we're coming up on another lake. Move you and your Song over the back hatch." She pulled up the nose to avoid another rain-lashed ridgeline.

"Scott unbuckled himself and helped Water carry the Song beneath the sled, no small feat on the pitching deck. "Is this the one we're after?"

"Inis Drum," Water confirmed, peering over his shoulder at the windshield.

Mara slowed the Surveyor. "Where do you want the drop, hon?"

"Anywhere," Water quickly answered.

Scott exhaled a relieved breath, feeling unduly blessed to have gotten this far. Another cityscape outlined against the bright gray came into view. Mostly towers. "Put us in the middle, Mara. Water, stand over your Song. We'll have to drop you fast to keep from getting scalded in here."

The siren bumped heads with him. Her voice sang softly like mournful violins. "You will always be my Song Guard."

I'm really losing you. Scott swallowed the realization with a shaky smile. His gut twisted. This wasn't what he'd expected to feel a couple months back when they first tried parting at the Temple. Somewhere an unjust God laughed, paying him back for his scorn. "You'll be Song Mother."

The ship swayed over agitated waves. "At hover," Mara reported. Her strained face warmed with a smile. "Nice knowing you, Water."

"You are Saint Mara, now," Water replied. "You must tell of the God Between who brought us here. Make your people not thieves."

A sharp series of rattling blasts overrode Mara's reply. "Scott, get back," she bawled. "Dropping the hatch *now!*"

Water's claws sank into him, and she threw him clear of the opening. Crying out from the sudden pain, he flew over the rear seat and slammed into the back of the copilot's chair. The rear hatch flew open, and Water vanished in a burst of steam. The hatch slammed shut again, cutting off a scalding blast of hot air.

"Hang on," Mara yelled over the alarms. She jammed the Surveyor's throttle forward with one hand while pulling a red handle above her with the other. The ship shuddered, the nose nearly burying itself in the waves.

They slewed violently across the water's surface toward the shore. An acidic-smelling smoke filled the cabin. "What happened?" Scott cried.

"Left engine's blown," Mara gasped, shaking her head. "Making for the city."

"What hit us?"

She pointed out the windshield. A hulking bat-shape ship three times their size swung out from behind them, a hard rain blurring the Valkyrie's armored sides. For an awful moment, he thought the assault ship would slide over and bash them into the lake. Instead, the pilot remained beside them until they hovered just off of a series of piers leading into a broad avenue. The warship swooped behind them again. Another clattering bang ripped through their starboard engine.

Shrieking, Mara slid *Alicia* across a pier. The stricken Surveyor skidded toward a main street bordered by towers and shops. A wing buried itself in a rounded orange building along a wharf, wrenching them around to point back toward the lake. Her screens were a devil's Christmas of red lights, but miraculously they lurched to a stop with an intact cabin.

Scott pounded the dashboard in front of him. Water was going home, but he and Mara weren't. "*You bastards!*"

Twenty

Water sank into the sapphire expanse of Inis Drum and watched the rippling outline of Mara's ship flee before a larger hunter. She clutched her precious Song and placed her trust in her newfound deity. The God Between rescued her people. She would see Scott and Mara safely home, too.

The Song was heavy, but fragile. Water countered her rapid descent with powerful counterstrokes of her swimming fins. She announced her arrival in fervent chirps. Hopefully, she would attract her Quan's attention. Was her Quan listening, or had it decided she'd been among the humans too long and become more like one herself? If her Quan heard her, it would surely give birth to more of her sisters as a precaution. They would be expecting a fight. She would have to be careful with her words.

Darkness surrounded her. Beyond the glow of her Song, dim as it might be, Water discerned a new illumination below her. Strings of blue beads stretched out as if across a domed stadium. Her Quan! Soon she would be a mote among its symphony of souls. Or crumpled beside it, a part of her ruefully pointed out.

Four aquamarine generation nodules flashed and darkened. Song Guards. A trio of sharp chirps rebounded off Water's armored plates. She frowned, holding the crystal close. Her ascending sisters would be but moments old and driven by instinct and borrowed memories. Killing them should be easy should worse come to worse, but only if she dropped her precious burden. "I am Water of Inis Drum," she sang out in Earth.

Her return chirp painted three lithe and lethal shapes arrowing toward her from below. Another followed. Her Quan sent a Quan Singer, too. There would be a chance for negotiation. "I am Water of Inis Drum," she repeated "I return our Song."

The first siren reared up before her, dorsal fins spread. "You will not take our Drum, Song Mother! I will kill you."

Of course, Water realized with sinking hope, Song Mothers

came to another Drum to conquer. That was how migrations ended when the lake was already occupied.

"Not when she carries our Song," a distant voice countered. It was the Quan Singer. His voice sharpened with command. "She is Inis Drum. Do not kill her."

"See what I carry, sister?" Water added, her scorn directed at the overly eager Song Guard. "You will help me. Do you have your name, yet?"

Cutting fins quivering, the glistening creature stared at the crystal, then at her. "I...I am Uncertain."

"Bring us to our Quan, Uncertain," Water pressed.

The siren gave a start. "You are not a Quan Singer to talk to me this way. I *will* kill you."

"But I *am* a Singer," the other voice spoke. A narrow-faced male appeared. His scalp was bald save for a long brush of silver hair running from the crown of his head to the small of his back. Gills worked along his neck. "I am Chur, and you both will obey me."

Oh will I? Water smirked inwardly. "I am much older than either of you. Now help slow my fall unless you would see our precious Song shattered."

"I am Question," a new voice sang out in Earth as Uncertain wrapped her arms around the glowing crystal. The second Song Guard darted by, twisted around, and dove down to confront the three of them. Her opalescent eyes widened upon seeing the precious cargo they carried. "How can this be?"

"We should kill her," Uncertain urged.

"No," Chur firmly repeated.

The third siren joined them. "Kill who?" She stared at their burden. "Our...Song?" She helped support the heavy crystal, running her hands over the dull surface. "So weak it barely sings. I will call myself Sorrow."

"The Song has been away too long," Water explained.

"Why are we not killing her?" Uncertain cut in, flicking her dorsal fins in exasperation.

Chur blinked slowly. "Because she is Inis Drum."

"Why not?" Uncertain protested. "Look at her. She carries others...she is Song Mother. She is migrating and will kill our Quan."

"I carry those of Inis Drum, too," Water pointed out with a dire glare. "Should we kill you for threatening them?"

Uncertain traded looks with the others. "But I am of Inis Drum!"

"You are all idiots," Water muttered in Scott's language. Was she really this stupid when she was born? She regarded Question, who still swam around them in indecisive circles. "Stop gawking and help us."

"She should not talk to us like a Quan Singer," Uncertain fumed as the other siren lent her support.

"You should have named yourself Disagreeable," Water snapped back.

Amber ripples ran up Uncertain's fins. "I do not like you."

Chur made a cutting motion with a webbed hand. "Enough. Silence, all of you."

"Silence yourself, Quan Singer," Water threw back. "I am Song Mother."

She ignored further bickering, her attention drawn to the grandeur below. Her most beautiful and mighty Quan. The humans might think it an immense turtle-like shell, save for the green-blue reception nodules beading its mottled gray skin. Indeed, her Quan held a resemblance to the crystal she carried, though many times larger. Each shining nodule was twice her height. Together they cast a soft aquamarine glow over a hemisphere outsizing the music hall where she and Scott had recently performed. The recollection made her think of the danger the two humans faced. Maybe the Quan would help.

The Quan Singer and four sirens gently eased their Song upon the Quan's surface between two of the glowing domes, the bioluminescent light casting them in ghostly colors. The sirens regarded each other with puzzled expressions.

"What do we do, now?" Question asked, looking around.

Chur folded his arms. "Song Mother, you will return to your Quan."

"I hoped we could kill her," Uncertain grumped, flicking her swimming fins. "I was supposed to kill something. That is why I became."

"We do far more than kill," Water returned, looking up into the darkness. "We heal, too. This is what the thieves want now. Not our Song. Us. The Quan must be warned not to send Song Guards to protect itself."

"The thieves will die at our hands," Sorrow sang.

Water scowled. "I died at *their* hands, sister. I sang myself into the Song, but ended up inside one of the thieves instead. They are strong…and greedy." A relenting tone crept into her singing. "Not all of them, though. Two are up there right now trying to protect us."

"Why?" Sorrow asked.

"Because they found a new God Between. One that can defeat

Kee and Anasa. The same one who brought me here and returned our Song."

"Did you not hear me, Song Mother?" Chur asked in testy tones. "You must return to your Quan."

"And our Song?" Water asked, resisting the urge to follow him over to the other nodule like a puppet. "We have come far, together. Let me hold the Song in my arms one last time as I come home."

Chur stared at her, as if not believing she hadn't immediately obeyed. He gestured to the other sirens. "Bring the Song. Her wish shall be honored."

Water swam beside him, listening as he sang in a mix of Earth and something she couldn't quite place. His song was beautiful. The reception nodule responded by brightening. She responded in emerald green ripples. She was going home. Finally. She would miss Scott.

"Just her," Chur ordered, beckoning Water to help him lift the crystal from their arms.

Together, they pressed themselves against the nodule's warm glowing surface. A section of the skin parted, allowing them inside along with a rush of water. Water gently set the Song upon the surface. The Quan Singer bade her lie beside it. "Those you carry will be reunited," he assured as she curled against the dim crystal.

Water smiled. The many souls inside her sang. Homecoming. At last. She sang, too. *Last Descent*. Scott's favorite.

~ * ~

Water watched the lost Shreen from Sanctuary rise into the Quan's consciousness as a golden stream of rediscovered salvation. She remained behind.

Her Quan wasn't used to something so...*human*. What was this shell around her? A barrier of alien memories, rendered as if in glass, defied attempts to merge itself. A...*fishbowl*? Gently, the Quan lifted the lid. Water smiled up at her creator. In her eyes shone the answer as to how she returned against all possible odds. The Quan paused in its absorption of these strange and new memories. *A God Between?*

The Song Mother rose from the fishbowl of her own accord, carrying into the Quan's consciousness a far greater gift of unprecedented hope. A way to escape Kee and Anasa's eternal wrath and destructive visitations to the world. All that this God Between asked in exchange was one final sacrifice. That, and the God's needed servants.

The lake around the Quan shook with its command. *Quan Singer. Find these humans...Scott and Mara. They have fallen within the city. Inis Drum must migrate.*

Twenty-One

Mara slapped at a control stick. "They shot up my ship!"

Scott unbuckled his harness. "Just tell me we're not blowing up,"

"Give me a sec. Intermix valves off. Check. Main bus shunts disabled. Check. Damn them!"

He breathed in acrid vapors. The cabin smelled like one big electrical short. The view outside looked no better. Sheets of wind-driven rain lashed the torn cobblestones before turning to steam. Half of a building's brick façade had fallen over the Surveyor's bullet-riddled starboard wing, canting the deck. *Alicia* wasn't going anywhere. Ever.

A large gray wedge swooped low overhead. The Valkyrie's wings wobbled as its engines swiveled downward, the assault ship obviously struggling to maintain a hover in the ferocious weather. The craft turned its nose toward the avenue's outlet and dropped to a rough landing.

"Our ride's here," Scott grated, wishing the Surveyor was armed. Right now he could do with a "just and righteous" God.

Mara wiped her eyes. "They saw us ditch Water and the Reliquary. We're useless to them, so why not leave us to die?"

He scowled. "I'm guessing we're bait. What else could it be? You think Jeremiah's leaving empty handed?" He looked back at the equipment rack containing his diving gear. That stuff was designed for cold, not the teakettle outside. "We've emergency gear, right?"

Mara gestured at a line of yellow cases bolted to the hull across from the shelves. "They're little more than sandwich bags with oxygen generators. We'd blow away out there." She exhaled a dejected sigh. "Where would we go, anyway?"

Scott peered through the windshield. A half dozen armored figures emerged from the Valkyrie's side hatch under the shelter of an overhanging wing. "Doesn't matter. We've guests coming aboard." He braced as one of the soldiers aimed something toward them. A muzzle flashed, followed by a reverberating clang against the *Alicia's* prow.

"Grapple gun," Scott guessed, raising a hand to squelch Mara's yelp. "They're running a cable." He watched the men affix their end of the line to the Valkyrie's strut. Two mercenaries attached themselves to the wire and carefully inched their way toward the stricken Surveyor.

"We're sitting on our belly," Mara stated, glancing at the cabin roof.

He followed her eyes to a yellow outline above them with the word "RESCUE" written in block letters. "You know those sandwich bags of yours? Best get in one. It's about to get really uncomfortable in here."

He glanced back outside. Their soon-to-be captors were halfway to the ship, and having a terrible time keeping upright. Good. Maybe they'd lose their grip and the storm would take the bastards. Movement in the water caught his attention. "Look at the lake. It's...rippling?"

Deep booms bombarded the world. The ship shook and thrummed, the seismic vibrations also knocking one of the approaching soldiers off his feet.

The sound faded. "What the hell's that?" Mara exclaimed.

"Came from the lake," Scott replied. "Drum. Inis *Drum*. Could that be Water's Quan telling us she made it?" A comforting thought in a room full of ugly speculation.

"Let's hope so. It doesn't look particularly great for us, though."

Mara was right about the emergency outfits. They were little more than heavy plastic bags begrudgingly accommodating appendages. The oxygen generator hissed like a snake, and the flashing lights reminded him of Christmas bulbs. He and Mara zipped their front seams closed, pressed against the rear bulkhead, and braced themselves.

It didn't take long. The soldiers disappeared beneath *Alicia's* nose. Scraping sounds preceded a loud pop. The ceiling hatch disappeared, letting in a rush of wind. The outside of Scott's suit beaded like a shower curtain in a steamy bathroom. Fortunately, the plastic kept the dangerous external temperatures at bay.

A hulking figure dropped into the cabin, shaking the deck with his heavy boots. Rivulets dripped from olive-drab armored plates.

Scott glowered at the black helmet's visor.

"Your boss wants a little chat," the mercenary rumbled through his helmet speakers. "Now. We're on the clock in case that noise from the lake was somebody's dinner bell. Good that ya had the sense to gear up. Saves time we don't have."

The thick plastic muffled the man's voice, but his urgency was quite clear.

They're afraid of sirens spawning. Hopefully, Water had warned her sisters not to show their faces.

Just climbing out of the Surveyor proved a harrowing experience, never mind the possibility of vengeful sirens or gun-happy mercenaries. He barely stayed upright while his flapping plastic suit battered him. Communication was impossible in the wind's constant roar. The suit fogged to the point where he had little choice but to trust in the cable. The two soldiers clipped Scott and Mara to the line. Together they half-crawled across broken cobblestones to the relative shelter beneath the Valkyrie's wing. He made out hunched figures setting up a wicked-looking cannon on a tripod near the landing gear.

Scott waited his turn to be jammed into a narrow airlock. He unzipped the top of his protective cover the moment the outer door shut. It felt like he'd been stuffed into a cramped sauna. Sweat dripped down his hair and onto the shoulders of his already damp flight suit. The inner door opened upon cooler air and mercs with drawn pistols.

Mara, half out of her suit, caught Scott's eye and pointed out activity in the large bay's rear quarter. Two soldiers braced sections of white ceramic bars while a third fused the sides together at the corner.

"A cage?" Scott observed with scorn. "That won't do a damn bit of good once those sirens start screaming."

"Which is why we brought other precautions," a new voice interrupted from their left. Jeremiah Jones stepped down from the flight deck in the white woolen sweater and slacks he'd worn at the press conference, his trademark blond hair disheveled above a grim expression. The Prophet stabbed a finger at a pile of thick gray blankets. "Acoustic dampers. Best we could do on short notice, thanks to you two. Fortunately, *Explorer* is on her way to help reap God's bounty."

He strode up to them, his lips curling. "How far my first Anointed has fallen. Mara, why did you turn your back on your Savior?"

"That's why," she replied, nodding toward the cage. "There wasn't going to be any ambassadors. Just slaves."

"The Song Guard are not coming up," Scott added. "I sent Water down with a warning. You're finished, Frank. No Reliquary and no sirens. Better find some snake oil to sell."

Mara gave him a venomous glare. "From now on, you get to grow old and die with the rest of us. Let's see how much God loves you, then."

"*I am His mighty Right Hand*!" Jeremiah thundered, raising his hand as if to strike her. "Enough. God still has a purpose for you sinners."

"You've got nothing, you sanctimonious bastard," Scott seethed.

"I have you, Mr. Rellant," Jeremiah purred. "I suspect you mean something to your pet, judging from how she obeyed you back in London. You will go into the lake and bring me these beasts as promised."

"Guess again, asshole," Scott swore. No doubt he seemed little more than an animal himself in this madman's eyes.

"Forcefully, if necessary," Jeremiah added with a serpent's smile. "God wills that His Church continues, and you *will* be His instrument." He glanced over Scott's shoulder. "Sergeant, I'm guessing the Surveyor has diving gear inside. Bring it, and the submersible sled, too."

"Can't get the sled out, sir," the mercenary behind Scott answered.

Jeremiah's face reddened. "Then tie him to a rock if you have to!"

"Yes sir."

"That lake water's near boiling, you idiot," Mara spat.

Jeremiah flinched. "Thou shall not steal, Miss Martinez. You will pay me my five oxen for the one you stole."

Scott gave a low whistle. "You really are out of your God damned mind."

Jeremiah raised his hand again. "Thou shalt not profane!"

"I didn't." Scott replied with a chilled voice. "There was truth in every word."

Jeremiah's fingers curled into a fist, then into a trembling finger aimed at Mara. "She will go next if you fail. Without a suit if need be. God's gifts must be *earned*."

"You'll kill him out there!" Mara protested. "Don't you understand? Those diving suits won't protect him, you psychotic ass!"

"Who are you to question God?" Jeremiah roared.

"So you're God now?" she hurled back. "Is this what I'm hearing?"

Scott pulled her behind him. "Easy," he hissed under his breath, seeing the Prophet's gaze travel to the other guard's pistol.

Jeremiah wiped a hand across his beaded brow then raised a hand to stop the Sergeant from entering the airlock. "At the end of the street is an old temple. Take this fallen saint there to contemplate her sins."

"Yes, sir," the soldier answered. "Suit up, Ma'am."

"And remove her suit after you leave her," Jeremiah continued.

The Sergeant returned a quizzical stare. "She'll slow cook in there."

"Penance is good for the soul. Incentive for Mr. Rellant to bring us our sirens before she does."

"Yes sir."

"Alright, I'll go," Scott broke in, hardly believing his ears. "You don't have to do this."

Jeremiah turned for the flight deck, speaking as if to himself. "God wills it."

"She'll keep her suit," the Sergeant assured in a low voice after Jeremiah left.

"What about Scott?" Mara's voice quavered. "He'll boil to death. Your boss...your *real* boss, Mackenzie, won't appreciate that."

The veteran's expression darkened. He grabbed his helmet from the bench seat beside them. "I'm not the miracle worker here. Get zipped in, lady."

"You'll kill him!" she cried before both guards forced the plastic back over her head.

"Mara, I'll be fine," Scott said, getting between her and the Sergeant before the man pistol-whipped her. "Just have to dive fast to avoid the heat."

The look in her eyes as they pushed Mara into the lock told him she didn't believe the lie any more than he did.

Scott slumped down on the troop bench and tried to put on a brave face. *Maybe* he could make it to the lake's bottom alive. He'd have to. Mara wouldn't last forever, even in that suit. Dehydration would set in quickly if he didn't rescue her. He clenched his teeth. Jeremiah wanted sirens, did he? How about an entire army of them?

The Sergeant returned within a half hour. Heat radiated from the man's dripping armor. He motioned Scott to the discarded emergency suit, giving a slight nod in the process, seeming to convey he'd kept his earlier whispered promise and hadn't left Mara without protection despite the Prophet's orders.

Taking a breath, Scott stepped back into the plastic and zipped it shut. Maybe this would work.

"You can hear me, right?" the Sergeant yelled over his helmet speakers once they got into the airlock.

He nodded and shouted back through the intervening plastic.

"You know Jeremiah's out of his mind, right?"

"He's also signing the checks, so don't bother. Here's how it's gonna go, slick. Your swim gear will be in a shelter at the end of the pier. Put it on then grab the gray box we've put outside the tent. It'll make you sink fast, just like the man said. If you're lucky, it won't be so bad deeper down."

"If I'm lucky," Scott derided.

"Life's tough all over. You make it, you bring those sirens back to us in single-file with their hands up. No more than four. We'll drop the ramp door in back. Bullshit us and you're dog meat, got it?"

Scott snorted. "You seriously expect everything to go so easy?"

"You seriously expect your girlfriend to be brought back if you screw up?"

The delightful conversation ended when they stepped outside. Once again, he couldn't hear anything over the maelstrom. A handful of mercenaries tried to create a wall of ballistic foam around the big gun they'd set up beneath the wing, but the wind kept tearing it away before the green stuff solidified.

The Sergeant wound a cable around Scott's waist and connected it to a line running along the red cobblestones toward the waterfront. Crouching in the wind, the two of them fought their way up the street. Ahead, Scott barely made out another cluster of mercenaries on the pier, the men obscured by storm-driven water and steam jetting across the cement surface. He heard the thunderous waves despite the wind-rattled suit.

If anything equaled being flung into the mouth of chaos, it was their arrival at the pier's end. The cement deck quivered. Great white twists of water lashed at bent metal railings. Soldiers threw themselves across a green tent to keep it from flying away while others shot tie-downs into the pier. Scott could imagine the curses flying over helmet radios. The umbrella-like shelter whipped about like a berserk mushroom, but held.

Crouching, his escort indicated a large piece of electronic equipment next to the tent. He swept his gloved hand from the box to a wide gap in the railing at the pier's edge.

Scott nodded and entered the wildly buffeting shelter. His diving gear was handed in, and the flap sealed shut. He unzipped the bag and gasped at the moist heat washing over him. Even breathing burned. Swearing, he tore off his clothes and put the blue-chorded diving suit over his rapidly reddening skin. Fins, gloves, and pack cost him dearly when even the tent's shuddering sides were hot to the touch. He reached for the helmet and pulled it on.

Something sounded like a rifle shot outside. A moment later all hell broke loose, along with the rest of the tent's tie downs. Tension poles shattered and fabric tore, sending him tumbling in a slow-motion horror over the pier's edge. Scalding water wrenched a scream from his throat. Thrashing free of the tent's remnants, he fought the urge to surface and dove down to escape the burning. His legs felt on fire with each kick, pain exploding everywhere in one prolonged shriek. He wasn't sure if he dove or sank, but the agony didn't stop until he passed out.

Renewed consciousness brought with it a feeling of puffy numbness. Was it getting dark? Was his suit stiffening from the depths, or just his muscles? He couldn't tell if he was even kicking his legs.

Three rainbows drifted by. Scott recognized green-and-blue ripples. "Song Guard," he slurred in Air, marshalling his blurred thoughts. Would they even hear him through the helmet's glass? The sirens were probably going to finish what the lake started.

Glittering hands held his head. Opalescent eyes, couched in swirling clear hair, peered through his faceplate. "You are Scott?"

"Yes," he managed. This didn't sound like Water. Too feral.

"I am Question. Stop dying. My Quan wants to see you." She grabbed his wrist.

He screamed with renewed pain. Something seemed horridly wrong with how his skin slid of its own accord beneath the blue fibers of her palm.

"You are beyond my heart's song," Question lamented. "I must call my sisters." She chirped.

Scott fought to stay awake. His throat squeezed tighter with each breath. Yes, it was getting darker, but he saw lights below. Aquamarine beads stretched across cobalt shadows. He drew rapidly toward the spectacle, be it real or the last hallucination in his melting mind.

Time disappeared for a moment. He lay on a gray stone floor beneath a glowing blue dome. Where was his helmet? What happened to the water?

"You must put your head down," Question's voice explained. "Travel out using the crystals our Song gave to you. My Quan awaits."

Firm hands pressed his forehead into the mottled surface. He felt himself...moving.

Such an odd way to die.

~ * ~

"Scott? You awake, honey?"

He pried open a bleary eye and pulled back the blue comforter tucked around his head. "Mom?" He rolled over and found himself staring at Water's crystalline smile where she lay next to him. Scott jerked upright.

Maiko stood beside his bed. She folded her arms over a flowery white apron he barely remembered from his childhood. "Water is difficult. She has brought me more knowledge than any of my people before her. You are difficult, too."

He bunched the comforter covering himself and glanced around the small upstairs bedroom. Pale green walls instead of blue. Old memories. He scrutinized the small Japanese woman. Not a gray hair on Maiko's head. *Very* old memories. His newer memories weren't much better. Was this death? Would Jehovah be dressed as his mother?

"You're Water's Quan?" he ventured.

Maiko nodded. "And you are Water's Quan. I know. It is difficult to understand, much like this God Between Water brings me. Is this hope? Can your god save us from ours?"

"You want to leave Petal," he stated.

"Migrate," Maiko clarified. "We are weak. When Kee's Sword is no longer in the sky, we will be few in number. The waters of Inis Drum are deep and coveted. Others will come to take our lake from us." She gestured at the resting siren next to him. "She will be Inis Drum's Song Mother. Water will take us where Kee and Anasa cannot touch us."

A plan formed inside Scott's head. One that might save Mara. "For that you will need a ship and a pilot."

Maiko beamed with recognition. "Mara Martinez, pilot."

"She is in the city temple. Give her enough Song Guard and she can take the ship from those who came to enslave you. Only she can fly us away from Kee and Anasa's touch."

His mother vanished.

Water threw off the blankets beside him. She stood, her dorsal fins spread and capped by bioluminescent fire. "I will not leave without you."

He looked down at his body. Just a memory. He'd been broadcast through the same tiny crystals that had first brought Water. "I can't. I think I'm dead."

"Trust our God Between, Scott."

Twenty-Two

Scott gazed up at the softly pulsing blue light. The last sight he remembered upon dying. Now the same gentle radiance greeted his rebirth. He reached back into recollections far deeper than he remembered, much like Water's racial memories when they had shared minds. His newfound knowledge was sharper. He looked around the compact hemisphere. This was one of the glowing reception nodules lining the Quan's skin. His entire life had been transmitted by the Quan into this body he found himself in.

He waved webbed fingers before his eyes, catching the powdery glint of tiny crystals. He touched a series of slits lining the outside of his throat. An empty vessel, yes, but not an exact copy. There was only so much a Quan could do, and replicating non-silicon life forms apparently wasn't included. Reaching back, he touched a narrow mane extending from his scalp to the nape of his neck. Hair? Hair didn't pull in sounds like nothing experienced in his previous existence. It felt as if he stood on a busy intersection listening to conversations around him. Or was it music? Hard to tell the difference. He even heard the heart songs of sirens swimming beyond the blue membrane, and knew their names. Sorrow, Uncertain, and Question.

Scott took a slow calming breath. With the body came new memories and knowledge. He'd been brought back as a Quan Singer. Was he truly himself, or just the patchwork consciousness salvaged from a half-cooked corpse? He was alive enough to feel the complaint of stiff muscles while uncurling from the fetal position he found himself in. He also remembered his previous conversation with the Quan. Fine. Freak out, later. Right now he had work to do. First on his list was getting Mara out of that temple before Jeremiah threw her into the lake as well.

He eyed the blue barrier inches from his face. Too hard to tear, but that wasn't how he was getting out. He worked his throat, searching through a library of new lessons until he found the right pitch and tone. He sang out a note. The hemisphere disintegrated into a wall of black water. A moment's choking panic was discarded for the reassuring throb of gills along his neck. He expected his eyes to adjust to the darkness. Instead, it was his hair filaments helping to paint a picture of his surroundings.

He floated above a great curving slope lined with strings of bright reception nodules. The individual beads of light winked out as he watched, as if someone walked around a house turning off lamps. *Migration*, he realized. The Quan was killing itself.

He caught the nearby melody of Sorrow's heart long before catching her crystalline glint approaching him. Her questing calls, a more benign version of a siren's chirp, tickled his body. Scott adjusted his throat to the pitch necessary to get both get her attention, and more importantly, obtain the siren's obedience. He sang in Earth with far more clarity than his previous human voice could ever hope for. "Come to me, Sorrow."

"I come, Singer." Sorrow's fins glowed with violet ripples of dread as she drew near. "Our Quan dies!"

"Our Quan migrates," he quickly corrected, pointing to a solitary upslope nodule gleaming like blue fire. He easily recognized the symphony emanating from the dome. Only one heart sang with such strength and familiarity. Water.

"Our Song Mother comes!" Sorrow exclaimed, flashing bright green waves of fresh exuberance. She shot toward the nodule at speeds his webbed feet couldn't hope to match.

Not just defenders, Scott reminded himself, recalling a distant conversation with Jeremiah. Conquerors. *And that's just what you're going to get, you son of a bitch.* He raised his voice in a general broadcast. "All Song Guards, come to your Mother."

He didn't expect the sharp slap of a siren's chirp rebounding off his skin.

"Who dares command us?"

That could only be Uncertain. He grinned, having some recollection of Water's own experiences with this particular siren. "Scott Rellant," he sang back, figuring this would pique her curiosity, if not her belligerence.

An orange bioluminescent meteor streaked through the blackness toward him, her heart's song strong and eager for a fight. He endured a disrespectful second chirp, letting her get a good taste of him.

Uncertain slowed her approach, gliding up to him with wary eyes. "Our Quan did this for *you*?"

"And we wouldn't want to disobey our Quan, would we?" he

returned, while part of him registered the fact he was completely naked. He glanced down. Reproduction was an obvious possibility with Quan Singers. While none of his embarrassment would register on a siren, Mara was another matter. The woman already had enough shocks in store for her. "I need you to find my flight suit."

Uncertain's eyes grew to indignant saucers. "I am Song Guard. I belong with the Mother."

Scott carefully shaped his words, using Uncertain's own emanations to customize the command into an irresistible mental vise. "Find my suit, Song Guard."

Shrieking, the siren spun around and vanished.

He continued toward the site of Water's rebirth, chuckling inwardly as he heard Uncertain's questing song recede into the distance. That ought to keep the little pain in the ass out of his hair for a few minutes.

Sorrow swam in circles around the dying Quan's remaining life light, joined by another siren he recognized as Question. He noticed another newcomer, and this one was a Quan Singer who regarded him with suspicion.

"I am Chur," the Shreen introduced with a scowl, swimming between Scott and the reception nodule. "I am older than you."

This was a challenge he knew he needed to take more seriously than Uncertain's insubordination. Quan Singers were the priests and leaders in Shreen society, and they maintained a strict hierarchy. "I am Scott," he sang. "Do you know how to attack soldiers armed with high speed weapons? Can you fly a ship? Negotiate with a madman?"

"I am older," Chur repeated, his voice lowering a pitch.

Scott noted with unease how both Question and Sorrow drifted closer to Chur's side.

Behind them, the nodule abruptly brightened, and not just in an azure hue. Every possible color shone forth, along with brilliant sparkles Scott couldn't even grasp at for a description. Water burst from her enclosure, her glistening crystal plates containing galaxies of iridescence. Her hair flowed about her in undulating waves, each strand tipped in light.

"I am Song Mother," Water stated in an orchestral voice, spreading her dorsal fins for effect. "We will migrate from this Drum and be free of both Anasa and Kee." She pointed at Scott. "He, and *only* he, shall speak for me."

Scott stared at the spectacle before him. "Are you really Water?"

She rolled her eyes. "Are you really my thief?"

Smiling, he bowed, joining Chur and the rest in a moment's adoration. No other siren infused Earth with such a sarcastic droll tone.

Scott caught Uncertain's return out the corner of his eye. A bundle of black cloth slipped from her left hand as she beheld the scene in front of her.

Mouth agape, the siren swam up to him, but her eyes were held by the darkness beyond Water's radiance. The Quan's giant bulk was completely silent and dark. "I found your...clothes..." Uncertain turned and raced along the Quan's body, calling out in plaintive chirps.

Water caught up with the distraught siren, quieting her cries with an embrace. Their foreheads touched. "I will be your Quan now. We migrate."

"I will die defending you, Song Mother," Uncertain sang in a mixture of grief and clinging hope.

Scott hurriedly put on his flight suit, not a small feat at such pressing depths. He looked down at the expanse of mottled rock. He wasn't sure if the sense of profound loss was his, or of those whose memories blended with his. One thing was certain. The Quan's choice for its people had been a final one.

Chur swam up to him, all hostility drained from his voice. "How do you fight these soldiers?"

"By not fighting them," he replied. "Is there a way we can get into the temple unseen?"

"Through Cradel Way," Chur replied after a moment's thought. "The passage is where we take our Shreen brothers and sisters to be merged into the Song."

Scott nodded but didn't prefer the odds. Four sirens and two Singers didn't make much of an army to throw against a squad of heavily armed mercenaries. *Three* sirens, he revised. There was no way he would allow Water to endanger herself. Lose her and Inis Drum lost everything. He swam up to their newly minted Song Mother. "Didn't the Quan make any more Song Guard than this?"

Water shook her head. "Many memories were consumed in our making. There were scant few to begin with. There will be even fewer lives reborn because of us."

"I didn't realize," Scott replied, mortified at the price exacted in his creation. His voice strengthened with a new resolve. "First off, we save Mara. Once that is done, we'll take the ship."

"You know how?"

"Working on it," he announced. Maybe, by the time they freed Mara, he'd actually have a plan. Right now the only realistic idea was to surrender. Scott smiled inwardly. Not a bad thought. "We'll give

Jeremiah what he wants. Just not in the way he wants it."

"I am hungry," Sorrow broke in, spreading her dorsal fins to take in Water's brightness.

"Head to the surface," Scott ordered, putting his webbed feet to good use. "I need you all charged up and ready to fight."

"Finally," Uncertain added with a degree of petulance.

Their ascent gave him plenty of time to worry about how much heat this new body of his could tolerate. The memory of his previous death made him want to curl up in a ball as the water's cobalt depths transformed into paler blues. Soon he made out the surface's frothing churn. The water flowing through his gills heated quickly. Soon it felt like someone lined his throat with chili peppers. His skin didn't feel much better, but at least he wasn't screaming with pain this time. He paused.

Chur swam next to him, regarding the turbulence above with a grimace. "We are not meant to swim beneath Kee's Sword."

"We are Song Guard," Water smugly sang, passing with her retinue. The four sirens rolled on their backs roughly thirty feet above Scott and spread dorsal fins with the grace of sparkling glass butterflies. They glided effortlessly, soaking in the nourishing light.

Scott smiled, drawing in a symphony of hearts playing against the deep bass rumble of overhead waves. Water's song outshone them all, filling the lake with her magnificence. A noisome buzz intruded on the performance. He glanced around, seeing nothing, but knowing too well what it meant. Drone. The Prophet had become impatient.

He motioned to Chur, who looked equally upset by the interference. "The thieves have sent a machine to hunt us. We need to get to the temple."

"Song Guard!" Chur commanded.

Water's escorts folded their fins and dove.

"You cannot command me, Singers," Water taunted.

"Never could," Scott agreed. "Now get your glowing butt down here before that drone gets a lock on you."

Water cut off Chur's aghast expression with a chuckle. "He is allowed to address me as he wishes." She grabbed Scott's wrist. "A Singer, yet you are still too slow. Sorrow, take Chur. We must be quick."

"Keep to the bottom," Scott cautioned as she propelled them through the depths. "I've had enough hot water for one day."

Water's fins edged toward crimson. "They should not have done that to you."

"Jeremiah's gone certifiable," he warned. "We need to get to

Mara before he does the same to her."

"I will kill him."

Scott shook his head. "You're done fighting."

"No, I'm not."

"Yes, you are…Song Mother. You're really going to become as big as your Quan?"

"My Quan was very old." Her opalescent eyes became wistful. "I like Haven. It will make a nice Drum for my people."

"Seriously? Haven?"

She nodded. Her fins reddened further. "I *will* kill him."

Gravel and rocky outcrops rose along a gentle slope as they approached the shallows. The heat grew worse. Clouds of sand rolled in the distance, accompanied by booming waves. Hopefully, they wouldn't have to go in that far. He glanced at his sparkling skin, appreciating the advantages of not being human. He'd have his nervous breakdown later, but right now being Shreen was a blessing.

Chur sang out from beside Sorrow, pointing toward the dim outline of dark columns in the water ahead. "Inis Way's pier. Cradel Way is just to the north, but so is that sound."

"Then we need to draw it off," Scott decided. He signaled Water to pause in her advance. The whining buzz grew closer now. Any closer and Jeremiah might see them, if he didn't already. "Uncertain! Time to kill something."

The siren was before him in a flash with bright eyes and a vicious grin. "Kill what?"

He pointed toward the sound. "Draw the thing south away from us, then destroy it."

"I am Song Guard!" She darted for the pier, disappearing into the billowing sand.

Her questing song sounded like two stones clacking together. Silence preceded a deadlier chirp. Minutes later, the siren burst through the roiling brown clouds heading south with a dog-sized ovoid close behind.

When the machine's wake dissipated in the currents, Scott gestured to Water, Chur, and the other two sirens. "Hurry!"

With Water doing the pulling, Scott swam over a bowl-shaped hollow on the far side of the pier. Sand agitated his gills, adding to the heat's discomfort. They passed a ring of serrated red crystals, his borrowed memories telling him this was where the Song used to be enthroned. Their destination was a marble-tiled tunnel above the blade-shaped hexagons. Cradle Way. Getting there proved frustrating. Each wave brought with it a surge of current they used to their advantage, but each gain was eroded by a subsequent undertow.

A murderous shrill ripped through the water, overriding the rolling thunder to shoot a jolt of discomfort up Scott's spine.

"Uncertain has killed the machine," Water reported with satisfaction.

"Let's not wait for more," Scott cautioned, imagining Jeremiah's reaction. Weather be damned, that nutcase would have those mercenaries scurrying up and down the pier like stirred-up ants. He pitched his voice to pierce the tumult overhead. "Uncertain, come join us." Then an inspiration struck him. "Uncertain, wait. Find a place to hide near the pier."

"Why?" came her ultra-low frequency challenge.

"Another diversion, Song Guard."

Uncertain's tone brightened. "I like diversions."

Scott wasn't so sure she'd appreciate this one. He motioned Chur to him once the four of them reached Cradel Way's mouth. "Here's the plan. Uncertain and I are going to appear like we're giving up. You get to the temple, make sure Water and Mara are safe, and then come back down with Sorrow and Question. Once you see our enemy open the back of their flying ship, you attack. Don't hurt the ship, understand? Just take it from the crew. I'll help once I get there."

Chur shook his head. "You said I do not know how to fight these thieves. You are right. I will come in with Uncertain at your call. Be quick!"

Scott's objection came after the Quan Singer's swift departure.

"He knows you are more important," Water explained.

"Prefer you didn't put it that way," Scott growled. *I hope to hell I know what I'm doing.* His father was the trained combat specialist, not him. "Come on, let's get this done."

The passage through Cradel Way should have been as beautiful as befit a dying Shreen rejoining their Song. Scott's deeper memories brought up images of sun-snails brightening the embedded gems along the wall. The little animals were gone now, with only Water's glow to reflect the tunnel's former glory. He swam in grim silence. Was Mara already being dragged down the pier? Would using Chur in an amateur hour diversion stand a chance of succeeding against the likes of Brothers?

Too soon for answers. Too late for cold feet.

The passage bent upwards towards a black mirror reflecting Water and her sisters' approach. He motioned Water to back off, afraid of seeing a helmeted head peering down to investigate the rising lights. Scott broke the surface of a round pool as quietly as he could. Gripping the basin's gem-studded rim, he peered into the darkness. The air was oppressively hot, but bearable when compared to the skin-blistering mess outside. The winds moaned from unseen corridors.

A painfully bright light shot into his eyes.

"Water?" Mara's voice quavered. "That you?"

Scott breathed a sigh of relief, but only for a moment. Mara had no idea what she was about to face, and neither did he. Her hesitant voice kept him from immediately diving to think this thing through. Too late. He coughed hard, flushing water through his gills. "Sc...Scott," he burbled between coughs. "Scott Rel...lant." Eyes blinking, he held up a warding hand, trying to adjust to the pinpoint of brightness.

"Scott? *Dios mio!*"

Great. She was running toward him as fast as her baggy suit would allow. *How in the world am I going to explain this to her?* He vacated his lungs enough not to sound like he was gagging. His skin threw back sparkles from her flashlight. He heard her stumble to a stop.

"You're not Scott."

He gulped in the humid air, spitting out a fine spray as he tried to explain. Fortunately, he found forming human words an easier chore than that last Quan Singer did out at Sanctuary. "Yes, I am. Call me Scott, version two. I was burned badly, Mara. The Quan couldn't save me. Instead, it used those crystals in my head to pull me out and deposit me in a new body. Not a human one, I'm afraid."

The light wobbled, but stayed on his face. Her voice filled with dread. "You don't sound like him."

"You don't look much like a saint, either," he retorted, lifting himself from the pool. He plucked at the sodden flight suit. "Remember how Water reconstituted herself back in Sanctuary? Same thing. Sorta."

"Maybe you do sound like him," Mara revised. "God, you even look like him... somewhat." The light lowered enough for him to see her through the plastic. She looked haggard and desperate, but thankfully alive.

Scott wiggled webbed fingers. "This was the best the Quan could come up with. Shreen call them Quan Singers. Crazy, yeah, but one miracle at a time. I hope you're alone, because I brought company."

She slowly nodded as if fighting better instincts. "Is Water with you?"

"Yes, and she brought friends. The sirens are newborns, so no sudden moves, okay? Water and I can keep them in line, but don't provoke them just the same. They're highly protective of her."

Question arrived first, sliding sinuously around Scott's left shoulder, her eyes centered on the disheveled human. Sorrow emerged in slow stalking moves to his right, her pelvic fins tinkling as she stood.

The room brightened substantially with Water's approach, cascading colors revealing surrounding alcoves containing what appeared to be giant glass lanterns. *Diving bells*, he realized. That was how the Shreen were taken to merge with their Song.

The Song Mother stepped from the pool. Her arrival drew a gasp from Mara.

"Mara," Water greeted with a grin. Waving a staying hand at her personal guard, the siren walked up and bumped foreheads with Mara through the suit's plastic.

"You're...radiant!" Mara exclaimed, stepping back.

"She's carrying every member of Inis Drum within her," Scott explained. "You're looking at the tribe's next Quan, assuming we can get her safely off this rock. Can you fly that Valkyrie parked outside?"

"Do I have a choice?" Mara gulped.

"You will be a saint again," Water promised. "You will show both our people the God Between."

Mara smiled. "I'll fly any ship." Her encouraging grin melted. "It'll take a miracle getting to the thing in one piece, though. Tell me you've a plan."

"I've a third siren and another Quan Singer outside preparing to surrender," Scott informed. "We'll get those bastards to drop the back door. Then me and the two ladies here will run in and take the ship."

"You? You're not in the same class as those guys," Mara pointed out.

Scott inclined his head toward Sorrow and Question. "They are."

Mara jerked a thumb over her shoulder. "What the hell. It's not as if we haven't always been insane, anyway. Door's that way."

"I'll give the word to start our diversion." Scott walked back to the pool and stuck his head beneath the water. Hopefully his voice would carry. He switched back to Earth. "Chur, are you with Uncertain?"

The answer was distant, but in the affirmative.

"Go to shore. Surrender yourselves. We will do the rest."

Water's head appeared next to his. "Be with my blessing."

"I am Song Guard," came Uncertain's faint reply.

"For you, Song Mother," Chur added.

Water nodded then beamed a smile at Scott. "Now they will be brave."

He and Water rejoined Mara and the other sirens, Question and Sorrow still giving Mara a predatory once-over until Water delivered a warning chirp. Together they crossed beneath a large dome. A solitary gray shaft of light lanced down to illuminate twelve statues whose upraised hands served as the dome's support columns. Winds howled above them. He imagined Kee and Anasa clawing uselessly at the safe haven to prevent their escape. Condensation dripped from uplifted granite faces three stories in height. Stone curtains flowed around each statue's base, mimicking pelvic fins.

"Dragons of old," Scott commented, recalling the Prophet's remarks upon coming face to face with Water. "The Shreen never forgot their Song Guard, they just relegated them to legends." His attention moved past benches to a large archway. Beneath the gate stood two iron doors, the rusting metal quivering and creaking. He switched to Air, grateful for Sorrow and Question's patience with a language that probably sounded like babble. "There are two winged ships below. We will hide behind the nearest damaged one. When the second ship opens its back door, we will charge. Don't harm the ship itself, understood?"

"We kill these thieves?" Question inquired with a smile.

Scott grimaced. Those bastards boiled him alive, and were fixing to do the same to Mara. There wasn't much humanity in vengeance, but then he wasn't human anymore. "Especially the one with yellow hair."

He waited a few minutes to ensure Chur and Uncertain's arrival then opened the doors to a combined blast of heated air and rain. "Water, stay put with Mara!" he shouted over the storm.

"I will not!"

"You will too, Song Mother!" Sorrow and Question chorused. Each seized one of Scott's arms and raced with him into the tempest.

Eyes squeezed shut, he had little choice but to be swiftly dragged down several flights of steps by his swifter escorts. The temperature was hellish, exacting a cry from his lips as they dashed for the side buildings. Once inside what looked like a small meeting area, Scott regained his composure in short breaths. Okay, he wasn't boiling this time. It just hurt. Raising a warding arm, he peeked out a paint-stripped window shorn of its glass. *Alicia* sat on the street just ahead. He pointed at the pile of bricks burying the stricken ship's left wing, seeing a small gap between the sheltering wing and the rubble beneath.

Sorrow nodded, pointing out the sparse shelter to her sister.

The two sirens hauled him back outside, lowering their heads against the wind while running along the sidewalk.

Even the cover of a broken wing was a luxury compared to being exposed to Petal's full fury. Crammed into the niche on his belly with both sirens beside him, Scott scrutinized increased activity around the Valkyrie. Yes, they were opening the back ramp! He could make out the waiting cage, along with several mercenaries hunkering down as the weather hit them.

And there was Chur leading Uncertain toward the cannon position he'd seen earlier beneath the Valkyrie's wing. Both were bowed and struggling against the torrent, but they had their hands up. The gun crew gesticulated wildly, trying to get the two to walk around them. More soldiers rushed out from the ship's side hatch with rifles pointed.

A sharp report disturbed the drenching rain. Did Uncertain just chirp? Scott watched in horror at what followed. Maybe it was all the guns. Or instinct. Or both. Uncertain pushed Chur aside, her dorsal fins spread flat like the wings of an avenging angel. Her scream rebounded off buildings along the avenue. Air fogged in a cone around both the cannon's crew and their re-enforcements. All but two of the furthest away mercenaries fell writhing to the ground. The survivors opened fire, cutting both Uncertain and Chur in half.

Screaming in rage, Scott scrambled to his feet and rushed for the back ramp before it closed. The two soldiers leapt over their fallen comrades and reached the cannon, attempting to swivel it around.

Sorrow skidded to a stop beside him, knocking him aside with a swift blow. Her fins flattened, as did Question's. Twin chirps rippled toward the defenders. Hell followed, born on blistering vapor trails. The cannon didn't explode, but the hapless mercenaries did.

A green cloud detonated in front of Sorrow's face. She rocked back, her screech muffled by a glob of hardening ballistic foam. Two more projectiles caught her legs, sending her tumbling.

Swearing, Scott saw three of the soldiers next to the cage ready another round of grenades in their launchers. So that's how they planned to neutralize their prizes. Unfortunately for him, he wasn't on the list. One of the men raised his rifle instead. Bullets sent up gouts of debris and water as they stitched across the ground toward him.

Question darted in front of him. She was struck twice before the soldiers ceased firing. The siren staggered but kept pace, shielding him as he ran beneath the wing and out of the shooters' line of sight. That only lasted for a moment. Scored, but still on her feet, the siren flattened her steaming dorsal fins for another scream. A succession of three grenades threw her back, each blossoming a gooey blob around her opened mouth. Eyes wide with rage, she fell.

Scott's webbed hands squeezed the cannon's handles, the barrel bucking as Question's assailants were hurled across the cobblestones in shattered suits. The ship's ramp began closing. Grabbing a fallen mercenary's rifle, he charged forward. His leap took him inside the troop compartment to confront an armored figure at a wall console. He squeezed the weapon's trigger. Nothing.

The mercenary's gloved fist slammed into his jaw, sending him reeling against the cage.

"Safety's on, ya dumbass!" the man shouted through helmet speakers, ripping the rifle from Scott's numbed hands. He aimed, a slow finger emphasizing the flip of a small lever behind the trigger.

A bright blurring arm severed the soldier's head in a horrid, crimson spray.

"I will not stay put," Water spat, kicking at the quivering body. "I am Song Mother."

Another cement grenade exploded next to her head.

Whirling, Scott saw Jeremiah standing in the hatch leading to the flight deck, his teeth gritting from the awful heat. "The Church is eternal!" the man screamed over the storm outside. "It *must* be eternal! I am God's will!"

Water collapsed against the cage's ceramic bars. Scott glared at the man. "You're out of your God damned skull, you son of a bitch!"

"Scott? Scott Rellant?" Wincing, the man dropped the launcher and shielded his face. "That you?"

"Back from the grave you tossed me in," Scott hissed, retrieving his rifle.

"Redemption," Jeremiah gasped. "Blessed redemption! Cage her, my child, and we will both share in His mighty gift."

"You're welcome to share this." Scott raised his weapon and fired. Jeremiah fell back in bloody spatters. The hatch door slammed shut. "Amen and Hallelujah to that."

The Valkrie's deck vibrated with the rumble of waking engines.

Water grabbed him from behind. The next thing he knew, they were both tumbling outside off the back ramp. The assault craft's engines added its forceful thrust to the hurricane-force winds.

"Told you to keep back!" he shouted, rolling the half-blinded siren away from the rising ship. He tried getting to his feet, but was repeatedly knocked down again. They needed to be elsewhere before that Valkyrie turned and used its cannons. Squinting, he saw the cable affixing *Alicia* to the Valkryie's left gear lift along with the assault ship. Shit. They *really* needed to be elsewhere. Spying Question pulling Sorrow toward a storefront, he grabbed Water by the wrist. "We can't stay here!"

Stumbling in blasting winds, he pulled the siren across the clearing just as the cable drew taut.

To Scott's left, the crippled Surveyor lunged forward with a wrenching scrape, bricks clattering off its hull. Overhead, the Valkyrie jerked sideways, tilting perpendicular to the road beneath it. The machine's engines swiveled desperately to compensate, their exhaust brightening with a gut-shaking roar. The fouled starboard gear was torn asunder. Scott pulled Water to the ground as the cable broke free, lashing the air over their heads.

Violent gusts sent the Valkyrie into a sideways arc over the lake, rolling the doomed craft on its belly. The ship fell, striking the pier with an outboard engine. A bright ball of plasma splintered the nacelle's supporting wing into reddened shards. The ship disappeared beneath the storm-tossed water as if it never existed, high winds sweeping the scorched pier clean of debris.

"God's will be done," Scott muttered, hauling Water to her feet.

The two of them joined the other sirens inside the shelter of a squat tower decorated by a sagging marquee, any signage having long since disappeared. Wooden shelving lay heaped along the back of a deep narrow room. Sorrow lay immobilized against a scarred green counter, angrily scraping at the green foam binding her legs. Question took a more direct approach beside her, repeatedly slamming her head into the counter's granite surface. Scott considered stopping her until he noted the cracks forming in the foam around Question's face.

He guided Water to a facing wall across from the other sirens and began to work on the confining cement with a metal rod pried from the wall – a piece of the Valkyrie's strut from the look of it. His initial elation at being alive darkened with the realization of what their victory cost them. They were effectively marooned.

The sound of breaking rock announced Question's unorthodox freedom from her encasement. The siren shook her head, then staggered over to inspect his progress with Water. She chirped then looked at Scott as if for permission.

"The idea is not to fry her," he cautioned.

"Silly Quan Singer." The siren emitted a burring series of chirps, sending a spider's web of fissures across the foam encircling Water's forehead and face. The cement fell away.

Water worked her jaw, spitting out bits of cement. "I will kill them!"

"Think Anasa did that for you," Scott replied. "What's left of Jeremiah is at the bottom of the lake." He turned to check on how Question was doing with Sorrow, and saw Mara half-collapse into the shop.

"Should've waited for help, damn it!" he admonished, leaping up to support her sagging body wrapped inside the emergency suit's plastic.

"Ship's coming," she managed between breaths, her voice muffled.

Scott's heart sank. Of course there'd be another ship. The *Explorer* was right behind Jeremiah. "Is it Mackenzie?"

She wiped at the moisture-fogged plastic and nodded. "He's picked up the Valkyrie's rescue beacon. Got me on my radio." She glanced around the room. "Anybody alive other than us?"

He shook his head.

"So now what?" Mara asked, sliding to a sitting position beside Water.

Water looked at them. "Now we have faith in the God Between."

Water's new god was heralded not by angels, but by an olive drab drone the size and shape of an oversized football with wings. The drone struggled to maintain a hover outside the gutted shop before giving up and seeking the room's protection, too.

"Be nice," Water quickly instructed her Song Guard as they closed ranks around her. "Wave."

Question turned to look at her. "Why?"

Water stood and kicked the siren's shin. "Wave. Smile."

Scott rose to his feet and helped Mara up before waving himself. "I'd like to see the face at the other end of that thing. Mara, please tell me someone's talking to you."

She nodded. "It's Mackenzie. He's over the lake checking for survivors. Wants to know our intentions."

"To get the hell out of this damn weather," Scott growled. "Tell him we've three ambassadors and...me. Not sure how I'm going to explain that last bit."

Mara grimaced. "You're about to find out. He's coming into the city. Says for nobody to make any threatening moves."

Scott regarded Water and her escorts. "Keep smiling. Especially you, Question. You saw what happened to your sister Uncertain when she forgot herself."

"They are thieves," Question returned through her forced grin.

"We're about to change that," he sang back.

The drone remained stationary, as if in a staring contest with the two sirens standing between it and Water.

The rain-blown wind outside swirled in all directions from an apparent downward thrust. The roar of engines overrode everything else. Moments later, Mackenzie's Valkyrie dropped to the torn cobblestones a scant few yards outside the shop. The back ramp dropped. Scott tensed as over two dozen heavily armed and armored men raced out to take flanking positions beneath the wings.

Question and Sorrow hunkered down.

"Song Guards," Water warned, rattling an admonishing chirp off their bodies. Both sirens immediately folded their dorsal fins in submission.

"Tell them the sirens aren't screaming," Scott yelled at Mara, who was talking excitedly on her suit's radio. "Get those goons out there to lower their weapons."

Nobody lowered their barrels.

A new arrival strode across the lime green troop compartment, pointed, and then made a quick gesture.

"That's Mackenzie," Mara shouted through her suit. "He's telling us to come in and kneel down at the center of the bay. Sirens have to do so walking backwards. You and I have to keep our hands behind our heads. Says it's either that, or he'll leave without us."

Scott looked back. "Water?"

Water nodded. "Inis Drum migrates."

Getting inside the Valkyrie was a chore. While the sirens were able to stagger through the wind-whipped rain, Scott quickly found it impossible to both keep his arms up and prevent Mara from sailing off in that bag of hers. He ignored Mackenzie's instructions and hugged her with all his might, exposing his back to a stinging mix of hot rain and ice. He was surprised when two soldiers broke ranks and helped them into the Valkyrie's interior.

Mackenzie, at least Scott guessed he was the person behind the helmet visor, walked forward and pulled Mara away from him. He was shoved to the deck. Water joined him, along with Question and Sorrow, the latter screeching in defiance at being repeatedly told to put her hands up as well.

"She doesn't speak the language," Scott explained, also telling the agitated Song Guard to submit before Water emitted another scolding chirp at her and got them all shot. Keeping on his knees, he watched nervously as the soldiers returned to their ship, their rifles pointed commando-style at the four of them. The ramp door closed with a thud, shutting out the howling wind and blistering heat. The mercenaries fell in behind Mackenzie, their aim never wavering.

Mara peeled off her suit once cool air whooshed down from ceiling vents. "Damn it, Mackenzie, knock it off! These are the ambassadors we came to get."

The armored figure removed his helmet to show Mackenzie's familiar brush cut festooned with a bandage across his forehead. His blocky jaw was tightly set below thin lips. He pointed at Scott. "What's this all about? What did they do with Rellant?"

"You're looking at him," Scott answered, taking satisfaction in Mackenzie's startled look at being addressed so clearly by one of the natives. "Your dear employer tossed me into yonder lake in just a diving suit. The Shreen reconstituted me as best they could. This is what I ended up as." He ignored a few warning shouts and stood. "By the way, Jeremiah was in that crashed ship."

"You sound like Rellant," Mackenzie half-muttered. He made a quick hand signal. The small army behind him lowered their weapons.

"What's left of him," Scott asserted. He placed his hands on Water's shoulders. "This is Water, carrying all of her people inside her."

"Thief," Water intoned, staring up at the man.

"Yeah, it's her, alright," Mackenzie grunted. "What about those other two pissed off sirens?"

"Question is on her left," Scott introduced. "That's Sorrow on her right. We've got the start of a new church here, Mackenzie." He inclined his head toward Mara, her brown curls still dripping with sweat. "You've also got a new Prophet, unless you managed to fish that bastard out of the lake alive."

"Cabin was flooded," the mercenary chief stated. He looked down at Mara next to him. "You want Jeremiah's job?"

She eyed the man. "You going to allow it?"

Mackenzie grinned. "Beats unemployment." He glanced back at his men. "Besides, I have the power of persuasion on my side, along with a big chunk of Hanza Corp stock."

"So why not run the church yourself?" Scott asked, imagining scenarios leaving both his and Mara's riddled bodies out on the street.

Mackenzie snorted. "Me? A Prophet?" His expression sobered. "If you're really who you say you are, you'll remember what I told you."

Scott smiled. "It's not about the money or power. It's about a man's honor."

Brother's Executive Officer folded his arms. "Damn right it is."

Epilogue

Scott watched Water's prismatic glow fade beneath Haven's placid waters. He plucked at his blue wetsuit. The unnecessary attire made him look more human, at least from a distance. Most in Haven thought him as simply "one of the Shreen arrivals." Only his parents knew better, after a very difficult introduction. He didn't want to impart any more physical difference than necessary between the son his parents knew and the Scott they were still getting used to.

"So what's next?" Mara asked, folding her arms over a prim, white blouse and matching slacks. The Church of Life's new Prophet had just returned from the third town meeting this week, Haven considering its refurbished future as the Church's new headquarters.

"Water will sleep," Scott replied, not looking forward to the inevitable. He would miss her presence. "She'll change into a Quan now that her migration's complete. What did Mackenzie say about the new sunlamp for this section of the lake?"

"He'll have it flown in tomorrow. All part of my church's renewed contract with Brothers."

"Prophet Mara and her two Saints." Scott chuckled. "I like the ring of that. Any objections from Hanza's Board on you taking over?"

"They were all smiles once Mackenzie tossed his vote in," she said with a sly grin. "One thing about Bob, he knows where the money is."

"And he'll expect a handsome price for his support, no doubt. How are our two new ambassadors getting along? Sorrow and Question haven't killed anyone, have they?"

Her voice softened. "Scott, you should've seen them in Tahoe. They're really getting into their new roles. An eleven-year old came in with burns over eighty percent of her body. It truly was a miracle for everyone, sirens included." Mara's voice steadied. "Something wonderful has begun. There is a God Between. Something for both our species to believe in. One not asking for your life savings, either. You could still be part of this. Especially now."

"I belong with my Quan," he replied. *Something I can finally believe in.*

"And your parents," she added, stooping down to pick up a granite chip off the shoreline. She skipped the stone across the lake's placid surface. "How are they taking your transformation?"

"Slowly," he admitted. "My father's starting to come around, but my mother's still having a problem accepting me for the real Scott Rellant. We've plenty of time to get used to each other. I'm even giving a concert."

"Without your oboe?"

He sang the first few lines of *Last Descent*, his voice catching subtle melodies even the Wolf couldn't match.

Mara's eyes widened. "That was all you?"

Scott grinned with pride. "All me."

"You could still go on tour, you know. You came back from the dead once. Do it again as a Shreen. Benny would be ecstatic."

He shook his head. For once he was truly content. "Anything else you want to tell Water?"

She shrugged. "We said our goodbyes." Her gaze skimmed the lake's surface. "She's really not coming back up again, is she?" Her wistful tone didn't go unnoticed.

His gut twisted. "No."

Silence stretched between them.

Mara put a hand on his shoulder. "You going to be okay while she sleeps?"

Scott put his webbed hands on his hips and glanced down. "Time to spend with my parents, I guess."

"So, when do the first Shreen appear?"

"A few years, after she's pulled in enough minerals. Luckily, the lake's packed with naturally occurring heavy elements. She'll have plenty to absorb and use." He sat on the rocky lip, trying to imagine what Haven would look like with Inis Drum reborn. "They'll need me as a liaison. Being needed is something I could get used to."

Mara placed a hand on his shoulder. "Go to her. I'll see you in a few weeks. Maiko wants you home for dinner tonight, so don't stay too long."

He hugged her. "Take care, Your Holiness, Chairman, or whatever they call you these days."

"Mara will do. Take care, Scott."

"You, too." Giving a final wave, Mara hopped into the electric cart that brought them here.

Scott watched her return to the housing area before diving into the welcoming water, his gills sucking in the metallic-tasting liquid. The darkness wasn't a problem for Water any more than it was for him, but the new colony would appreciate the sunlamp's radiance as would his human side.

The lake vibrated with Water's greeting. He spied Water's glow far below him on a bowl-shaped section of lakebed she'd carved for herself. She lay curled up in the middle of the depression, a blissful expression on her face.

He drew up next to her. "So, my Quan, when does it start?"

"My change?" She studied her flowing swimming fins. "Soon."

Scott could see the thin crystals already fusing together. "That supposed to happen?"

She nodded. "Imagine the future my people will have. They will build and grow without Kee's Sword to cut them down again. We're free, Scott. Just as free as you wanted to be."

He bumped his forehead head against hers. "Freedom can get lonely."

Water pressed a hand to his temple as if sensing his foreboding. Her voice echoed in his mind. *You will never be rid of me, Scott Rellant.*

About the Author

K M Tolan is a science fiction and fantasy author with six books published through Burst Books (Champagne Books SF/F imprint). His first two novels in the *Blade Dancer* series were both finalists in the EPIC E-book Awards for Science Fiction. *Blade Dancer* was accepted into the Cushing Memorial Library and Archives at Texas A&M. *Rogue Dancer* received his publisher's award for best novel of the year. Mr. Tolan is a software engineer, a combat veteran, and lives near Austin, Texas.

K M loves to hear from readers. You can find and connect with him at the links below.

Website/Blog: http://kmtolan.com/
Facebook: https://www.facebook.com/kmtolan

~ * ~

We hope you enjoyed *Siren's Song*. If you did, please write a review, tell your friends, give another book by K M a try or check out the other offerings at Champagne Book Group.

Now, turn the page for a peek inside *Tracks*, the book that introduces readers to the steam child world of Hobohemia.

Tracks

Vincent's sister is swept away by a steam locomotive riding rails that vanish along with her. Ten years later he rediscovers those tracks, and heads down them to bring her back.

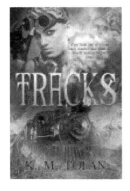

Ever look out of a train car's window and think the world rushing by isn't yours?

Welcome to Hobohemia, where hobo kings vie with rail barons over the value of the human spirit and steam engines still ply the living rails.

Vincent arrives searching for his long lost sister, but quickly finds himself immersed in a battle to stop the Erie Railroad from unleashing a horror that will see the end of hobo jungles and craftsmen alike.

Excerpt

Vincent swore the railroad tracks hadn't been there a moment ago. He glanced back at the low bushes hugging the meandering creek, and then across the bright rails toward a dusty country lane bordering the open field. That was his road, wasn't it? Yes, the street ran by a gray house with a small barn out back. The building sure seemed like his home.

He turned his attention to his seven-year old sister, unconvinced. "Dad said not to go beyond the creek."

"We didn't," Katy retorted. She brushed a fleck of mud off her blue play dress and retrieved a clouded jar of tadpoles from a knot of grass next to their impromptu trail. Her brown eyes widened. "Maybe this is one of those ghost trains."

"That's just old railroader tales," he replied, parroting Mom's often used admonishment when Dad told his stories.

Vincent's sneakers crunched through bright white ballast rock. He kicked at the rail. Why was it humming? Pulling an unruly sweep of coal-black hair from his eyes, he hunkered down for a closer inspection. It would be great if even one of Dad's stories were true. Mountains made of rock candy. Railroad barons and knights. Vincent's lips pursed. Truth was, he'd been thinking of those sort of things a minute ago. Daydreams and fairy tales. That's what Mom always said. Now he had gone and gotten himself and his sister lost.

He let out a breath and decided to head back to the creek.

Katy was not having any of it. Clutching her jar, she ran up on the roadbed and jumped up and down on a tie.

His nostrils drew in the tang of fresh creosote in the heat of an Indiana summer. "You're getting your shoes sticky, stupid."

"I'm not stupid, and you're not Dad."

"I'm twelve, and so I'm smarter than you."

His sister stuck out her tongue. "Vincent Baloney!"

He wished he could hop on one of those trains Dad always talked about. Mom would backhand them both if Katy tracked goo on the carpet. "Maloney, stupid. It's your name too, so grow up."

"I'm not stupid."

The rails wavered like molten silver as they merged in the distance. He sensed a sort of humming. The sound was constant—a tugging, natural rhythm matching the beat of his heart.

Katy set her jar on a tie and crouched. "I can hear singing."

"Huh?"

Grinning, she gingerly pressed an ear against the left rail, her curly brown hair spilling across the bright metal. "It's singing! Come here."

The excitement in her voice only brought dryness in his mouth. "I don't hear anything," he lied.

"Vin, it's so pretty. Like at church."

Caught by the wonder in her eyes, he knelt and pressed an ear against the surprisingly cool metal. No church, just the same odd quivering hum set to the pulsing rush of blood to his face. No, wait. Something, but more like the echo of a summer storm than any choir.

He looked down the rails again, and this time saw a baleful yellow ball dance like a mirage above the tracks. "Train coming."

"Train coming!" Katy squealed, clapping her hands. "Train coming!"

He rose and brushed the white dust from his patched jeans. No question now. He felt the steel's vibration, the noise in his head rising as if in anticipation. The approaching light was bright enough to challenge the overhead sun, the vision gaining substance until a gray bulk surrounded the lamp. It was big, whatever it was.

"Katy, off the tracks."

"They're singing my name." His sister giggled, her little body bunched up along the rail, oblivious to the oncoming behemoth.

"Katy, get up."

She stuck out a bottom lip. "No."

He grabbed her arm and yanked the girl to her feet. "Get *up!*"

"I want to hear." She tried to pull away. "Let go of my arm."

"Dad said I was to take care of you." Vincent kept his grip despite her struggles.

"My tadpoles!"

Sighing, he let go. Of course, she ignored the jar completely and put her head on the rails again. One look up the track was all he needed. Spouts of white smoke and steam jetted up from the engine, accompanied by a chuffing sound he rarely heard. The last steam engine he remembered was the one they had brought down to the town park a couple years back. He used to play on it. Now a fence surrounded the old steamer. The locomotive rumbling toward them was easily twice that engine's size. Fending off kicks and bites, he pulled his sister away from the tracks.

Vincent mustered authority into his voice. "You want me to tell Mom?"

Katy immediately settled down at the threat. Mom could really hurt when she got mad. Glowering, Katy let him take her wrist again. He stood well clear of the tracks.

The electric feeling in his head became lost within a greater rumble and shake of the approaching locomotive. The ballast leapt and spun along the quivering ties, the rails appearing to flex in eager anticipation. The steam engine's great pistons drove four wheels taller than he was. Brass lines ran along a lustrous black boiler like attentive serpents. Billowing white gusts exhaled from iron cheeks behind the black teeth of a broad cowcatcher, each breath adding to the shaking in Vincent's belly. He stepped closer, wanting the thrill of swirling vapors enwrapping him.

A geyser erupted next to the locomotive's main stack, and with it came a whistle's mighty blast. The engine fell on them like an earthquake, shadowing everything in iron and steam. He let the smell of oil and heated metal lift him, the moist clouds so thick he saw little beyond the rush of wheels and pistons. He caught a brief splash of green as the tender passed. Bright yellow letters inside a diamond spelled out "Erie".

Shaking like a leaf, he paid little mind to the clatter of brown freight cars passing by on screeching wheels. The bright red caboose brought him out of his rapture. He stared at his left hand, his fingers clenched around nothing but air. Guts cramping, he looked at the receding train, then back at the tracks. "Katy?"

Vincent stumbled along the tracks. Even the train was gone. Whirling, he dashed back to where he and his sister had stood. Had she gotten scared? *Tadpoles.* His throat threatened to close up on him as he ran back to the creek, ignoring the tug of brambles and grass on his pants legs. Heart pounding, he nearly fell into the shallow thread of water coursing its way through a tangle of scrub trees. Tiny shapes darted unmolested in miniature backwashes.

She wasn't here. "Katy, where are you?"

Stifling a sob, Vincent headed back to the tracks but couldn't find them. Chest heaving with pain, he ran back to the creek, and then returned to where the grass had been pressed in by his and Katy's feet. His foot crunched on something in the tangle of weeds and wildflowers. Wiping the blur from his eyes, he stared down at several tadpoles flopping around in a fruit jar's shards.

"Kaaatyyyyyy!"

We hope you enjoyed the taste of *Tracks*. Both books are available now at Champagne Book Group and other major retailers.

~ * ~

Interested in getting advance notice of great new books, author contests and giveaways, and only-to-subscriber goodies? Join https://www.facebook.com/groups/ChampagneBook Club/.

Made in the USA
Columbia, SC
01 May 2022

59591787R00137